MOUNTAIN
THE ENLIGHTENED
(Volume II)

DAVID A STOUT

Mountain: The Enlightened (Volume II)
Copyright © 2021 David A Stout
[To the Reader © 2021 David A Stout]

ISBN   9798590507757

This is a work of both fiction and historical nonfiction. While reporting on actual historical events, I have either stood by names for the purpose of authenticity or changed them to avoid offence. In the latter case, I have gamely applied the names of colleagues and friends to the fictional characters in the book. In no way do these reflect their real life personas. The decision to use their names is purely a mark of respect.

I have provided a glossary at the back. It is by no means exhaustive but will help with language, terminology and jargon.

First published in Great Britain:
2021 Amazon Kindle and Paperback formats.
Cover Design © David A Stout and Susan Abraham
Cover Artwork and Maps: Susan Abraham
Illustrations: Gina Brees-Marcovecchio
Back Cover Photography: Ben Ealovega

To the Reader,

I owe it to you to provide answers to some of the riddles posed in **Eagle**: Volume I of **The Enlightened** (and maybe pose a few more). The concept behind writing these books germinated from a desire to share my experiences of growing up in what now seems, in the midst of a global pandemic (Jan17th 2021), like a parallel universe.

Regarding the **Mountain** storyline: much of it is based on contemporary ideas with a factual basis, and some are far-fetched. We have become a species obsessed with conspiracy theories, social media, algorithms and fake news. Nevertheless, the dividing line between fact and fiction is as thin as it has always been. We ought not to forget how quickly we have progressed from Galileo's heretical theory of the Earth orbiting the Sun to the Moon landings. (I'm pretty sure it actually happened).

Since time immemorial, it seems that Mankind has fought wars in the name of its gods: invariably for power and wealth, land grabbing and the control of both natural and synthetic resources. This has (mistakenly) been deemed an inevitable characteristic of advanced burgeoning cultures, and certainly not a survival device. What people choose to believe, whether it is a faith-based doctrine or other, is drawn, and has always been drawn, from subservience, wonder, aesthetic (in its broadest sense) or an innate thirst for knowledge born out of the study of scientific disciplines, secular histories and Holy Scriptures. But from whence does this thirst for knowledge spring, and what is its purpose? The more we look into our past it appears that our ancient ancestors were asking the very same questions. And, perhaps, they left us a few answers – but have we, and are we interpreting them correctly?

—

3

Resonance...

'A mountain is composed of tiny grains of earth. The ocean is made up of tiny drops of water. Even so, life is but an endless series of little details, actions, speeches and thought, and the consequences whether good or bad of even the least of them are far-reaching...

...be good, do good.'

SIVANANDA SARASWATI
(Hindu spiritualist 1887-1963)

The Story so Far...

In the summer of 1987, a thirteen-year-old boy-chorister called Samuel Walker began to hear sinister voices and experience strange recurrent dreams that evoked memories of an ancient frozen world, and its last surviving inhabitant: a mysterious, tall woman with bulbous eyes. In his dreams he would transform into an eagle flying high above the African continent.

The shocking poisoning of the Science master, Anthony Greenwood, led to the forging of an unlikely friendship between three of Sam's contemporaries. The boys set to work finding out who was responsible, and in so doing discovered a young African man called Mukwa hiding in the foetid tunnels beneath the Abbey cloisters. It turned out that Mukwa was Anthony Greenwood's adopted son. Mukwa left a series of clues before disappearing, worried that he might suffer a similar fate.

The clues pointed to the gruff Australian 'Games' master called Lester Hendricks as the culprit, but he turned out to be a South African citizen and trusted friend of Anthony and Mukwa. He was wrongfully arrested but deported to South Africa before the police could interrogate him thoroughly.

Before Anthony Greenwood succumbed to the poison, he confided in Sam – giving a lengthy account of his family history – and most importantly, he introduced Sam to the fabled Stonelore: a trove of books, maps and journal entries recording the potential existence and eventual unearthing of three mysterious spherical stones in southern Africa at the turn of the last century by a pair of Welsh mineral prospectors, Samuel Morgan and Huw Williams.

Anthony's father, William Greenwood (a direct descendant of Louis Groenewald, a Dutch fleet navigator and astronomer – and the first to theorise the existence of the stones in the late 1650s), had obsessed over the Stonelore to such an extent that in 1938 he absconded to Austria to recover his family legacy.

The grounds of Westminster Abbey then became the backdrop for an adventure, culminating in the discovery of an unremarkable-looking stone, a silver key and two cloths that had incomprehensible writing on them; one of which was a map. Relinquishing the stone reluctantly to British Intelligence, Samuel smuggled the two cloths and key out of the grounds and took them home to southern Africa.

Dramatis Personae

Ckan Premek	Leader of the Premek clan
Hekket Premek	Wife of Ckan Premek
Lek Premek	Cousin of Ckan Premek
Sul Premek	Wife of Lek Premek
Thetu Premek	Premek musician, sculptor, poet, visionary
Yuriy Kuriagin	Russian-born soldier; son of Boris Kuriagin
William Greenwood	British military cartographer
Anthony Greenwood	Son of William Greenwood
Rosalind Schmidt	(or Stollwitzer); sister-in-law to Dr Knapp
Dr Alexander Knapp	Austrian museum curator; adventurer
Gerhard Stoltz	Gruppenführer; Austrian Nazi.
Oliver Stollwitzer	Austrian soldier; nephew to Dr Knapp
Babette Stollwitzer	Austrian biochemist; niece to Dr Knapp
Gernot Bauer	Austrian soldier
Samuel Walker	Former chorister of Westminster Abbey; zoologist
Franco de Villiers	Game Ranger; Letaba Camp manager
Lester de Villiers	(or Hendriks) Franco's father
Maxwell Vongai	Samuel Walker's co-intern at Letaba Camp
Mercy Tawanda	Letaba Camp receptionist
Greg Erasmus	Phalaborwa Head Ranger (Kruger National Park)
Dr Mukwa Greenwood	Adopted son of Anthony Greenwood; trauma surgeon
Dr Mostapha Nkosi	Egyptian museum curator
Boris Kuriagin	Russian Anthropologist based in Kiev
Dr Eric Chamberlain	British Foreign Office liaison in Zanzibar
Jameel Jayasinghe	Personal Assistant to Dr Chamberlain
Temba Schmidt	Adopted son of Rosalind Schmidt
Edward Haskins	Businessman based in Francistown
Dr Rhona McTaggart	American doctor and adventurer
Roderick McTaggart	American big game hunter
Andre de Swaart	Safari guide employed by Roderick McTaggart
Dr Mark Watts	British forensic scientist (divorced from Sinead Watts)
Sinead Watts	British geophysicist
Dan Roberts	British geologist
Dr Leo Marcovecchio	American forensic scientist
Dr Anna Wagner	German physiologist
Dr Jan Schneider	Head of the EU research facility on Antarctica
Timothy Gordon	Former chorister of Westminster Abbey; civil servant
Dr Magnus Nedregaard	Norwegian geophysicist
Machel Ramaphosa	South African Ambassador to Norway

Delegates of the Dar-es-Salaam Convention: Dr Teodoro Alvarez (Peru), Dr Mateo Gomez (Argentina), Prof Kirstin Blanch (Australia), Prof Kioko Kamau (Kenya), Dr Yoshi Morimoto (Japan), Henry Tan (China), Dr Stephen MacDougall (New Zealand), Prof Ravinda Singh (India), Dr Giorgio Rizzo (Italy), Dr Kasper Iversen (Norway), Dr Jesùs Rousseau (Mexico), Dr Quentin Baraise (France), Dr Thys Myburgh (South Africa).

CONTENTS

MOUNTAIN

—

For S.L.W, N.R.S and O.M.S

MOUNTAIN

Steep cliffs rose above the ship as it bobbed aimlessly and unmanned into the bay. The sky was dark, the sun obscured behind thick billowing clouds. The change in motion was registered by one of its crew.

Burnished rock discs – cold, inert.
Fashioned by unfathomable skill.
Crystal interspersion.
Interconnectedness: long-since understood.
Golden gossamer threads: hermetic innervation.
Sentience growing and diminishing in precarious equilibrium.
He must succeed.
He was born to succeed.

Ckan coughed and winced at the pain in his throat. His arms were lashed to the bow mast and rudder. Struggling to breathe, he cleared his lungs of water. The ropes had cut deep: the blood had clotted, fusing cordage to flesh. He gnawed at a knot. It loosened. Gritting his teeth, Ckan pulled slowly – flaying his own skin.

He reached for the crystal tied around his neck.

It was gone.

His cries roused several of his kin – adrenaline coursing through his pulsating arteries.

Ckan wrapped his mutilated wrists in strips of penguin hide and cordage, and searched among the bodies. He found an unconscious woman and tipped her onto her side. Relieved to see her stir, he dived from the prow of the ship into the frigid water below. Surfacing, he gasped in shock. The salt water stung his wounds – excruciating and yet revitalising. With powerful strokes he caught a wave that bore him to shore.

Time is inconsequential.
Life is paramount.

—

At the top of the beach, above the tidal margin, was a brackish pool. It tasted foul, but quenched his thirst. Ckan turned to see his wife stagger out of the breakers and collapse. He carried her up the beach and plunged her delirious body into the pool.

"*Hekket!*"

She spluttered and swallowed the olid water with painful gulps.

Leaving her to recover, Ckan strode back into the breakers and swam out to the stranded vessel, hauling up slack rigging suspended from a fractured mast. Stepping over more unconscious bodies, he crouched down at the central hatch to the hold. He removed an iron pin from the latch and lifted the heavy wooden trapdoor. It was too dark to make out any detail. Ckan clambered inside. As his eyes adjusted he could make out the four corners of a large rectangular granite box. His hands caressed the smooth cold stone, searching for cracks and blemishes.

This is my legacy: my gift to you.
My curse.

The cargo was intact.

Ckan's wife, Hekket, now revived, revitalised her Premek kinsfolk with water transported from the pool in capacious sealskin bladders. Ckan stood tall above her, shadowing her from a ray of light that had pierced the clouds, scalding his skin. In spite of the discomfort, Ckan interpreted the beam as a good omen.

The Premek numbered sixty-two. Only two of the clan had died in the crossing – a woman of more than seventy years and her unborn child. Amid lamentations, her battered corpse was wrapped in sealskin pelts and hauled through the breakers onto the beach.

In distant generations it would have been deemed injurious for the Premek to conceive at such an advanced age, but the Premek's dark subterranean world, while shielding them from the hostile post-cataclysmic environment, had forced them to adapt from a millennia-old maritime existence to one of perpetual darkness. Over generations, the stygian habitat had given rise to peculiar physiological traits including longevity, tough scaly skin with an olive-green hue and light-sensitive bulbous eyes.

The Premek had survived for more than a thousand years in bitter cold and meager sunlight.

IMPLICATION

Ckan — my dearest child.
I cannot explain why I was chosen,
nor can I see what the future holds.
I cannot make sense of the wonders we have witnessed,
nor can I be certain of their purpose.
What I am certain of, dear Ckan:
our destinies are intertwined.
Interconnected.
Deliver the gifts to those who survived the purge.
Help them: enlighten them.
But is not our duty as Premek to decide the fate of Mankind,
neither should we meddle with incomprehensible forces.
We are mere survivors, messengers,
pawns in a struggle against a violent and treacherous world.
We can only prepare humanity for what is to come.

My life ebbs away.
I feel no contentment, nor am I ever at peace.
My days are filled with self-pity, sorrow and crying.
A poor reward for the onus I bear:
the heartache and guilt I feel for ignoring the wisdom of the elders.
But I was drawn deep into the innards of our world:
not by negligence and selfish delight,
but by an instinct that I fought against
every twist and turn of the serpentine coils
that nipped and pinched; squeezing me deeper into its belly.

My time has come.
Time is inconsequential.
Life is paramount.
Your life — dear Ckan.

I pray that the Gods deliver you safely across the ocean.

Farewell, my child.
Go!
Save our kin.

I: Yuriy Kuriagin

Kruger National Park, Republic of South Africa
October 23rd 1998

Yuriy Alexander Josef Kuriagin operated alone. A gun for hire, he carried the obligatory array of fake passports and conversed fluently in several languages. His kill list numbered more than one hundred – some of them household names. He had little empathy for gender or status, neither was he mindful of self-preservation or personal wealth. The only matter on which he would not compromise his moral integrity was the abuse of children.

Slowly and deliberately, Yuriy clipped a magazine into his silenced prototype SV-98 single-shot sniper rifle. Lying prostrate and camouflaged on a warm flat rock against the side of a ravine, he took aim and slowed his breathing rate. Yuriy adjusted the gunsights to accommodate a gentle southerly breeze... a lizard slithered in front, interrupting his view. He took a second to admire the colourful little rock agama, which snapped at a fly before dashing off.

Yuriy blinked to moisten his eyes in the dry heat. Wiping away an eyelash, he took aim and fired. He cocked the bolt back and forth thrice, in quick smooth succession.

Crawling backwards into a patch of tough grass, Yuriy dismantled the rifle into a felt-lined case and assessed the situation through the sights. A khaki-green jeep sped below him, sending up a trail-cloud of dust. Yuriy capped the sight's lenses, pinched his nose and squinted until the dust had cleared.

Taking an apple from his rucksack, he put on a pair of earphones and inserted a tape cassette into a battered Sony Walkman. He hoisted his pack onto his back, picked up the rifle case and made no attempt to hide his tracks as he slid down the side of the ravine to the dusty road. The plucked guitar strings of John Denver filled his ears: 'Take me home, Country Roads'.

The apple was sweet.

II: On the Run

Schwarzenberg, Vorarlberg
Austria
August 27th 1939

William Greenwood braced himself as the vehicle veered around another corner towards the town of Dornbirn. Belted and hemmed into the back of a post van, William cast his eyes over two large trunks containing a trove of books, journals, maps, historical accounts and interpretations written, collected and collated by his family (among others) over a period of nearly three hundred years.

Map of Switzerland and Western Austria (circa 1940)

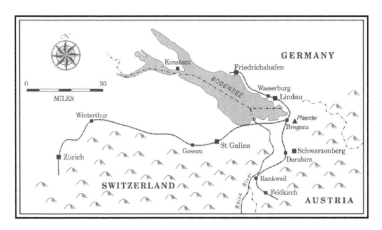

The trove had been handed down the Greenwood (or Groenewald) lineage until eventually it was sold in the late 19th century to a mineral prospector called Samuel Morgan. Morgan had removed salient extracts, before gifting what remained to a fellow Welshman named Huw Williams.

Not long after the First World War Armistice was signed, William Greenwood had travelled from England to southern Africa to retrieve what he could from Huw's house in the town of Mafeking in British Bechuanaland. Having located and searched the boarded up derelict ruin from top to bottom, he recovered fragments of a journal that Huw had written, documenting the discovery of three curious stones. Evidence that the stones had affected Huw's mind was scrawled all over the walls.

Unbeknown to William, Huw had absconded and died somewhere remote in the Pilanesberg region of South Africa – north-west of Pretoria – but not before bestowing the entire Groenewald trove and two stones upon a young Tswana boy called Temba.

At his home in Dorchester, England, William had spent years studying the fragments in the hope that they might lead him to the trove and the stones. In the autumn of 1938, a letter had arrived from an Austrian museum curator explaining that he was in possession of the trove and that it should be reunited with its rightful Groenewald heir. Or that is how William interpreted it.

The museum curator in question, Alexander Knapp, was seated opposite William in the rear of the post van. A greedy Wehrmacht Gruppenführer called Gerhard Stoltz had subjected Alexander to several rounds of brutal cross-questioning.

In Alexander's jacket pocket was one of three stones that Huw had unearthed from archaeological dig sites in South Africa and Southern Rhodesia. It was housed in a small cubic lead-lined box. The whereabouts of the other two stones were moot points, but William believed that he had located one, using Huw's journals, at the bottom of a lake in the Pilanesberg region. The third stone, it was assumed, was still in Temba's possession.

With a soiled handkerchief, Alexander wiped away a crust of dry blood from his nose. "I'm sorry that we had to meet like this, William. That Nazi bastard was onto us as soon as he saw the research facility in Wasserburg. He didn't believe a word of my cover story. Stoltz is so self-absorbed. With any luck, he hasn't mentioned the stones to his superiors. Then again, if they find out, he might receive the punishment he deserves. The Nazis are notoriously unforgiving when it comes to insubordination."

William didn't know what to say. As far as he was concerned, he had been duped into giving away a possible location of another stone: a ruse that had been concocted by Gruppenführer Stoltz. Thanks to some quick thinking, the tables had turned. Stoltz's elaborate bluff had backfired, but not before William had been forced to put his ancestor's legacy at risk – not to mention his own life – to rescue Alexander.

"What's your plan, Herr Knapp?" asked William. "Are we really going to Africa?"

Alexander's sister-in-law, Rosalind Stollwitzer, relinquished her grip from the side of a crate and sat back. The post van swung around another corner, and she caught hold of the crate again. Rosalind was responsible for lugging the Groenewald trove from her Christian Mission in the Pilanesberg region of South Africa after the death of her husband Rev Rudolf Schmidt. There, she had fostered the Tswana boy Temba. She made it plain that she wanted nothing more to do with the Groenewald legacy and the 'cursed' stones that the little lad had brought along, tucked into numerous saddlebags and crammed into a capacious rucksack. She blamed the stones for hastening the death of her husband, Rudolf, who had exposed himself to their pernicious nature.

"I hope you enjoy flying, William," yelled Rosalind over the din of the engine. "We'll be in Trieste by nightfall. We'll board a steamer to Piraeus. Then it's down to Cairo."

"Cairo?" enquired William.

"Yes, William. Cairo," she confirmed arrogantly. "I hear the pyramids are quite something."

Alexander was anticipating William's confusion and threw an unspoken 'shut up' at Rosalind.

Why Cairo?

Then it clicked.

"The Eagle and the Pyramid. The Giza Plateau!" William did nothing to hide his excitement. "You think there's a link between the stones and the Egyptians. Do you think they crafted the stones?"

Rosalind dismissed William with a smirk.

Alexander clambered over the luggage into the vacant seat next to William. "Rosalind's only reason for returning to Africa is to find Temba. To her, the stones are a waste of time, effort and life. We believe the pyramid symbol in Huw's journals is key, somehow, and I can't believe that I'd missed its significance until now. That's why we need you along for the ride, William."

William was giddy. He had been waiting his entire life to have this conversation, and was suckered in by the flattery.

Alexander continued. "References to pyramids and triangular symbols are rife in Huw Williams's notes but less so in previously written documents. The symbol suffused his manifestations. Granted, he was a very complicated and confused man."

William raised his voice to include Rosalind in the conversation, but she deliberately tuned out. She had William marked as a charlatan and there was nothing he could do about it.

"Agreed," confirmed William to Alexander. "Nevertheless, I'm sure there are significant elements to my ancestors' stories. The Khoi-San of southern Africa had a belief system based on a heaven-sent stone that conferred some sort of spiritual intelligence. But what led Huw to find stones in the burial pits at Mapungubwe? I have no idea."

Alexander took over, "My guess is that part of the jigsaw puzzle is missing. What did Samuel Morgan discover? Why is there such a conspicuous lack of his analysis in these crates? I wager that Morgan knew what to look for and where to find it, and convinced Huw it was worth a great deal of money. Huw was seduced by mythology and captivated by intrigue."

"Too bad your father had to kill him," interjected Rosalind, bursting into a fit of ironic laughter.

There followed a sobering exchange of glances. Alexander looked apologetically at William, but the comment had jarred. It was true. William's father, Johannes Groenewald, was responsible for Samuel Morgan's premature demise.

William slid open a side window to allow in fresh air, but torrential rain put paid to that. He closed it sharpish. A moment later the post van skidded and then accelerated. Rosalind stubbed her finger and swore.

"We have company!" yelled Oliver from the driver's seat. "Black Mercedes!"

Alexander's nephew, Oliver, was a demoralised Austrian soldier in his late twenties, and had smuggled William over the border from St Gallen, Switzerland. He battled to keep control of the post van on the slippery tarmac while trying to identify the pusuit driver in the side mirrors.

Alexander cocked his pistol. The black car flashed its lights on and off.

"How far to the airstrip, Oliver?" bellowed Alexander.

Oliver couldn't hear his uncle over the engine. Rosalind unstrapped and clambered awkwardly into the front passenger seat to relay the question.

"Ten minutes tops," was the reply from Rosalind.

"It's Babette and Gernot!" yelled Oliver, hitting the brakes.

William caught a glimpse of the car as it pulled in front of them, pummelled by rain. It was the same black Mercedes that had chased him and Oliver out of Switzerland. Gernot, a family friend and army colleague of Oliver, was slumped against the passenger door. Babette, Oliver's younger sister, had been instructed by Alexander to dispose of Stoltz' henchmen in the woods.

The back doors of the van flew open to reveal Babette supporting a sodden and groggy Gernot. He had taken bullets to the right leg and arm.

"It was a patrol car looking for Stoltz," said Babette, bracing under Gernot's weight. "We took care of them and their bodies, but not before they opened fire."

William helped Gernot into the van and strapped him into his seat. Rosalind plundered a medi-bag for bandaging material, disinfectant and scissors while Alexander ordered William into the front passenger seat vacated by Rosalind.

Alexander shut William's door and shouted, "I'm not coming with you. Take the plane with Rosalind as agreed… yes?"

William looked bewildered.

Alexander put on his macintosh and removed his luggage from the van, placing it on the back seat of Babette's bullet-ridden car before getting in. Babette started the engine and pulled out, but stopped abruptly. Alexander got out and dashed towards William's window. William obliged him by winding down the window, tolerating the cold shower.

"I forgot. Take these." It was the small cubic box and a letter. "You have the entire collection in these crates. Find out what we're missing." He blew kisses to Rosalind and Oliver and waved goodbye.

The car raced away leaving William in disbelief. "He was never coming with us, was he?" He repeated himself assertively. "Rosalind! He was never coming to Cairo with us, was he? Rosa…"

William felt a warm hand on his forehead and a sharp prick in the back of his neck.

III: Calling Card

Kruger National Park, RSA
October 23rd 1998

Yuriy Kuriagin removed his Walkman earphones. He scanned the scene: a Rest Area comprising three picnic tables, an oildrum bin and a wooden toilet shack lined with bamboo. Parked in the centre was a white 4x4 Landrover with blacked-out windows. Next to a brick sentry box with a thatched roof was a red-white striped barrier laid horizontally across the road.

A muscular, shaven-headed man was sitting with his back to the front right wheel of the Landrover with a neat hole in his forehead. A burned-out cigarette wedged between his fingers had singed his trousers. Yuriy removed a set of car keys from the dead man's breast pocket before dragging him to a line of neatly spaced and roped fence posts. The body toppled over the edge of a cliff into a wooded ravine twenty metres below. It struck several branches before clattering into a thicket.

Seated at a picnic table was a second man. Dressed similarly to the first, his head was flipped back. A pair of binoculars slung around his neck had snagged on a broken table slat, preventing his body from keeling backwards. A spatter of blood led all the way to the steel bin behind him. Nonchalantly, Yuriy kicked away the blood spatter to examine the bin. Two holes had punctured the steel. Yuriy swore before releasing the binoculars and tossing the dead man into the ravine.

The third deceased man was a Tsongan security guard dressed in army fatigues. He was lying face down next to the thatched sentry box. Yuriy rolled him over with his foot. A wad of US Dollars was stuffed into his top pocket. As the last of Yuriy's kills, there had been enough time for the man to react and draw a pistol. Yuriy pocketed the bank notes and pistol and scanned the brickwork for the bullet, gouging it out with an ostentatious combat knife. The Tsongan's corpse was next to tumble into the ravine.

Yuriy's fourth and final target was not dead: a gut-shot had incapacitated an elderly white-haired man. Ignoring the man's distress, Yuriy loaded his rucksack and rifle case into the front passenger seat of the Landrover, before retrieving the binoculars.

"You're too late, Yuriy!" The old man spluttered blood into the sand. "Do you hear me? Your father was right all along."

Yuriy snapped. He picked up the frail man, swung him over his shoulder and ran towards the edge of the ravine. The man's screams ceased as he struck a stout branch before plummeting into the bushes below. In a final act of defiance, the broken man gazed up and mouthed, 'I forgive you'.

Stepping back from the edge of the ravine, Yuriy shook violently. A flock of birds scattered. The sand around his feet began to crackle and fizz. Insects scurried out of the dust and withered into husks. Yuriy's Walkman burst into life, emitting a shrill, high-pitched squeal and the Landrover's alarm activated. The buttons on Yuriy's shirt scorched his skin. Clenching his fists, he breathed deeply to gain composure.

The car keys were warm in his pocket. He pressed the clicker to turn off the car alarm. Taking a last look at the corpses below him, Yuriy got into the Landrover and engaged the wiper blades to clear dust from the windscreen. They made a peculiar tap-tap as a lump of distorted metal jumped from one blade to the other. Yuriy got out, and dropped the crumpled bullet into his jacket pocket. Driving out of the Rest Area and down through the ravine, he stopped at a chain-link barrier. He unclipped it and drove through, replacing it tidily. A junction signpost read 'Phalaborwa 60km'. The needle on the fuel gauge indicated that the Landrover had been filled recently. From a pocket in his rucksack, he pulled out the cassette tape from the Walkman and inserted it into the dashboard stereo: Sergei Prokofiev's ballet music to 'Romeo and Juliet'.

IV: Sedation

South Tyrol, Austrian Alps
August 27th 1939

William came round from a crudely administered dose of anaesthesia and watched in horror as a snowy mountain loomed in front of him. His entire body stiffened. He inhaled so fast that he snorted and dislodged the headset that someone had furnished him with to dampen the roar of the propeller engines. Strapped into the front seat of a light aircraft high above the Tyrolean Alps, William searched his pockets. His pistol was secure, as were his wallet, passport, letter from Alexander and the cubic box containing the stone.

"I'm sorry my aunty drugged you." Oliver spoke through the headset, piloting the aircraft over a spectacular glacier.

Rosalind was in one of two rear seats tending to Gernot.

"She gets cross very easily. You picked the wrong time to start demanding answers. You'll have to apologise to Gernot though. The anaesthesia was meant for him!"

William settled his nerves and admired the view. Patchwork fields and dark pine forests had given way to stark grey rock, glaciers and snowy peaks. It was of such staggering beauty that William puffed out his cheeks. Oliver chuckled to himself. William turned round again to see Gernot scowling at him; his arm in a sling and his leg heavily bandaged.

William opened the cubic box and took out the spherical stone. He rolled it into his hand, registering a look of concern from Oliver. "It's that bad, is it?"

Oliver shrugged his shoulders. "I don't know. Maybe now is not the time to find out."

The plane bumped up and down portentously in a thermal as they crossed what seemed to be the apex of the Alpine range. Oliver pulled back on the steering yoke to gain altitude.

"We refuel in Toblach. Then it's down to Trieste while we have daylight."

William checked his wristwatch. How long had he been unconscious? Two hours! Rosalind was engrossed in a novel. William decided against engaging her. Oliver prepared the aircraft for landing.

Why had Alexander absented himself? In spite of Rosalind's awkward comments regarding his father's fatal encounter with Samuel Morgan, William knew he had met a kindred spirit in Alexander. But how did Alexander know about his father's involvement? Perhaps Huw had recorded it in his journal. Whether William liked it or not, his father, Johannes, was responsible for Samuel Morgan's death. The guilt of strangling Samuel's lady-friend was impossible for his father to reconcile, and had transformed him into a manic-depressive monster.

William's mother had protected him from his father as best she could. William had been shepherded off to boarding school and various camping excursions during the holidays. As a result, he remembered precious little about his father, only his bad temper, manic episodes and his speeches regarding 'Stonelore' – as he put it. During one of their father-son talks, Johannes had recounted the macabre events that took place that fateful night. William had every detail etched in his memory, including the moment when the whisky bottle slipped from his father's grip and the ensuing whiff of urine, indicating that his father was too inebriated to control his faculties. Johannes Groenewald's suicide was arguably a saving grace.

Pushing back a tear, William said a silent prayer in memory of his mother. His thoughts turned to his own wife, and son Anthony. It would only be a matter of days before they would declare him missing – if not already. What would Anthony make of his father's decision to walk out on them? William consoled himself in the understanding that absconding was better than the seventeen or so years of brutality that he had just about avoided.

V: Decision Time

Letaba Rest Camp, Kruger National Park, RSA
Republic of South Africa
October 23rd 1998

Samuel Walker stared at the dashboard of his khaki-green jeep. It was over ten years since anyone had mentioned the two cloth maps and a key that he had smuggled out of the grounds of Westminster Abbey under the nose of the Ministry of Defence. Less than one hour ago, an elderly man had done just that – only to be gunned down a heartbeat later by an unseen assailant.

The maps and key were all Sam had to remind him of his Science teacher, Anthony Greenwood and his adopted son Mukwa. Apart from three Greek words that Sam had translated as 'those who are leaving', he had given up trying to understand the symbols drawn on the maps. He had stuffed them in an old tin lunchbox and buried it.

Should he report the incident? Yes. But what if anyone else should turn up asking questions? Sam might be forced to relinquish his possessions. And why wasn't he dead?

A spatter of blood on Sam's shirt had coagulated. Repulsed by the image of the old man's guts imploding in front of him, he punched the dashboard and swallowed hard to stop himself from vomiting.

Whoever had killed the men in the ravine had picked their targets with military precision. Sam remembered hearing the whistling bullets make their targets, his eyes fixed on the old man kneeling in front of him and the look of shock on his face. Instinct had kicked in. Sam had run to the jeep and driven off as quickly as he could, barely checking his mirrors for reprisals.

Should he report the incident?

No.

Sam checked his watch. It was 3.30pm. Dashing to his digs – a rondavel at the back of the managerial side of Letaba Rest Camp – he stripped and scrubbed the blood out of his clothes, dumping them in a pile outside for the Camp laundry. It was a nosebleed should anyone ask. Sam took a fresh shirt and ran a brush through his hair, dabbing some cheap eau de toilette on his neck. Grabbing a stick of mosquito repellent, Sam locked the door behind him and walked swiftly to the main Reception area. Sam was booked to serve drinks and snacks on a private Game Drive at 4.00pm.

Sam's boss, Franco de Villiers, a dashing South African in his late thirties, was always impeccably turned out, punctual, and expected the same from his Staff. Franco oversaw the private operation as well as the scheduling and accommodation of self-drive tourists. His linguistic proficiency was perfect when catering for wealthy Europeans who wanted 'that little bit extra'.

Map of Kruger National Park, Central Region
Republic of South Africa (circa 1998)

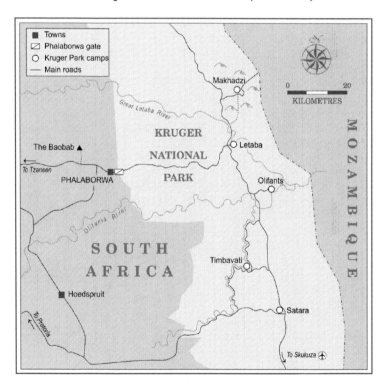

Sam arrived at Reception and collected his thoughts, sipping from a bottle of water. Over the years, Sam had grown to understand that the contents of the tin he had liberated from the grounds of Westminster

Abbey were linked somehow to a recurrent dream in which he transformed into an eagle, soaring above the African savannah. He couldn't fathom the connection, and was reluctant to think about it. His teenage years had been tough enough without having to explain to his dormitory schoolmates why he would awake in the middle of the night screaming gobbledygook. In time, he learned to suppress any thoughts of the eagle, and the nightmares went away.

He was equally reluctant to think about his time at Westminster Abbey Choir School. He hadn't made any effort to contact Timothy Gordon with whom he had shared his adventure: code-breaking in the foetid tunnels underneath the Cloisters and the final showdown in the Abbey Library. Without fail, a Christmas card would arrive from the retired Headmaster, Mr Sandbatch, and he would thumb through the annual school magazine. But, aside from fleeting phone conversations with James Bunton and Scott Arnold, he had lost contact with the Choir School sleuths.

Years of rough and tumble at Uppingham School and backpacking around southern Africa had put his Abbey escapade into perspective. He had since been in tighter scrapes: held at gunpoint, mugged, malaria and too many rugby concussions to count on both hands.

Franco strode into reception.

Now was Sam's chance. "Franco!"

"Sorry, *boet*. I've gotta take a call. Chat later?"

VI: Trieste

Adriatic Sea
September 2nd 1939

Rosalind eventually apologised for drugging William and made a point of being aloof – not that he minded. In Alexander's absence, he had inherited the onus of her irritability and her hatred of the stones.

The German charter cruise to 'popular spots' on the Adriatic Coast turned out to be a restful if not luxurious respite from the incident in the Bregenzerwald and the showdown with Gruppenführer Gerhard Stoltz. William travelled under the pseudonym, Willi Schneider. What little contact he had with the paying passengers, he used the opportunity to practise speaking German. It helped him to translate Alexander's analysis of the trove.

Over the course of three years, Alexander Knapp and his colleagues had sifted through, ordered, and restored almost all of the available journal entries and maps. They had interspersed the documents with their own remarks on separate sheets of paper. William agreed with some postulations and dismissed others, balancing zeal with sleep. The plentiful food and wine were hard to resist, and after five days William had skim-read the entire trove. He turned his attention to his own dossiers: the extracts that he and his father Johannes had retrieved.

A couple of Rosalind's comments made in their first meeting jarred in his mind. One of them was her use of 'astrology' instead of 'astronomy' when she had described William's ancestors' meddling. Was it a slip? And this was complemented by a comment about how the stones must have affected the first people who stumbled upon them. Her sentence had stopped abruptly. William couldn't help thinking that she knew much more about the stones than she was prepared to let on.

Filling in the gaps, William made a breakthrough of his own. Samuel Morgan had made a discovery. With his father's journal fragments inserted, William pinpointed a megalithic site near Nelspruit in South Africa called Blaauboschkraalspruit. The evidence suggested the presence of ancient monoliths – 'a calendar' in Morgan's words. Could Samuel Morgan have discovered a fourth stone?

William lit a victory cigarette and poured a stiff gin. The euphoria was short-lived, when in comparing the timeline with Alexander's notes, he saw that his Austrian colleague had arrived at a similar conclusion. William finished his drink and changed focus. Aside from the copious references to triangles or pyramids, he couldn't fathom why Egypt was significant. After deliberation, he decided to pluck up courage and to approach the subject directly.

It was late when William found Rosalind in the galley with the kitchen staff, playing cards and drinking whiskey. "You couldn't beat the Irish out of the girl," he thought.

"I'll be with you in one minute, Sweet William."

William withdrew and retraced his steps up to the main deck. An elderly couple clocked him and headed his way. He saluted them and retreated, making it clear that he wasn't in a talkative mood.

"They don't bite!" mocked Rosalind.

William choked on his cigarette smoke in surprise.

"Cairo. I'd like to know why we are…"

A swift finger to his lips cut him off. "Not here." Rosalind beckoned him along the deck to her cabin. She entered, only to return moments later with a slim black leather briefcase. "Alexander told me to give you this. Run along."

With that she returned to her card game.

Dear William,

I instructed Rosalind to hand you these dossiers once you were at sea. Hopefully they will cast more light on what we are dealing with and answer the question you must be asking: why Cairo?

The legacy of the stones is far more intriguing than I ever imagined. Three years ago, I put out feelers to see if anyone could cast any light on the stone that Rosalind brought back from Africa. In hindsight, it was foolish. Nevertheless, it jogged the memory of a friend and colleague, Boris Kuriagin, who had a stone that fitted my description that was unearthed in an ancient temple in Cambodia. He had considered it a worthless artefact but, with some encouragement, he commenced analysis: a tough outer surface protecting a spherical crystalline core. He, like Huw, has curious dreams, one of which has led him to a location in Yugoslavia. I'm going there to meet him.

Please minimise your exposure to the stone. The effects of short-term exposure are unclear, but we think that the stones interfere with our dream state as well as our cell biology.

When you arrive in Alexandria, an Egyptian called Mostapha Nkosi will supervise you. I have spent many years working with Mossi to recover relics looted from Egyptian excavations and sold on the black market.

Recently, I spotted a photograph in a collector's inventory, confiscated during a Customs check in Geneva. A golden Eye of Horus pendant, reputedly worn by Hemiunu (Hemon) chief architect to Pharoah Khufu (Cheops) some 5000 years ago. The inset Eye is identical in form and dimensions to one of our stones. The implications are profound.

If we are to retrieve Huw Williams's Mankwe stone we need financial backing, and Nkosi is the only person I know who has access to significant resources. Does that answer your question? I hope so.

In these dossiers you will find a set of archaeological papers, extracts from scientific research journals, maps of the Giza Plateau and recent deliberations on The Great Pyramid itself, also known as Khufu's Horizon.

God speed. A.

The letter had been written in a hurry, judging by the writing. If the inset stone of the Eye of Horus was indeed another 'Groenewald' stone, it placed their discovery or manufacture before 2650BC, the reputed commencement date of Khufu's pyramid. And if Samuel Morgan had indeed found another stone, it brought the tally to five.

There was now plenty to suggest the stones affected the subconscious mind – but if they encapsulated and disseminated information in the form of memories, who put them there?

Under the dossiers was a newspaper. Germany's Luftwaffe had bombed Poland, and the army had occupied the port of Danzig on the Baltic Sea. Brushing the newspaper aside in disgust, William poured a second gin. He stepped out of his cabin and watched the azure water slipping underneath the hull of the ship. Carefully removing the stone from its box, William recalled Alexander's warning about exposure and potential ill effects. Rolling the little ball in his hand, he felt its inert coldness. He squeezed it and stroked it.

VII: The Quickening

Letaba, Kruger National Park, RSA
October 23rd 1998

Choosing a road following the banks of the Letaba River, Sam and Franco encountered a large herd of elephant. A few of the calves were sustaining some rough treatment from their older siblings. To the delight of the clients, an elderly matriarch waded into the fray to chastise the mischievous teenagers.

Having parked a safe distance from the herd, Sam prepared sundowner drinks. One of the French clients mentioned that she would love to see a big cat and Sam explained, in slow overly enunciated English, that big cats were rarely seen in the vicinity of an elephant herd.

Franco opted for a cut-road under a copse of mahogany trees and suddenly hit the brakes. In the dust below the driver's side wheel was a set of footprints.

"Wild dog!"

Sam couldn't hide his excitement. Franco sped after the dogs while Sam reported the sighting on the jeep walkie-talkie. Suddenly, a reedbuck bolted across the road. A pack of patchwork-furred dogs careered out of the bush in pursuit. Although the light was fading, it didn't stop the four French clients firing off copious photographs. Franco snuffed the engine so that they could all listen in. The dogs had brought down their quarry tantalizingly just out of view.

It was an enigma to Sam that clients were so animated at the prospect of witnessing a kill. He had seen several in the ten years that he had lived in southern Africa, and in spite of the thrill of experiencing nature at its most raw, it was a gruesome event that brought on deep and profound emotions. In most cases it was the young, weak or aged animals that were exploited and terrorised before they were ultimately dispatched. Wild dog were particularly undignified when it came to the kill, ripping off chunks of flesh or feasting on innards before their prey succumbed to its injuries.

Sam was yet to see a leopard kill. He had seen many buck carcasses hanging from treetops, but never an actual kill. Leopard fascinated him – he often dreamed about them. It was his way of shifting focus from his eagle familiar. It was also one of the main reasons he had selected a site on top of a ridge, not far from the Rest Area where the shooting had taken place, to bury the tin containing Mr Greenwood's cloth maps and key. It was the perfect terrain for the elusive cat.

Suddenly, Sam squealed: Franco's hand clenched Sam's right inner thigh in a vice-like grip. The clients were too engrossed in the wild dog to notice anything. Franco withdrew his hand and Sam sat in shocked silence, trying to work out what he had done to cause Franco to react so violently.

"What was that all about?" asked Franco as the clients retired to bed.

"What do you mean?" asked Sam.

"You went all queer, *bru*. One minute you're rabbiting on about wild dog, and then you start spouting some *kak* about two leopards and a lake. And who is Hugh?"

Sam looked bewildered. "Hugh?"

"I don't know, *boet*, but it was freaky."

"Maybe it was the beer, or something I ate." Sam excused himself quickly. "Night-night."

Sam slipped off to his rondavel, leaving Franco looking on concerned. It wasn't the first time that someone had rescued Sam from some distant world. For ten years, Sam had been on and off medication for migraines and out of body experiences. Once or twice, he had found himself in hospital – clueless as to how he had got there. His nocturnal disturbances had scared off any long-term girlfriends, and without any rational medical explanation Sam had been told to grin and bear it – "cut down on booze and fags, and take half an aspirin if you feel a headache coming on".

Sam's clean laundry had been delivered to his front door. The blood was gone. Slipping off his boots and socks, he performed a routine scan for any unwanted invertebrates or worse (vertebrates) and brushed his teeth. After a quick smear of mosquito repellent, he flicked off the light and clambered into bed under the net. No sooner than he had lain back, the room began to spin. He pushed the net aside and dashed for the toilet. Up came his supper. The spinning stopped and was replaced by paranoia. What happened up in the ravine? Was it another dream? Why hadn't he told Franco?

He remembered smoking a cigarette by the picnic site toilet, conjuring a leopard, when a white Landrover with tinted windows had pulled up. Assuming it was Park Security, he had extinguished his cigarette and prepped himself for a bollocking. Four men had got out of the vehicle. One was wearing National Park Security camou-fatigues. Two of the men were burly with shaved heads – but the last man was strangely familiar.

"Good afternoon, Samuel." He was either British or spoke with a British accent. "I'm glad we found you."

He would have been in his seventies by Sam's estimation, but his eyes looked older – wizened and glassy. He reminded Sam of poor Mr Greenwood, his Science Master. Could he be a relative?

One of the men took out a pair of binoculars and sat at a picnic table. The driver lit a cigarette and leaned against the driver's door. He had an ostentatious tattoo on his arm: a hammer and sickle with some Russian Cyrillic writing underneath.

The old man continued, "Samuel, I need your help with something. It concerns two cloths and a little key."

Sam remembered four high-pitched whistling noises. The driver of the Landrover fell back against the bonnet and slid onto his backside by the front right wheel. Sam blinked as he felt a shower of something wet hit him in the face. The old man lurched forward on his knees clutching his gut, and the security officer was thrown back against the wall of the brick sentry box. Terrified, he sprinted towards his jeep. The next thing he remembered was clutching his keys in the Camp car park by Reception.

Sam shuffled out of bed again and ensured that his door was firmly locked.

The ravine road to Makhadzi had been cordoned off pending a safety check for erosion, and was only ever used by a handful of Park Staff as a short cut. It was the reason why Sam had chosen it as a place to bury the cloth maps and key – up on the ridge.

Who were the men, and how had they found him? How did the old man know about the contents of the tin? Would the killer come for him?

It was too late to wake Franco or any of the Camp staff so he tucked the mosquito net firmly under his mattress, took an aspirin and hatched a plan.

CLOSURE

Streaked white rollers of the southern seas,
batter the cliffs of the Cape of Good Hope.
The eagle soars above rugged-rock peaks,
people process – sparsely wooded slopes.
Scorched earth, pocked with stagnant water,
defiant grasses and forsaken trees.
North he flies over viridescent woodland.
A circle of stones: the people – he sees.
Smoke: burning settlements,
pogroms in a far-off land.
Maniacal beasts hurl fire through sky:
Gouging vast craters, vitrifying sand.
A fertile plain: fruit-laden trees.
A mountain? A Pyramid? What is this he sees?
A sandstorm ruffles feathers.
He flaps with all his might.
Melting rock and boiling seas,
Titan wields his bolt of light.
Down he plummets – his feathers torn.
His wings are hands: he is reborn.
Ice and snow: he stumbles, falls.
Ahead walks Tsuk, frail, gaunt and tall.
He runs to her, but slips and slides.
Intense cold: he shortens his strides.
In pursuit, he keeps apace:
Explanation? Closure?
Her glassy eyes betray her guilt
– Stricken from exposure.
He reaches out with trembling hands:
She recoils in fear and shame.
A tinnitic hiss obscures her words,
but "Sam" he comprehends.
He understands.

Sam sat bolt upright. His sheets were soaked through. He got out of bed, shivering, and took two tablets from a packet labelled 'chloroquine'.

VIII: Mostapha Nkosi

Port of Alexandria,
The Kingdom of Egypt
September 15th 1939

The crossing to Alexandria was rough. Unlike the German charter
vessel, Rosalind and William had boarded a container ship at Piraeus,
and their cabins were cramped. Rosalind was civil, but found William's
presence irritating. Occasions where they were forced into each other's
company were awkward at best. William worried that his seasickness
had been exacerbated by exposure to the stone. His fears were allayed
when the ship docked at Alexandria and his stomach settled.

Map of Eastern Mediterranean Sea (circa 1940)

Just as Alexander had stated in his letter, a well-heeled Egyptian in
official-looking fatigues met them at the dock. He ordered a mob of
porters to convey their luggage and cargo crates onto horse-drawn
wagons, and ushered the pair into an open-backed jeep with a loosely
flapping canvas canopy. The seafront Cecil Hotel was only a mile from

the dock – William was relieved to see his belongings and the trove trunks materialise in the foyer. He was furnished with a glass of lemonade and a damp flannel. The Egyptian gentleman joined Rosalind and William at an ornate table. The shutters were open and the breeze made the heat just about bearable.

"My apologies for not introducing myself sooner, William. My name is Mostapha Nkosi – Mossi to my friends and Nkosi to my work colleagues. The port authorities are very cautious at present – the British are mobilizing troops to the Libyan border and tensions are high. The Italians appear belligerent." Mossi paused long enough for William to absorb the information. "You need time to relax and prepare for supper. I'll join you at seven o'clock sharp. In the meantime, I have mouths to feed." He bowed flamboyantly to Rosalind who seemed unimpressed. As he left, Mossi detailed the hotel porters as to where to convey the precious cargo.

William attempted pleasantries with Rosalind. "Nice chap, Mossi? Or should I say, Nkosi?"

He was relieved to find Rosalind amenable. "He was educated at Oxford, and uses his beautifully cultivated accent to charm both the British and the Egyptian authorities. Do you know what Nkosi means?"

William shook his head.

"It means rules and regulations in Arabic."

"So he plays by the rules, and shares information with Alexander?"

"William, there are clearly several things you have failed to grasp. My brother-in-law is not just a curator and relic hunter. He worked in Cairo for several years as a consultant in antiquities to the Museum. Alexander helps Mossi by monitoring the flow of Egyptian relics into and around Europe. Secondly, didn't you note how fast we sped through Customs without our luggage being strewn about the dock; and our visas processed without hours of scrutiny and 'official' bribery?"

"I'm sorry…"

"Another thing, William, Nkosi is an Arabic word that, like so many others, has been adopted by languages such as Swahili, Xhosa and Zulu. You should familiarise yourself with Arabic as soon as possible. Nkosi also means sir, god or chieftain." Rosalind smiled ironically and left leaving William to nurse his lemonade and absorb her truculence.

Spotting a writing desk, William considered sending a letter home, but quickly dismissed the idea before retiring to his room for a pre-supper nap. He lay back and tried to balance the stone on his forehead.

It rolled into an eye socket causing him to wince. He placed it on his pillow and closed his eyes. Within minutes he was asleep but was woken abruptly by the stone rolling into his nose.

"What the hell am I doing?"

He got up, dressed for dinner and popped the stone in his jacket pocket.

Mossi was already seated when William arrived. He stood up and shook William's hand. "Rosalind is delayed. She went for a walk, caught the sun and is administering the necessary soothing balms."

William detected a hint of fondness and familiarity in Mossi's tone. He was a handsome chap but 'with mouths to feed' he guessed that any former relationship or even congress with Rosalind had been unlikely.

"I gather you were up at Oxford?" said William, assuming that Mossi was aware of his *curriculum vitae*.

"Merton 1928 to 1932," replied Mossi. "Although I worked predominantly from Cairo – A DPhil in Egyptology and Middle Eastern Linguistics. Yourself?"

"Hertford 1922 to 1925. Geography and Mineralogy – though purely undergradate. I was all too eager to get to work."

A waiter arrived to take the drinks order and William didn't hesitate to engage Mossi in business.

"So, tell me about this pendant."

"Not now!" Mossi replied curtly. "After supper."

William noted other patrons filing in.

Mossi continued, "I've had a little opportunity to study the Groenewald Stonelore. From what Alexander says it seems that you've discovered what your ancestors were looking for."

"I believe so, though most of the work was done for us by a pair of mineral prospectors in southern Africa. We believe we know the location of three such 'discoveries'".

William's hand edged toward his jacket pocket.

Mossi clocked it. "Might I be right in thinking we have a guest?"

William retracted his fingers sharply and gasped, feeling a hand on his shoulder.

"Relax, William!" said Rosalind. "At ease."

After supper, Rosalind excused herself, and Mossi ushered William to the bar. Several fine whiskies caught his attention. Mindful of his host's generosity and unsure as to who was funding his employment, he plumped for a modest blend. Mossi abstained and helped himself to a jug of water. They both took to the veranda and sat comfortably.

"We can be frank here," said Mossi. "I've a man posted at the door."

William continued to waffle on about the stones until Mossi raised his hand to signify that he had heard enough.

"William, I know that the Stonelore means a great deal to you, as it does to Alexander and me, but I wish to divert your attention. It was my idea that Alexander should bring you on board, so to speak. I need someone in my employ that has a first class grounding in Geology, Geography and Natural History, as well as an instinct for reading terrain through photographic and aerial reconnaissance. More specifically, evidence left behind by megalithic cultures."

William took a moment to consider the offer. Surely Egypt was full of such experts. "Forgive my reticence, but I was under the impression that I was *en route* to southern Africa to unearth part of my family legacy?"

"In good time, William. I need to impress on you that your family legacy is just the tip of the iceberg. Recovering the stones is just one piece of a very complicated jigsaw puzzle. I'm offering you the chance to be part of something much greater."

"Which is?"

"If I knew that for sure, you wouldn't be here. I've spent all my life researching Egypt's antiquity. Suffice it to say, William, what is taught in schools is mostly, if not all, codswallop."

"So you think the stones are in some way connected to the establishment of pre-dynastic Egypt?"

"I do."

William smiled. "Then count me in." He stretched out his hand for Mossi to shake.

"Excellent," remarked Mossi. "You won't regret your decision. But our adventure will not be without slings and arrows."

"And outrageous fortune?"

Mossi laughed and ushered a waiter onto the veranda. "I'm funding your research, so please order a proper Scotch. And, for the record, I admire your frugality."

William wasted no time in choosing an Islay single malt, gulping down what was left in his glass.

"Make it a double." Mossi waved away the waiter.

"So where do we start?" asked William.

"There are many who are satisfied with the *status quo*, and the vast majority wish to keep it that way. Very few of my colleagues tolerate progressive thinking about the founding of our civilisation – to the point where expressing one's point of view can be deemed sacrilegious to the point of blasphemy." Mossi pointed to his man. "Hence my guardedness."

The waiter returned with a double-measure of the more sophisticated whisky.

"Forgive me for stating the obvious, William, but what the European treasure hunters did and continue to do under the banner of Archaeology is not only desecration but it has near obliterated any chance of determining how my forebears managed to live, love and – for want of a better expression – build all that from scratch. It angers me that my people were powerless to stop the whole damned imbroglio and the subsequent thieving… looting… robbery. Call it want you want. If I can help you discover the truth about your family legacy and the stones, can I count on you to help me in return?"

William savoured the spiced peaty flavour for a moment.

"Of course. It's all I've ever wanted."

"Good," stated Mossi. "We start tomorrow." He hesitated and pointed to William's right jacket pocket. "And I insist you put that stone back in its box."

EMERGENCE

Ckan-Premek scanned the restless, mottled sea. Periodically, the sun would peek through the clouds. Ckan would absorb its warmth and recoil in irritation, longing for the dark frozen world in which he was raised.

Rudimentary sunglasses protected his eyes, fashioned from bone and shards of ground polished glass. He knew from what his ancestors had told him that the sun was vital to his survival. It did little to assuage his loathing of its prickly radiance.

Ckan took cover under a rock ledge, investigating a clump of green bushes and their small ripe fruits. He nibbled at one tentatively before spitting it out and collecting as many as he could. As with any harvest, he would have to wait another day or so before his kin would be permitted to ingest its flesh.

The Premek's clothing was rudimentary: pounded monitor lizard skins sewn together, smeared in fish oil and lined by hyrax pelts. It provided them with protection from the sun as well as warmth at night. Frustratingly, the oil attracted squadrons of flies. The mouthparts of the insects couldn't penetrate the Premek's scaly skin, but their persistence was enough to drive the Premek to distraction.

He clambered down from a bluff with his basket of fruit and a brace of snared hyrax. It wouldn't feed the entire tribe but others were fishing or gathering what they could. Stiff grasses grew out of crevices in the limestone, dissipating the heat under foot and providing islands of comfort. Ckan reached the beach and dipped himself in the cold surf. A plume of smoke caught his attention, snaking out from under a grove of coconut palms. The palm fronds had been stacked and knitted together to provide cover from squally rain.

He plucked a moist coconut husk from the beach and pondered: once beaten flat with a rock, dried and lined in hyrax pelt, it could be fashioned into a shoe to protect his feet from the hot, sun-scorched rocks. All he needed was some cordage and tar, and that was salvageable from their ship that had carried them across the tempestuous ocean – now a skeleton, beached beyond repair.

He hurried under the canopy of the coconut grove and into the smoke to dodge a swarm of flies, slaking his thirst from a hollowed-out treetrunk reservoir. The water was fresh and clear, filtered through sand and boiled to remove any sickness-causing entities. Two Premek children greeted him: they had eaten shellfish tainted by poisonous algae and been stricken for days. Ckan was relieved to see them full of life, nourished by plentiful fish soup and coconut milk.

A clap of thunder was a prelude to a cloudburst. It was the signal for every able-bodied Premek to operate their rain collectors. Once set, the Premek ran onto the beach to indulge in whatever conceivably reckless activity they fancied: singing and dancing and hurling themselves into the breakers. The rain cooled their skin and washed off crusted fish and coconut oils. The music made Ckan smile. In spite of the Premek's precarious struggle to survive, there was one constant that united them and brought joy: the singing of songs – songs of their ancestors, songs of their time in the icy caverns, The Song of Tsuk, and songs of the new world.

Ckan's attention was drawn to the granite sarcophagus-like box, salvaged from the ship's galley and part-obscured by a pile of dry palm fronds. Calling out for assistance, he slid the lid aside to examine its contents. Ckan took out a wooden box that contained powdered medicines. He tipped a selection into a clay cup, added some fresh water and swallowed its contents. Then he pulled out a heavy leather sack and removed a small spherical stone. Heaving the granite lid back into place, he sent his helpers away to play in the rain.

He soars above a pyramid,
rising up amid myriad waterways.
A bolt of lightning strikes his breast,
he tumbles to the earth.
His ashes: washed away by a sleepy river,
that snakes out to sea.

Ckan juddered as images flooded his mind. He popped his stone into a leather pouch and climbed to where an outcrop of rock jutted from the cliff, forming a natural shelter. Its walls were chiselled and daubed in faded berry juice, ochre and charcoal – paintings from a time before the cataclysms. He wrapped himself in a pile of buckskins and lay down. Breathing deeply, he closed his eyes.

VISION

Jagged pinnacles of rock pierce a mantle of ice.
A stout wooden door.
An eagle, a pyramid and a river runs beneath.
Caverns, dark and eerie.
He senses desolation: her loss and regret
sadness, exhaustion, resignation.

The Sky God flies, its white tail flaring,
falling through cloud, roaring in distress.

The leviathan breaches, spewing malevolence – contagion,
none are immune to its wickedness – deception.

Down they slide into the dark recesses.
Despairing, they chatter in some unfamiliar tongue.
Deeper they descend – the innards of the beast,
its guts rumbling – hissing in irritation.

They stumble on in fear.

He feels her presence, her touch, marking the way.
Hope, curiosity, bewilderment and awe.

Fear gives way to accomplishment.

He sees.

IX: The Eye of Horus

The Cecil Hotel, Port of Alexandria
Kingdom of Egypt
September 16th 1939

William took a newspaper and was shocked to see how quickly matters had escalated in northern Europe. Great Britain had declared war on the German Reich. To the south, Jan Smuts had been elected Prime Minister of South Africa, and had been quick to declare his support for the British Empire.

Mossi was absent from breakfast. It was eleven o'clock when he eventually wandered onto the veranda. William was reading Alexander's instructions and thumbing through a series of photographs. Rosalind kept to the shade.

After pleasantries, Mossi beckoned William to a private drawing room. Water had been provided alongside two cool lemonades and a plate of figs and sugared dates. Mossi produced a leather briefcase containing photographs, which he laid out deliberately.

"What do you see, William?"

"I see an aerial photograph of the Giza Plateau, taken recently judging by quality of the print. Royal Air Force?"

"Go on."

"It looks as I would expect it to. The pyramids are, quite rightly, wonders of the world."

"Do you notice anything curious about the construction of the pyramids?"

"I'm no Egyptologist, but I suppose the idea of ancient people dragging blocks of stone around and placing them with a precision that we would struggle to achieve today does leave one scratching one's head. And then there is the issue of their purpose, their astronomical alignment and the equinoctial riddle of the sphinx."

"Bravo, William! You know your Egyptology."

"I read Flinders Petrie in my early teens?" William brandished a smug grin.

"Hm. Well, let us not dwell on his predeliction for flight of fancy." Mossi took water. "Soon it will be Ramadan and I will lose this luxury. Change of scene."

The next photograph was of a 'sugar loaf' mountain and a city in the clouds.

"Machu Picchu!" exclaimed William.

"Correct," said Mossi, laying out more photographs. "And these were taken at a site called Sacsayhuamán on the outskirts of Cusco, Peru; these are from a temple excavated by the Italians called Abydos between here and Luxor; these are first dynasty Valley of the Kings; these are pyramids in Mexico; and these are from an area of the Indus Valley called Mohenjo-Daro."

William took out a magnifying glass and scrutinised the images. The resolution was good. Assuming that Mossi was testing him, he separated the photographs into piles. "I see three distinct forms of architecture. The photographs on my left show massive interlocking limestone and granite-like blocks set without mortar – Mexico, Cusco, the Abydos temple and The Great Pyramid. On the right we have the use of mortar and fired bricks, including several sites in Egypt and Mohenjo-Daro."

"So what's your conclusion?"

"That the monoliths and stone blocks were placed in the same technological epoch and added to later."

"Good," said Mossi. "Any anomalies?"

"It's possible to see different styles of architecture within one epoch – you're less likely to see one particular style in different epochs." William re-examined the walls at Sacsayhuamán. "The lower parts of the walls are significantly different in construction method to the upper walls. The lower appear to be mortarless, older and weathered. The upper stonework could be a repair job – or an extension?"

"Agreed. Anything else?"

"The people who set the original stone were more adept at building walls than the people who did the repair job. The original technology was lost, perhaps?"

"Speaking of technology," said Mossi. "We think work started on The Great Pyramid around 2650BC. Cusco and Machu Picchu were reputedly built in the fourteenth century AD and yet possess similarities in quarrying, cut and setting. After what you have just said about styles and epochs, how do you account for the technological gap of over four thousand years?"

"Gosh," exclaimed William. "I suppose it's never occurred to me. I'd like to examine the stone cuts *in situ*. It's one thing to moot how they shifted, crafted and positioned the stone, it's quite another to work out how they quarried and shaped it so precisely with rudimentary copper tools. Steel blades were first forged around 1800BC."

"I could show you similar examples of miraculous stonework in Syria, India, Turkey and the Far East," said Mossi. "Later, the Greeks and Romans quarried stone into smaller blocks and carted it using horses and, significantly, wheels. I believe they learned most of their skills from the Egyptians in the latter dynasties. We know that the Romans rebuilt parts of Baalbek in Lebanon between 100AD and 200AD, but there is no explanation as to how their Persian predecessors quarry-cut two thousand tonne obelisks and erected them."

William paused for thought. "I suppose wooden axles would not have been strong enough to support the weight of rock. That discounts wheel usage. So when do you think the original foundations of the Djoser Step Pyramid were laid? Assuming it is the oldest recorded pyramid?"

Mossi smiled. "That, William, is a key question. Imhotep built the Djoser Pyramid before Khufu, around 2700BC, but where did his inspiration come from? I'm beginning to wonder if our little stones might have had a role."

William couldn't wipe the grin off his face.

Mossi continued. "I believe we are looking at three distinct cultural epochs. Current thinking is that these examples of architectural design manifest between 2700BC and 1450AD. That's a four thousand year window, during which time the standard of masonry declined significantly and spontaneously improved in a series of peaks and troughs – but it's not that simple. Picture the great cathedrals of Europe, built at the turn of the Second Millennium AD with steel hammers and chisels. A comparable quality of masonry was accomplished in Meso-America a thousand years before the New World was 'discovered' in the late 15th century AD. Sacsayhuamán was reputedly built by the pre-Inca Killke culture between 900AD and 1100AD with obsidian and copper as their cutting edge. Egyptians used similar materials to build the pyramids in 2700BC. If the academically accepted timeline is correct, what caused the troughs – and more importantly – the peaks?"

William selected a fig and stared out to sea, enjoying the cool breeze. He glimpsed Mossi smiling at him.

"Could it be that the Peruvian monoliths were fashioned around the same time as the Egyptian ones and that Archaeologists might have got the timeline wrong?"

Mossi swung his head from side to side and shrugged, tapping the photograph of Machu Picchu. "Why did the Inca build a fortress at eight thousand feet?"

William replied. "Some scholars think Machu Picchu was built to hide the Inca King from the invading Spanish. The theory doesn't cut the mustard with me. If the timelines are to be trusted, it couldn't have been a knee-jerk reaction to invading Spaniards. The photographs suggest separate epochs of masonry. So what was its function? A temple is built to venerate a deity. A town is built to exploit something of value – a commodity such as gold, trade goods, or a water source – or maybe an observatory with ideal conditions for stargazing. In the case of Machu Picchu, judging by the amount of terracing, the conditions might have been right for specific crop propagation. Let us say, coca? It might not be the correct crop but the reasoning is logical. Check skeletal remains for excess coca usage and if they test positive for cocaine, you have your function."

"I like your thinking, William – and especially the idea that the people were 'high' for two reasons. I prefer your observatory suggestion. Whatever its function, would you agree that some of the stonework is relatively recent?"

"Certainly. Maybe five hundred years old."

"What about Sacsayhuamán? How did they build the irregular polygonal mortar-free walls, and set those vast stones in place?"

"I simply don't know," chuckled William.

"The Inca had a cultural renaissance about seven hundred years ago which thrived for two hundred years until it was obliterated by the Spanish Conquistadors. Scholars suggest that it was on the brink of collapse anyway. Why? Disease is probably a factor – famine too."

William nodded. "So? The connection to the pyramids?"

Mossi didn't reply, and instead extracted a small cubic box from his briefcase. "This was found in Cusco."

Mossi opened the box. William's brow furrowed and then his eyes popped out of their sockets.

"I don't think I need to elaborate, William."

William shook his head in disbelief.

Mossi closed the box and cleared away the photographs. "Imagine trying to present my theory to the Museum. The logical thing to do would be?"

"Not bother." said William. "I see your dilemma."

Mossi finished packing his briefcase, while William ambled towards the open veranda windows, lost in thought.

––––

"I'm not finished," said Mossi, placing a photograph on the table. "This came to light three months ago."

"The Eye of Horus pendant."

"Correct, William – part of a private collection stolen from a dig that I supervised at Tanis in the Nile delta. The courier was detained and questioned, but he couldn't shed any light on the identity of his employer. He was merely a broker. It seems the real thief went to great lengths to mask his identity. Close examination of other items lead to Salisbury in Rhodesia."

The pendant in the photograph was large, measuring almost eight inches across. The separate gold elements were interspersed and backed with what looked like ivory and lapis lazuli.

"I've heard that it's supposed to represent the 'six' senses," stated William. "And collectively something more profound."

"Indeed," replied Mossi. "There is a mathematical resonance too – not to mention a possible association between Horus, the falcon God, and soapstone artifacts discovered at Great Zimbabwe in Southern Rhodesia – incidentally, also built around 1100AD. Look more closely."

William reached for his magnifying glass and looked again. "Well, I'll be! Alexander was right – the pupil is a stone. Is Tanis significant?" asked William.

"It was reputedly one of the resting places of the Ark of the Covenant. Sadly, I didn't find anything fitting the description – neither did my German colleagues. Another significant detail is that this Eye of Horus should not have been found in Tanis. The entire Tanis trove was fashioned out of silver. The golden pendant is clearly a relic from a previous dynasty. Before it was stolen from the inventory, it was recorded under 'anomalous anachronistic artifacts' – 'triple As', as I like to call them. It belonged to a man called Hemiunu or Hemon, Khufu's chief architect. How do I know that? Quite by chance, I uncovered his serdab or tomb at Giza six months ago. It had been looted many years prior, but the hieroglyphs depict what I believe to be the presentation of the pendant to Hemiunu by Khufu himself. I haven't informed my colleagues about the serdab. I need to get you in there first to build a convincing case linking the pendant to Hemiunu. If you succeed, we might be able to persuade the Museum authorities to sanction a recovery mission to southern Africa."

William looked pensive. "Might the Eye be just another trinket from another looted serdab?"

"Yes, William, it might. But that's of no use to us. I believe the stones have the power to rewrite history. If you can connect the Eye of Horus to Hemiunu and 'Khufu's Horizon', I have no doubt we will be granted the resources."

"I see," said William awkwardly, scratching his head. "And the stones?"

"They are not yours by right, William." Mossi was earnest. "The written Stonelore chronicles in your hotel room, however, are. We both know that the stones aren't just museum pieces. If I'm right, these stones pop up at the beginning of each new surge in global sophistication. We are on the brink of discovering something astonishing."

William sat down, mulling over the implications. Could he trust Mossi? Or Alexander? Miles away from home and pursued by Nazis, his family didn't know if he were dead or alive. And now he had been ask to gamble everything he had on a theory – a whim.

Perfection.

"William, it's high time you let your family know you're alive and well. As far as the Egyptian immigration authorities are concerned, you are William Greenwood once more. We can push papers at the Consulate tomorrow. Is that agreeable?"

"Of course," replied William. "I need to lie down."

Map of The Kingdom of Egypt (circa 1940)

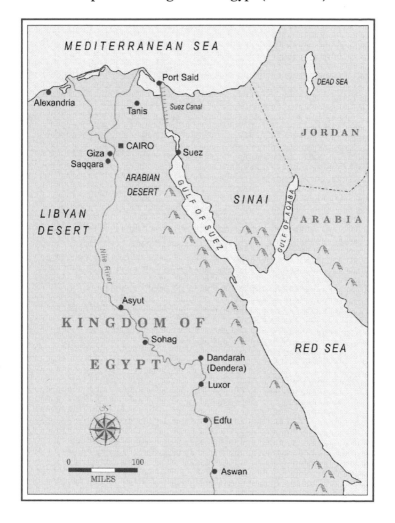

X: The Enquiry

Museum of Antiquity, Cairo
Kingdom of Egypt
December 15th 1939

It took three months of intense scrutiny for William to decipher reams of paperwork, photographs and maps – keeping a journal of sketches for his own records. He correlated evidence retrieved from Tanis with artifacts found in and around Giza. Mossi translated the hieroglyphs from the Tanis excavation as well as Hemiunu's serdab, and held himself solely accountable to their claim. While William provided evidence to link the Eye of Horus pendant to Hemiunu, he was unable to find conclusive proof linking the pendant to the construction of The Great Pyramid. It didn't dampen his spirits: the Eye of Horus was a significant and priceless find.

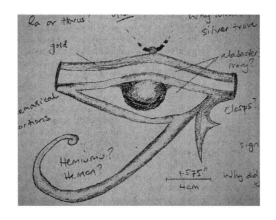

The Eye of Horus Pendant

At the hearing in front of the ministerial committee and Museum authorities, William commenced proceedings, presenting both his and Mostapha Nkosi's research. Afterwards, he was ushered out and sat nervously, waiting for a recall. William opened a letter from his son: Anthony was thriving at school, but sorely missed his father. William shed a guilty tear. He had assured sufficient funds for Anthony's education, and their reunion would have to wait. His mind wandered to

Rosalind, who had absconded a month ago. Any attempt to ascertain her location was dismissed by Mossi. Contact with Alexander was reduced to the occasional telegram that Mossi relayed.

A portly Egyptian gentleman summoned William into the courtroom.

Mossi sidled up and whispered, "Trust me."

William nodded and took a swig from his hip flask, earning a disapproving glance from Mossi.

"Don't worry – it's just water!"

The Director of the Museum cross-questioned in Arabic and Mossi translated. The atmosphere in the room was tense as the committee mooted political instability in Europe, Africa and the Levant. The British were pouring troops into Alexandria to fortify defences on the Libyan border and along the Suez Canal. Several committee members were hell-bent on dismissing anything that Mossi had to say. They appeared hostile to William, seemingly personally motivated. He saw first hand just how gargantuan a task Mossi had imposed upon himself.

After several calls to order, Mossi gave his closing speech. The Director of the Museum addressed the assembly in Arabic. He pleaded with the members to demonstrate common sense. Arguments became heated, and a fracas ensued. The Minister for Foreign Affairs threw a pile of papers across the room. Once peace was restored, a man who had up until this point remained silent stood up. The hubbub on the floor ceased immediately, and the assembly sat up reverentially. William guessed that the man must have a royal bearing, and was surprised when the man spoke in flawless English.

"We have heard all the evidence, and I am indeed indebted to the toil of our esteemed and learned friends Mostapha Nkosi and William Greenwood. Gentlemen, the strength of your conviction is admirable, and I have no doubt that the Eye of Horus was once bestowed upon our long since deceased father Hemiunu by King Khufu – may they be at peace. In this time of uncertainty, however, a rescue attempt draining national resources cannot be sanctioned. It is my decision, as Chairman of this committee, that we postpone the retrieval of our sacred property to a later date."

The assembly stood in respect and filed out, leaving Mossi and William to a private audience with the Chairman. Two strongly built men dressed in traditional garb stood either side of him, carrying hefty scimitars, sheathed in ornate scabbards strapped tightly to their flowing crimson robes.

Mossi's head dipped in reverence. He encouraged William to do the same, but William felt a compulsion to study the Chairman. He had smooth oiled skin, a fine moustache and wore a silver silk tunic with a traditional fez hat.

Mossi spoke. "May I formally introduce King Farouk the First, King of Egypt and The Sudan. Sov…"

"That's quite enough, Nkosi," interrupted the King. "Egypt is on the brink of being ripped apart once again, and we can't throw thinning resources at heroic quests."

William looked towards Mossi who appeared calm.

The King continued. "Nevertheless, I have a considerable personal interest and resource at my disposal." He settled into his chair. "Nkosi, please enlighten me. You have something else to say?"

"Your Majesty, may I take some water?"

The King authorised one of his men to replenish their glasses.

"My loyalty to you, my King, and to our Ancient Kingdom is unswerving. It is my belief that the pendant of Hemiunu is the key to deciphering many mysteries, including the purpose and design of The Great Pyramid – not to mention its value."

The King looked unimpressed. Mossi took another sip and pulled out a wad of papers. William didn't recognise them. The armed men stepped forward and clasped their sword hilts, only to be stood down by the King. Selecting a photograph and a couple of pages of hieroglyphic script, Mossi stepped forward.

"If I may?" asked Mossi

The King beckoned him over.

"This relief states that the pendant was a gift from Khufu to his chief architect, Hemiunu. It was the sacred ornament through which he could commune with the creator gods, once bestowed upon Imoteph and the forebears of Khufu by the Seven Scribes, our founding fathers, by order of Osiris himself. How else could Hemiunu have designed and built the greatest monument ever constructed on our planet?"

William did his best to hide his amazement. What a boast! He had never seen the relief, nor had Mossi ever mentioned it.

The King read the script and translation, matching it to the hieroglyphic in the photograph with care and attention. He placed the papers back on the table. "Continue."

Mossi took out several more photographs and finally the stone found at Cusco. "Stones like these have been found at several key megalithic sites across the world. William has another stone that was found either amongst the ruins at Great Zimbabwe or an Iron Age trading settlement in South Africa called Mapungubwe. We are not sure which, but I believe there is a connection. Look again at Hemiunu's pendant, my King."

King Farouk asked one of his men to convey the stone and a magnifying glass. William also offered up his stone for inspection and comparison. The King examined the stones, rolling them around in his hands, testing their weight and enjoying their smooth spherical perfection.

"You held this back from the committee, Nkosi. Why? Was it your trump card?"

The King studied William who was fighting to control his nerves while staring blankly at his notes.

"What do you need?" asked the King.

Mossi didn't hesitate. "Majesty, we need a ship and a crew, enough money for fuel, and supplies for a year-long recovery expedition."

King Farouk coughed in amusement. William dug his thumbnail into his index finger. The King stood and paced around the chamber. He looked up several times, as if trying to work out the overall cost in his head.

After several minutes, the King sat down and put his hands together as if in prayer. "In four months from today you will have a ship, crew, fuel and enough money to see you through six months. In the meantime, I'll make available funds for logistics and supplies. After six months have elapsed, I insist that you report to me personally with your findings, Nkosi. I pray that we will have the Eye of Horus in our Museum long before then."

The King stood and was ushered out of the chamber swiftly by his entourage. William and Mossi bowed in unison.

Mossi slumped into his chair and let out a long sigh.

"You had this worked out all along didn't you?" said William under his breath.

Was that a tic or a near-imperceptible wink? William drained his hip flask and let out a long controlled puff of air.

Mossi sniffed and smiled. "That's not water, is it?"

XI: No Picnic

Letaba Camp, Kruger National Park, RSA
October 24th 1998

Sam's alarm bleeped at 5.30am. His mouth was parched. He poked his head through the curtains: it was still dark, but light enough to see one of the Camp staff carrying breakfast provisions to the kitchen *boma*. Private clients were scheduled to take coffee and toast before embarking on their morning drive at 6.00am, whereas self-drive guests were only permitted to leave the Camp gates at 7.00am. He dressed smartly in all khaki: shirt, shorts, long socks and *veldskoens*, and placed his laundry basket outside his door before locking up.

The French clients were at the *boma* hosted by fellow-intern, Maxwell, enjoying toast and coffee. Maxwell and Sam had grown close. The Zimbabwean knew more about The Bush than Sam could ever hope to. He had been born and raised in the Mana Pools Conservancy on the southern banks of the Lower Zambezi. He was waiting for his South African work visa to clear before he, like Sam, could commence full time employment within the Parks Board infrastructure.

"*Bonjour*," announced Sam. "Did you sleep well?"

The most charismatic of the French clients, a lady in her late sixties replied, "*Oui, merci!* We all slept well. Did you hear the lion last night?"

Sam nodded, even though he hadn't. It was the same lady who had enquired about big cats the previous day.

"Maybe there was a kill! The roar travels many miles."

The clients were animated and collected their cameras and binoculars.

"*Mesdames et Messieurs*," It was Franco. "*J'espère que vous êtes bien dormi et que vous êtes plein de café?*"

The quartet was visibly impressed with Franco's command of French.

"I have to go to the Main Gate at Phalaborwa to fill in some paperwork for your departure tomorrow, so Sam is taking you out this morning for your game drive. Make sure you ask questions *en Français*. He needs to learn!"

Franco ruffled Sam's hair, pulled him to one side and muttered, "There's a problem over in Phalaborwa – something about a

51

Landrover and a missing Ranger. Could be poachers. Keep safe and radio me only if necessary."

Sam's heart raced. What if Franco was referring to the white Landrover that had intercepted him at the picnic site Rest Area? What if the bodies were still there? Ushering the clients towards his safari jeep, he left the fenced encampment over a cattle grid and onto a tar road. A heavily pregnant warthog scurried by, and the clients demanded that Sam stop for a photo. The warthog had other plans and scuttled into long grass. Sam was itching to get away.

The view ahead was lit spectacularly by the dawn sky: a range of ancient hills mottled with trees, bushes and exposed rock. Sam noted several large droppings on the road ahead and slowed: a large buffalo bull sniffed the air menacingly. Indicating that the clients should keep still and silent, Sam lifted the handbrake and rolled as close as he dared to the *dagga boy* and his thick mantle of horn. The buffalo posed for photos before barrelling its way into dense bush. Sam accepted a congratulatory pat on the back from one of the clients.

At the foot of the low-lying hills, Sam pulled over by the chain-link fence. The ravine road to Makhadzi was closed to all but essential traffic. The rains had eroded the surface making it treacherous in places. The Parks Board staff, anti-poaching units and scientific research teams used it sparingly. That was another reason it appealed to Sam – it was off-limits. He unclipped the chain, moved a 'no entry' sign and drove through, replacing them carefully.

Sam continued up the incline for several hundred metres and slammed on the brakes, jolting the clients out of their seats. Skulking across the road in front was a large male leopard. Sam cut the engine and all looked on, enthralled by the magnificent beast, replete from a recent meal. Sam couldn't believe his luck. The leopard spread out on a flat rock above them to bask in the sun, sniffing curiously before yawning and revealing an impressive set of canines. Sam wondered if he might get a larger tip for laying-on a big cat to order.

One of the clients requested a comfort stop. Sam started the engine and drove swiftly up along the ravine road towards the Rest Area. It had been built on a natural ledge. He was relieved to see that the white Landrover had gone, and there was no sign of the carnage that had befallen.

As Sam's jeep rolled in it disturbed a venue of vultures. What replaced them was a foul smell. He hopped out of the vehicle and began to read the sand for spoor, clapping his hands to startle any other fauna out of hiding. Nothing so much as stirred. Waving for the clients to disembark, he handed over a roll of toilet paper and a pack of wet-wipes, directing them towards the long-drop toilet *boma*.

Sam strolled over to a picnic table and spotted a bloody smear. Someone had made a considerable effort to clean up. He spun round to see where the old man had been gunned down and found a trail of blood spatter leading to the edge of the ravine. Peering over the edge he found the source of the smell. A pride of lions were lying some sixty feet below him. Next to them were the unmistakable remains of the men: a pair of trousers, snagged in a thicket and a bloodied white shirt hanging from a bush. Then Sam spotted the camouflage jacket of the Tsongan security guard. He felt a wave of electricity surge through his body and began to convulse.

"Back into the jeep!" He battled the words out of his throat and retched as a draught of warm air carried up the stench of carrion. The clients dashed back to the vehicle. Sam spat out a mouthful of vile-tasting vomit and clambered in. He spun the car into reverse and drove back down the hill, only stopping briefly to replace the chain and reposition the 'no entry' sign.

"Something happened up there. I insist you're all quite safe."

Sam parked up by Reception and led the clients hurriedly to breakfast, begging Maxwell to look after them. Sam dashed into the office and called the National Park's office in Pharlaborwa.

"*Boet*, what is it?" asked Franco.

"I took the clients up the Makhadzi track into the hills. The Letaba pride is up there. I saw the remains of a camouflage jacket. It could be your missing security guard. There are other remains too."

"'*sus* Man! Go on…"

"Two bodies at least."

"OK. Hang tight and don't make a fuss. Did the clients see anything?"

"Apart from regurgitated toast, no."

"*Ja*! I get the picture. I'll get Anti-Poaching to do a recce. I'll call you when I'm done. Stay by the phone. Wait…"

Sam put the phone down but it rang immediately.

"Where exactly?" asked Franco.

"The picnic site before you drop down into Makhadzi."

"OK. Roger that."

Franco hung up. Sam aggravated a split fingernail. The phone rang again minutes later.

"The *okes* (guys) are on the case. The Landrover has been traced – a hire car from Jo'burg. Came through Paul Kruger Gate three days ago, stopped in Skukuza and left yesterday. Old guy with two inked Russian dudes. Car registered under the name of Anton Groenewald."

"Who?" Sam dropped the phone. By the time he recovered the handset, the line was dead.

Sam occupied himself with chores until Franco returned from Phalaborwa.

"Shut the door!" ordered Franco. "The police found the Landrover Discovery, burned-out, 10km west of Phalaborwa."

"Any sign of the occupants?" asked Sam.

"That's a negative, Ghostrider," said Franco, glancing at the faxed report. "We'll see if the Park Rangers make any IDs in the ravine." Franco looked up at Sam. "*Boet*, I can't help thinking that you know more than you're letting on."

Sam shrugged awkwardly.

"Look, Sam, I'm no Nancy Drew, but you said you saw what was left of a security guard. I didn't mention anything about a security guard – I said 'a ranger'. I only found out that he was security when Greg briefed me at Phalaborwa."

Sam blushed.

Franco exploded. "Why the hell didn't you radio it in on the walkie-talkie? Normally we can't get you off the *bluddy* thing."

"Shock, I guess?" said Sam. "I saw a khaki uniform in the ravine…"

"Which could have meant rangers or patrol or anti-poaching. Sam! Be straight with me. What happened up there? Did you stop there for a *skyf* (smoke) on your way back from Makhadzi yesterday?"

Sam searched for a suitable dodge, but his mind went blank. He indicated for Franco to follow him out of the office and outside to the back of the laundry block.

"Yesterday, I took a stock check over at the Makhadzi and helped fix a fence – a honey badger has dug a hole under the mesh. I buy a couple of cokes, a pack of smokes and drive back via the picnic site. I stop there for a cigarette. A white Landrover pulls up with blacked-out windows. Four men get out - a Tsongan security guard, an old man and two big Russian dudes. I assume they're lost, so I offer directions. Next thing – all four are shot dead in front of me."

Franco rubbed his eyes in disbelief. "And you didn't think to mention it when you got back? Or when we were out with the clients?"

"No, Franco! I didn't know what to do. I took the clients up there thinking…"

"Thinking?"

"I don't know what I was thinking. I thought maybe I imagined it."

"You imagined it? *Kak, man!* You took the clients with you."

"They're OK though."

"They're OK? What about the Tsongan guy – or the old guy – or the Russian *okes* for that matter?"

"No. I mean…"

"I know what you *bluddy* mean. What did they want?"

"No idea."

Franco shepherded Sam back into the office, shoved him into a chair and paced about. "Look – in terms of the clients, you took a stupid risk. I'll wait until the Park Rangers have completed their investigation and then decide whether we reveal your involvement. Maybe you just happened to be in the wrong place at the wrong time. Is there anything else I should know?"

"No."

"Good. Take my Game Drive at 4.00pm and stick to the tarmac. I'll stay here and wait for Greg's call."

"Thanks, Franco. I'm sorry."

"*Nee, man* – don't apologise. Just get your head back on task – you're too strong an asset for me to lose – that's until Maxwell gets his permit."

Sam shot a look of distress at Franco.

"I'm pulling your leg, *Soutie*!"

"Ah – OK. Good."

Sam stomped off to his rondavel and threw himself petulantly on his bed. Several wild permutations flooded his brain. The old man that had been gunned down was certainly not the Anton Groenewald or Anthony Greenwood that he had known. But the old man's knowledge of the cloth maps and key was too much of a coincidence. The more Sam thought about him, the more he discerned similarities – a relative… a twin? But who was the shooter? Why kill the men? Why not me? What if the shooter was protecting me, and if so from whom or what? Why had Mr Greenwood's legacy suddenly become an issue? The tin was buried up on the ridge. Perhaps I should check on it?

Sam didn't fancy the trip by himself. He jumped: there was a knock at the door.

"Franco wants to see us," called Maxwell.

When Sam and Maxwell entered the office, Franco was on the phone but wound up the conversation. "Guys, that was Greg over at Phalaborwa. The forensics have almost finished up in the ravine. They've recovered four bodies or what's left of them. The missing Tsongan has been ID'ed, but they haven't ID'ed the other three bodies. Greg says the shooters must have cleaned up after themselves."

Maxwell glanced at Sam. "What happened?"

"Sam will fill you in, Max. Change of plan. I'll take the clients out at 4.00pm while you take a trip over to the ravine. Something might jog your memory. Take my car. I want you back by 6.30pm to fire up the braai. *On y va... Voetsek...* Bugger off!"

Sam apprised Maxwell of what he had seen in the ravine. Arriving at the picnic site, they watched a Parks Board flatbed truck pulling out. In the back were ten or so Park staff straddling clear plastic bags filled with forensic evidence – mostly ripped clothes and bones.

Sam parked in the exact place where the white Landrover had parked. He got out and peered over the ridge before selecting several sizeable sticks, which he positioned carefully in the sand.

Maxwell monitored Sam's curious behaviour. "What are you doing?"

"I was here."

"I know... What? You saw the shooting? I thought..."

"I don't remember much." Sam stepped back several paces and planted another stick by his feet. "Four shots – there was no report so I'm guessing the weapon or weapons were silenced – four distinct whistling sounds. One came very close to me and hit the old man. It made me flinch." He pointed to the picnic table. "I saw this guy's head jerk backwards. The shots must have come from behind me. Next, the old man fell to his knees." Sam pointed to the hut by the barrier. "I saw the Tsongan security guard draw his pistol. He was thrown backwards against the wall and then fell forward." He walked over to Franco's car. "The driver was already down. I was parked here next to the toilet. I dashed over and got the hell out."

Maxwell pottered around and beckoned Sam over to the thatched booth where the security guard had been dispatched. Sam watched attentively as Maxwell poked his finger into a small recess.

"What'cha got, Max?"

"The bullet impacted here, but it's been gouged out. There's residual blood-spatter on the wall. Judging by the angle of the bullet's entry, it came from high ground."

Maxwell pointed to a rocky outcrop on the side of the ravine before digging out a pair of binoculars from the glove compartment of Franco's car. "Sam, stand exactly where you were when the shooter opened fire."

Maxwell walked to where each victim had perished and focused the binoculars on the side of the ravine. Walking along the road, he stopped underneath a tree. "A leopard was up there."

"I saw him this morning. He was fat."

"*Eish!*" exclaimed Maxwell, realising why. Noting a disturbance in the sand, he selected a game trail that led up the side of the ravine. It was dusty and mottled with footprints. Maxwell paused to look back towards the picnic site, before continuing higher to a large flat rock. He studied the area.

"Single shooter – took the shots from here. Footprints lead to the road. Size 11. Probably male."

Sam peered at the road below. It was the same flat rock that the leopard had settled on that morning. The picnic site was a little over a hundred metres away, and in plain sight.

"Good vantage point, Max."

"Agreed. How long between the shots?"

"Couple of seconds?"

Maxwell confirmed what Sam was thinking. "Sniper. He must have cleaned up and taken the Landcruiser. But if this was a stakeout, how did the shooter know to be here? And how did he get here? On foot?"

Sam felt his skin prickle. The tin was buried up on the ridge. "Just going to check on something, Max."

Maxwell continued to search for evidence. Sam clambered up a few metres only for Maxwell to call from below, waving a small clear plastic bag.

"What is it?" asked Sam.

"Apple pips. Not a Kruger endemic."

Sam walked over to a familiar-looking tree stump. The rock and branch he had positioned to obscure signs of digging had been rolled aside. The tin was gone.

Is this what you are looking for?

Sam heard the words, but took a moment to adjust, feeling dizzy, as if a migraine was coming on. He turned expecting to see Maxwell, but in his place stood an old man with white hair.

And then he vanished.

"What the…?" exclaimed Sam.

Maxwell called from below, holding a sliver of torn white fabric. "They cut themselves on an acacia thorn. There's blood - I bagged it."

"I just saw him."

"Who?" asked Maxwell, looking around nervously.

Sam began to hyperventilate. "No one… I was entrusted with something… I buried it up here in a tin. It's gone."

Maxwell pointed to where he had found the bloodied thorn. "Whoever took it, they dragged acacia to hide their tracks. The British are famed for it. It's like placing little white arrows next to cups of Earl Grey tea."

Sam forced out a smile and took a few deep breaths. "I think I just saw a ghost."

"Ah! Sam, it's just shock. Besides…" Maxwell paused and lowered the pitch of his voice. "I have a confession to make."

"Yeah?"

"The Tsongan – I saw him in Camp a week or so ago. Mercy was on Reception. He asked after you. He was carrying a package. Mercy said you were in Makhadzi. I overheard her mentioning the shortcut through the ravine." Maxwell shrugged and added coyly, "She was just being helpful."

"You like her don't you, Maxwell."

"Very much, Samuel. Please don't be cross with her."

Sam wiped away tears. "I thought all this was just childish fantasy. Yesterday changes everything." He sat on a rock and removed a thorn from his boot. "When I was fourteen we'd often visit the Pilanesberg. On one trip I buried the tin out the back of Mankwe Bush Camp – I can't say why I thought it appropriate – it seemed as good a place as any. I'd often stay there, I suppose, so it was easy to keep an eye on it.

Last year, a mate of mine tried to get in touch. He was supervising a Field Course there with Durham University. I was up in the Makgadikgadi Salt Pans at the time, so it took a few days for my folks to relay the message. The nearby Mankwe lake had almost dried up in the drought, so the Parks Board were digging boreholes. My mate mentioned that they had uncovered a body by the Bush Camp, close to where I'd buried the tin. Worried they might uncover it as well, I took leave and retrieved it in the nick of time."

Maxwell sighed. "'*sus!* So what was in the tin?"

"Maybe another time, Max." Sam looked at the apple pips and the fabric. "At least we have a lead. Not a word to Franco about the tin!"

"You go easy on Mercy, and your secret is safe with me."

"Deal," said Sam as he headed down the trail to the road.

"Wait, Sam," called Maxwell. "I'd like to check something."

Maxwell retraced his steps along the ridgeline, stopping occasionally to check the terrain. Lying down on the leopard rock, he focused his binoculars on the Rest Area and then made a beeline for the picnic table where the Russian had taken a headshot. On inspecting the bin behind the table, there were two holes though which a bullet had passed and disappeared into the ravine. Max crouched by a nearby fencepost to the side, behind the picnic table. He took out his bush knife and wheedled it around.

"There we are," said Maxwell. Out popped a lump of twisted metal. "The shooter missed this one. Franco should be able to ID this bullet before the forensic report comes back."

XII: Hard Truths

Dorchester, England
February 15th 1940

On his return to England and Dorset, William Greenwood had much explaining to do. Mossi had furnished him with a work visa and a letter of employment from the Museum in Cairo. It gave him a cast-iron alibi for his disappearance, but it did little to assuage his wife's fury. William suspected that she had found contentment in an old acquaintance. Although it upset William, he knew it was only a matter of time before he would be called away again.

To ease his guilt, he invested quality time in his son Anthony, and in spite of a rigorous schedule interpreting air surveillance footage for a Royal Navy Marine detachment in Dorchester, Captain William Grenwood was home for supper every evening without fail. Against his better judgement, and certainly the wishes of his wife, he began to confide in Anthony.

The reconnaissance work took William's mind off the Stonelore – it had been a month since he had received any news from Mossi or Alexander. With the Stonelore chronicles safely stowed in Egypt, his little stone was locked away in the family safe.

The next morning, a car arrived at the Naval base, decked in official looking regalia and a standard that William didn't immediately recognise. A courier was ushered through to the detachment office and handed William a dossier. It bore the royal seal of King Farouk of Egypt, and there was a cover letter from Mossi.

Museum of Egyptian Antiquities
Cairo
10th February,

Dear Captain Greenwood,

I trust this letter finds you well. King Farouk has agreed our embarkation on May 17th.

The Kingdom of Egypt is preparing for War. The British have all but commandeered the Port of Alexandria 'at their disposal' and King

Farouk is incensed. This has only strengthened his resolve to maintain business as usual. He is a stubborn man: an appealing trait!

I have secured passage and official documentation for you to travel to Cairo, setting out at His Majesty's pleasure on the 4th May from Southampton on the Egyptian coaster, Isis. It has been converted into a heavily defensible vessel so don't expect luxury. I anticipate it docking in Alexandria on May 15th, if not before.

Tension is high in the Mediterranean. The ship bears Egyptian signals, so neither Allies nor Axis powers have reason to interfere.

If you have any reason why you do not feel fit for duty then please contact the Consulate in London by 1st March. If this is the case, I request that you return your stone.

Yours faithfully,

Mostapha Nkosi

The dossier contained various maps and drawings, a lengthy handwritten document from Mossi and several commentaries that William recognised as Alexander's handwriting. He dismissed the courier before locking the dossier and cover letter in the office safe.

Southampton, England
May 4th 1940

Just as Mossi had stated in his letter, the Isis was docked in a berth in Southampton. After signing paperwork for the port authorities, William boarded the vessel.

The coaster measured one hundred feet long and had a robust, steel hull. It bore the signals of the Kingdom of Egypt as well as the symbol for Isis and an ankh, a cross with a hoop at the top. It had been equipped with a cumbersome armament on the bow, while the windows had been modified to accommodate steel cladding, protecting the occupants of the wheelhouse were they to sustain attack. William was ushered on board and taken below deck to his quarters by the captain: a stocky, swarthy gentleman in his fifties. He wore a royal blue cap and a thick navy woollen jumper, and was struggling with the cool spring temperature, wringing his hands irritably for warmth. His English was limited, so William retired to his quarters to unpack.

The smell of smoke and the rumble of the ship's engine signalled imminent departure. William headed up to the deck: the tide had risen significantly. He covered his nose and mouth with a handkerchief. Squinting through the miasma, he gazed across the marina and saw a familiar face staring back at him. It was Anthony – he was waving. William waved back and kept the handkerchief firmly pressed to his face, masking the tears rolling down his cheeks. Father and son held each other's gaze until the fog obscured them.

William had spent weeks pondering how he might break the news of his imminent departure to his wife and only son. Eventually, he engineered orders to second himself to the North Africa campaign. Somehow the Egyptian Consulate had convinced some high-ranking official in the British Government or military intelligence that William would be better employed *in situ*. The official documentation arrived, and William accepted the post. His wife was dismissive; their relationship already strained to breaking point. Anthony was a different matter entirely. His esteem for his father and his work had strengthened their bond, forged in the months since William's return from Cairo. When William broke the news of his departure, the boy wept bitterly. As a token of appeasement, William made the difficult decision to enlighten him with the truth. He took care to separate fact from fiction, allowing Anthony to form his own opinions. The boy was intelligent and a fast learner, and proud to be associated with the Groenewald legacy. Naturally, he was disappointed when William had to cite 'matters top secret' regarding his affairs in Cairo. It didn't stop William dropping hints.

Once the ship had cleared the Solent Sea Forts to the east of Bembridge Point, it bore south-west towards Brest. William spared a thought for his own sailing boat, that he had sequestered in a small harbour near Granville, France – now retrieved and berthed in Weymouth Harbour. The sea was rough but the sky clear. Clinging on to the bow armament's casing, William fixed his gaze to the horizon and tapped the little cubic box in his coat pocket.

That night the ship docked at Brest to take on more coal. The harbour was sheltered, the sea calm and William relaxed. Reading at his desk, he was interrupted by a knock at the door and summoned to dinner. Donning a jacket and tie, he ate on his lonesome. The food was intensely spicy – probably to hide the quality of the ingredients and the cook. On returning to his quarters, William swallowed a sachet of magnesia salts.

Mossi had sent a batch of paperwork including a transcript of a letter from Alexander to Mossi, written in German. Having met with his acquaintance in Sarajevo, Alexander had travelled to several archaeological sites in Bulgaria and Turkey, all under the auspices of the Museum of Cairo. The letter had been written and posted in Aleppo, Syria, where Alexander had located several relics confiscated from a black-market dealer. Alexander was confident that he would arrive in Alexandria on time. He expressed concern that he had not heard from Rosalind in months, and assumed that she had made plans to travel to South Africa by any means at her disposal.

Port of Alexandria
May 17th 1940

Docking in Alexandria was tougher than William had envisaged, in spite of the warning. The harbour was crammed with military vessels, and the Isis was forced to find an alternative berth. At sea for two weeks, and without academic nourishment, William had made headway learning Arabic at Rosalind's suggestion. Frustratingly, the crew of the Isis showed no interest in interacting with him.

Eventually, the Isis dropped anchor and lowered the tender boat. William watched from the lower deck, but was told sternly by the captain to return to his cabin. William obliged, but not before noticing the crew had begun to remove the steel cladding. It hadn't occurred to William that the Isis was the vessel that Mossi had commandeered from King Farouk. He had, however, figured out that the coaster was equipped with a diesel engine as well as a coal-powered boiler.

Using the time to annotate a few of his own sketches, William saw out of his porthole window that the tender had returned, and watched it being roped into place by the burly captain, tugging on a foul-smelling cigarillo. Alexander boarded, followed by another man.

"William, good to see you! This is Boris Kuriagin. We've been on quite an adventure. I'll tell you more once we're settled in."

Boris, like Alexander, was deeply tanned. Thickly set and sweating profusely, he grinned and shook William's hand before being ushered to his cabin.

The tender pushed off and returned an hour later with Mossi and a pile of luggage, wooden crates, the Stonelore trunks and diesel drums.

"William! Are you ready for adventure?" crowed Mossi.

"Yes, indeed. Tenterhooks. Any developments?"

"Plenty. Fancy a drink? I'm parched."

Mossi led William to the upper deck. William stared in disbelief at the metamorphosis: the steel cladding had been fully removed; the 'salt-caked smoke stack' had been scrubbed clean and supported a mast; the upper deck had been fitted with wooden struts supporting canvas shade cloths and equipped with tables and cushioned *suffa* chairs.

Mossi clocked William's stupefaction. "I made some modifications. Wind will save on fuel."

William was speechless. Mossi laughed and poured him a long gin. Two of the Isis' crewmen reported for duty. They had shaved, donned pressed white suits and busily arranged snacks.

"Let's sit," said Mossi. "I'll bring you up to speed."

The ship's claxon abruptly signalled departure, startling William, who spilled his gin on his trousers. Guffawing, Mossi eased into a *suffa* while William dabbed himself dry.

"I need to come clean, William," said Mossi, enjoying his choice of words. "I couldn't show the pictures in my folio or the stone to the Committee at the enquiry because one or two of my colleagues might smell a rat. The true Eye of Horus that I discovered at Tanis is now safely stowed in a case at the Museum, having been located in a lock-up outside Geneva. Should we need to produce the relic, my wife has instructions."

"But Hemiunu and the stone?" asked William.

"I have no doubt that the stone helped in the design of Khufu's pyramid. As for the link to Hemiunu – I had to take a leap of faith. You provided the paper trail."

"I had my suspicions," said William, settling himself.

"So did my King. But as you will appreciate, William, a good story is sometimes more appealing than reality. I needed this ship."

"And the vendor?"

"Oh, the vendor exists – but all in good time. We will continue to use the Eye of Horus ruse as cover."

"The Seven Scribes?"

"All in good time, William!" Mossi pointed up at the sail unfurling in the wind. "We are permitted to travel through the Suez Canal to the Red Sea. I'll tell you more at this evening's debrief."

Mossi's voice tailed off as Boris and Alexander joined William on the upper deck. It had been more than six months since William had seen Alexander. The Austrian had put on weight.

"I've been dreaming of this day for many years," announced Boris Kuriagin. "Alexander and I spent the last few days reliving our youth. Our livers have taken punishment."

"*Ja*, Boris! *Genau*," agreed Alexander, pushing aside his gin. "Boris is Professor of Archaeology and Biological Anthropology in Kiev – under the watchful eye of his Soviet colleagues. He met me at the Yugoslavia border, and we travelled south-east to Sarajevo. There's a man there who wanted us to look at some curious hills. He believes they might conceal pyramids."

"Pyramids? In Yugo…"

"They are huge," interrupted Boris. "The problem is that they are hidden below thousands of years of forest growth. We've taken readings and samples for you, Mossi, should you wish to delve deeper."

"Fascinating," said Mossi with a wearied expression.

No one attempted conversation for an awkward few seconds. Mossi broke the tension by excusing himself, citing a matter of urgency.

"I think it's time I explained, William," said Alexander, leaning forward in earnest.

"I'm aware that Mossi has shown you other stones. He discarded them as irrelevant curiosities, as did Boris and I, until we read the Stonelore. Boris…"

Boris was sound asleep. Alexander smirked.

"Boris's father was an Archaeologist and adventurer before him. Years ago, Mossi, Boris and I collaborated on dig sites in China, Vietnam and Cambodia. Being a Soviet, Boris was able to get us access. We took up from where his father had left off. Together we uncovered many ancient temples and pyramids in the Far East, bearing similar structural hallmarks to the ancient builders in Meso-America as well as here in Egypt. Have you heard of the Seven Sages or Scribes?"

"Mossi mentioned them in passing," replied William.

"There is a temple at Edfu near Aswan dedicated to the god Horus – reputedly built by Imoteph nearly five thousand years ago and added to, bit-by-bit. The façade was constructed in the Ptolemaic period about two thousand years ago. The original site, excavated in the 1860s is much, much older. The inner sanctum offered up a library of scrolls that predate Khufu's dynasty. They speak of a once fertile land, crisscrossed with waterways, and destroyed by cataclysm – lost to the 'sands of time'."

"The Sahara?"

"Indeed. North Africa was once a vast wetland. The scrolls refer to travellers from a far off land that bestowed knowledge on mankind. Sound familiar? The hieroglyph for this knowledge was the precursor to the Eye of Horus, which has now come to represent divine protection and health. Whether or not the Eye was used by Hemiunu is conjecture, but what we can say is that Hemiunu was either a genius who understood the dimensions of the planet, had advanced understanding of mathematics and engineering techniques, or he received help."

"So, my time was not entirely wasted then," said William, trying to process the information. "And then you made the connection to the pendant stone found at Tanis?"

"Let me finish, William. The Seven Sages, also chronicled by the Sumerians, were reputedly giants among men – survivors – refugees from a cataclysmic flood that inundated their world, 'The Homeland of the Primeval Ones'.

"A continent beset by deluge?" asked William. "You're not referring to Atlantis, Plato's mythical continent? Santorini in the Aegean Sea, perhaps? Surely a metaphor for the dangers of capitalism and greed?"

"Plato recorded what Solon had found in the Library, here in Alexandria, and suggested the catastrophe occurred nine thousand years before his time. The Bible, The Qur'an and myriad historical texts both secular and sacred from all across Asia describe a catastrophic deluge. Boris and I saw further evidence of this in Mesopotamia only three weeks ago. What if Noah's Flood really happened, and Plato conveniently put a date on it?"

"That would mean it occurred eleven and a half thousand years ago – around 10,000BC. Have you any proof? It's an incredible theory."

"Exactly! Where else better for Boris and I to start than ancient Sumer?"

Boris stirred at the mention of his name and tuned into the conversation.

Alexander continued. "It wasn't easy, but we managed to get access to a museum in Baghdad that stores excavated ceramics from Shuruppak in Iraq. They were crudely dated to 3000BC, found under several feet of riverine sediment. We interviewed (Alexander rubbed his fingers together) one of the scientists at the museum who had examined pottery fragments dredged up from the Persian Gulf. He

66

suspected some of them to be more than twice that age."

"So what's to stop the scientist publishing his research?" enquired William. "If the Iraqi museums are in accordance…"

Boris cleared his throat, stopping William. "Imagine a catastrophic deluge so powerful it rips humanity from the land and tosses it into the sea; covers the plants and trees in saltwater and silt and destroys all habitation. Eventually the deluge subsides and the few survivors start from scratch. Civilisation is dependent on collusion between humans, each man and woman performing a skill that is useful to the population in a struggle to survive the most basic pressures – shelter from the elements, food, water, disease *etcetera*. In this theoretical model it's the hunter-gatherers that flourish; the bow and dart hunters of the Amazon; the Aboriginal people of Australia; the Bushmen of southern Africa. They can feed and harvest medicine from the scarcest of sources – their lives are inextricably linked to the land. This cycle of events may repeat itself time and time again every twenty five thousand years or so – until someone is smart enough to write down a list of instructions."

"Are you saying someone did?" asked William.

"Not just one person," Boris beamed haughtily. "Hundreds of texts have come to light depicting catastrophe and rebirth from Mexico to Egypt; from Sumer to Japan; The Bible; Qur'an; Vedic texts. They're not just tall tales – they are historical accounts. We've just been too pig-ignorant to accept them for what they are. Communication is key here – civilisation is dependent on verbal as well as pictoral and textual communication. There are, however, inherent problems that arise from such sophistication – politics, religion, propaganda and ultimately… tyranny."

William took a moment to process Boris's revelation. He agreed – throughout history, empires had risen and fallen just as Plato had described in *Timaeus* and *Critias*. Assuming that Boris was citing the reasons why the Iraqi scientist could not simply announce his theory, just as Mossi had been forced to improvise in Cairo, William elected to steer Boris back to flood mythology. "So are you suggesting that there were two separate deluges, five thousand years apart? And where do the stones fit in?"

"There may have been more deluges, but two significant ones, yes," replied Boris. "What's more curious is this – we are led to believe that there was a Megafauna extinction that occurred about 10,000 years ago; mammoths and sabre-toothed cats *etcetra*. Bear in mind the timeframe of Plato's cataclysm. Were humans responsible for the eradication of these beasts? Or was rapid climate change the culprit? What if humans were put on the brink of extinction as well?"

William found himself, at once, enthralled. He visualised a map of the world with isolated pockets of humanity, each struggling to survive for thousands of years while adapting to their post-apocalyptic, rapidly changing environment.

Boris saw that William was warming to the concept. "When Alexei alerted me to the stones' significance I was, at first, dismissive. I'd carried such a stone with me for years – my father brought it back from Cambodia before the Great War. Nevertheless, I began analysis in Kiev last year. The internal structure is crystalline and the outer coating, whilst smooth, is extremely tough like a nut, but not impenetrable. And then the dreams began – nothing like I'd experienced before. I handed the stone over to a colleague in Kiev – an authority on electrical signalling in the brain. He records and analyses brainwaves – electrical oscillations produced during meditation or sleep. He found that if the stones were subjected to certain frequencies or mechanical pressure, they vibrated and emitted radiation. I put myself forward as a test subject."

"Stone Age survival texts and crystal telephones?" scoffed William. "That's a big leap."

"And I'm sure you are familiar with how a radio works, William?" Mossi made a timely appearance at the top of the flight of stairs to the upper deck.

"Yes, but that took years to develop, with detailed knowledge of electrical circuitry and frequency modulation." William wore a pained expression. "The mica is wafer thin and you need a battery, wiring, numerous electronic amplifiers, valves, switches, bells and whistles."

William staggered towards the drinks table to compose himself. Pouring a large scotch, he turned to his colleagues. "There are more things in heaven and earth, Horatio."

"Irony that you should quote Hamlet, William," said Mossi. "Because it is during our dreams that communion occurs, and it's my philosophy that we try to extract the information."

"Point taken," acknowledged William. "So to summarise, Mossi – you think pre-dynastic Egyptian, Olmec, South American and Indus societies were handed instructions on how to reconstruct society through communion with the stones, thousands of years before mainstream Science has it cemented in the mind of every schoolchild?"

"Sort of," replied Mossi.

"Well, then – where did the stones come from? And when were they handed out?"

"That, William, is what we intend to find out. By my estimation they were in circulation over ten thousand years ago. There's evidence here in Egypt to corroborate my theory – but as to who handed them out? The evidence is rather thin. But our journey should shed some light on our mysterious travellers, or as Boris puts it so romantically, 'The Seven Scribes'."

DELIVERANCE

Ckan-Premek awoke from communion with the stone and wiped away tears. The eldest and most respected Premek matriarch, Tsuk, had passed on owing to her tremendous age and compounded by exhaustion and starvation. Tsuk was the sole reason that the Premek had survived for more than a thousand years in the caverns, locked in post-cataclysmic darkness. As new leader of the motley band of survivors, Ckan was duty-bound to lead the Premek into the unknown – his stone would be their guide.

Each Premek loss left an indelible mark on Ckan. He delivered the news to his kin. Numbering fifty-six men, women and children, he took responsibility for each and every one, and in return the Premek placed their trust in him without question – all but one – Ckan's cousin Lek.

Since arriving in the bay aboard the now stricken ship, several of Ckan's kin had perished. Two had succumbed to infected wounds sustained on hunting trips; three to poisoned berries; two to snake bites; and one man simply disappeared. The man in question, Lek, was scouting for resources in the north. A search party was dispatched, and in the dead of night they stopped in the foothills of a mountain range. A stream in spate had washed away Lek's tracks. There was no indication of a struggle or any trace of his belongings.

At the behest of Lek's mate Sul and their two adult offspring, Ckan suggested they widen the search, but after consultation with the elders it was decided that the entire clan should leave the relative safety of the bay and travel north into the unknown. After all, local sources of food and firewood were fast diminishing.

The ship's timbers were recovered from the surf and fashioned into litters to transport their bivouac shelters, tools and food. Spring water was stoppered into gourds and loaded onto four tamed buffalo. The younger Premek carried backpacks crammed with cured meat, medicines and ointments. The last and most precious litter housed the granite box, protected by acacia wood panelling and lashed onto two stout wooden poles with sinew and palm frond cordage. It took four of the Premek's strongest to bear its weight.

It was dusk when Ckan called his kin to prayer and gave the signal to leave. Several young women went ahead as scouts to select the safest route out of the bay. Armed with bows and arrows they were fleet of foot and quick to supplement food and firewood. The remaining Premek women were tasked with carrying the young, and being just as strong and athletic as their male counterparts, took over the burden of the litters when required. The few remaining elders carried what they could and sang to lift spirits.

The caravan moved steadily inland in darkness over the saddle of a flat-topped mountain and north through cool forest, until they reached a grassy plain. The starry sky outlined the mountain range into which Lek had disappeared.

One of the scouts had brought down a *quagga* and was busy stripping skin and meat from its carcass with a sharp forged blade. Such cast metals were vital to the Premek's survival and keeping them oiled and well tended was high priority; they were irreplaceable.

It weighed on Ckan's mind how the Premek might be received if they were to run into other cataclysm survivors. In the two years that the Premek had spent in the bay they had only found remnants of pre-cataclysm human settlement: petroglyphs and the skeletal remains of *strandlopers*. What if the mountains were home to roaming bands? Would they be hostile?

Ckan removed the stone from its pouch, fashioned from bushbuck scrotum and tied round his neck with strips of dried twisted hide. Losing the crystal that Tsuk had given him during the ocean crossing, he felt a pang of remorse. But all was not lost. Each of the stones' crystal cores seemed to be impregnated with memories of the Premek's predecessors – a wealth of information. Decades of communion with her stone had taught Tsuk how to extract pertinent information to keep her kin safe – and she had passed this gift on to Ckan. It was Tsuk's parting wish that the stones be given to those who were worthy; those who might have the capacity to comprehend the information locked away for millennia.

By dawn, the Premek had reached the escarpment and sought protection from the sun.

Prolonged hibernation in the dark polar caverns had brought significant changes to the Premek's physiology and, despite their physical prowess, their eyes suffered in the glare of the sun. The sun's curse was also a cure and, combined with the domestication of the buffalo, milk strengthened their brittle bones. Lotions such as coconut oil and the consumption of seeds, fruits and nuts softened their scaly skin, alas, making it easier for pestilential insects to penetrate. One of the Premek elders had discovered a root extract that made an effective repellent, and when ground and mixed with aloe sap, a soothing balm.

The Premek giants had graduated from a struggle to survive to walking tall through the southern African *veld*, albeit at night. Each man and woman was tasked with a role, whether to hunt, build, carry, repair or craft tools and weapons. In Tsuk's absence, the elders schooled the clan in history, astronomy, and how to prepare food, cook and concoct medicines.

The Premek fed well and rested under a natural rock ledge until, at dusk, one of the scouts brought news. She had spotted small sets of footprints including a far larger Premek print. There were spots of blood amongst the spoor. Ckan immediately called his kin to prepare: every man, woman and child armed themselves with spears, swords, bows and arrows and rudimentary armour fashioned from all manner of dried hide, bone and lightweight wood. Leaving the beasts, caravan and children under the supervision of an elderly matriarch and four of Ckan's most skilled fighters, Ckan moved out under the cover of darkness up a ravine.

They followed the trail until they could hear voices. Ckan discerned a group of four diminutive men skinning an antelope. Judging by their percussive tongue-clicks, they were Khoikhoi Bushmen.

Ckan ordered his scouts to hold their position and waited until the Bushmen had finished their butchery. When they moved off, Ckan followed for several hundred metres until he caught a whiff of wood smoke. Passing a signal to the outermost scouts, he commanded them to outflank the hunting party and locate the source of the fire. Word returned that there was an encampment ahead numbering twenty or so individuals, but no sign of Lek. Ckan gave the signal to intercept the four Bushmen with blow darts tipped with a sedative extracted from beetle larvae. The Bushmen dropped noiselessly into a deep sleep. Ironically, it was from Khoikhoi that the Premek's predecessors had learned the art of poison-tipping arrows. If Lek were held captive, Ckan had four souls to bargain with.

Silently, the Premek surrounded the camp, using their enhanced night vision to search for sentries. There were none – the Premek outnumbered the Bushmen two to one. Swiftly, they descended and restrained them.

The eldest of the Khoikhoi was first to utter anything recognisable to Ckan as language. There was enough light from the fire for him to see his gigantic Premek assailants, and he immediately surrendered; wide-eyes filled with terror. Ckan dragged him aside, like an infant, while the Premek bound the other Bushmen. Without women and children accompanying them, Ckan surmised that the group was merely a hunting party, and their village would be nearby.

Ckan sat the Bushman elder by a small fire and pulled out a stoppered gourd. He took a drink and offered it to the man. Sniffing suspiciously, the Bushman took a swig and spat it out. He savoured the spice infusion, and satisfied that it wasn't poison took another swig. Ckan rolled out the stone from its pouch and closed his eyes in communion. Several minutes passed before Ckan uttered a series of strange clicks. The Bushman coughed in disbelief and replied.

The Premek's petrified prisoners listened attentively to the conversation and their manner changed. Ckan ordered his kin to release the Bushmen, who remained in a huddle. He then ordered them to relinquish the bag containing their antelope meat, and for the sedated men to be brought forward. Selecting five of the Premek to stay the night with the Bushmen, he sent the others back to mobilise his kin at the base of the ravine. It would take several hours in the cool of the night to ascend with the heavy litters.

The Bushman elder spoke and Ckan translated for his kin. The Bushmen had found Lek delirious, his body fighting the venom from a mamba bite. They were tentative, not knowing what to make of Lek's size and elongated cranium. The elder had administered herbal anti-venom, before carrying Lek back to their village. They had left him in the care of the Shaman or *Sangoma*.

The Bushman elder offered to take Ckan to Lek at dawn. Ckan asked if they could travel immediately. The Bushman spat in disgust and cited Lek's predicament as a good reason why his people stayed by the fire at night. Ckan respected the elder's wisdom, but then explained that the Premek's skin would suffer in the glare of the sun. The elder reconsidered Ckan's proposal and gathered several of the hunting party. Ckan instructed the remaining Premek to stay by the fire and await the caravan. Within seconds he was running with the Bushmen, clattering bows on quivers to announce themselves to critters concealed in the bush. After an hour, Ckan heard rhythmic beating and the ululating voices of women.

The village had been fenced with acacia. Leaping through a breach, the Bushmen led Ckan through a maze of thatched mud-huts. The music and singing stopped. The people looked at Ckan in awe and fear.

A baby's cry broke the silence, and its mother held it close to suckle. The throng parted to reveal a stricken, prostrate Lek. He was sweating profusely and writhing in agony. The elder Bushman indicated that Ckan should approach the *Sangoma*, his body daubed head to toe in white and yellow paint, shivering in unison with Lek. Suddenly, the Shaman's shivering stopped, as did Lek's torment. Ckan crouched beside Lek and felt for a pulse. It was weak but regular. Lek's breath was fragranced. The *Sangoma* collapsed and was tended by several women who forced him to drink a gourd of similarly fragranced fluid. Opening his eyes, the painted man looked calmly towards Ckan, got up and disappeared into one of the huts.

The Bushman elder indicated for Ckan to help him lift Lek gently. With assistance, they took the frail Premek into one of the huts and laid him on a woven grass pallet. Ckan took his gourd and attempted to administer some herbal water to Lek, but the elder pulled back Ckan's hand and shook his head, pointing to the door flap. The elder led Ckan away and sat him by the fire amongst a group of scarcely clothed women who giggled at Ckan's elongated head, beard and tightly bound hair. One mischievous little boy poked Ckan's head with a stick. Ckan flinched and laughed, scaring the little boy off; silencing the jittery women. The Bushman elder reached forward for Ckan to hand him his gourd, and took out a leather wad containing a powder. The elder explained that it was the same *muti* that the *Sangoma* had imbibed and used to treat Lek. He dropped a pinch on his tongue, another in Ckan's gourd and told him to drink it all. Ckan resisted for a second, but was overcome by a sense of willingness. He drank the potion.

XIII: Communion

Suez Canal, The Kingdom of Egypt
May 20ᵗʰ 1940

It wasn't the first time that William had deliberately exposed himself to the stone, but this time he had a better idea of how it might take effect. If Boris were to be believed and the stone emitted radiation affecting the brain's neural pathways: meditation and sleep might just enhance William's ability to interact with it. He was all too aware of the stone's more pernicious nature. He consoled himself that there was no indelible proof either way.

The waters of the Gulf of Suez were calm when William sat at his cabin desk to attempt communion with the stone. He experimented with different states of mind and proximities. Each morning he would wake from a deep sleep expecting to marvel at his dreams, but after four nights he was none the wiser. He revealed his disappointment to his colleagues.

"Boris, how long were you exposed to the stone before you became aware of the dreams?" asked William.

"In the clinical trial? – maybe a week. But I didn't try to commune with the stone – it had been stowed in my travel bag for years. I can't explain why I was drawn to Sarajevo, just as I can't conclusively say that the pyramidal features we saw are manmade. When we left, the dreams stopped, but that may have something to do with quantity of alcohol I consumed."

Alexander clutched his liver and agreed. "*Genau*! I'm not as young as I used to be. You Russians were suckled on vodka!"

After breakfast, the Isis docked. Mossi excused himself to meet a colleague in Suez: largely to ensure his cover story was in place and to keep King Farouk apprised of their progress. He returned shortly afterwards. "Gentlemen, our first port of call will be Stone Town, Zanzibar. William will coordinate and collate our work documents. Alexander, Rosalind was spotted in Dar-es-Salaam. She is alive and well."

Mossi drew their attention to three named briefcases. "Please don't open them yet. I need to inform you of their contents. I've compiled three sets of research that will occupy us for most of the

75

journey. I'd like you to analyse the contents, but not discuss them. You are only to address questions to me. Is that clear?"

The men nodded in agreement.

"There is one last thing. I don't think it's fair that we leave William with the sole responsibility of communing with a stone. Before we departed Alexandria, I dispatched a colleague from the museum to bring these to Suez."

Mossi opened a case and handed Boris and Alexander a small cubic box each.

"Boris, this is your stone that led you to Sarajevo. Stick with it – I'm interested to see if you are able to reattach to its wavelength. If there is no response, you will act as a control for the experiment. Alexander, take this – it's the inset stone from the Eye of Horus. I will experiment with the Cusco stone. Good luck. I hope we all find the experience profitable!"

XIV: The Meeting

Letaba Rest Camp, Kruger National Park, RSA
October 25th 1998
Dawn

> *He screams in anguish.*
> *The steel chains crackle and spark.*
> *His disciples fall.*

"Sam!" yelled Franco as he banged on the door to his rondavel.

Sam woke suddenly, checked his watch and cursed. "Sorry, Franco. With you in five."

"I'll be in the jeep."

Sam dressed and dashed out.

Franco was sitting behind the steering wheel. "We had a call from Makhadzi this morning. A guy checked in five days ago and hasn't been seen since. He left his keys in the ignition. The car was empty apart from a note in the glove box addressed to you."

Sam's eyes lit up. "To me? Did he give a name?"

"*Ja.* Fax arrived this morning."

Franco handed it to Sam. It was a photocopy of the man's passport.

Sam smirked. "Jimi Hendrix?!"

"Do you know this man?" asked Franco, pulling out of the car park.

"No."

The photo showed a Caucasian man in his late twenties.

"His parents might be Hendrix fans?" said Sam. "I had a Maths teacher called Hendriks once, but he must be in his late sixties by now."

"What say we have a look at this note?" said Franco.

It was only a half hour drive to Makhadzi 'Wild' Bush Camp on the ravine road past the picnic site. Franco insisted on having a nose around before driving on.

Sam collected the note from the Makhadzi office, and returned to the car. "It says, *Call JH*."

"Did he leave a number?" asked Franco.

Sam checked the paper thoroughly and the envelope. "Nope."

Once back in the office, Franco examined it under ultraviolet light and heated it with his cigarette lighter.

"I give in," exclaimed Franco, tapping the telephone as if he were going to 'phone a friend' for help. "Any ideas?"

Sam picked his thumbnail for inspiration. "Can I borrow your phone?"

Franco looked surprised, but turned his telephone towards Sam who tapped in the corresponding numbers to the letters in JIMI HENDRIX: 54644363749. There was no dialling tone.

"I see what you're doing," said Franco. "Put a 00 dialling code in front."

This time the call connected and rang.

"Sam?"

It was a man's voice.

"Yes. It's Sam."

"Are you alone?"

"Yes," replied Sam, holding a finger to his lips.

"Good. We should meet."

Sam noted a Russian accent. "When and where?"

Maxwell entered the office. Franco did his best to silence him but it was too late. The phone went dead. Sam redialed, but there was no response.

"*Jeez!*" Franco held his head in his hands.

"What did I do?" asked Maxwell.

"Next time, knock!" yelled Franco.

Suddenly, the phone rang and Sam picked up.

"Hello?" said Sam.

"Don't lie to me, Sam. Is that clear?"

"Yes. I'm sorry. My boss just walked in." Sam screwed up his face.

After anxious seconds, there was a reply. "Did your boss read the note?"

"Yes," replied Sam.

"OK. He needs to leave now."

Sam waved Franco and Maxwell out of the office.

"He's gone."

"Write down these instructions," said the voice. "Take the road from Phalaborwa east towards Tzaneen. After nine kilometres turn north and look for the baobab tree about four hundred metres on the left. Park your car and walk due east on foot for ten minutes up the hill. If anyone follows you, it's over."

"What do mean, 'over'?"

The line went dead and Sam replaced the handset.

Franco walked in. "He's given you instructions, hasn't he?"

"Yes. Can I borrow the jeep?"

"Only if you tell me where you're going."

"I can't, Franco. He says if anyone follows me 'it's over'."

Franco shook his head. "What if he's bluffing and wants you dead?"

"I guess if he wanted me dead he'd have killed me at the picnic site."

"What if his rifle jammed?"

Sam couldn't think of a good reason.

Maxwell produced the evidence bags. "We found where he took the shots and these – a bullet, acacia thorn, torn fabric and apple pips. We thought you might be able to ID the bullet."

"Where did you find it, Max?"

"In the fence post behind one of the victims."

"I'm impressed, Max. I'll need help to ID it. Here's the deal, *boet*. We'll take the jeep to Phalaborwa. Drop me off at Greg's office, and I'll have a go at ID'ing the bullet. Maybe we'll get some DNA off that thorn. If you're not back by 5.30pm, I'm calling the police. Deal?"

"Deal," replied Sam.

"That means your rendezvous point can't be that far away."

Sam grimaced and rolled his eyes.

Franco unlocked the office safe, took out an old-school radio collar, and unclipped the tracker. Then he took a pistol out with a fresh magazine and handed it to Sam.

"Load it in the jeep. *Avanti! Hardloop!* Run!"

Sam dropped Franco off at Phalaborwa Head Office. Noting the odometer reading, he drove out of town towards Tzaneen. It wasn't long before he had clocked nine kilometers and turned north. The road was quiet. As instructed, Sam parked the car near the baobab and headed due east through the bush, climbing over a barbed-wire fence into an over-grazed field. Scrambling uphill through thick bush, Sam looked for any signs of habitation or tracks. He waited several minutes before pressing on up a rocky scramble and into a copse of mopani. Ahead was a small corrugated iron shack. He drew his pistol and approached slowly, pushing gently on the ramshackle door. Steadying himself, he popped his head inside. There was a smouldering fire, an empty can of baked beans and a brown sleeping bag tucked into a canvas roll mat.

"Don't move!"

Sam froze, feeling a prod in the middle of his back. He raised his hands in surrender as an unseen hand wrested the pistol from his grip.

"You had the safety on!" mocked the voice.

Sam turned slowly.

"I said, don't move! Anything else I should know about?"

The man had a Russian accent.

"Bush knife on belt."

"Good boy! What's this?"

"It's a tracker."

"Drop it."

Sam did as he was told.

"Now turn around. We haven't much time."

The man wore camouflaged army fatigues, a baseball cap, aviator sunglasses and shouldered a khaki rucksack. He looked nothing like his passport photo ID. In his right hand was a stick.

"Lesson one, Sam – don't assume your attacker is armed. I took your pistol with this." He snapped the stick in half and threw it onto the fire.

"Who are you?" asked Sam

"The ghost of Jimi Hendrix!" The man laughed and removed his aviators. "My name's Yuriy. What time are you expected home for tea?"

"I have to be at the Gate by 5.30pm."

"That gives us two hours."

Yuriy led Sam ten minutes further into the bush until he found a suitable patch of shade. Sam studied Yuriy's features. He looked familiar – tall, strikingly handsome, with short brown hair and dark menacing eyes.

"Have you eaten?" asked Yuriy.

"Yes thanks," replied Sam.

"You're a terrible liar, Sam. Lesson two – only lie when you have to, and make sure it's a good one. Here, take some biltong."

Sam took the meat. "So… are you going to kill me or what?"

Yuriy laughed. "No."

"Do you have my tin?"

"Two cloths and a key?"

Yuriy pulled the tin out of his rucksack and handed it to Sam.

"Why did you take it?

"Take it? I got it back for you. They've been watching you."

"Who?"

"Specifically… the security guy. I watched him dig the tin up on the ridge."

"Ah!" exclaimed Sam. "I went up there a few days ago. What did they want with me?"

Yuriy took off his cap and rubbed his head. "I was hoping you could tell me."

Sam shook his head. "My instructions were to bury the tin."

"And you did well…" Yuriy's accent morphed into 'to-the-manner-born' English. "Right up until the moment when you lost your nerve and gave away its location. Lesson three – don't give the enemy…"

"Stop!" shouted Sam. "Who are you, and why am I here?"

Yuriy gave Sam a wry smile, rolled his eyes and whistled, switching to deep-south US drawl. "Funny. I've been waiting for this moment for many years. In my mind I knew exactly what I was gonna to say – but now…" Yuriy stopped and made a 'bip… bip… beeeeep' noise. "I'm just pulling your leg," said Yuriy, reverting to his native Russian accent. "My name is Yuriy Kuriagin. Born, Moscow 1966 – and educated in Paris, London, Berlin and the Soviet Union. My father worked as a scientist in Kazakhstan. I served Spetsnaz, Russian Special Forces, until 1995. And then… I got bored."

"So? Who were those men, and why did you kill them?"

Yuriy rolled his eyes again before appearing to select an answer from an unseen list. He shrugged his shoulders and made a silly childish face. "They were greedy – evil men." He cut some more biltong for Sam before continuing. "The project my father worked on involved crystals that he collected over many years."

Sam's eyes lit up. "The stones?"

"Bzzz. Correct. He had seven."

"Seven? I held one of them once," said Sam. "It belonged to an old teacher of mine."

"Anthony Greenwood. Yes, Sam, I know your story. He stole it from my father's research facility in Moscow. When I heard that the British Secret Service had been compromised, I tried to get it back."

Yuriy threw his hands up in mock exasperation and rubbed his brow. "I failed!"

"Woah!" exclaimed Sam suddenly realising the implications. "So who has it now, if not your father?"

"That's a conversation for another time. But understand – I am here for your protection. You've been part of a cruel game all your life, and I want to help you set things straight."

"Who was the white haired man?"

"He was part of it." Yuriy halted Sam. "You've been deceived and manipulated. You should know the truth."

"I don't understand. Does this have anything to do with what's in here?" Sam checked the contents of the tin: nothing seemed amiss. "And my dreams…"

"An eagle? Africa? Icy peaks? A glassy-eyed lady who follows you around?"

"Yes! How could you possibly know that?"

"Her name is… Tsuk."

"Tsook?"

Sam felt his fingers numb and his head spin. Lurching forward, he retched out a meaty soup. "Yuriy? What've you done?"

XV: Deception

Queen Maud Land, Antarctica
October 8th 2016

Mark Watts lit the fuse and ran as fast as he could to where his colleagues cowered behind a snowcat digger. Shielded by steel plates and robust caterpillar treads, Mark used the countdown to review his life; excelling at school; drunken high-jinks at Cambridge University; Medical School in Newcastle; the injury that curtailed his rugby career; his first day at KPMG; his recruitment into the Ministry of Defence; his marriage to Sinead Watts (née O'Reilly) and their subsequent divorce; meeting his current partner and the births of his two boys…

A cloud of needle-sharp ice fragments shook the snowcat and caused a whiteout. The blast had brought down a huge section of overhanging ice on top of three frozen corpses, and obscured a mysterious wooden door.

Leo Marchovecchio, Doctor of Forensic Medicine from Caltech, calmly unzipped the hood of his parka jacket. "I hope that was the right decision."

"Only time will tell," replied Mark. "I don't have a great deal of sympathy for Nazi soldiers dead or otherwise. Besides, it's where we found them."

Sinead Watts checked her watch. As team leader of the excavation and extraction party, if the plan failed, the buck stopped with her. "We've thirty minutes before Schneider arrives with the tow trucks." She pulled a hipflask from her down jacket and toasted her team. "If we pull this off it'll be a miracle. Here's to a lengthy jail term." She swigged back a tot of rum and offered it to her colleagues.

"What the hell," sighed Dan Roberts, Sinead's assistant, grabbing the flask. "I'm gonna miss begging for research grants."

"Don't be so melodramatic!" snapped Mark. "My boys are expecting me home in two days."

Sinead snorted.

"And you can keep your sodding opinions to yourself!"

****

"Dr Schneider!" yelled Sinead over the din of diesel engines. "I see you brought the cavalry."

An array of tow-trucks parked up, designed to pull the units of the mobile research base back to Neumayer Station III HQ. Each mobile had been equipped with its own power source, and all were mounted on sleds: living quarters, kitchen, laboratory, office and storage depot.

"Ready when you are!" called Sinead, uncoupling the last of the power cables.

Jan Schneider glanced up to the icefall. "What happened?"

"It seems we got the bodies out in the nick of time."

"Well done, Miss Watts. Are they in cold store?"

"As you requested. But we've taken extra precaution to keep them in the best condition possible. They're mummified in foil and cellophane. Best we don't expose them until we get them to Berlin."

"How thoughtful of you," replied Dr Schneider. "The extraction plane is fitted with an thermoregulated deep freeze with its own backup generator – so you need not have bothered." He retreated to the warmth of his vehicle.

Sinead took out a walkie-talkie. "He's taken the bait."

Mark watched the Hercules LC-130 circle and make its approach towards Neumayer Station III. "You're sure you're OK with this?"

Sinead nodded. "Yup."

"Dan?" asked Mark more forcefully.

"Yeah, sure," replied Dan, marching over to where Leo was overseeing Dr Schneider's team loading three unidentified bodies into one of two crates for deep freeze extraction.

"Sinead," said Mark abruptly. "Stick to the plan. As soon as we're airbourne, get back to HQ and make the call. We should be well on our way to Cape Town."

"Thanks. It needed mansplaining," said Sinead sarcastically.

Leo intervened hastily, preventing Mark from biting back. "We have a problem. Schneider is sending one of his team with you to oversee delivery."

"Who?"

"Her name's Anna. She was with Schneider when they did their inspection. It was her I overheard saying 'widen the search'."

"She's one of Schneider's team," replied Sinead. "She was the one originally assigned to check on the Nazi bodies. I suggested that we needed someone who wasn't German, and she got pissy. That's when you got the call from HQ, Mark." Sinead coughed. "It's one fewer person to dodge in the canteen queue."

"Fine," said Mark. "I'll find a way around her."

Sinead turned while sucking on her cigarette and muttered, "To be sure."

Mark boarded the four-prop aeroplane via the hydraulic cargo ramp and inspected the crates through a frosted window in the deep freeze compartment. The second crate contained an array of ice core samples destined for Oslo. He stowed his belongings in a cargo net as the pilot gave the command to shut the cargo door and pressurise. The hold was full of machinery and cellophane-wrapped boxes crammed with files and samples for further scientific analysis, strapped down to every available lash point. It left little room for the five other passengers.

Light was fading. Within minutes, the plane taxied for take off. Sitting just behind the cockpit, Mark watched out of the window until he lost sight of the Neumayer Base. Once the plane had reached cruising altitude, Mark unclipped his safety harness and took out a pair of noise-cancelling headphones from his bag – and was startled by an attractive young woman. She extended her hand assuredly in spite of the turbulence and clatter of the propellers.

"I'm Anna."

"Mark. You were with Dr Schneider the other night."

"Pleased to meet you, Mark – or should I say Doctor Watts?"

"Mark's fine. I gather you're chaperoning the bodies back to Berlin."

"*Ja*. I guess even Nazis deserve a funeral."

"I guess so," replied Mark unconvincingly, nodding politely to the other passengers.

XVI: Unanswered Questions

Phalaborwa outskirts, Mpumalanga, RSA
October 25th 1998

Sam swatted away a fly from his nostrils. Belted into the driver's seat of the jeep, he noted his pistol and tracker on the passenger seat next to him, along with the tin and an open packet of mints. The taste in his mouth was vile. He got out, spat on the ground and popped a mint. Sam checked his watch: 17:04. Where was Yuriy? He got back into the car and opened the tin. Both cloth maps were there, as was the key. A note on the dashboard read…

Lesson 3: Don't give enemy opportunity to gain upper hand.

On the back was a childish drawing of two stick men holding hands. Sam revved the engine and spun out of the layby.

"You left that a bit late, *boet*. How are you?" said Franco, tugging on a roll-up cigarette outside the Main Gate at Phalaborwa.
"Fine… confused but fine," replied Sam, getting out of the driver's seat. "Maybe you should drive."
"So?" asked Franco. "How was Jimi Hendrix?"

Lesson 2: Only lie when you have to and make sure it's a good one.

"I found an old shack with a sleeping bag and roll mat. I waited for ages but he didn't show, so I went back to the car. I read the instructions again, returned to the shack and found a note saying he'd been compromised. It said he'd been sent by the British Government to protect me, and I must call him if I'm in any danger. I burned the note. When I got back to the jeep, I found this tin and its contents on the passenger seat."
"British Government?" exclaimed Franco melodramatically. "'*sus*. If the South African Defence Force finds out there'll be an international incident! What's in the tin?"
"A packet of mints, my pistol and the tracker," replied Sam, clutching it firmly.
Franco pulled a funny face. "Bizarre! I checked the bullet. It's Russian military issue. Clever, hey! The SADF won't trace that to

London." He chuckled to himself and pretended to grab Sam's thigh again. "*Nee, man*. I'm just glad you're back in one piece."

Sam didn't answer – he just smiled and instinctively scanned the bush for animals.

"Even so, *boet*," added Franco. "You're going to have to find a better place to hide that tin."

Sam looked quizzically at Franco. "What?"

Franco didn't answer.

Suddenly Sam felt anxious. "What…"

"If your life depends upon it, *boet*, my office safe is as good as anywhere."

Sam felt weak. Had Maxwell mentioned the tin? Had Franco seen through his lie? Did Franco know what was really in the tin?

"Your tin – your choice." Franco's voice tailed off.

As the jeep pulled up in front of Reception, Franco sprang out and headed for the office. Sam felt his strength return. He took the cloth maps and key from the tin and stuffed them into his pockets, replacing them with a mint and his handkerchief. He left a thread poking out.

"You know, Franco. Maybe you're right," said Sam. "Your safe is the best place. Please don't open it."

Franco nodded and stowed it along with the tracking device. If Franco were to be inquisitive, Sam would know. He then pulled out a shoulder holster from his desk drawer. "Keep the pistol, *boet* – just in case."

Sam spent the evening revising what Yuriy had told him. If he had been deceived all his life, how much did his parents know? Had they deceived him too? Franco seemed to know more than he was letting on. Sam toyed with the idea of calling *JH*, but his priority – to keep the maps and key safe. He bought packaging, bubble-wrap and sellotape from the Camp general store and bound the maps and key tightly, waterproofing it with some plastic sheeting from the motor depot. When completed, the package was about the same size as his wallet and fitted comfortably into his zipped trouser pocket. 'From now on, they stay with me.'

****

Franco and Maxwell were eager to interrogate Sam over a beer. They chose a table outside on the veranda overlooking the Letaba River, next to a colony of noisy weaverbirds.

"Do you think anyone else will come looking for your tin?" asked Franco, stealing one of Sam's cigarettes from under his nose. "If so, shouldn't we post a security guard?"

"I don't think so," replied Sam. "It would only draw attention. *JH* wrote that I should only call him if I was in trouble. Besides, I've so many questions for him, including the identity of the old man at the picnic site. There was something familiar about him." Sam didn't mention his hallucination.

"So, Jimi Hendrix didn't show?" asked Maxwell.

Sam ignored the question, opting to hail a waiter.

Franco clocked Sam's dodge. "Maybe the forensics will be able to help? The Park's Commissioner has declared the incident 'an internal matter pending enquiry' to keep the Press away. Your name wasn't mentioned so you're in the clear for now."

Maxwell cleared his throat. "Might I ask what is in the tin?"

Franco shifted uneasily. "Don't pressure the boy! He's been through enough without having to divulge his best kept secrets."

"I'd love to tell you guys," said Sam, noting Franco's unease. "But the previous owner went to great lengths to hide its contents, and told me that if I retrieved them, I was in grave danger. I thought it a little OTT, but within an hour he was dead and several days later someone tried to kill me."

"So the shoot out on Makhadzi ridge wasn't the first time you've been up *kak* creek?" exclaimed Franco.

Maxwell looked unsettled. "Maybe it's better you keep your secret to yourself."

"Thanks, Max," said Sam. "And if you notice something suspicious let me know ASAP."

Sam ordered a cheeseburger and a beer from the waiter and changed the subject to the duty roster. Franco divided the workload evenly. He was keen to keep Sam on the premises for his safety, but Sam resisted. Soon they were all ready to turn in.

Sam prepped for bed and secured his mosquito netting. Then he remembered the name, 'Tsuk' and visualised her. How could Yuriy know about Tsuk? Could they share dreams?

88

COHERENCE

Arms and legs shackled;
Hands and feet numb;
His mind removed, abstracted.
He lies there, distant, dumb.
A star hewn into rock:
Resonance: stability.
Atoms cluster into molecules,
Growing in complexity.
Three orbs hover over him,
Dowsing him in light,
Converging in a single point that burns in brilliant light.
Chatty people!
How they love to chatter!
Tubes releasing perfect spheres
Drip slowly – like the leopard's tears.
He can't understand their language.
"Why?" he cries, but no one hears.
His heart rate quickens: people flee,
Fire strips flesh from bone.
Swept away, a cleansing gust.
Bodies are but cosmic dust.

Sam woke with a stinging sensation behind his eyes. Again, his mosquito net had been kicked aside, his bedding damp with sweat. Reaching for his glasses on the bedside table, he stumbled into the bathroom. It was not yet dawn but the sky was light enough to avoid flicking the light on and exacerbating his headache. Glugging water directly from the tap, he noticed a strange brown colouration on his fingers and feared the worst. Hitting the light, he checked himself, but couldn't find the source. The substance was oily and took some scrubbing to remove. In doing so, he noticed that the skin on his right index finger was red and swollen. He returned to his bedside and jumped as something brushed against his foot. Squinting to protect his eyes, he turned the light on to discover an open tin of brown boot polish with its lid and buffing brush nearby. Confused, he replaced the lid. Sam froze. Daubed on the wall were drawings – none of which he recognised. Instinctively, he reached for his pistol.

89

XVII: Code Breaker (Part One)

Abyssinian Coast (Italian East Africa)
May 27th 1940

"William! Wake up. Come quickly. You need to see this."

"Coming, Alex."

William rubbed his eyes and rolled out of bed. The ship had listed under sail at night, and he took a moment to adjust his balance. Dressing swiftly, he left his quarters in the moonlight and followed voices to the upper deck, where he found Mossi passing Boris a cup of what smelled like coffee.

"Boris's cabin! Record what you see," said Mossi.

William found Alexander already there, doodling on a pad. Daubed in toothpaste on the wood-pannelled wall were three separate pictographs. William began sketching. Each one appeared to be a befuddled amalgamation of emblems and symbols. He had seen similar drawings in Huw Willliams's diaries. He dashed back to his cabin, but Mossi intercepted him.

"I asked you not to discuss your findings, but this is different. Let's hear Boris's testimony."

Boris was shivering despite the balmy air. "Where to start?" He shot glances into space, as if he were trying to recall his dream as it unfurled. "Sorry, gentlemen, but this is harder than I anticipated." He closed his eyes and drew breath. "I'm cowering in the dark... anxious... scared... hiding from something... something big... something terrifying. I'm trapped. People are shouting... howling.... I'm crammed in. I can't move.... I can't breathe. There's a high-pitched whirring noise... electrical... a hot wind... a deafening boom. Every bone in my body is shaking until I can bear it no longer... the screams are bloodcurdling. Then silence... darkness. I feel myself falling... balance... symmetry... geometry... resonance. People are humming... singing... chanting... worshipping... the night sky... stars. I can't see what they see... just stars." Boris stopped, took a deep breath and shook his head. "I woke up on the floor of my cabin with a sore finger and covered in toothpaste."

"Gentlemen, I think we should give Boris some time to himself," ordered Mossi.

William hurried back to his cabin to study the symbols and cross-refer them with the ones in the journals. It had taken less than a week for Boris to express sensitivity, reattach to his stone and provide fresh evidence. Sure enough, the symbols bore distinct resonance with Huw Williams's journal entries.

The first pictograph appeared frequently with a series of associated flecks, which looked ostensibly cuneiform in origin. William jotted down different permutations to isolate its basic root. He selected a book from the shelf above his desk on Mesopotamian script and interpreted the symbol as *Unknown* or *Door*. The associated wedges seemed to be a sequence of numbers, but without any frame of reference, he could only guess that they were either measurements or coordinates.

The second pictograph appeared to be a story told in Nordic runes. He isolated a few characters: *Ice. Journey. Birth/Beginning. Knowledge.*

The third pictograph resembled early Chinese script. William found a similar drawing in Samuel Morgan's diary. It was a compound pictograph, and in isolating the individual elements William deduced the meanings *Origin* and *Mountain*. The mountain icon was uncannily similar to the three pyramids on the Giza Plateau.

William put down his pencil. Sunrise had brought a stiff easterly wind, which caused the ship to roll abruptly. A thud startled him. His stone had slipped from the bed linen and rolled towards the door. He snatched it up and pocketed it. Opening the cabin door, he squinted into the rising sun. The crew was adjusting the sails, and the sudden thrust forward indicated they had maximised propulsion. Crossing to starboard there was no sign of land, and after a week at sea he was relieved that he hadn't succumbed to seasickness or cabin fever. He peered over the rail and watched the hull cut through the swell.

Mossi spotted him and beckoned him to the upper deck. "I trust you slept well?"

William appreciated the irony and smiled as he laid out his work. "Not a wink."

"Ah! I see you've been busy deciphering Boris's message. Let's have a *shufti*."

"Each of the three pictographs seems to be derived from three separate language systems. I've seen similarly hybridised drawings in Huw's journals. In this case we have distinct Mesopotamian pictographs, Runes, Cuneiform and Chinese pictographs. *Caveat!* I'm no expert and have very little reference material to help me translate, but they appear to me to be individual characters superimposed onto each other or, in the case of the runes, amalgamated. They appear to tell a story. I've circled elements that I am more confident about, and I've left the rest for interpretation by the better-qualified."

Mossi pulled up a chair and looked at William's notes.

"Reading the symbols left to right, I've put together a list of seven words: *Journey. Ice. New Beginnings. Unknown. Door. Origin. Mountains.* The last symbol, by the way, is drawn in a curiously similar formation to the pyramids at Giza."

"I can't wait to see what the others make of it," remarked Mossi. "Keep it under your hat. Linguistics is Boris's area of expertise." He smiled and winked.

The smell of fried fish made both men reel in anticipation. It had also roused Boris, who looked surprisingly fresh after his night activity.

"Morning, gentlemen!" crowed Boris. "I've just knocked on Alexei's door and he's snoring soundly."

"How do you feel?" enquired Mossi.

"Good. I mean really good. My liver doesn't ache any more."

"Excellent! Fresh fish, coffee and sea air," rejoiced Mossi. "Debrief after breakfast? It's time we all had a chat."

Mossi cleared his throat to indicate that the meeting had begun. "I've decided to call a halt on our research today. It's clear to me that only Boris is exhibiting sensitivity to his stone, and the rest of us should stop forcing communion with ours. I have two reasons for this. First, we don't know how the stones might affect us if we continue, and secondly, we need to be objective and untainted by anything pernicious."

Alexander quickly relinquished his stone to Mossi, but William was reluctant.

"Maybe I should try for a couple more days."

Mossi held his hand out and William dutifully handed over his boxed stone, which was then stowed in Mossi's briefcase with the others.

"Good!" piped Mossi. "Now, I'm sure that you've all dwelt on the meaning of these symbols. William has had a crack at deciphering them, but admits it's not his field of expertise."

"Might I be permitted to glance at William's notebook?" asked Boris.

Mossi granted permission, and William handed it over.

Boris turned the pages slowly, studying them carefully and looked up, impressed. "I agree with you, William. This is the symbol for *doorway*, but *unknown* can also be translated as *foreign land* or *untrustworthy*. The cuneiform wedge-flecks could be numbers, but there are no units associated. I think together they refer to *journey*, if we interpret *unknown* to be *foreign land*. There is a symbol here that I'm struggling to see the significance of, but I've seen it on clay Sumerian tablets – perhaps *knowledge* as you say. The upside down triangle with a line is a symbol for *woman*, but can also mean *origin*."

William looked pleased with himself. "What if all three symbols are part of the same tale?"

Boris pointed out the Chinese pictographs. "I think you're right, William. They all tell of a journey, but not *to* a foreign land, *from* a *foreign land* – a land covered in *ice*. Curiously, the symbol for *mountain* is, as you say, repeated on various oracle bone-scripts that were discovered in pyramidal mausoleums in China. I've always considered them to be a reference to the Giza pyramids, so I don't understand the connection to *ice*. The cross represents the number *seven* and the grid shape represents *man* or *men*. It's a bit of a jump, but what if the symbol tells of a journey by seven people. The Seven Scribes?"

"Let's not get ahead of ourselves, Boris," chuckled Mossi. "We all know how much you love our theory of Egypt being built by the Seven Scribes of Edfu. Alexander, you're next."

Alexander excused himself, returning moments later with a series of drawings that he had transcribed from Huw Williams's journals. "I've seen runes similar to these carved into monoliths near Icelandic burial grounds. I agree, the message suggests that the travellers sought the *origin* or *beginning* in a land of *ice*. In my view, William has correctly interpreted this symbol as *knowledge*, but this *journey* failed. These additional symbols can signify *hunger, death* or *disease*."

Mossi stopped Alexander. "I'm sure the Vikings charted the Arctic Circle, and visited North America long before the Italians. And I have reason to believe that they may have come further south. Are you suggesting they were looking for this 'origin', but had to give up the search?"

"More or less," replied Alexander.

"If so, how did this information become imprinted in Boris's stone? It cannot be that Chinese, Viking and Sumerian adventurers exchanged information? Do the stones communicate with each other?" Mossi reached into a satchel by his chair. He pulled out a stone and tossed it up into the air several times until all three researchers were focused on it.

Mossi eyeballed each of the men. "Gentlemen, I have deceived you. As, of course, is permitted in a game of my design."

They all looked bemused, until Boris crossed his legs nervously.

"Aha!" erupted Mossi, threateningly. "Boris, would you care to explain yourself, bearing in mind that we are in international waters, far from land and any authority."

Boris shot a glance at two burly crewmembers who had made a timely appearance. "I didn't mean any harm, Mossi! Forgive me."

William and Alexander exchanged bewildered glances.

Mossi broke the tension with a laugh. "You must be aware of trust games?" He held the stone up. "The stone in Boris's pocket was found in a mine in Klerksdorp, South Africa and was polished by one of my men to resemble Boris's keepsake. It has no curious properties and certainly doesn't emit brainwaves. It's a placebo."

Alexander and William looked at Boris, aghast.

"You, bastard!" barked Alexander. "Don't tell me I've been chasing after bogus pyramids for nothing?"

"Please!" pleaded Boris. "No! You have it wrong. My stone led me to Yugoslavia. The stones do emit radiation – I assure you – I have the research with me to prove it. But, alas, I have deceived you. Those symbols are composite drawings I fabricated from pre-existing symbols that I found in the journals. I thought it might help me to explain my dreams. Forgive me."

Mossi smiled menacingly. "One of my men saw you creep into William's cabin when he went for a smoke."

William's eyes bulged.

Mossi continued. "I'm well aware that the reason we are here is because I deceived my King, so let us not dwell on the matter any further. I need you to be straight with me. There is no room in this expedition for secrets, lies, heresay and idle supposition."

"I'm sorry Mossi." Boris sounded sincere. "Gentlemen, I meant no harm."

Despite Boris's contrition and Mossi's absolution, Alexander was not in a forgiving mood. He stood abruptly.

"Stop, Alexander!" rasped Mossi. "You are in no position to be judgemental. Be seated!"

Alexander sat down quickly as if reprimanded for something specific, eliciting a gaze of intrigue this time from William and Boris.

Mossi pointed to the three newly issued dossiers. "Back to work. Digest these materials after lunch and we'll discuss them after supper. In the meantime – get some sleep." Mossi withdrew to his cabin as Alexander gathered his notes angrily.

"You owe me a night's sleep!" snapped William, stomping off to his cabin.

William slumped down into the chair where he had spent most of the previous night, and picked up a research paper written by a Mexican Archaeologist called Jesùs Rousseau translated into English by Mossi. William struggled to grasp the finer details. The paper compared and contrasted excavated ruins from Mayan and supposedly Olmec temples and their foundation stones. In every case, the quality of construction deteriorated with the passing of time.

He annotated his sketches with his well-gnawed pencil. 'Upper stonework more eroded – curious – exposure to thousands of years of sun, rain and living organisms. Significance? High quality foundation masonry – evidence of machine-cut stone? Geological movement: localised or tectonic? Alignment?'

Why was there no record of their construction? Did the ancients take their ingenuity for granted? Without sufficient evidence of how ancient Olmec, Toltec or Maya were able to seemingly machine-cut, move and lay massive rocks with such remarkable precision and symmetry, it seemed bizarre to William that these ancient people hadn't bragged about their talents. Then a peculiar idea popped into his head. 'Perhaps rock weighed less?'

He pondered awhile – and crossed the thought out. Pushing back his chair, he poured a whisky from the shelf, adding a drop of water from a little jug. He noted how the liquid clung to the lip. A thought lingered. 'Perhaps the ancients didn't brag about their ingenuity because it wasn't their ingenuity to brag about – but if they received guidance, who were these enlightened master-builders? Did the ancients give thanks by building temples in remembrance? Or did the master-builders erect temples and icons as a self-indulgence?'

That didn't make sense. 'God didn't give Noah instructions on how to build the Ark for it to simply sit on top of mount Ararat as a divine memento. No – the Ark was designed to carry precious cargo. Or perhaps it was a metaphor. Perhaps Noah was an antediluvian Darwin, collecting specimens from all over the world in response to an imminent cataclysm? Like the Ark, did ancient temples, monoliths and dolmens have a functional purpose other than places of worship? Why to this day do we still build mosques, temples and cathedrals of such garagantuan proportions and exorbitance?'

William shut his eyelids. It was clear to him that Mossi was steering his research team into the realm of antediluvian civilisations. 'Perhaps Neolithic dynasties existed far, FAR before the mainstream theoretical date of 10,000BC – or does *Homo sapiens* owe its survival to co-existing hominin societies or… gods?'

But how and where did the stones fit into the puzzle? 'Were the stones gifts? If so – from whom? Who had the technology to design them? Who, in some bygone age, had the requisite understanding to load them with information that could be extracted as brainwaves?'

THE GIFT

Ckan awoke to the sound of animated clicking. He was no longer by the fire in the company of Khoikhoi, but was lying on the floor of a mud-brick hut with a thatched roof. His feet were protruding out of the door and were tingling in the sunshine. He pulled them in and smothered them in aloe and coconut juice. Suddenly aware of his predicament, he checked his belongings and scanned the village nervously for Lek's hut. Squinting through the glare, he dashed towards it and whipped open the buckskin doorflap. Lek was gone.

Ckan's head spun – a hangover from the psychotropic poison that the Bushman elder had administered.

The villagers were gathered by the woven acacia perimeter-fence. Some had left its confines and were pointing to the hills. Towering above them stood Lek. Ckan marched over, giving a small boy the opportunity to cling to his ankle and be carried into the throng. The game caught on, and by the time Ckan had reached Lek, several infants were squabbling to gain a better purchase on his torso and limbs.

"*Tak, Amagatha*," whispered Lek, still weak from the snake venom.

Ckan was suddenly distracted by the appearance of a caravan of parasol-wielding Premek and his wife Hekket.

Lek's kin were first to bolt from the caravan to embrace him. Their behaviour affected several of the Khoikhoi women, who began to ululate and rhythmically gyrate their arms towards the sky, stamping out a dance of jubilation.

The Khoikhoi welcomed the Premek through the breach in the acacia fence and bid them discard their belongings to drink blood with them, spiced with herbs. Several young Bushmen appeared with strips of biltong and a basket containing ostrich eggs, which they cooked over a fire.

The Premek enjoyed the attention of the Khoikhoi and tolerated bravely the burning sun. They accepted the hospitality, in spite of being prodded and poked incessantly.

As night fell, Ckan gathered the Premek around him. They sang to the Bushmen, who giggled nervously and in fascination as Ckan translated the lyrics as best he could. The Premek sang of their forefathers and their life on the high seas, the cataclysm and their survival in the frozen caverns across the ocean. To finish, Ckan told the story of Tsuk-Premek who had saved them from oblivion.

As the caravan moved out of the acacia enclosure and north-east along a well-beaten track, Ckan stayed behind with Lek to offer thanks to the *Sangoma* and elders. As they clasped hands Ckan produced a small buckskin bag with a leather strap: inside was a stone wrapped in coconut husk for protection. It looked like a pinecone. With permission, he handed it to the *Sangoma*. The painted Bushman looked wide-eyed at Ckan, understanding immediately the significance of the parting gift.

XVII: Code Breaker (Part Two)

Abyssinian Coast
May 27th 1940

William woke to find papers scattered about. At first he thought there must have been another intrusion into his cabin, and then it dawned on him that he must have knocked them off the desk as he had rolled into bed.

He contemplated Boris's story. What if Boris really had experienced powerful visions and dreams, and used the symbols in Huw's journals to reverse transcribe them into a format to make them sound plausible? His interpretation was fanciful, such as the coincidental reference to the pyramids, and even Mossi had seen this to be a case of forcing a round peg into a square hole. If Boris's stone had elicited memories of a journey undertaken many years ago… by whom exactly? Vikings? That would explain the runes, but what of the other linguistic structures? Maybe it was the same people who laid the foundations of the pyramids, survivors of the fabled Atlantian purge, or the mysterious bearded white man Viracocha, Quetzalcoatl or Kon Tiki, who brought wisdom and understanding to Central America.

William suddenly felt restless and mischievous. What if he were to interview Boris? Clear the air, say. Strictly speaking, Boris's dream was not part of their prime directive.

"Come in."

As soon as Boris saw it was William knocking, he pushed him out onto the starboard deck. "Just a moment!"

A couple of minutes of paper shuffling ensued until Boris opened the door to find William taking a final drag on a cigarette and tossing the butt out to sea. He invited William inside and offered him a chair. "I'm sorry, William…"

"Boris, let's forgive and forget what happened last night. You are quite welcome to share my reference material, but please let me know in advance."

"Thank you. It was bad judgement on my part. I needed a way to express my dreams."

"It's your dreams that I'm here to discuss. I don't think it contravenes Mossi's 'game' rules. I'd like to know just how much of it is genuine, and how much is… poetic licence."

"Of course," Boris replied candidly. "Sometimes I wake up and feel like I'm falling, and other times I feel a crushing weight on my chest as if I'm drowning."

"There are sleep-related disorders that cause symptoms like that," said William. "I've suffered sleep paralysis and nausea before, and I suffer from apnoea if I smoke too much."

"I know, William. But these manifestations seem so real. Well, more specifically, they were real for someone or something. I know you think that I'm over-egging the theory of the Seven Sages, but it makes so much sense to me. The pyramids in my dreams are glorious, either bound in ice or towering above lush vegetation – jungle, yes jungle – and yet sometimes they are dusty desert edifices. I see men and women building and worshipping together." Boris stopped and laughed.

"What it is?" asked William.

"In one dream I see a large, wood panelled box with golden-winged eagles on top."

"You mean?"

"Yes, William – The Ark of the Covenant. I know how risible it sounds. I see the people revere it – worship it. I feel their joy, desire, piety and strength, but I also sense their struggle, despair, fear and pain. Something terrible happened long ago, William." Boris paused. "Or maybe…"

"What?" urged William.

"No. It sounds crazy."

"You mean… like the Ark of Covenant, for instance?"

"No – even more fantastic," marvelled Boris. "What if they are glimpses of that which is to come?"

William shook his head in disappointment.

Boris continued in earnest. "Something catastrophic nearly wiped out humanity – I have no doubt. As to the rest…" He shrugged. "The dreams can be heroic and euphoric, but some are appalling and terrifying. The one thing that unites them is that they start with ice and end in fire."

"So where do you suggest we start looking for answers?"

"Somewhere covered in ice," replied Boris emphatically. "But not as the Norsemen knew it. Somewhere inaccessible to them."

William pondered. "The Himalayas? The Antarctic?"

There was a knock at the door and both men jolted in surprise.

"What are you two up to?" Alexander appeared at the door and looked suspiciously at the cabin occupants.

"Come in, Alexei," said Boris. "It's only right that I share something with you."

Understandably, Alexander was unimpressed with Boris's account. He was, after all, a museum curator who dealt with relics that one could see and touch, as opposed to obscure dreams and idle heresay. Regardless, Boris was adamant about the veracity of his dreams, and Alexander and William knew that his expertise was vital to Mossi and the expedition.

"Should we tell Mossi?" enquired Alexander.

"I'll do it," replied William. "It'll add weight to Boris's testimony. My ancestors were hardly scientific in their quest to find the stones, and look where we are now. I think we should give Boris the benefit of the doubt."

****

Mossi listened attentively to William's defence of Boris, and was delighted to see that his research team had put their grievances aside. He was quick to ask if any of his game rules had been breached, and each man assured him that they had been discreet.

"Excellent!" exclaimed Mossi as supper was laid out. "Don't ask me where I sourced this beef. It would create an international incident. Incidentally…" he chuckled to himself. "It's high time I stepped up the pace. You've had plenty of time to analyse each of your case studies. Time to exchange materials – Alexander and Boris – straight swap. You have the rest of the day to assess the new research material. Make sure your comments are kept separate to prevent cross-contamination of ideas. They will be used later for our discussion group meetings when we arrive in Dar-es-Salaam. In the meantime, I'll be interviewing each of you at a time that best suits. I'd like to start with you, William, if that's all right?"

"Happy to oblige."

"Studies by eminent Egyptian Archaeologists, geographic anomalies in Peruvian and Bolivian civic centres as well as Meso-American archaeo-technology: for my first point of study, I focused on dating stonemasonry in Peru and Bolivia based on Geology and local topography to see if there could possibly be a link between the age of early Egyptian and American constructions. The weathering of Andesite rock dolmens in the high Andes initially led me to think that they might have been positioned as far back as five thousand years ago.

In all cases, from Machu Picchu to sites in the Cusco region, I see unbelievable quarrying and craftsmanship interspersed with repair work performed at a much later date. I found myself lulled at times into thinking that the stone had been gouged and carved using some lost technology, but weathering serves as a more logical answer."

Machu Picchu, Peru

"You say 'lulled'?" interjected Mossi.

"Let me come back to that. The Great Pyramid was alledgedly one of the original constructions on the Giza plateau, completed around 2600BC, but I doubt that its purpose was a glorified tomb. Sorry, Mossi, it just doesn't make sense to lay vast stone blocks in a desert on a whim. I haven't seen any evidence for how your ancestors could have quarried the stone and dragged it mind-blowing distances over such rough, uncompromising terrain. They had to have used water as a transport medium, without a wheel in sight, and there isn't sufficient evidence that this actually occurred or the water table was high enough. Months working in and around Hemiunu's serdab hardened my resolve on this matter. Your predecessors were highly systematic when it came to keeping records. Why not record how Khufu's 'lighthouse' was built – its purpose – and how much everyone liked it? Why not brag about it? They couldn't stop bragging about Ramesses 'The Great'. Was Egyptian society so tyrannical that their King was their God, and they, like ants, were born merely to serve the greater good? So it would seem. I warrant that whoever laid the foundation stones of The Great Pyramid did so a long time before Khufu, and for a very specific purpose. The construction and rock setting that came after could well be attributed to Khufu and Hemiunu. It must have been a gargantuan engineering task and thirsty work."

William took a sip of water and smirked at the irony of his actions. Mossi was grinning like a Cheshire cat. Had he said something daft?

Giza Plateau, The Kingdom of Egypt

"My second point concentrates on the purpose of geo-shock-proof or flash-flood-proof stone fortifications at Tiwanaku and Puma Punku, Bolivia and the interlocking walls at Sacsayhuamán, Cusco in Peru. The reason for their robustness is self-explanatory. As to how they were quarried, carved and set, I have no idea. For the Inca to have cut such perfect right angles is an astonishing feat, and why they did it is just as important a question. Cuts, incidentally, that have been exposed to the elements for hundreds of years and survived remarkably well. Judging from their composition, the 'H-shaped' stone blocks at Puma Punku were quarried and carted, or dragged, more than six miles to where they were set – and if they weren't, there must have been an abundance of water. I would say the same for the pyramids at Giza – even if it were just seasonal flooding. An obvious source of water for Tiwanaku is Lake Titicaca or an artificially damned tributary. Basic floatation devices strapped to cut-stone blocks would reduce their weight and allow them to be set more easily. But I refer to my first point – the suggestion of a group of master stonemasons operating in Egypt at the same time as in the Andes... I don't have enough information on water diversion or climate to propose a theory on how it could possibly be the case.

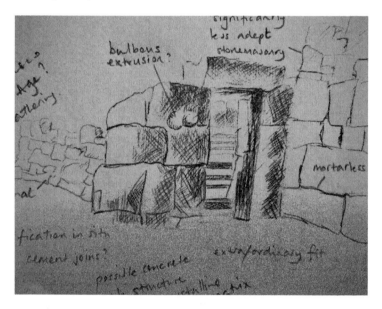

Interlocking 'polygonal stone' walls – Sacsayhuamán, Cusco

"But you think that Egyptian, Incan and pre-Incan megalithic cultures built these structures at a time when the land was significantly wetter or colder?" inquired Mossi.

"Yes. It makes sense. Going back to Egypt, why would an ancient high-tech culture in Egypt build solely tombs, temples and shrines to venerate gods? If they had the know-how, why not build grain silos, irrigation culverts, sanitation, markets, and houses *etcetera*? Are all these surviving structures just expensive mausoleums? Why don't we seek other functional reasons for them? Or have I missed the point entirely and they are purely decorative expressions of high culture. Art, if you will."

"Do you have a timeframe for the South American stonework?" inquired Mossi plainly.

"According to these research papers, the Tiwanaku Empire hit its peak between 400AD to 500AD, some three thousand years after the supposed completion of Khufu's pyramid. I'm not sure how this age was calculated but photographic evidence shows that in nearby Puma Punku, some of the walls are covered in several metres of silt. This would indicate a catastrophic deluge of Gilgamesh proportions. What if the deluge wiped out the original Puma Pumku settlement, and the stone blocks were used to rebuild at a later date?"

"Here's another postulation. The elevation of Puma Punku is thirteen thousand feet. What if the original blocks were cut and set while this part of the Andes was covered in ice and glaciers? The collapse of a glacier would be cataclysmic. Also, Ice Age conditions might provide a solution for the quarrying and transportation of the andesite: drill several holes in the rock in a straight line with a copper rod, using sand for friction or a dowel tipped with a robust gemstone. Fill the holes with water, wet wood or sawdust, stopper with plugs of hot metal and hey presto! Let sub-zero temperatures split the rock for you. Then drag the cut rock on sledges across the ice. I appreciate it's rather Heath Robinson but if the climate were several degrees colder, it's plausible."

Mossi made several notes while William gathered his thoughts.

"Regarding the polygonal Sacsayhuamán wall monoliths – I'm pretty much stumped. The Killke people that performed these remarkable feats of engineering were either damnably smart or – like the H-blocks at Puma Punku – I'm willing to accommodate the possibility of some third-party instruction here. My snap judgement regarding the near-impossible precision was vitrification – melting the rock and pouring into moulds to be shaped and sculpted *in situ*. I've seen evidence of vitrified rock in Egypt, incidentally. But there are two reasons why I have my doubts – the colossal amount of heat required to melt rock and the lack of trees, thus wood, to burn. Combine that

with a gaping paucity of evidence to substantiate any counter-theory..."
William stopped mid-flow. "Maybe the Inca stripped the land of trees and changed the climate? Sorry Mossi – guesswork. Thus, I have no reason to disagree with the *status quo* and conclude that the Killke and then Inca were responsible for the fortifications at Tiwanaku and Sacsayhuamán between 900AD and 1400AD."

William watched Mossi's eyes for any discernable flicker. Instead, he remained aloof and thoughtful. William couldn't help but think back to the time he was interviewed for a place at Oxford University.

"You said you'd explain why you used the word 'lulled'."

William avoided the question again.

"We have little or no record of megalithic construction in Egypt before 3000BC. Long before that, modern man was allegedly hunting mammoth with spears and living in caves – and then domesticating livestock and selectively breeding crops. I think clues to Egypt's founding are in Mesopotamia. If we assume that a cataclysm destroyed what was already an established civilisation in Mesopotamia, and the survivors took their knowledge elsewhere to re-establish their culture. How long would it take for a band of one hundred survivors to achieve a population of, say, a million?"

"Indulge me."

"Allowing for inevitable immigration and trade interests, only five or six hundred years, given sufficient milk and honey."

"An Empire," said Mossi, nebulously.

"Puts it in perspective, doesn't it? What if, ironically, Egypt was the original land of milk and honey, after a deluge that drowned Mesopotamia? What if the pre-dynastic Egyptians were the descendants of displaced Sumerians and, for that matter, other fugitives from the African continent?"

"It's a theory, William. Now answer my question."

"I used the word 'lulled' because something has been nagging me ever since I took an interest in Stonelore. Modern man didn't evolve overnight. There is plenty of evidence to suggest that *Homo sapiens* has been around for over a million years, struggling to survive. It is inconceivable that humanity was suddenly whipped up into a frenzy of technological advancement 'in the twinkling of an eye'. In our accepted timeframe, humanity went from mammoth worrying, to creating doomsday weapons within a period of five thousand years. That is one five thousandth or less than 0.5% of our entire existence."

Mossi was quick to reply, "I couldn't agree more, but please stick to the evidence. Have you looked at the Mayan pyraimids?"

William grimaced. "I have, and I'm sorry to say that my third and final point is even more speculative and requires more information regarding the Maya and their Olmec predecessors. There is no doubt that the pyramidal construction at Cholula is similar to that of Giza – and Señor Rousseau suggests that this was built in stages starting in the third century BC – but to propose that the Maya built it with help from Egypt is impossible with the evidence I have at my disposal."

"A shame," said Mossi. "I think Rousseau may have stumbled on something highly significant. But I respect your honesty."

"Nevertheless," added William. "There may be some clues as to when the older structure were built – and it might be worth pursuing Rousseau for more information."

Mossi smiled. "Go on."

"I read his analysis on other stone structures – Olmec or Toltec temples – I forget which. They had dilapidated over time, for various reasons. He documents clearly different ages of stonemasonry, and what catches my eye, as it does his, is that each successive construction is subtly off-kilter with its foundations. The observation forced me to re-examine all Jesùs Rousseau's research material. Most of these Meso-American structures seem to be aligned to the pole star, or the vernal and autumnal equinoxes. If I'm right, we have a methodology: the monoliths were set carefully, aligned meticulously – like sundials or 'moondials' or 'stardials' – positioned to track the sun, moon, stars and ultimately the precession of the equinoxes. With each successive construction the alignment changed by a small but significant amount. If we work out how much the planet has altered in its precessional journey, we can extrapolate back to when these buildings were originally set in stone."

At last, Mossi betrayed a flicker of interest. William knew for certain he was on the right track.

"The Greek astronomer, Hipparchus, concluded that the earth tilted on its axis, to a greater or lesser extent, over long periods of time. A wobble, if you will. At the commencement of each twenty six thousand year cycle, a new star is revealed as the pole star. If we were to find a structure that had been built to venerate a particular celestial deity, or oriented to a particular star cluster, constellation or individual star, such as Polaris, we should be able to work out when it was built by plugging the numbers into a suitable equation. Unfortunately, I don't have access to such an equation – but I could find out easily enough."

Mossi looked up and laughed, staring out into the Arabian Sea. "I'd like to see you try!"

William realised the folly of his words and laughed. "Well, maybe not easily! But what if humanity became aware of how the earth fell into repeating cycles of cataclysm, meteorite impact or volcanic or tectonic activity? What if they used the stars as a countdown sequence to the next calamity? Didn't the Aztecs create such a calendar? If so, it might provide compelling evidence."

****

Returning to his cabin, William dwelt on the conversation. One thing hadn't occurred to him at the time: 'If humans had been working stone for thousands of years, without the ability to cast and temper metals, they would have become rather good at it.' And, secondly, as with any degree of craftsmanship: 'If the people weren't practising it, the skill and knowhow might have been forgotten.' This tied in with what Boris had said about post-cataclysmic rekindling of society. 'Maybe someone stumbled upon the process of mining ore and forging it, and, thereafter, humanity was forced to develop metallurgy competitively. Perhaps, as a consequence of this discovery, the master stonemasons were forced into retirement, or they left and took their knowledge with them.'

XVIII: An Unexpected Visitor

Letaba Rest Camp, Kruger National Park, RSA
November 3rd 1998

Aside from an evening game drive with a private client, Sam's duty involved coordinating a litter pick, a stock check for the kitchens and attending to a slow puncture on one of the safari jeeps. That allowed enough time to add another lick of paint to his rondavel wall. In spite of the unnerving nature of his night activity, Sam compartmentalised his anxiety and accepted it as inevitable. Knowing that Yuriy had experienced similar dreams somehow made the burden lighter – if not more intriguing. When the dreams manifested, Sam would wake well rested, take a photograph and apply a layer of paint. When he ran out of boot polish he weaned himself onto washable whiteboard markers.

With no way of discerning the meaning of his 'night art' he was aware of the similarity of some of it to the symbols on the cloth maps. But as far as he was aware, they bore no correlation to the narrative of his dreams. Aside from Yuriy, he didn't know anyone who might be able to help, and it gnawed away at Sam – had he been exposed to one of the stones? And if so, when and how?

Sam fixed the slow puncture with resin and prepped the vehicle for the evening game drive. As he 'signed out' in Reception, Mercy pointed out his client, sitting alone at the bar in a wide-brimmed Stetson, supping on a beer. With a few minutes to spare, Sam checked the reigster for unusual game sightings. The wild dog hadn't been seen for a week, which could indicate that they were denning, ready to produce a litter.

"Hi! Sam Walker. Pleased to meet you!"
The client turned, stood and extended his hand. "Hello, Taff!"
Sam's heart skipped a beat. "Mr Hendriks?"
"Call me Lester." He drew closer to Sam, as he always used to, revealing the same awful tobacco breath. "And it's 'de Villiers' now. The SA authorities thought it was for the best. How's my son looking after you?"
Sam's mind raced. "Your son?"
"*Ja*, Franco! Hasn't he told you anything?"

Sam sucked his teeth.

"Obviously not," chortled Hendriks. "We've lots to discuss."

"Whoa!" Sam pushed his Prep School Maths teacher back onto the barstool. "So you're Franco's dad?"

"*Ja.* He probably hasn't told you because he wanted you to think you got the job here fair and square. Which, of course, you did." Hendriks winked and tapped his nose thrice.

Sam ushered Hendriks out of the bar towards the jeep. "I know a place we can talk."

Sam hardly spoke a word until he had reached the ravine picnic site. He cut the ignition. "Right. Start at the beginning."

"Well it's good to see you looking so well and grown up."

"Cut the bull, Hendriks. Why are you here?"

"I heard Yuriy showed up."

"Jeez! You know him?"

"Apple pips? One bullet – one kill? It's Yuriy alright."

"He said I've been lied to all my life. Looks like he was right! Did Franco tell you to come?"

"He told me about Jimi Hendrix. It's a double code: telephone number and an order to fetch me."

Sam frowned. "What? Jimmy as in winkle out? Bloody hell! Does Franco know Yuriy?"

"No, but I do. Well, to be precise, I know his father's work."

"Russian scientist?"

"Correct." Hendriks paused to collect his thoughts. "Look, Taff. It's probably better if I just spill my guts."

"Good – because that's literally what happened to an old man on this very spot two weeks ago."

Hendriks looked around nervously. "*Eish!* Franco knew you'd met up with Yuriy, despite what you'd said. He followed you on the tracker."

Sam puffed out his cheeks.

"I don't know what Yuriy told you, Sam, but I hate to say he's probably right – you've been lied to, my boy. It's no coincidence that Anthony and I were your teachers at the Choir School. We were supposed to protect you. Unfortunately, Anthony took matters into his own hands, and that is why Yuriy killed him."

"Yuriy killed Mr Greenwood?" Sam regressed into his memories. "Bellingham Sports Ground, July 1987. That was Yuriy talking to you under the trees by the pavilion. And he watched the cricket match too."

Hendriks looked surprised. "For sure! *'sus* – I didn't think anyone had noticed us. He came to warn me what Anthony was up to and that I should get him to safety – but by then it was too late."

"But I thought Vanderbeck killed Anthony Greenwood. How does he fit in? He knew about the stone."

"Huh – that's another story. Vanderbeck, or Stoltz, was the reason that I was brought into the Choir School – to keep an eye on his idiotic machinations. He got himself caught up in the whole debacle."

"What 'debacle'? What 'machinations'? He was a Nazi fugitive. This doesn't make any sense. What was he doing working at a Choir School for boys."

"Look, Sam, if you keep interrupting me, we'll get nowhere."

Sam shook his head petulantly and lit a cigarette.

"We were all involved in a cover up. Anthony came into possession of several items that date back thousands of years. They were collected by a delegation of men and women from different countries culminating in a paradigm-shifting discovery in the autumn of 1940. The next thirty years were politically unstable with Wars, and both the Soviets and the USA making window dressing concessions regarding nuclear disarmament and espionage. The delegation fell apart and Anthony's father William disappeared – presumed dead. In the early '60s, Anthony found out that William had defected to Russia, and was working on a top-secret project in Kazhakhstan. It involved the stones and their arcane capabilities. When William witnessed the horrors they unleashed, he fled with one of the stones, gave it to Anthony and went into hiding."

Sam got out of the car, extinguished his cigarette and tossed the butt into the steel bin. He took two beers out of the cool box and handed one to Hendriks. "Go on!"

"That's when Vanderbeck got involved. The Russians paid him to find out where Anthony had hidden the stone."

"But MI5 intercepted him. Brigadier Gordon took it."

"Brigadier Gordon and Vanderbeck were in cahoots. It was the Brigadier who sanctioned Vanderbeck's interception – the poisoning – and it was he who handed over the stone to the Russians. He washed up a week later near Canvey Island."

"Poor Timothy!" exclaimed Sam.

"He's doing fine by the way – working for the civil service, if you catch my drift. Anyway, everything was quiet for years until two weeks ago. Mukwa saw a familiar face at work. He recognised the man immediately as a Greenwood."

"Mukwa? Wait. Are you saying that the old man killed here was William Greenwood?"

"Using Anthony's Namibian passport and considerable resources, he was hiding out in Argentina for years."

"But the two men with him were Russian."

"Correct. They must have got to him eventually. I'm guessing he was here under duress. He must have gone into hiding when he heard that Yuriy had assassinated Anthony."

"Wait. How old was he?"

Hendriks cleaned his shades and slipped them into his breast pocket. "This is where you need to keep an open mind, Taff. The stones have peculiar properties that only work on certain people. As well as altering perception they cause physical changes. In William Greenwood's case, exposure seemed to have prolonged his life. He can't have been far off his one hundredth birthday."

"But why did Yuriy kill him?"

"To stop the Russians getting to you and your tin. I strongly suspect that Anthony had no means to decipher the codes on the maps or he would have taken matters into his own hands long ago. Maybe William bluffed the Russians into thinking he could precipitate something to spare his life? There's another reason. The project that Yuriy's father and William worked on involved exposing children to different levels of the stones' potency. They believed that communion with the stones facilitated the downloading of memories from a time when... I don't know when – a *bluddy* long time ago – and only by those who were receptive. Because Yuriy's father, Boris, could interact with the stones, he put forward his own son for clinical trials. The boy proved to be a revelation. To cut a long story short, there were unforeseen side affects to Yuriy's exposure, and he broke out of the research facility leaving a wake of destruction. Boris feared that he might return one day and exact revenge, so the Soviets put out a warrant for Yuriy's arrest and moved the project to Moscow. But Yuriy broke in and killed his father. He stole some floppy disks containing classified information and a transcript of a letter from Anthony Greenwood saying that he had continued to research the stones' impact at a genetic level. Yuriy feared the worst and came after him too. I'm sorry to say that I was unaware of Anthony's contact with Russia, and totally unprepared for what transpired at the Choir School. When I found out it was too late. Yuriy triggered the fire alarm at St Thomas' hospital, silenced Anthony, returned to Russia and handed himself in. He was sentenced to two years in a Siberian gulag, but being a marvel of military medicine, he was pardoned, released and re-enlisted as a covert Spetsnaz operative. He managed to extricate himself in 1995 and sold his talents to the highest bidder."

"What happened to Mukwa?" asked Sam reluctantly as the penny began to drop.

"Yuriy got to him before the Russians, and smuggled him out of the UK."

Sam lit another cigarette and drained his beer can. "I suppose the next question is – was I one of Mr Greenwood's test subjects? It would explain the peculiar dreams and…" Sam stopped.

"And what?" Hendriks's tone was severe.

"It doesn't matter," replied Sam.

"It *bluddy* does, Taff! Anthony may have exposed you to the stone for nearly four years. I was under the impression that you hadn't exhibited symptoms. *'sus!* That's why William Greenwood needed to speak to you!" His face morphed as if he had had an epiphany. "He needed to know."

"Know what?"

"Know if it had worked!"

"If what had worked?

"According to Anthony, roughly half of all test subjects experience dreams, or what they called Stage One symptoms. A few survive to Stage Two: enhanced physical and mental development – like Yuriy. In nearly every case, Stage Two test subjects experience psychotic episodes or develop cancerous lesions and die. But there were a couple of instances where test subjects reached Stage Three. They were able to transcribe data in the form of text, mathematical symbols or code. Anthony referred to Stage Three subjects as Scribes."

Sam kept calm and threw his cigarette butt out of the jeep. "You said there were a couple of instances of Stage Three."

"One of the reasons that Yuriy spared Mukwa's life is that Mukwa confessed to being one of Anthony's Stage Three test subjects. He draws in his sleep but can't explain what the symbols mean. He's a Scribe."

"Is he OK?"

"He has regular check-ups. He's fine – he lives with me in Hout Bay, Cape Town. You must have been exposed to the same stone."

Sam put his hand up in defeat. "Too much information. Time out."

He binned the beer cans and excused himself for a pee. It was getting dark. Sam started the engine and drove out of the ravine. If Mukwa was OK, then God willing so was he.

"How did Anthony do it? I mean… expose me," asked Sam.

"I've no idea. I would have stopped him if I'd known. I was too preoccupied working out where to hide his damn things."

Sam pulled over at the chainlink fence and took two beer cans out of the cool box. He cracked them open, took a large swig from one and handed the other to Hendriks.

"And cancer?" asked Sam. "What are my chances?"

Hendriks put his hands up apologetically. "Please, Sam – be patient. Anthony worked on the theory that the stones cause inheritable mutations in DNA. Years before, Boris had theorised that progeny of those who survived prolonged contact with the stones would have enhanced ability to commune with them, and like him, immunity from their harmful charcteristics. If you put the two together – one of Mukwa's parents must have inherited the mutation, making Mukwa more susceptible to the stone's influence. Anthony began to screen Mukwa's DNA for abnormalities. It was one such batch of results that the Russians tainted with poison."

"Or mine?"

"It's possible," replied Hendriks.

"But if Anthony was working for the Russian establishment, why would they want him dead?"

"I've no idea," replied Hendriks. "Yuriy was just out for revenge."

"Why me?" Sam asked forcefully. "Did one of my parents possess a stone?"

"No, Sam. Your parents are utterly oblivious to any of this. Your maternal grandfather is a different story altogether. He was given a stone by your great-grandfather. Both men survived long exposure to the stones and understood their potency so, when you were born, Anthony intercepted a plan to kidnap you and take you to Kazakhstan. Having witnessed the effect that exposure had on Yuriy, Anthony confessed his involvement in the project, and turned himself over to British Intelligence. Brigadier Gordon was tasked as his handler, and facilitated the position as Science Master at the Abbey Choir School."

Sam pulled over. "And you were called in to protect his secrets?"

"*Ja!* Anthony hid his stuff as life insurance. He knew that the Russians had got to Vanderbeck and Brigadier Gordon. They must have spent years fathoming how to get the information out of Anthony.

114

It was a stalemate that lasted years – until they lost patience and poisoned him. It must have been a shock to them to find out that Yuriy finished the job! I'm certain it caused a flurry of activity in London and Moscow – and I can only assume that the Russians didn't come after you because they had no idea you had smuggled Anthony's maps out. I'm guessing that William Greenwood worked it out eventually."

Sam mulled over Hendriks's statement. "You said my grandfather changed his name. What was it before Chamberlain?"

Hendriks lit his roll up cigarette. "Morgan. Your great-grandfather was Samuel Morgan."

"And you've always called me Taff." Sam slapped his forehead. "So I'm Welsh after all!"

XIX: The Gods

20 nautical miles off the coast of Mombasa
June 6th 1940

The second briefcase that William received from Mossi contained anthropological studies. It was outside his area of expertise, but he took care to read the research papers and journal extracts. Occasionally he spotted pencil impressions in the margins. Intrigue gave way to nosiness, and William attempted to read some of them in the meagre candlelight. They were mostly in Russian Cyrillic or Arabic, and William soon lost interest.

The main context of the research highlighted the different stages of human evolution, including postulations regarding coexistence of not just *Homo sapiens* and *Homo neanderthalensis* but several other homanin species identified from their skeletal remains.

Attached to one paper, was a handwritten note from Mossi saying 'Don't disregard'. There were photographs of giant skeletons from North America, and drawings of diminutive 'hobbits'. One article in particular drew William's attention – not because of the content – but rather because Boris had written copious notes on top of it and left imprints in Cyrillic. It concerned a set of elongated skulls unearthed in the Cusco region of Peru. The author of the article, Teodoro Alvarez, had made the discovery in 1928. Native to the region, he had noted that in spite of the elongation, the skulls had a different morphology to 'normal' human skulls. They had no saggital suture. Though aware of artificial cranial deformation and modification, Alvarez suggested that the skulls might not be the result of mutilation, but congenital defects.

Again, William filled in a few of Boris's indented characters. Soon he had extracted a few sentences, but without a means to translate he slipped the notepaper into the back cover of an old textbook of cartographic symbols. "Time and place," he muttered to himself.

The second briefcase also contained articles on ancient mythology from Native American 'Indians', Polynesian Islanders, to the mythical continent of Lemuria or Mu. William was surprised at the extent that Mossi had gone to: some of the articles were far-fetched folklore in William's opinion.

Mossi had added interpretations of creation myths to the dossiers. In almost all cases they refered to 'beings' descending from the sky in gaudy chariots or spacecraft, gifting humans with wisdom and understanding – or tyrannical entities subjugating humanity and demanding veneration in exchange for benevolence.

One of the authors, Stephen MacDougall, went on to describe religion as an artificial construct based on autocratic power mongering – or in the case of Buddhism, spiritual enlightenment based on virtue and morality.

There were tales of fallen angels, servitude, liberation, giants, archangels, miracles, plagues, heroes, demons, vimanas (flying machines), divine punishment and purge by cataclysm, paradise, heaven, hell and so on.

William thought that Sumeria might be a more credible source of information; cuneiform being the oldest recorded scripted account of a belief system. William enjoyed its resonance with the biblical creation story: primaeval waters or 'soup', as had been coined by contemporary Science, giving birth to the earth god *An* and sky god *Ki*. They mated to produce the god *Enlil* who divided 'the heavens from the earth' and claimed the land as his domain. His half-brother, *Enki*, created 'man' – and upon death, 'man' descended to a dark place, deep below the ground. This race of gods was known as the *Anunnaki* – and William interpreted their story as a metaphor, freeing him from the shackles of timescale and reality.

Another text, translated from Akkadian, described the *Apkallu*: a group of seven sage demigods banished to the underworld by younger gods called *Igigi* – but not before furnishing mankind with wisdom and culture.

Something struck William as pertinent, and it wasn't just the reference to 'Seven Sages'. He flicked back to a paper written on Native American deities, and noted the name *Abenaki* in oral tradition which was a ligation of words meaning 'dawn sky' and 'earth'. Other similarities began to unfold. William accepted that humans must have eventually spread across the planet by land bridges or sea from Asia into the Americas. But to have such connected belief systems in seemingly unconnected continents was surely no coincidence. William continued to note similarities in Egyptian deities. The ancient world religions resounded with the same basic premise: humans were created by gods or interventionist extra-terrestrial beings.

William was a Christian, at least he'd been brought up in the Christian tradition, and yet he was largely ignorant of its resonance with the creation myths of the Egyptians, Babylonians, the Greco-Roman Empires, Judaism, Islam, Janism, Zoroastrianism and Hinduism to name but few. He had never considered such an important detail – their intimations converged – and in William's experience, such correlation was unlikely to be coincidental.

****

The third briefcase contained piles of maps. William was irritated by further references to Atlantian legends and sunken continents, but the maps' transcripts were impressively drawn. Glancing through, he began to query their authenticity. He couldn't be sure if he was looking at planet earth or something out of a Jules Verne novel. Rivers traversed North Africa, and Lake Chad was drawn as a vast inland sea covering most of the north Belgian Congo. William had already tuned to the idea that water levels had fluctuated dramatically over millennia – but when were the maps drawn, and by whom? Romans? Greeks? Egyptians? Surely the maps must predate even Mesopotamia.

Mossi had sketched depictions of Upper Egypt, Edfu, Luxor and Lower Egypt, with the Giza Plateau looking like a water garden. If the maps were to be believed, water would have been plentiful and yes, maybe the pyramid builders didn't require wheels after all. The massive blocks could have been shipped in directly along the Nile to the construction site, and dragged over slippery log beams.

The next series of maps included a dossier marked '*Kitab-i Bahriye*' or Book of the Sea. William had heard of the cartographer, a sixteenth century Ottoman navigator called Piri Reis who had copied the maps from records held by notable explorers including Christopher Columbus. One such Mercator map seemed to depict the coast of South America contiguous with an ice-free Antarctica, complete with elaborate drawings of animals and birds (and yet free of 'Here be Dragons'). Rather more perplexing were the accurate measurements of longitude. If the map had been copied in the sixteenth century, who had made the original measurements?

The scale of tectonic displacement necessary to lift the seabed to conjoin South America to Antarctica could not have been an over-night occurrence, never mind the necessary colossal drop in oceanic water level. The coincidence of lower sea levels and melting polar ice seemed counterintuitive. The map was truly an enigma.

Finally, William opened up the last set of maps and papers entitled *Atlantis Mythology*. He poured a large gin in preparation, and began to read extracts from *The Lost Continent of Mu* by James Churchward. There was a footnote written by Mossi, 'Could Churchward and Le Plongeon

118

have been on the right track?' The extracts described a vast continent, incorporating modern day Hawaii and Polynesia, Easter Island, Fiji and Samoa that had sunk beneath the waves in some bygone age. It didn't make much sense to William, but he continued to read, if only to garner a perspective. If such an exposed tectonic plate existed – or some gigantic bulge of the earth's crust – it would have raised oceanic levels around the Antarctic, not lowered them. To expose Antarctica, as the Piri Reis map showed, global temperatures must have been significantly higher to melt the coastal ice. But with increased temperature should come an increase in sea level.

'So,' wrote William. 'What if a bubble of mantle pushed up the ocean floor? What if it suddenly burst in a massive underwater volcanic eruption? Not only would the turmoil wrought be cataclysmic on a scale similar to the catastrophe that wiped out the dinosaurs, it would have as good as wiped out any form of humanity and any trace of habitation – unless, of course, the habitation was made of stone.'

It was all fanciful conjecture, and the concept bothered him. Mossi was obviously steering the researchers' attention to Antarctica. What had he found? Whatever it was, it certainly fitted in neatly with Boris's dreamland of ice.

XX: Tintswalo

Letaba Rest Camp, Kruger National Park, RSA
November 3rd 1998

Sam picked the same table for Hendriks on the veranda, knowing that their conversation would be masked by noisy weaverbirds. Accepting that Franco was aware of his background made it easier for Sam to discuss his feelings openly. Maxwell had arranged a date with Mercy from Reception, and gave his apologies.

"So… Boet!" mocked Sam. "You've known about my predicament all along?"

"I knew you got into trouble at school," replied Franco. "But *Pappie* didn't tell me that you were entrusted with any of Anthony's stuff until now. As for what it is? – I'd rather not know. Regarding your appointment here – *Pappie* gave you an excellent reference on top of your grades. You had the credentials, and it was all done by the book."

"What about Yuriy?"

"*Pappie* warned me about him, but I had to make sure it was him before making the call. The bullet and apple seeds confirmed it."

Sam put his hands behind his head and cracked his neck. "So many questions."

The trio ordered steaks and several rounds of beers before Sam felt a burning desire to air a particularly nagging question. "How did Yuriy know to stake out the picnic site? The Russians unearthed the tin – they got what they came for – but how did Yuriy know where and when? "

"*Ja.* That puzzles me too," replied Hendriks. "I think that's a question for Yuriy."

"Hmm. I'm not prepared to trust him quite yet." He wasn't sure whether his nausea and blackout was a result of his manifestations, or if Yuriy had laced his biltong.

Hendriks finished a mouthful. "Have you wondered why Yuriy gave the tin back to you? He could have kept it or copied the contents."

"True," said Sam. "What do these Russian fanatics know? What's happened since Yuriy killed Anthony Greenwood?" Sam stopped as a thought popped into his head. "Scott Arnold saw you trying to break in to Mr Greenwood's laboratory storeroom. Why?"

"*Ag!* I remember." Hendriks chuckled. "Scott Arnold! *'sus* his father was so desperate to question me! I knew that Anthony had something hidden in the storeroom." He thought for a moment. "I'm guessing it's now in the tin?"

"It might be. But that doesn't answer my question."

"I installed the storeroom door for Anthony. He did all the electrics. When Yuriy appeared at Bellingham and confirmed my suspicions that Anthony was up to no good, I wanted to see if I could bypass it – just in case."

"I heard you arguing about it in the Common Room. There was a small key in there. Any idea what it opens?"

"Not a clue," replied Hendriks.

Sam changed tack. "How is Mukwa?"

Franco caught the question on his return from the toilet. "I think you should find out for yourself, *boet*. The other reason *Pappie*'s here is to give you the option of some time out. Maxwell and I can cover you while you get your head straight."

"What do you mean?" asked Sam.

"Come with me to Cape Town," said Hendriks. "Meet Mukwa properly – see if you guys can make sense of it all."

Sam suddenly felt insecure. "Can I think about it?" The last thing Sam wanted was for Hendriks to find out how the stone affected him, but if Mukwa was also a Scribe it might provide him with answers.

"I leave tomorrow morning," said Hendriks. "If you want to come, let me know first thing and we'll get you booked on the flight from Skukuza. Don't worry about the money. Consider it a long overdue apology."

Sam excused himself and had hardly stepped inside his rondavel when he realised he had forgotten to pay for his supper. Returning, he saw father and son talking at the bar. It made him smile. Suddenly, Hendriks began to choke. Franco handed him some water. It seemed to do the trick, but the cough persisted until it became uncontrollable. Hendriks struggled for air. Franco called for help, and Sam came running with the medi-pack.

Hendriks slid from his bar stool and hit the floor hard, dragging several glasses with him. He clutched at his throat, wild-eyed. His body shook violently and abruptly calmed. The white froth on Hendriks's lips and the faint smell of almonds could only mean one thing. In spite of Franco's attempts to resuscitate his father with CPR, intubation and a shot of atropine, Hendriks was dead.

*

The shattering of glass had alerted Maxwell. Passing by the office, he found the door broken in and papers strewn everywhere. Whoever had entered had done their best to crack the safe, but failed.

*

Sam and Maxwell coordinated the removal of Hendriks's body out of the restaurant while Mercy consoled the bar staff. The coroner from Phalaborwa arrived an hour later escorted by Head Ranger, Greg, and two security guards.

****

Franco sat at a table on the veranda, nursing a whisky and the rest of the bottle. Tears streamed down his cheeks.

Maxwell sidled up to Sam at the bar. "I'm sorry, Sam. I gather Franco's Dad was your teacher."

"He was. Thanks, Maxwell. What do we do about Franco?"

"I think he needs some 'alone' time." Maxwell hesitated. "Do you want to talk about the office break-in, or should we wait until tomorrow?"

"Have you secured it?"

Maxwell nodded.

"I guess that's all we can do, Max."

"Sam, Mercy didn't tell me everything. She said that when the Tsongan security guard came to find you, he was carrying a package."

"Yes. You said so."

"There was someone with him."

"Who?"

"His nephew, Tintswalo. He was looking for work. He hung around for an hour while his uncle drove off to run an errand. A couple of the men in the motor pool have flu so, having verified his paperwork, Franco signed him up. Mercy saw him later in the car park. His uncle was waving the package in his face. She doesn't speak much Tsongan, but she thinks that it contained something bad because Tintswalo was scared to touch it."

"Where is Tintswalo now? Does he know about his uncle?"

"Yes. Mercy sat him down and gave him the news this morning. She says the boy's reaction was not what she expected. It was as if he was scared – not relieved, sad or angry."

Suddenly, Sam leapt up from his bar stool. "That poison was meant for me!" He looked around, processing the scene. "We all had beers and we all had steak – medium rare." He then looked toward the table on the veranda where Franco was sitting. He bolted to the slide doors and banged on the window. "Franco! Stop!"

Franco was rolling a cigarette from his father's tobacco pouch.

"Stop! Franco!"

Franco couldn't hear Sam through the glass, and continued to toy with his father's zippo. Sam hurtled along the veranda and knocked the cigarette from Franco's mouth.

"What the..?" exclaimed Franco.

"It's laced!" shouted Sam.

Franco sniffed his hands and dashed to the bathroom.

Maxwell smelled the tobacco pouch cautiously and nodded at Sam. "You're right."

Sam collapsed into a chair, his heart booming inside his chest, staring into the dark water of the Letaba River,

Franco returned chugging on a carton of milk. "Thanks, Sam. Is it laced? Does it smell weird?"

Sam's gaze remained transfixed on the river. "I'm sorry Franco. It's all my fault."

"What do you mean?" asked Franco.

"It's my fault. I killed him," repeated Sam more earnestly. "Your father kept leaving his tobacco roll on the bar, and I kept fetching it for him. The killer thought he was lacing my tobacco. It was meant for me."

"You can't know that for sure, Sam," said Maxwell.

"Yes, I can." Sam jumped up. "We need to find the boy. What's his name? Tintswalo?"

Sure enough, the Tsongan boy had been seen loitering near the restaurant earlier and had absconded. His body, or what was left of it, was recovered the next day, several kilometres from Camp.

XXI: Sloppy

Cape Town, Republic of South Africa
October 9th 2016

The Hercules LC-130 landed at Oliver Tambo International Airport. Mark switched his phone on to find three unread messages. One was from Sinead.

> Booked u and A in Waterfront
> Breakwater Lodge
> Separate rooms obvs lol S

Anna was first to disembark and reclaim her baggage from the tarmac. Mark informed her of the booking only to receive an ironic smile, a rattle of her phone and a curt, "I know."

She made her way to Customs and began the necessary paperwork for the cargo.

Mark's phone buzzed.

> Depart tomoz 2130 to Zurich
> Core samples tb collected by Dr Magnus Nedregaard
> Freight Dock 3B
> Connection to Berlin 1030
> Security passes issued on arrival S

Mark waited by the deep freeze until the South African immigration authorities granted permission to transfer the crates to an intermediary frozen storage unit in a secure hanger. Once his own paperwork had been signed, Mark passed through Immigration and found Anna waiting for a taxi outside the terminal building.

"Leaving without me?"

Anna feigned surprise. "I can manage by myself. Big girl now."

A taxi pulled up and they both got in.

"Got any Rands?" asked Mark, pulling out his wallet.

"Of course," replied Anna, with a wink.

Mark noted the brightly painted houses on the outskirts of Cape Town, and pointed at an exit ramp off the N2 motorway.

"Langa Township. I played rugby there – years ago."

Anna didn't react. Mark's intrigue grew.

Eventually, the taxi turned into the Breakwater Lodge forecourt and Mark ushered Anna towards the Check In desk. She tied up her fulsome brown hair to reveal a sleek neck and thin gold chain. Having collected her keycard, she turned to Mark. "Dinner at seven? Give me your number in case I'm running late."

Mark broke the ice with a cocktail. As the alcohol took effect, Anna bored him with details of her education, travel and the effects of intense cold on the human body. After supper he hedged his bets and followed her to her room. It was a warm night. He opened the sliding door to the balcony. Table Mountain was floodlit majestically, and a wispy tablecloth enhanced its beauty. Anna slid her hands around Mark's waist and buried her nose in his spine. Mark was aroused but fought the urge, allowing her to choreograph the ritual. He was in good shape for nudging past forty years old, and despite a numbing guilt, he had been hooked.

****

Mark slipped out of bed, checked that Anna was asleep and stepped naked onto the balcony. Gazing up at the floodlit mountain, he dialled a number that connected immediately.

"I need a favour," whispered Mark.

The voice on the other end of the line coughed, took what sounded like a sip of something, and spoke. "I'm all ears."

"Jane, John and Pointy are set to arrive at Freight Dock 3B at 0800. I need an extraction detail."

"Your wish is my command," replied the voice. "Oh… and put some clothes on. It's chilly here in London."

Mark tutted and hung up.

****

The next morning, Mark loitered in the breakfast bar, reading the paper. When Anna failed to materialise, he returned to his room to pack and Check Out of the hotel. Leaving his bags with the concierge, he took a stroll through the Waterfront shopping mall to buy gifts for his boys before settling down with a coffee to read the newspaper.

"Find anything suitable?"

Mark jumped out of his skin. Anna took a seat opposite him and pushed several bags of curios under the table.

"Trinkets," replied Mark, settling his nerve.

Anna ordered a coffee and a refill for Mark before clearing her throat dramatically. "About last night…"

"No need to discuss," interrupted Mark. "I'm not sentimental."

"Good. Glad we cleared that up."

Mark took an unwanted sip of painfully hot coffee.

"So what do you do when you're not collecting bodies from Antarctica?" enquired Anna.

"As little as possible these days. I inherited handsomely and bought in the Highlands of Scotland. I choose when and where I work, and invest time in my boys."

"Nice," said Anna. "And your wife?"

Mark's eyes lit up. "What makes you think I'm married?"

"A hunch."

"No, Anna. I'm not married. I made that mistake once. My partner and I are happy as we are."

"Does she see it that way too?"

Mark smirked, tossed a few Rands onto the table and collected his shopping. "What makes you so sure it's a 'she'?"

Several hours later, a taxi arrived at the Breakwater Lodge. Anna was nowhere to be seen, so Mark got in. His phone rang – the number was withheld.

"Yes?" asked Mark.

"I've pulled strings as requested. Café Suisse."

A knock on the passenger side window startled Mark.

"Thanks for waiting!" said Anna sarcastically, catching her breath. She put her suitcase in the boot and clambered into the back seat.

"I thought you'd made your own way," said Mark, pocketing his phone.

"No. I climbed Table Mountain and got stuck in traffic on the way back."

Mark could feel the heat radiating from her body. Perfume had been applied liberally to mask her body odour, mingling politely with her coconut sunscreen. He opened the window for effect as the taxi pulled away.

Zurich Flughafen
October 11th 2016 - 7.30am

Mark awoke as the Boeing 747-400 series touched down. He had upgraded to Business Class, annoying Anna. He waited for her at the arrival gate, but she ignored him and made her way with the other passengers towards Passport Control.

"And that was that," said Mark to himself.

He had requested that his luggage be automatically transferred to the Berlin flight to avoid suspicion so, unburdened, he asked directions to Cargo and Freight. Sure enough, as Sinead had stated in her text, the crate containing the ice core samples had been listed on a charter flight manifest to Oslo from Dock 3B. He collected his security pass from a Customs official and headed to the Dock. There was no sign of Anna.

A tall bearded gentleman was sitting alone, tapping away on a laptop. Mark guessed that he was his Norwegian contact.

"Dr Nedregaard?"

"Yes. Magnus. Pleased to meet you, Dr Watts."

"You're here for ice core samples?"

"Yes. They're being loaded as we speak." Dr Nedregaard pointed out of the window. "I was just emailing Dr Schneider and my colleagues in Oslo."

Airport staff were milling around a twin-prop de Havilland cargo aircraft. Below was one of the freezer crates, connected by a thick cable to a power supply truck.

"The temperature was kept well below zero," said Dr Nedregaard. "I'm grateful."

"Good. I'll leave you to it then. Safe flight."

Mark shook hands and returned to the main passenger concourse. It was 9.15am – half an hour until he was due to board the Berlin flight with Anna.

In Café Suisse, Mark spotted a scruffy unshaven man in his mid-forties sitting at a table reading a Swiss newspaper. He was wearing an ill-fitting suit and a waistcoat that accentuated his paunch. Mark sat opposite.

"The ice samples have been loaded onto Nedregaard's jet, and we've pulled the bodies and your bags off the Berlin flight manifest. How are you shaping up, Mark?"

"Fine. I saw Nedregaard. We ought to go."

"Wait. Sit down," said the man quietly and assertively.

"Wait for what?" asked Mark.

"Wait for whom," corrected the man deliberately, eyeing a woman queuing at Passport Control on the concourse below.

"Anna?" exclaimed Mark. "Why?"

The man moved his hand: a gesture for Mark to be silent. "German Intelligence are everywhere. One of them is sitting at the bar behind you. Who passes through Zurich Flughafen without hand luggage? Really? I must have a word with my German counterpart. Anna put a tracker on our crate. She doesn't trust you."

Mark looked confused.

"Fortunately for you, Mark, our man in security found it so now she can't tell if the crate's been loaded onto the Berlin flight or not." The man's mobile phone zoomed in, tucked out of sight behind his newspaper. "She's looking for you... now she's on the phone... probably her handler... she's good. I should have recruited her years ago."

Mark screwed his face up, knowing that he'd been played by a twenty-something-year-old with pretty eyes and a cocksure smile.

"Highland life's made you sloppy, Mark. Too much haggis and single malt." The man adjusted his glasses while lifting his newspaper. Sleight of hand revealed a fresh ticket, which Mark tucked into the breast pocket of his leather jacket. "Ah! She's boarding. Let's give our German spook something to do."

They were followed from the cafe, as anticipated, and down to the lower concourse. Their tail stopped well before Passport Control. Having descended the escalator, Mark looked to see where Dr Nedregaard had been sitting. Dock 3B was deserted and the de Havilland had taxied from its stand.

"Mark! We have a problem!"

Mark looked to where his contact was standing by their Gate. The man swore through his teeth before pocketing his phone. In the corridor behind the desk, two pilots and a cabin steward were sitting on the floor, bound and gagged.

Mark's watch vibrated on his wrist: Bon voyage. A

He calmly slid the watch up his sleeve and pursed his lips. "Looks like I'm not the only one who's got sloppy, Timothy!"

CONSOLIDATION

Ckan gave the order for the Premek to make camp in a wood at the edge of a plateau. The land fell away steeply as if a receding flood had washed it away. The Premek had never seen such dense, lush vegetation: thickly wooded rolling hills as far as the eye could see. Birds flew in vast flocks under the watchful gaze of mighty eagles.

It had been over a thousand years since the land had been inundated, and the view that lay before them was testament to how quickly it had recovered from the extreme weather: tsunamis and tidal surges, melting ice caps, and earthquakes that had emptied and filled great inland seas.

The Premek were tired. After ten months, they hadn't encountered any survivors other than the Bushmen, in spite of finding many abandoned circular stone ruins, similar in shape and size to the dwellings of their ancestors.

As they had journeyed further to the north and east, so the skies had begun to clear, forcing them to move only by night or suffer agonising blisters by day. Though treatable, the discomfort slowed them down. Travel by night brought them into inevitable contact with predators, but nothing more lethal than hippopotamuses in the river courses.

Lek had recovered fully from his ordeal, and his rescue had brought him closer to Ckan. Whatever differences, dislike or distrust they had harboured seemed to have vanished. Not that they had ever been conspicuously at odds with one another, but in the dark confines of their frozen world, Lek had allowed a seed of envy to grow into resentment for his cousin. Tsuk-Premek, their maternal great-great-grandmother had favoured Ckan and ultimately chose him as her successor, sharing her knowledge of the diverse, bioluminescent, polar underworld with him alone. The two giant warriors now stood together, proud and fierce, protecting the Premek caravan from territorial elephant and wild buffalo herds.

Their unanimity had been cemented by chance. Ckan had dashed into a river to assist a stubborn buffalo calf, unaware that a huge crocodile had clamped its jaws around the calf's leg. When Ckan realised the danger, it was too late – he was waist deep and the current was strong. The crocodile let go of the calf and launched at Ckan. Losing his footing, Ckan narrowly missed a snap from its lethal jaws.

Without a thought for his own safety, Lek leapt onto its back, preventing it from lunging again at Ckan who was flailing helplessly in the slippery silt. The crocodile spun, but Lek held firm; his legs wrapped around the reptile's scaly body. Lek plunged his sleek blade behind the beast's eye socket, severing its brainstem. The calf escaped with barely a scratch.

Ckan found his footing, only to shriek as a floating log brushed against him. It was the source of great hilarity amongst his kin, especially his wife, Hekket. Once the hysteria had faded, Ckan embraced Lek; relieved and awestuck at his cousin's heroism.

Lek's wife, Sul, extracted the crocodile's ivories. She polished and drilled them, and set them on a leather cord. Fashioning the crocodile's skin into a garment, Lek's new attire earned him the name 'Lek-Sobe-Kwe-Na-Malu-Ra-Ki' (the crocodile who walks like a man on the path of the sun-god).

As a reward, Ckan bestowed upon Lek a stone from the acacia-lined granite box. Pouched in bushbuck leather, it hung around Lek's neck and looked impressive, dangling in the midst of the crocodile tooth necklace.

It was one of Tsuk's commandments that the stones should be awarded to the Premek's most worthy. Lek had proved his worthiness – designing and building the ship that carried the Premek from the ice; surviving the voyage; recovering from the mamba's neurotoxic venom; demonstrating fearlessness in battle; and putting his own life at risk to save others. Most importantly to Ckan, he sensed that Lek had let go of any trace of resentment. Ckan now trusted Lek like a brother, and mentored him on how to commune with his stone and filter pertinent information. To begin with, Lek's mind resisted. He avoided sleep and would distance himself from the stone when he did. With constant encouragement from Ckan, Lek accepted his responsibility. Together they discussed the meanings of their dreams and manifestations. Ckan was able to share his burden at last. When in trancelike state, the men's minds melded.

The Premek cleared an area of trees on the edge of the plateau and used the abundant wood to build shelters. In doing so, they uncovered a ring of standing stones. Some were cracked and fallen. Many millennia ago they would have been positioned to track the stars and the rising sun. Ckan conferred on his kin the task of repairing and replacing the massy monoliths.

The clear night sky permitted the Premek to view the cosmos as well as intermittent shooting stars and auroras. The elders taught their kin the names of constellations. Up until now, to all Premek, the stars and their astronomical significance had been figments of imagination and the stuff of legend. The elders embellished their stories with characters in the image of star clusters, while the younger Premek carved records of their stories into the monoliths, leaving an indelible account of their passage from the polar icecap.

XXII: The Haskins Residence

Francistown, Bechuanaland Protectorate
January 21st 1930

Temba Schmidt was overwhelmed to see how much the Haskins family had grown in the five years since he had been smuggled over the border into Southern Rhodesia. A month with the joyful, hyperactive brood had quickly restored his faith in humanity.

Several years earlier, during a period of 'self-exile' (Temba's words) from the Driefontein Mission in the Pilanesberg region of South Africa, local businessman, Edward Haskins, had saved Temba from an awkward spat in Francistown. A local dignitary with substantial influence and a roving eye had grown insanely jealous of Temba. The married man in question had become obsessed with an attractive young English widow who, in turn, had become fixated on Temba. Interracial relationships were frowned upon, so Edward hadn't wasted any time, knowing what might befall Temba if she pressed her suit. Edward had spoken to a friend in Bulawayo, and without further ado, Temba was smuggled over the border into Southern Rhodesia and began working at a printing press, but not before mentioning Temba's considerable prowess with a hunting rifle to his new boss.

The subsequent year had changed Temba. Although guilt had driven him away from his adoptive mother, Rosalind, he missed her terribly. He was in no doubt that his adoptive father Rudolf's deteriorating lung condition and eventual demise had been hastened by his meddling with Temba's 'cursed' stones.

Temba eventually returned to the Mission to find the nearby village had been deemed uninhabitable due to cholera in the water sources. Rosalind had made the tough decision to depart for Austria with the Groenewald trove. On parting, Temba had tucked one of Huw Williams's stones into her luggage: a peculiar memento in the light of the evil it had wrought, but a symbol of Temba's steadfast love for his mother. It left him with the quandary of what to do with the last remaining stone. He had already failed to launch it into the cascades of Victoria Falls, as instructed by Huw Williams, when the opportunity had presented itself. Now he had another quandary: he had inadvertently taken a priceless rifle called 'Trusty Girl' from an American big-game hunter called Roderick 'Roddy' McTaggart. The Winchester rifle had been presented to Roddy as an adoslescent by none other than President Theodore Roosevelt, and had been fired twice to save Temba from a near-fatal mauling from a huge dark-maned Cape lion by the Limpopo River. Roddy's sister, Rhona, had nursed Temba back to health – and in so doing, learned of Temba's curse.

Map of Bechuanaland Protectorate and Southern Rhodesia (circa 1930)

"What have you decided?" asked Edward.

Temba didn't hesitate. "I have to find McTaggart."

"What if he accuses you of stealing Trusty Girl?"

"I'll cross that bridge when I come to it. I owe him my life – and his sister for that matter."

"So long as you understand the consequences, my friend."

Temba stirred his hot brew and watched as the tealeaves spread out, only to gather in the middle when he stopped. "I think some form of retribution is inevitable."

"I've put feelers out," said Edward. "The McTaggarts are moving north to the Okavango Delta with their hunting entourage. We could intercept them at Orapa. It's a few days ride. I'll come as your advocate."

Temba smiled and nodded. "You're a good man, Edward, and a better friend. I know He's watching over me."

"Good. We'll need 'Him' along for the ride. I don't know much about these Americans, but I know they've invested a great deal in a mining operation down in Jwaneng. The locals say the McTaggarts have a nose for diamonds, and neither the British nor the Batswana want the Americans sniffing around elsewhere."

"When do we leave?"

"First light. I've made arrangements."

Temba couldn't sleep. Although he was nervous about the reunion, his stone kept infiltrating his thoughts. Since he had relinquished possession of the Great Zimbabwe stone to Rosalind, his dreams had become clearer if not more unsettling.

When dawn broke, Temba went out to saddle his horse, Tshukudu, and was dumfounded to find the stallion already prepped for departure.

"I thought I'd get a head start," announced Edward. "I had to process some paperwork, and once I'd finished it was too late to doss down."

"I couldn't sleep either."

Edward's eyes drifted to the stone tied around Temba's neck.

"No – not that," lied Temba. "Just anxiety."

The housekeeper bustled into the yard with a heavy rucksack, packed with provisions for the journey.

"I'm hoping the McTaggarts might be hospitable and replenish our water supply. If not, it's going to be a thirsty return trip. There's precious little water out there. We'll be reliant on rain."

Once the horses were loaded, Edward popped inside to say his farewells. Temba nuzzled his cheek against Tshukudu's, and pulled at his mane. "We'll be all right, old friend."

XXIII: Eric Chamberlain

Stone Town, Zanzibar
June 10th 1940

At long last, the captain of the Isis signalled for disembarkation. Manoeuvring the ship through the treacherous Zanzibar reefs and swells into Stone Town harbour had absorbed another precious day. Safely moored, William planted his feet on dry land and was immediately overcome by the heady scent of spices packed into bundles on the dock.

"Ah! Makes it all worthwhile," exclaimed William.

"Quite something, isn't it," replied Mossi. "Have you all the documentation with you?"

William lifted up a briefcase. "All accounted for. I could do with some directions, though."

The whitewashed Customs House gleamed in the sun. A massive orb spider had built a vast web pulling together the fronds of two adjacent palm trees. William studied it in awe. Close inspection revealed hundreds of desiccated beetle carcasses.

"Incredible aren't they!"

William spun on his heels, relieved to hear an English accent.

"The locals use its silk to weave scarves. *Nephilia* spiders are docile and harmless – unless, of course, you're on the menu."

The gentleman was dressed in a cream flannel suit.

"Eric Chamberlain – pleased to meet you, Captain Greenwood. Mossi told me to look out for you."

Eric took William by the arm and escorted him brusquely into the Customs House, and into an office. "I work for the British Residency here. Mossi and I were up at Oxford together. I monitor antiquity trafficking for him on the side – a hobby of mine. Make yourself comfy: back in five."

William sat beside a large desk. He noted an array of letter-writing paraphernalia, maps and a brass name plaque:

NCO Dr R.E. Chamberlain DPhil (Oxon) FRCS.

Map of East Africa (circa 1950)

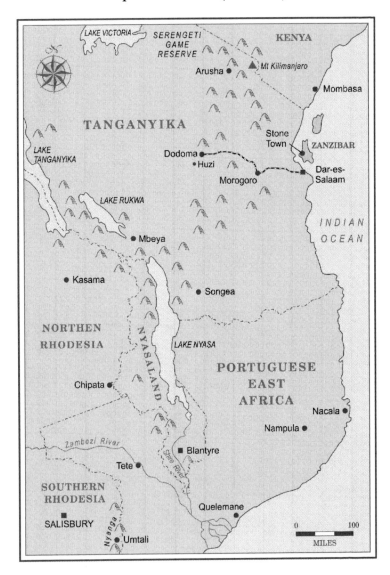

Eric returned with a young Asian gentleman. He was dressed smartly and his hair was cut, parted and pomaded immaculately.

"William Greenwood – Jameel Jayasinghe. JJ for short. As my personal assistant, JJ will be processing our papers for the next leg of the journey."

William shook JJ's hand.

"JJ was born in Dar-es-Salaam. He'll be our escort through Tanganyika, Nyasaland and down to the Rhodesian border."

William looked surprised. "Our papers? This is all news to me, Dr Chamberlain. Mossi keeps me on a short lead."

"Ah!" exclaimed Eric. "How very Mossi. It's no secret. Over to you, JJ. I'm off to arrange the transportation and safe stowing of your 'Stonelore' chronicles – fascinating. See you at dinner!"

JJ sat at the desk and took William's paperwork.

"So how did you get roped into all this, JJ?" William immediately regretted his choice of words.

"Fate, Mr Greenwood. I have relatives in Dodoma. My family owns a network of orchards and tea and coffee plantations. With me as guide, we won't be pestered."

"JJ, your English is impeccable," said William, attempting to redeem himself. "Is Sinhala or Tamil your first language?"

"Thank you, Mr Greenwood," replied JJ, stamping a visa document. "We speak Swahili at home. My mother's side of the family has been in East Africa for generations. My father came to Tanganyika in his early teens from Ceylon."

"So you know our route?"

"Yes, Sir. We'll employ Maasai porters in Dodoma and travel south to Lake Nyasa."

"Porters? What about the train?"

"Only as far as Dodoma. Mr Nkosi has business in Blantyre. I have an uncle there. He'll be accommodating us and organising our passage into Rhodesia."

JJ finished processing the travel documents and handed them over. "I gather you know Mrs Schmidt."

William was caught off guard. "Yes. Is she here?"

"Was, Mr Greenwood – she passed through here a few months ago. She's a remarkable lady."

"I know," William chuckled. "Where was she heading?"

"Lusaka. After that, I've no idea."

"Was she alone?"

"Yes, Mr Greenwood. She speaks fluent Swahili. I doubt anyone would…"

"How is everything?" interrupted Eric from the doorway. "All finished? Ts crossed and Is dotted?"

"Yes, Sir," replied JJ, sheepishly.

"There's a change of plan, William. Mossi wants us to assemble before dinner. *Tutaona baadaye*, JJ."

"Indeed, Dr Chamberlain. See you later." JJ smiled in appreciation of his boss's attempted Swahili. "Adieu, Mr Greenwood."

XXIV: The Test

Francistown, Bechuanaland Protectorate
Jan 22nd 1930

It didn't take long for Temba and Edward to pass through the farm settlements surrounding Francistown, and into sparsely wooded grassland. They headed west with the rising sun on their backs.

"We must be vigilant, Temba. I've lost two horses to snake bite in the last few months."

"Tshukudu steers well clear. Remember I told you the story of how I met Huw Williams?"

"I do."

"That all began with a snake bite – a puff adder – shame for Oubass Coetzee to go that way. He wasn't a bad man – his boys on the other hand... *Eish*! I'd love to have been a bystander at the Pearly Gates."

"So you don't feel remorse for dispatching them, Padre?"

Temba didn't reply.

By dusk, clouds had rolled in and passed by, negating any chances of a cooling cloudburst. The vegetation was lush, greened by summer rains and full of insects, birds, impala and wildebeest – and the highlight – a herd of fifty or so elephant making their way east towards Francistown's fields and orchards.

"You'd think they'd have enough food out here, wouldn't you? I mean, in the winter months you'd expect them to be hungry, but they seem to prefer plundering crops to reaping nature's bounty. It says something about the way our world is changing. They're protected, but who knows how much damage they'll cause. They ruin livelihoods on a daily basis, and fences don't stop them."

The men camped in the open, near a small copse. Edward lit a fire while Temba scouted for wood. He returned with a tidy bundle and a handful of mopani worms for the pot.

"Regarding the elephant," said Temba. "I forget who wrote it... '*Nature is no saint. She comes eating and drinking and sinning.*' Who are we to judge nature?"

"I agree. You don't blame the lion for attacking you, then?"

"Not at all. I stood in the way of his dinner."

Edward laughed. "And how do feel about hunting?"

139

"When I was in Matopos, it was a means to an end," replied Temba. "I needed money, stability and an opportunity to build a good reputation. We only shot what was plentiful. Once, we lost a client to a buffalo. I advised him not to take the shot. He ignored me. He didn't like being told what to do by a 'native'. I killed the beast, but not before it had charged the man, gored him and crushed the life out of him."

"I take your point. I think."

The men fed and slept well, serenaded by the call of jackals and nightjars. At dawn, they broke camp and continued into the grass savannah – escorted by hornbills and drongos that snapped up insects disturbed by the horses' hooves. There were few trees to shade them from the relentless sun, and by midday there was no cover at all. The tough grass and thorn trees scratched and irritated the horses' legs. Temba noticed several ticks gathering near an abrasion on Tshukudu's flank.

"Time for a rest."

Edward agreed, dismounted, and poured water into billycans for the horses. The sun baked the men as they stood, and a menacing westerly wind had picked up the red dust of the Kalahari.

"We'd better find shelter," said Edward. "There's an outpost about five kilometers west of here, if I can get my bearings. The Bushmen have been seen there once or twice. They're moving closer to the towns – fascination probably."

Temba remounted, having tended to Tshukudu's abrasions. "I've only heard stories. Are the Bushmen as mysterious a folk as people make out?"

"Probably. I've only come across them once, and they fled as as I drew near. They left behind a gemsbok carcass that would have fed thirty. They do well to keep to themselves – one bad disease could wipe them out. On the other hand, they've survived in the desert for tens of thousands of years – maybe hundreds of thousands – who knows? We wouldn't last a week without water and provisions."

Soon Temba saw what Edward meant by 'outpost'. Several petrified trees had been uprooted and woven together with rope to form a squat bivouac frame. Someone had laced desiccated fan palm fronds through the struts, providing a framework but offering no protection.

A dust devil whipped up sand, forcing them to squint.

"Quick, Temba. Let's get the canvas rigged."

Temba set to work while Edward settled the horses underneath the palm struts. Forcing the horses to lie down was no easy feat, and left very little room for the men. Securing the canvas with rope, Temba battled against the wind's increasing ferocity. All of a sudden, the full force of a sandstorm buffeted him backwards. Edward caught Temba's arm and dragged him into the shelter. The sky turned orange-red as visibility fell to a couple of metres. All at once, a deafening thunderclap startled the horses. Edward commanded Temba to lie on top of Tshukudu to calm him. Rain spattered the canvas with noisy droplets until it came hard and fast, roaring in intensity. Earsplitting bolts of lightning struck near and far, rocking the earth.

Both men were simultaneously aware of a presence, and caught each other's look of astonishment. Something had joined them under the canvas. Hunkered down by the entrance flap, were several balls of fluff, eliciting high-pitched squeaks.

"Suricates! Meerkat pups!" shouted Edward.

Temba scooped the furry bundles into his lap and yelled, "None of His creatures deserve to be out in this."

No sooner had Temba stopped talking than the wind abated, leaving a torrential downpour that lasted several minutes. The lightning continued to rumble around them, but as quickly as the storm had arrived, it passed. Stepping out from under the canvas and into a small pool that had formed around the canvas bivouac, Temba selected a dry burrow in an island of tough grass. He stowed the bewildered meerkat mob and gasped: the clouds had parted to reveal a shimmering mirage.

"Sua Pan," called Edward. "It floods occasionally – twice in my lifetime. Then the flamingoes fly in from the Skeleton coast. How they know to do it is beyond me. They feast on brine shrimp and then bugger off. Isn't nature something?"

Something caught Temba's attention. Beside the meerkat burrow was a small vertical stick. It had been placed deliberately.

"Don't touch it!" yelled Edward. "It's a Bushman water collector. There'll be an ostrich egg buried underneath. Like I said – one bad disease…"

Temba marvelled at the contraption for a second and then noticed something glimmering in the sand. "Is that Bushman too?"

Edward picked up a couple of colourful, polished stone beads.

"According to Tswana elders, many moons ago this whole area was submerged under a vast inland sea. Now they call it Makgadikgadi based on the word *kgala* meaning thirst. It's also how the Kalahari gets its name. These beads are the remnants of an ancient

141

people who flourished here, hunting and fishing to their hearts' content. There are some extraordinary animal skeletons to the north, but no human remains as far as I'm aware. These beads and the odd arrowhead is all we have left – and this saltpan."

"It's beautiful. I've seen it in my dreams."

"You've what?"

"That's right," laughed Temba. "Crazy isn't it? One minute, I'm an eagle, flying high over mountains to the south, and the next I'm crossing this white-crust saltpan on the wing. I've even seen your flamingoes – they must sense the humidity inland, somehow, and smell the shrimp. But whoever's vision I'm experiencing, they were here long after the inland sea you speak of had dried."

"That's pretty far-fetched, my friend."

"For sure. Can we camp here tonight? Tshukudu is tired."

"Of course. You can keep an eye on those pups."

While Edward cooked up a stew, Temba took the horses out to graze in the tough sparse grass. He knew that predators would gather at dusk, so he felt it prudent for them to eat their fill before anything spooked them. He looked towards the west and the setting sun, and was suddenly overcome with anxiety.

"How far is Orapa?" asked Temba.

"We'll be there by sundown tomorrow."

"What's there?"

"Not a great deal. I sunk a borehole and erected a few shacks several years ago, but I've no idea what condition they might be in. If we're to intercept the McTaggarts on their trek north, it's our best and safest bet."

"And if we don't."

"They are motorised, but the main party will be on horseback and wagon – they'll still need to stop for water. There's nothing between Serowe and the Delta. And they would be fools to cut corners in the sands of the Kalahari. My borehole at Orapa is their only option."

Temba fetched the horses and manhandled them under the bivouac canvas. "There's something I need to do."

"Be my guest. There's paper and soap in my saddlebags."

"Not that!" Temba chuckled. "I need solitude to pray."

It was warm, but grew cooler the further Temba wandered away from the grass islands. Soon he was far enough out into the sodden saltpan to lose the flicker of firelight and the buzz of insects.

It was silent. He lay back on the moist crust and broke through into cool damp silt, instantly soothing his aches and pains. Gazing up at the vast milky expanse, he marvelled as a shooting star blazed across the firmament, snuffing out in the atmosphere high above him. It brought thoughts of happier times: Rudolf, Rosalind and Tshepe at the Mission. He clasped his stone and recited:

> *"Yea, though I walk through the valley of the shadow of death,*
> *I will fear no evil."*

The verse of psalm eased his anxiety.
He closed his eyes: his mind wandered...

> *Bound in chains – hopeless.*
> *He must escape.*
> *He yearns for his animal familiar.*
> *The eagle. No! He is himself.*
> *Ropes burn his wrists: his eyes fill with blood.*
> *The chains crackle and spark. His disciples fall.*
> *Confusion. Disconnection.*
> *Out of the darkness: an orb of light.*
> *A humming sound.*
> *The chatter of men and women –*
> *The buzz of unfamiliar voices.*
> *A pair of leopards appear on the rocks above him.*
> *Teardrops fall into an azure lake.*
> *Water wells up from the earth.*
> *Rivulets coalesce into a mighty river, flowing out to sea.*
> *He stands before a mountain – gleaming in the darkness.*
> *It illuminates the heavens.*
> *He senses a colossal force – Titan takes aim.*
> *The thunderbolt strikes him, but he does not falter.*
> *He will survive.*
> *He was born to survive.*

Temba came to and pondered the significance of his dream. None the wiser, he sensed that he would be tested – and soon. He had to stay strong. Gathering his thoughts, he followed his footfalls back to the margin of the saltpan, tracing his way through the grass islands to the safety of the fire and bivouac. Edward was fast asleep, and Tshukudu barely acknowledged Temba as he opened his bivvy bag to check for critters.

He couldn't sleep.

Sleep could wait.

Thunder rumbled in the distance. Temba sat up. Disturbed, he wriggled out from under the canvas and peered into the darkness. The air was intense. Hot. His nostrils were filled with a strange sweet smell – like cooking corn. He saw someone… something… neither man, nor beast: something ethereal, non-corporeal. It was searching in the grasses, noiselessly. The horses had sensed it too from under the canvas. Temba felt his fingers tingle. The entity stopped to acknowledge his presence, radiating a blueish hue. A ghost, lost in a wilderness of sand, salt and grass. Temba reached out towards the apparition. It had no face. Formed from energy alone, it backed away as if shy. He took tentative steps towards the manifestation and reached his hand out again, shaking, as if every cell in his body was pulsating. The entity drew closer, inspecting Temba's body; infiltrating his every thought. He was rooted to the spot, perspiration beading on his brow and suddenly aware that he was observing himself from the perspective of the entity. Time slowed. Temba watched a drop of sweat fall from his brow to the earth.

At once, a deafening crack launched him backwards through the air. The stiff grass broke his fall. Regaining consciousness, he looked to one side: it was the meerkat burrow containing five charred little bodies. Temba leapt up, furious, to engage the entity – but it was gone.

Frighted, the horses had taken off, pulling the rope tethers and pegs from out of the soft ground, levelling the bivouac.

"What are you doing?" called Edward, extricating himself from under the collapsed canvas.

Temba started towards him, threateningly.

Edward took a step back. "Temba! What's wrong?"

"I saw something."

"There's nothing out here. You're dreaming!"

"That was no dream."

Temba showed Edward a burn mark on his right hand before snatching Roddy's Winchester from under the canvas. I'm going to find whatever it was, and blow it to kingdom come."

"Blow what?"

"That abomination."

"Stop Temba. You're not making any sense."

Temba loaded Roddy's rifle. "What was it then?"

"I've no idea." Edward grabbed Temba's shirt, stopping him. "Describe it."

Temba stared into Edward's eyes. "It was blue, hot – a ghost – a wraith – a demon without feeling or emotion. It had no sense of right or wrong. It just moved about, looking for something, and then…" Temba stopped, noting Edward's attention had been diverted.

On a patch of canvas, illuminated by the fire, was a sticky sap-like substance.

Edward sniffed and tasted it. "Sweet."

"Tell me, Edward. What is it?"

Edward began to laugh quietly. "It's amazing."

"What's amazing? It burned the meerkat pups to oblivion."

"You are amazing, my friend."

"What do you mean, I'm amazing?"

"You truly are a wonder of nature. And the first person I have ever met who's gone toe to toe with the Tokolosh and survived."

"The Toko-what?"

"How have you not heard of the Tokolosh?"

Temba drew a blank.

"The Zulus believe the Tokolosh comes in the night and kills people indiscriminately."

"The Bogeyman? Rosalind would read me stories at bedtime. She was more into Leprechauns, though."

"Yes. The Bogeyman. It leaves burn marks, strange sugary residue and dead bodies in its wake." Edward scoffed. "I'm sure there's a rational explanation for it all."

"Well, whatever it was, it murdered those poor pups."

****

Sua Pan, Makgadikgadi
January 24th 1930

Once the canvas was stowed and the horses watered, Edward led Temba towards Orapa in the hope of finding the McTaggart safari expedition and potable water. Sporadic islands of towering makalani palms provided shade, but the heat was unbearable. Both men were drooping in the saddle by the time Edward recognised the terrain.

"We're not far," said Edward. "Start praying that the borehole is operational, Padre."

Ahead, the heat-haze revealed a circle of wagons and several wood shacks. Mounds of earth were piled up to the north.

"You were right, Edward. They're here. Let's stop and drink. I need to get my head straight before I make my apologies."

"No. We must press on. Here – finish my canteen. I have another." Edward dismounted and wandered towards the *laager*.

Temba accepted and drank sparingly. Was the Tokolosh sent to test his resolve, or was something more deadly waiting for him? The closer he drew to the McTaggart *laager*, the more his sense of dread intensified.

"Something's wrong," muttered Edward. "They've been digging here – for a while it seems. It looks like they've found diamonds. If they have, they're mining without permission."

Temba was too busy mustering the courage of his convictions to hear Edward. What if Roddy were to ask to see the stone? He untied it from his neck and pocketed it.

Edward ordered Temba to stop while he cantered ahead. Temba dismounted and watched Edward scan the scene, cover his face with a bandana and return swiftly.

"Did the Tokolosh come for them?" asked Temba.

"No. But something else did. Tread carefully, my friend. Tell me what you see. You know far more about disease than I do."

Temba felt fear for the first time since being mauled by the lion. He pulled a *shemagh* from his saddlebag and wrapped it around his face. Then he covered his hands in soap. "I'll take a look."

Flies buzzed around two of the wagons. Roddy's truck was nowhere to be seen, and the horses were gone. Suddenly, a cough made him swivel. Tentatively, he pushed aside the canvas of the nearest wagon. Two Tswana porters were lying prostrate on mats. Crusted blood seeped from their eyes: both were dead.

146

"Jesus!" exclaimed Temba under his breath. "What pestilence is this?"

He approached the fly-ridden wagons slowly, presuming the occupants were also dead. A quick recce proved him right. He spotted something familiar. Poking out of the back of one wagon was a piece of furniture belonging to Rhona McTaggart. He peered inside and found the source of the cough. Running back to Tshukudu, he called Edward for assistance. When Edward refused to budge, he grabbed a bag of medicines and returned to Rhona's wagon. She was burning up, but alive. Pouring some watery *muti* between her cracked lips, Temba scanned the wagon for clues. Whatever had infected the others had clearly not had as dreadful an effect on Rhona. Selflessly, Temba sat her up before gently lifting her out of the wagon. She wheezed. Her breathing was awkward but sure; her heart rate slow but steady. Temba carried her away from the *laager* towards Edward and the horses.

"Don't come any closer!" yelled Edward.

Temba ignored him and laid her in the shadow cast by Tshukudu. Using what was left in his canteen, Temba revived her. She raised her eyelids momentarily and fell into a deep sleep. Temba covered her with a blanket.

"Don't worry. Whatever infected her has done its worst. She's fighting it. If she wasn't, she'd be dead by now."

Edward hesitated before dismounting.

"Keep her in the shade of the horses, Edward. I'm going back for answers. Roddy may have gone for help… or fled. Either way, he's in trouble. Whatever killed the others is going to slow him down and disorient him – if it hasn't killed him already. Rhona understands medicine. She's alive because she stayed put and rested to fight the infection. There's evidence that she's been treating herself with quinine amongst other drugs."

Temba covered his hands with more soap and returned to the *laager*. There were vehicle tracks leading north. An array of bootprints suggested that four or more souls had made it out alive with horses. Temba spotted the iron-corrugated shacks that Edward had mentioned, next to what looked like pumping machinery. A gust of wind brought a whiff of something deeply unpleasant. Temba retreated a safe distance.

One of the wagons had been stripped of its contents. Judging by what remained, it had contained weaponry, ammunition and fuel for the truck. Temba threw out what was left and took hold of the draught pole. With every ounce of strength, he lifted the front wheels of the

147

wagon and manoeuvred it round in the soft sand, pulling it free from the *laager*.

"Edward," called Temba, exhausted. "Time for the horses to learn how to tow. Tether them while I get Rhona comfortable."

Edward was reluctant, but did as he was told. When they had dragged the wagon a safe distance, Temba lifted Rhona into the back of the wagon and dosed her with more watered-down *muti*. Once the horses were tethered to the yoke, Temba took out his bivvy bag and hemmed Rhona in between the horses' saddles.

"We should check the borehole, Temba. Maybe it's operational."

"No! It may be the source of the infection. We should get out of here as quickly as possible. There's a dire smell coming from the shacks."

"Your choice, Padre, but we have maybe four litres of water left, and the horses are going to need most of that."

"True. We must find the truck, and fast."

Temba clicked his parched tongue and the horses responded awkwardly, unsynchronised and ungainly. Soon they got the hang of pulling together, and followed the tyre tracks and hoofprints in the hard baked earth. After several hundred metres, Edward forced Temba to rein in the horses.

"Reality check." Edward pulled out a map. "There's a village north of here called Gweta. It's our nearest source of water, but it means taking on the main Nwetwe Pan. Once we break through the salt crust, the sand underneath is going to be damp to wet, and near as damn impossible for the horses to pull us through. Our best bet is to head north-west to the spit of land that separates the eastern Nwetwe Pan from Sua Pan. We'll still have to cross the salt, but it'll be at its narrowest."

"What about the truck?" asked Temba.

"What if we don't make up the ground? If Roddy has any sense left in him, he'll do the same. Chasing him is too much of a risk. If Rhona means anything to you, Temba, save her and make your peace with Roddy some other time."

"You're right, my friend."

Edward steered the horses north-east, away from the tyre tracks. The air cooled as the sun dropped on the horizon. After an hour of silent progress, they saw the white dry crust of the saltpan. Temba clambered into the back to check on Rhona. She was feverish, but nothing like Temba had feared. He forced some more fluid between her dry lips, and was relieved to see them part and swallow without resistance or suffering. He watched her eyes roll under her eyelids. Her breathing was constant and deep, and her heart rate had elevated. She seemed to be responding well.

As the sun set, Edward reigned in the horses once more. "They need to feed. It's just grass for you, my beauties!"

"How much light do we have?" asked Temba.

"An hour?"

"I'm going to look for tracks. If you're right and the truck turned east, then…" Temba stopped. It was unmistakable – the roar of an engine somewhere to the north.

"That could be thirty miles away," said Edward.

"Or closer. Let's press on."

"Fine. I'll give them some oats, or you can argue with them when they don't want to pull any more."

The sun seemed to have dropped out of the sky, leaving a pink aura and a peculiar greenish glow. It was blissfully cool: moisture sucked out of the atmosphere by the salt-caked sand. By midnight, the wagon had reached the southernmost extent of the spit. The wagon wheels resisted as they cut through the salt crust into the soft sand, clogging them. Several pools had survived the heat of the day, but the water was unpotable.

Tshukudu stopped – ears pricked to the north-east. Something had caught the attention of Edward's horse too.

"He can smell water," remarked Edward. That's why I call him *Diviner*."

"Let's take their lead."

"I'll water them first. You get praying."

Temba checked on Rhona and placed a cool, damp rag on her forehead. He loosed the plaits that bound her hair and laid her head down softly on his *shemagh*. She swallowed and moaned.

"Rhona?"

Again, she stirred. He repeated himself, but she didn't respond.

Temba pulled a blanket over her, curious to see what Edward was doing outside: he was greasing the wheels with fat.

"Good thinking, Edward."

Stepping up to the footplate, Temba took the reigns and clicked the horses into action. Edward clambered aboard. It was pitch dark as the unburdened wagon slid across the pan in whatever direction the horses were taking them.

Just before dawn, both men were roused by a thud as the wagon wheels struck bare rock.

"Where are we?" asked Temba.

"No idea."

"I'd better investigate. Stay here with the horses, Edward. They could do with a rest."

The stars lit the surrounding land just enough to make out three baobab trees and a gentle incline up a granite outcrop. Temba wandered further until a glow in the east revealed more details. Twenty minutes later, at the northern limit of the outcrop, the granite had eroded to form a natural amphitheatre surrounded by gnarled trees. In a shaded recess was a pool of rainwater. He scrambled down and wet his lips. It was brackish and unpleasant, but if boiled it would serve them well. As he retraced his steps he heard a twig snap. Ducking down for cover, he scanned the outline of the rock.

"Don't move!"

Temba recognised the accent to be that of the Afrikaners.

"I have no intention," replied Temba. "I'm unarmed."

"No quick move or I *mooer* you. *Verstaan*?

"*Ja. Ek verstaan.* (I understand)" replied Temba.

"*Goed.* Stand slowly and raise your hands."

Temba stepped out of a rocky depression and discerned the silhouette of a man toting a rifle.

"Come into the open."

Temba walked slowly towards the figure, his arms raised. Some twenty metres below on the saltpan, he could see the outline of the truck, but there was no sign of the horses. He heard another voice. This time, the accent was American.

"Roderick McTaggart? Is that you?" Temba looked down at a man sitting in a chair, shivering in the cool of dawn. He had a rug drawn about him, and a medicine chest by his feet.

"Who's askin'?" replied Roddy, his voice weak.

"Temba. Temba Schmidt? What happened?"

"Temba?" Roddy tilted his head. "The prodigal Preacherman returns. How the hell d'ya find us?"

"The horses must have smelled the truck, I guess. I thought they were heading for water."

"Horses? Where? Keep them away. I lost four beasts just

getting to this rock... and three men. It's just me and Andre left. He hasn't had so much as a sniffle."

Andre lowered the rifle. "We call it *die siekte* – the sickness. I suffered from it when I was young. My mother wasn't so fortunate. They say it's spread by the Bushmen to stop the settlers grazing cattle out here."

Temba remembered what Edward had said about the gemsbok carcass – abandoned for no apparent reason.

"Man, that's bullshit!" said Roddy. "We found hundreds of wildebeest carcasses north-west of Serowe. Next thing – the horses start coughing and my men drop like flies."

Temba noticed Roddy shift his rug to obscure the medicine chest by his feet. What had he done? Temba's mind began to race.

"What brings you out here, *monna*?" asked Andre.

"I had a tip-off that you were headed this way. I thought I'd return something. Something I took by mistake... and make my peace."

"My Trusty Girl? It'll be good to see her again. Where are your horses?"

"Not far," replied Temba, nebulously.

"You here on your lonesome?" asked Roddy.

"Yes," lied Temba.

"Good."

Temba felt a crack on the back of his head...

OLD WORLD

They came from far: crossing the void,
Hungry and thirsty, their world destroyed.
Millions perished through no fault of their own,
Countless more succumbed to dangers unknown.

Survivors flourish, reap and multiply,
Exploiting weaknesses, they reach out, diversify.
For millennia they thrive, unfettered, unconfined,
Asserting their dominance – subjugating Mankind.

The meek rose up, overthrew the oppressor,
And grew fat on the spoils of bloodthirsty wars.
In victory they spared no one, granted no quarter,
Raising great edifices in stone to their Lords.

They reclaimed that which was theirs "By Bloodright!"
"Murder thy neighbour! Fulfil thine own desires!"
Orisons of praise to counterfeit gods,
An orgy of profligacy: compassion expires.

"The Day of Judgement" arrives – as foretold:
With avarice comes pride, the folly of old.
Contrition of the few: acknowledgement of crimes.
Circumvention of wrath in dismal confines.

Those that prevail are rewarded, reprieved –
Enlightened with Wisdom
– the Will to succeed.

The Worthy ascend, disseminate the Word:
Sow their seed, strengthen the herd.
Cultivating humanity, like as the grain,
Restoring harmony to Mankind's domain.

NEW EARTH

The balance of power starts to shift,
A fragile equilibrium begins to drift.
Time trickles by: it is inconsequential.
Life is paramount: quintessential.

How we forget the lessons of the past,
Taking such beauty for granted:
Burning Her forests, polluting Her seas, befouling the atmosphere:
Nature supplanted.

Nations lose faith in one another,
Revering false prophets and shapeshifting deities:
Corporate manipulators, the twisters of Truth –
Greed, mistrust, baseless claims and disease.

"Catastrophe Unavoidable!" – as light is dawning,
We ignore, at our peril, Her tempestuous warning.
Fools scoff in the face of extinction,
Refusing to acknowledge their gluttony, addiction.

"Good people, we are fashioned from earthly clay –
Like an oasis in the heat of day –
The blue-green Rondure is not ours to possess;
Yoke, bend, disfigure, distress."

Mankind, to Her, is but cosmic dust –
Flecks on a parchment – a patina of rust.

Betrayed, unforgiving, She beats her breast.
The sprawling masses are a virulent pest.
Arrogant, cruel, beyond repentance –
She wipes from Her face the ignominious guest.

Harmony ignored?
There shall be No more reward.
She will slay us all.

XXV: Homecoming

Oliver Tambo International Airport, Cape Town
Republic of South Africa
November 10th 1998

Franco had arranged his father's funeral in a small church in Hout Bay on the southern slopes of Table Mountain. Lester Hendriks had bought a house under Tierboskloof, near the township of Imizamu Yethu. Sam had flown down with Franco and Lester's body three days prior to organise friends and family, and a boozy wake – just as Lester Hendriks would have wanted.

A funeral company took custody of Hendriks's body at the airport, and Franco went to find his father's car. Sam stayed in the Terminal building, nursing a coffee, until eventually his phone lit up with directions.

Franco was quiet. The pair drove west towards Table Mountain and south onto the agapanthus-lined M3 motorway, skirting the University and Rhodes Memorial, before turning right amid purple-blue flowering jacarandas into Kirstenbosch. The road to Constantia Nek passed the Botanic Gardens and twisted through towering eucalyptus, until it dropped down into Hout Bay. The security gates opened automatically and Franco parked up.

"Just bung your bags anywhere. I'll give Nomsa a call – she'll know where the fresh bedding is."

"Nomsa?"

"She organises *Pappie* – or she used to." Franco's voice wavered. "*Pappie* took her on as a cleaner when he retired. She'd help with Mukwa. You know… it was tricky to justify the graffiti when the neighbours popped over for 'a bowl of sugar'."

Sam understood the euphemism.

"In return, *Pappie* helped Nomsa start her own cleaning business. She's formidable. In the meantime, make yourself at home – have a cup of tea and a swim. I'm off to the shops. Want anything? I'll get beers and smokes."

Sam shook his head. "No. I'm good."

The house was substantial and had been maintained lovingly. Built on a slope, it had a garden, front and back. Sam was no stranger to Hout Bay. His parents had owned a small cottage closer to the beachfront in the early '90s. He had fond memories of playing cricket in the driveway, substantial seafood platters at Mariner's Wharf and drunken staggers home from Dirty Dicks.

Nosing around, Sam couldn't help but notice a citrusy chemical smell. He knew immediately what it signified. He went upstairs to the landing where the smell was stronger. There was a sizeable study, Lester Hendriks's master bedroom with small balcony and ensuite, and another locked bedroom. Sam felt drawn towards it, and an inexplicable frustration that he couldn't see inside. He knocked but no one answered. Where was Mukwa?

Sam went downstairs, made a cup of rooibos tea and sat comfortably with his Wilbur Smith. The pool on the veranda looked tempting, but he didn't have the inclination. He was too preoccupied with meeting Mukwa.

Franco returned an hour or so later with shopping and immediately cracked open a beer. "Want one?"

"I've got a tea."

"Nomsa says to put you in the downstairs spare room. It has an ensuite. I'll just put some bogroll in there, and you can crash."

"Where is Mukwa?" blurted Sam.

Franco put away the groceries. "Work – probably due back in an hour or so. I've got some calls to make. I'll be up in the study. Help yourself to stuff."

Sam's fascination with Mukwa began to unsettle him. He hadn't seen him in more than ten years. And when they eventually clapped eyes on one other it was fleeting and under a bizarre set of circumstances, never fully resolved. Sam picked up his novel and put it down immediately. Pacing around, he studied the art on the walls. Opening a drawer containing photograph albums, curiosity got the better of him. Sam nosed through hundreds of Franco's school photos and family holiday snaps: the beach at Muizenberg, kids playing in the surf, university cricket and rugby, army colleagues pictured with a large dead eland and surfing the Namib dunes.

A second album contained wedding photos. Franco's mother was a tall attractive woman with striking blonde hair. There were numerous black and white shots of her with baby Franco taken in different locations around southern Africa, mostly in the back of safari jeeps. It was no wonder that Franco had trained as a Game Ranger.

The third album was not so joyful. It was clear that Franco's mother had fallen ill when he was young. Hendriks was conspicuously absent – probably because he was behind the lens. Sam guessed that it was about the time when Hendriks would have met Anthony Greenwood, in the early '60s. After that, there were no shots of Franco with his father apart from a small, loose colour photograph. It was similar to one he'd seen at the Choir School in Hendriks's apartment, showing Mr Greenwood, little Mukwa on crutches, a young Franco, a middle-aged African gentleman and an elderly lady with grey hair and dark glasses. On the back was written: 'Umtali 1973'. Sam had never heard of the place. He tucked the photograph into the back of his novel.

The electric gates opened and a blue VW Citi Golf drove in. Mukwa stepped out with a briefcase. 'He looks older', thought Sam as he peered out of the window. Mukwa spotted Sam and waved. Sam returned the compliment awkwardly and settled himself.

"Sam! It's been a while."

"It sure has. Sorry it's taken so long for us to meet up – and under such circumstances." Sam had been rehearsing his introduction, and the formality seemed daft in hindsight. "I mean... I've been coming to Hout Bay for years. It's just a shame that..."

"Yes, Sam. I know what you mean." Mukwa smiled and shook Sam's hand. "Lester wasn't a well man, but he had a few good years left in him."

"Can I make you a cuppa?" asked Sam.

"That would be *lekker*," beamed Mukwa. "I'll just freshen up and join you now-now. Is Franco in?"

"*Hier, boet!*" yelled Franco from the upstairs study. "Beers in the fridge."

Sam brewed the tea, and sat on the veranda, nervously. Moments later, Mukwa returned.

"We had a busy day at the hospital. Gun crimes are on the rise in the Western Cape."

"Is that what you do?"

"Gun crimes?" Mukwa laughed. "No. I'm a trauma surgeon at Groote Schuur Hospital in Cape Town. I finished sewing up my last victim this morning, but the paperwork is endless."

"Jeez," remarked Sam, removing a cigarette from a fresh pack. "That's intense."

"So, Sam. Where do we start?"

Sam inhaled and shrugged. "At the beginning, I guess. I know I'm not who I thought I was. How about you?"

"It's complicated. Anthony kept stuff from me. I've pieced some of it back together, but as to the bigger picture – let's leave that for now. I don't remember my biological parents. My memories... and by that I mean the truth... are of pain and suffering. Anthony always maintained that I fell down a mineshaft. But he was hiding something. Whatever happened, I was in a bad way and needed fixing. I was on crutches until I was seven."

"You were in Botswana?"

"Sure. They found diamonds up in Orapa in the late 1950s, but large-scale mining didn't take place until the early '70s. So what Anthony was doing up there is a bit of a mystery, and it involved Lester. I was born in '68 – so whatever it was my biological parents were up to – they were also caught up in it. I've spent years reading up on the area and my suspicion is that they weren't looking for diamonds."

"Stones?"

"Funny how everything comes back to them. I started digging, so to speak, to find more about my parents but kept drawing blanks. It's as if someone had gone to great trouble to wipe out any evidence of them."

"So, now?"

"Unfortunately, the only people who know the truth are dead. Lester resisted any opportunity to tell me, citing it was for my own good." Mukwa took a sip of tea. "Tell me about William Greenwood. What happened up in Letaba?"

"The old man?" Sam scratched his head. "He looked really old – a wizened version of his son, Anthony. Glassy eyes – skin and bone. Yuriy took him out."

"Yuriy?"

"You've not met?" asked Sam, confused.

"Not that I know of – but I've a gut feeling that is about to change."

"He's crazy. And I'm not sure I can trust him, but I don't think I have much choice. He may be able to throw some light on why we know so little about our ancestry."

"William Greenwood," said Mukwa, pensively. "So he was hiding in Argentina all those years. I saw him at Groote Schuur Hospital. My first thought was it was the ghost of Anthony! I'd put in a long shift. I didn't tell Lester at first because I knew he'd overreact." Mukwa looked back into the house nervously and continued in a whisper. "He left me a note."

"Who? William Greenwood?"

"*Ja.* All it said was 'trust your instincts'. Infer what you will, Sam. I eventually mentioned it to Lester – next thing, he absconds and turns up in Letaba a week later."

"A week? But Franco 'jimmied' him as soon as I'd divulged the shooting incident. What was he doing in the interim?"

"Your guess is as good as mine. Tell me more about Yuriy."

"Messed up – obviously intelligent. He's caught up in a world of espionage, and clearly not averse to killing people. Lester told me that his father, Boris, had used him as a test subject in a facility in Kazakhstan. Yuriy killed his own father in revenge some years later in Moscow, as well as William Greenwood in Letaba last week and, if Lester is to be believed, it was Yuriy who finished off Anthony at St Thomas' Hospital. Wait!" Sam paused for thought. "Lester said Yuriy helped smuggle you out of London, and that you'd admitted to being…"

"That was Yuriy?" exclaimed Mukwa. "He said he was a British agent – tall, dark hair, handsome chap?"

"That's him!"

"I seriously thought he was a Brit! And what is it I'm supposed to have admitted to being?"

Sam considered his words carefully. "A 'Stage Three Scribe'."

"A what? I did nothing of the sort. Did Lester tell you this?"

Sam nodded. "You write in your sleep, but have no idea of what you're drawing."

Mukwa looked distraught. He started to shake.

"I'm sorry, Mukwa, no offence," said Sam. "I'm just regurgitating what Lester told me."

Mukwa stood, beckoned Sam inside and climbed the stairs, moving quietly so as not to disturb Franco. He took out a key and opened his bedroom door. Sam entered. There was nothing unusual about the room's contents. It was tidy and exuded a strong citrus smell – the walls were whitewashed and the curtains tied back. Sam saw nothing out of place.

"Bear with me," said Mukwa unlocking a small safe. He pulled out a light bulb and inserted it into the central fitting. He then pressed a hidden button: Sam heard the click. Aluminium shutters began to fall on the windows until it was pitch black.

Mukwa whispered. "So, what do you see?"

"Er… nothing."

"How about now." Mukwa flicked on the light. Sam's jaw dropped. In ultraviolet light, every wall, cupboard and even the shutters were covered in emblems, symbols, equations, weird pictograms, and something that Sam recognised – a star – a six-point geometric shape with concentric circles and lines joining the points.

"The star? You recognise it, don't you?" Mukwa pressed the button to raise the shutters. Light poured in. "I had to check. You draw as well?"

"Yes. It started a couple of weeks ago."

"We have something in common. I wonder if that's why William Greenwood came to find you, Sam. How much do you know about your family?"

"Lester told me that my great-grandfather was Samuel Morgan, and that my grandfather changed his name."

"Samuel Morgan! *'sus.*" exclaimed Mukwa. "Shame I know nothing about my forebears."

"What do you mean by 'William Greenwood came to find me'," asked Sam. "Lester said it too."

"I think he was trying to precipitate something," said Mukwa. "You don't hide out in Argentina for thirty years only to appear suddenly in a packed hospital, and then in a remote valley in the Kruger. I think he had a message for you, Sam, and from what you've told me, Yuriy silenced him before he had a chance to pass it on. I think you're right, we can't trust him."

Ushering Sam out, Mukwa turned the light off, locked the door and led Sam downstairs to the kitchen. He opened a panel on the wall with a key. It housed two pistols and a rifle. "This house has a five minute security response time. If the alarm goes you take this." Mukwa shoved a pistol into Sam's hand and quickly snatched it back. "Follow me."

At the back of the veranda there was a wooden sauna. Mukwa opened the door and lifted the wooden floor to reveal a steel plate trapdoor with a coded locking mechanism. "The code is 1211. Don't worry – it's not significant." Mukwa heaved it open and stepped down a ladder. Sam followed. "This is the panic room. It's a bit leaky and smells fusty in the winter, but it'll serve you for a few months should you need to hide out."

Shelves were crammed with tins of food, bags of pasta, bottled water and toilet paper. There was a TV in the corner and a single camp bed, made up.

"Just like my room in the cloisters!" said Mukwa.

"But without a booby trap!"

"*Ja!* Sorry about that." Mukwa laughed. "It all seems so childish, now; puzzles, codes and crossword clues. Aside from the poison, that is." He rolled his eyes. "You press this button to release yourself, and this one for armed response. Hopefully, you won't need to use either. Another cuppa?"

"Perhaps a beer?"

"For sure." Mukwa locked up the sauna. "Your dreams suggest that you, like me, were exposed to the stone at the Choir School. You were supposed to be enrolled there for protection."

"I know. Lester told me."

"I'm sorry that Anthony went rogue. He kept it from me too."

"What's done is done," said Sam nonchalantly.

Franco appeared on the veranda. "You've shown him the upgrade?"

"Yes," replied Mukwa. "He's one of us, now."

"Us? What…" Sam felt his hair stand on end. "Franco? You're…"

"Going to make supper, *boet.*"

****

"So I guess my mother had a stone too," said Franco. "All *Pappie* had to say on the matter was that she was hiding something. I kinda assumed it was a stone."

"And you're a Scribe too?"

"*Ja,* about that – I've learned to control my manifestations through a magical substance called *dop* (alcohol)," chuckled Franco. "I still get the odd bout of creativity."

"Lucky bastard," quipped Mukwa.

"Franco, do you think Lester might have given your mother's stone to Anthony Greenwood?"

"It's possible."

"So where does that leave us all?" asked Sam "And what are we supposed to do about it?"

"I think your friend Yuriy has answers," said Franco. "But I'm in no hurry to summon him. What about your tin, Sam? Did you bury it in the Bush again?"

Sam scratched his stubble. "I buried the tin and its contents – a packet of mints and a hanky. If anyone unearths it…" He shrugged, reached into his shorts' pocket and pulled out a small wad of bubble wrap. "I thought it best to bring this along."

Mukwa looked dumbfounded. "Do you understand how hard we worked to hide them?"

"*Yassus!*" exclaimed Franco. "*Ag*, well. No time like the present."

"That was a bad idea," said Mukwa nervously. "We have no idea who might have followed you here."

"True. But Yuriy's seen Anthony's cloths and he knows I have the key – I bet he's not far away. He has an uncanny knack of turning up at the right moment, like a bad penny, and then disappearing. Besides, we have his number." Sam rattled his mobile phone. "What do you know about the map that you hid in the Abbey Library?"

Mukwa shook his head, unconvinced. "The map was always Anthony's best kept secret. I've no idea who drew it, or what it depicts. I've no idea what the key opens either, but I'm glad you rescued it. The writing, however… it's a prayer written in different languages – something about a group of cataclysm survivors who set out on a journey asking for divine protection. Whoever they were, it was a long time ago. I suspect it has something to do with a land of ice and…"

"A tall skinny woman called Tsuk," interrupted Franco.

"That's right, Franco!" exclaimed Sam. "Sorry, I just find it bizarre that people can share dreams of things they have never experienced or heard about before. Of course, I should know better."

"Let me guess," said Franco. "Yuriy told you that he has the same dream."

XXVI: The Funeral

Church of St Peter the Fisherman, Hout Bay
November 13th 1998

The funeral service was a remarkably jovial affair and brought together people from across the Cape community. Sam met Nomsa and her family, as well as a legion of Hendrikses from near and far. Lester's Bishops' students and old school pals put in a good showing, as did the rugby club. Franco was visibly humbled by the turnout and equally concerned, sending Sam and Mukwa to the Chapman's Peak Liquor Store with a wad of Rands.

The wake was held in the Church Hall. Franco stayed in the Church with close family to observe the burial rites before joining. A couple of local DJs kept hips swinging, while a huge *braaivleis* sated appetites. Mukwa greeted everyone and plied the guests with alcohol.

The gardens were awash with colourful garments and happy laughter.

'Makes a change from black suits and renaissance choral music,' thought Sam as he slipped off for a smoke.

No sooner had he lit up than a familiar face caught his attention. It was Yuriy. He was talking to some of the older Rugby Club members. Sam watched him ingratiate himself into the conversation with ease.

Puffing out his chest, Sam wandered over. "Gentlemen. Yuriy. So glad you could all come. I'm Sam."

"Yuriy says you work with Franco up in Letaba," said one of the men. "And Lester taught you at Westminster School."

"The Abbey Choir School," corrected Yuriy in a flawless English accent. "Sam was a little choirboy in those days. He's put on some height since."

"*En djou ballas het gedrop!*"

The men laughed. Sam got the gist.

Yuriy broke the awkwardness. "Join me for a drink, Samuel?"

"Gentlemen, catch you later," bid Sam. As he left, he heard one of the men mutter the word *moffie* meaning homosexual. Sam was visibly ruffled by the insinuation.

"It's just banter, Sam!" quipped Yuriy. "Get over it."

"Bullying is how I remembered 'it' at school. I couldn't wait for my voice to break. Not that I…" Sam suddenly realised to whom he was speaking. "Still, it can't come close to what you've been through."

"My issues started after I left school." Yuriy changed tack. "We need to talk. All of us."

"This is hardly the time or place."

"You're right. But it has to be soon. There's been a development."

"A development?"

"A power shift. I'll explain tomorrow. And be careful. We're being watched. Talk to the others. Tomorrow 7.00pm. I'll let you know where."

Yuriy left quickly. Did he know about Franco's sensitivity to the stones? 'Others' suggested so.

Chapman's Peak Drive, Hout Bay
November 14th 1998
7.00pm

Mukwa and Sam pulled into a viewpoint car park, halfway up the winding coastal road from Hout Bay to Chapman's Peak. There were four other cars parked up: families enjoying a picnic in the warm sea breeze. Sam got out and searched for Yuriy. Mukwa stayed in his car and kept the engine running. The viewpoint looked out across Hout Bay towards The Sentinel, standing some three hundred metres above the breakers.

Another car parked up and Yuriy stepped out. "Where's Franco?"

"How did you know?" asked Sam.

Yuriy smiled. "He's up there, isn't he?"

"We're not quite ready to trust you yet, Yuriy."

"Is he armed?"

"Sights trained," confirmed Sam. "Mukwa's carrying as well. This is a big leap of faith."

"I understand. Good work, Sam. Now you must search me for concealed weapons, and make sure Mukwa trains his pistol on my skull. If I move, he must shoot." Yuriy said it loud enough for Mukwa to hear.

Sam patted down Yuriy. "More lessons?"

"Of course, Sam. Satisfied?"

"Yes."

"We need to move before we lose the light. Mukwa!" shouted Yuriy. "Come – you've nothing to fear."

Yuriy led the men up a path through *fynbos* and flowering protea, higher and higher, until they met Franco brandishing a rifle and kitted out in his old army fatigues.

"Franco de Villiers, or should I say Hendriks?"

"Franco is fine. Why are we here, Kuriagin?"

"Answers – or at least some. It's not much further."

Yuriy stopped by a large vertical rock slab. The land fell steeply towards the road, several hundred feet below them. On the mountainside, a fissure above them indicated that a large chunk of overhanging rock had collapsed in a landslide.

"Look at the rock closely. What do you see?"

Sam inspected it. There were signs of chiselling and discolouration. "Petroglyphs?"

"They were left by *strandlopers* thousands of years ago."

"You said you had answers, Yuriy," said Franco. "Speak."

"Take a seat." Yuriy sat in the dust, took a sip from a hip flask and offered it around.

"Do you mind if I don't, Yuriy," said Sam. "Last time we met, you drugged me."

"True, Sam. I did. But I needed time to cover my tracks in case Franco sent out a search party." Yuriy took another swig. "To business – we all have something in common. We have the ability to commune with a set of crystals. We know that they cause cancer – but judging by the fact that we are all fit and well – we are probably immune. Many were not so lucky. The project my father established was responsible for the deaths of scores of young men and women. Many of them were my friends. Boris was blinded by superstition – as were the Greenwoods. They had no idea of the purpose of the stones. Instead, they gathered as many stones as they could by fair means or foul, and subjected us to varying doses of their radiation. Only a few of us survived."

"*Ja!* We know all this," interjected Franco.

"Can we all agree on something?" asked Yuriy. "We've all seen the geometric six-point star with the concentric circles?"

They all nodded.

"Good. My grandfather saw this symbol in ancient temples all over the world, from China to Peru. He also found a stone, and in time suffered from nightmares and contracted cancer. He gave it to my father when he was young, not knowing that it was the stone that had caused his illness. My father had manifestations but didn't contract cancer, and gambled that, as his son, I'd also survive exposure. I now believe he was right, but it doesn't change my mind. He was a monster – I have no regrets. Anthony proposed the concept that the passing on of susceptibility is through inherited chromosomal mutations, but Boris could never have known this, the Science wasn't available to him. Anthony began work on his theory in London in the 1980s by subjecting Sam and Mukwa to the stone's potency, and comparing their DNA over time."

Sam and Mukwa looked at Yuriy with a mixture of confusion and incredulity.

"It's true, whether you like it or not," said Yuriy plainly. "Anthony was supposed to be protecting you both. Not even Franco's Dad knew. You were lab rats!" Yuriy took a bite from an apple, while the others let the information sink in. "Boris was sure the geometric star was a template for how to position the stones for maximum effect."

"What effect?" asked Mukwa.

"He thought he could create superman, for lack of a better expression."

"This is bullshit!" exclaimed Franco, throwing a rock over the edge of the cliff. "You see why *Pappie* and I wanted nothing to do with this *kak*?"

"And you were both right," said Yuriy. "But please listen. Because my father's stone gave him bizarre dreams and permitted him to recall episodes from a bygone age, he believed that it might have other arcane powers. Sure, the stones distort brain biochemistry, mutate DNA and give us weird dreams – but they were only designed for one thing. They were filled with the memories of an ancient people who lived on this earth well before the Ice Age. Not twenty thousand years ago, not one hundred thousand years old…" Yuriy paused. "I believe the stones were fashioned more than two hundred and fifty thousand years ago."

Franco laughed. "Whatever. You're loco *my boet*."

"Carry on, Yuriy," interrupted Mukwa sternly. "Give him his chance, Franco."

"My father wrote, in intial studies, that only boys survived long term exposure to the stones as all the girls died. But he persisted."

"Sick, twisted bastard," mumbled Franco.

"So? Was he wrong?" asked Sam.

"William Greenwood said something to me – before I threw

him into a ravine. 'Your father was right all along.' I thought that if I killed my father, I'd stop his research. With seven stones at his disposal, it was Boris's hypothesis that if he determined the exact spatial arrangement of stones, and under ideal conditions, women might also survive the mutation process."

"Why? To bring Tsuk back from the dead?"

"I don't know what he thought, Sam. He was deeply disturbed. But judging by William Greenwood's reappearance after all these years – someone must have made a breakthrough."

"Does this have something to do with Franco's mother?" asked Mukwa nervously.

Yuriy took a long swig from his hipflask and nodded almost imperceptibly. "Remember – Boris couldn't have known at the time that the stones caused genetic abnormalities." He hesitated. "Franco, your father told you that your mother died of cancer, correct?"

"Yes. She underwent treatment, and was sick for several years, but that was the '60s."

"OK." Yuriy took a deep breath and extinguished his cigarette. "We are all testament to the fact that certain men can survive the mutation. After many more tragic, failed attempts it was Boris's conjecture that the only way for a girl to acquire the mutation was for the father to be first or second generation 'sensitive' and the mother untouched… intact… normal… pure…"

"Well, that can't be right!" butted in Franco. "How could I have inherited the mutation? Assuming *Pappie* wasn't a freak too."

Yuriy ignored the question, and turned his attention to Mukwa. "William Greenwood came to Groote Schuur Hospital, correct?"

"Yes," replied Mukwa.

"I found this in the boot of his Landrover up in Letaba among his belongings." Yuriy took out some folded medical records from his jacket pocket, and handed them to Franco. "This is what William Greenwood was looking for at Groote Schuur. Like I said…" Yuriy cleared his throat. "Let's assume that Boris was right and that Anthony corroborated his theory at a genetic level: for a girl to inherit the father's mutation, her mother's DNA must be untainted unless…"

"Unless the mother is born with the mutation?" queried Mukwa.

"Possibly," Yuriy became animated. "Or?" He lit another cigarette. "I, too, was under the illusion that only men had survived the trials. Now, I'm convinced that a woman survived the transformation process – your mother, Franco. I found a paper trail confirming that

Anthony Greenwood smuggled a young woman out of Moscow, and a stone, and hid her where no one would come looking."

"My mother…" Franco's voice wobbled.

Yuriy nodded more assertively. "And I'm willing to bet that Lester Hendriks was tasked as her guardian. Franco – they fell in love."

"Namibia!" exclaimed Sam. "Anthony had a bank account in Windhoek."

Franco began to weep.

"What do her medical records say, Franco?" asked Mukwa.

Franco struggled to speak. "It says my mother committed suicide after several failed attempts – 'overdose brought about by severe depression and substance abuse'."

The men were quiet. The buzz of cicadas did little to muffle Franco's sobs.

"I'm so sorry, Franco. I had no idea," said Mukwa. "Your father must have known all along… it must have broken him."

"So she didn't have cancer?" asked Sam.

"No," replied Yuriy. "Not a trace, according to her medical records."

"So? *Ma* had bad dreams." Franco hesitated, trying to hold himself together. "Tsuk was a woman…"

"True," confirmed Yuriy. "And if I'm right, Tsuk spawned generations of gifted children. Or, as my father called them, 'The Seven Scribes'. Franco, if your mother was a breakthrough test subject, who's to say that her eggs weren't harvested? Franco could have half-siblings. There could be many more just like us."

"*Yassus*, Yuriy. Just stop already!" shouted Franco, his face wet with tears. He stood and wandered several metres from the group. He was still grieving for his father. Now he had another truth to reconcile.

The sun was low on the horizon – the light fading fast.

"I'm sorry, Franco," said Yuriy. "But I must continue."

Franco rejoined reluctantly.

"I was subjected to years of torture at the hands of my father and his cronies – pumped full of stimulants and God knows what else. The combination of the mutation and the drugs affected me strangely – both good and bad. I get the dreams. Sometimes I write them down and interpret them as best I can." Yuriy looked to Mukwa and Sam for reassurance. "What if Franco's mother went one stage further? What if she understood their meaning?"

"Where's the proof?" asked Franco.

"I'm guessing Sam has it with him."

Sam clutched his pocket.

"Anthony Greenwood hid the evidence," asserted Yuriy. "In spite of his treachery, he knew the risks. I fear that what we see in our dreams is a doomsday message – design plans for a lost technology that has the potential to wipe out humanity. I think it nearly did – once upon a time. If that information gets into the wrong hands, we have a problem. I've studied the map and the cloth inscriptions. I'm sure the clues are there, but I've no idea what that key is guarding."

"One of Africa's greatest secrets," mumbled Sam.

"I've not heard that in a while," said Mukwa with a wry grin.

"It's what Anthony said to me at St Thomas' Hospital, Yuriy," said Sam. "*One of Africa's greatest secrets.*"

Yuriy screwed up his face and rubbed his eyes. "Franco, I fear Anthony Greenwood may have been referring to your mother."

"And then you killed him." Mukwa cocked his pistol and pointed it at Yuriy's head.

Yuriy didn't flinch. He calmly raised his head and smiled at Mukwa. "You'd be doing me a great favour – you have no idea of the horrors that plague my dreams! I'm sorry I killed Anthony, but he went too far: his meddling nearly sold us all out to the KGB. Brigadier Gordon tried to clear up his own mess, but failed. Mukwa, it was me that smuggled you out of London. I risked my life for you. Killing me now would only hasten your deaths and worse. We have an opportunity to stop what otherwise will be a systematic destruction of our world. We have to stop it. It's our destiny. We were born to survive."

Yuriy's last words struck a chord – a distinct series of harmonic vibrations – as if classical music was being performed nearby. They were all aware of it. Sam felt his body numb and slump back against the rock of the cliff. His mind drifted in and out of consciousness. The last rays of sunlight picked up the spectral form of a man clambering towards them – unnaturally tall and lithe. The man cursed as he stumbled. Sam noted the land around him: barren except for a few woody shrubs. The ghost lay beside Sam, wrapped himself in animal pelts and began to repeat an incomprehensible yet sonorous monotone mantra. Sam regressed in sympathy. In his vision he saw a dimly lit room and a writing desk. Tsuk blotted her ink dry and shut a large, leather-bound book. Standing abruptly, she placed a stone into a pyramid-shaped recess on the tome. Her torment caused Sam's body to convulse. He witnessed her leave a dark cavernous world, and stagger onto an icy plateau, pierced by towering rocky pinnacles. She fell, pulled up her knees to her chest and breathed her last.

When Sam awoke, Yuriy was gone. Franco and Mukwa looked about groggily in the darkness. Sam snatched at his pocket. The bubble wrap containing maps and key was intact.

"Tsuk?" asked Sam. "And a phantom dude?"

They both nodded.

"Yuriy must have a stone, or we have sorely underestimated his capabilities." Mukwa dragged himself to his feet. "Unfortunately, what he says about Anthony makes sense. I remember he and Lester would leave Orapa for weeks at a time; saying they were visiting friends. I saw photos of them with another woman. She was much older – she always wore shades – and a Tswana man that I just knew as 'Kats'."

"I know that photo," said Sam. "Lester had it in his apartment at WACS, along with a photo of 'Mafeking Station'."

"Mafikeng was where I received the last of my rehabilitation treatment from my fall. I must have been only five when Anthony moved us all to the Cape in 1972. It was only then that I became aware of Franco's existence. And one day, out of the blue, Anthony announced that we were moving to England. That was 1974."

"The year I was born," said Sam.

Franco got up, lit his torch and headed down the path in silence.

Mukwa's eyes followed Franco down the path. "Franco went to stay with his granny in Bellville. It was for the best – believe me."

XXVII: Childhood Memories

British Consulate, Mambo Msiig
Stone Town, Zanzibar
June 10th 1940

"I think it's best we go round the room and introduce ourselves." Mossi asked those assembled to give a short account of their background and circumstance.

William did a headcount before it was his turn to stand. There were eighteen personnel gathered inclusive of Mostapha Nkosi: Alexander Knapp, Boris Kuriagin, Eric Chamberlain and Jameel 'JJ' Jayasinghe. What struck William immediately was the multi-ethnicity of the group: delegates from Argentina, Peru, Mexico, The United States of America, India, China, Japan, Australia, New Zealand, France, Italy, Norway, South Africa and Kenya; men and women handpicked by Mossi to represent their country in whatever he was planning to reveal.

"Captain William Greenwood, from England – Air Reconnaissance Cartographer – currently seconded from His Majesty's forces. I'm here to record and map our journey, and consult on Geology and topography." He left out his relationship to the Stonelore. Anyone who had read Alexander's research paper would have made the connection.

"Thank you, ladies and gentlemen," said Mossi. "I'd like to start by thanking you all for coming and providing us with such wonderful accounts of your research. I'm looking forward to getting to know you all better… on safari!" He raised his voice in excitement, and the company applauded. "I'm grateful that you were able to join me in this time of great uncertainty. Some of my intended guests were not so fortunate – for reasons that I'm sure you are painfully aware of. I hope my reasons for this gathering will become evident soon enough. There is so much that we don't understand about our history, and judging by what we do know – we don't seem to have learned a jot."

The delegates began to murmur, bobbing heads in agreement.

"Let me assure you, I haven't summoned you here to debate politics and hostility, nor will I tolerate grudges or enmity. We are here to share knowledge freely. Any contravention of this directive will result in immediate rescinding of your right to be here. Do I make myself clear?"

William watched all the delegates nod in accordance. Although there was a sense of relaxed conviviality, he feared it might be a one-way ticket should they step out of line.

Mossi continued. "When I was young, my father worked on an excavation site at Dandarah in the Nile Valley. I would watch as he methodically and painstakingly documented his findings. The team he worked alongside was a mix of French and Polish Archaeologists, so I rarely understood their conversations, but I would listen nonetheless. In the heat of the day I would sit in the cool of the Temple of Hathor. One day, a peculiar little man caught my eye. He wasn't part of the research team, so being young and inquisitive, I decided to spy on him. He would stare at the reliefs for ages and chuckle. With nothing better to do, I copied his mannerisms. This amused him greatly, and he gave me this." Mossi showed the assembled what looked like a small coin. "I didn't speak much English – my head was full of Polish and French – but I understood that I should keep it safe. And then he said something that still resonates in my mind today, 'I'm going to change the world'. The man pointed at a hieroglyph, smiled and left. I never saw him again. To cut a long story short, this coin is made from two identically sized pieces of copper and zinc welded together. It's part of a penny battery – a pile of coins, separated by paper soaked in vinegar and salt. Assembled correctly, the stack produces electricity. The relief he pointed to was the Djed, the backbone of Osiris – the symbol for rebirth. I found out, some years later, that the man in question was none other than Nikola Tesla."

The assembled began to mutter; brows knotted and smiles beamed until laughter filled the room.

"Whether or not the event happened is for you to decide." Mossi smiled, winked and flipped the coin.

William wasn't sure what had just happened. The story was far-fetched, but irrespective of its veracity or meaning, it tickled the delegates.

"Sadly, I've never had the chance to ask Mr Tesla if he remembers me. But he went on to change the world, and I still have his penny as a memento. The point that I'm trying to make, of course, is that we must not be drawn into supposition or superstition. We scientists need empirical evidence, or we are wasting time. What I intend to show you all will challenge us scientifically, spiritually and emotionally. We need to be focused on our area of expertise, and at the same time open minded."

Mossi showed the delegation an overhead projector map of the route they were to take, and introduced JJ as their guide from Dodoma to Lake Nyasa. The second overland stage would take them into a range of mountains to the east of Southern Rhodesia called Nyanga on the border with Portuguese East Africa. He chose not to reveal their exact destination, or what they would find. Frustratingly for William, there was no mention of a retrieval operation for Huw Williams's Mankwe stone, further to the south in the Pilanesberg.

Eventually, Mossi called an end to the meeting and bid everyone a good evening. The delegates filed out into the Consulate lobby and dispersed.

William headed straight to the bar. "Gin and tonic, please."

"How very British of you." Eric Chamberlain sidled up to William. "I'll have the same. What did you make of that, Captain Greenwood?"

"William, please. He certainly knows how to impress."

"He certainly does! And the safari?"

"This is the trip of a lifetime, but it's not quite what I signed up for."

"I assure you, William, I'm in the dark as much as you are. But whatever Mossi is planning to reveal, the British Consulate here is aware of the importance of this expedition, and you are a key part of it. Just don't mention the war!" Eric winked and beckoned William to sit with him. He looked about nervously. "I'm curious. As part of the delegation, I read the article that Alexander Knapp wrote on the 'Stonelore'."

"Yes," replied William. "I co-authored it. In the light of my ancestors, I felt I had as good a grounding in it as any."

"Good," said Eric snappily. "Because this may come as a bit of a surprise to you – it certainly was to me. When my parents passed away several years ago, as their only child they left me a great deal of money and paperwork. Sifting through their belongings, it turned out that they were not my real parents. They adopted me when I was a babe. No explanation, but I'm too long in the tooth to bear a grudge. I found a letter addressed to my adoptive parents from a lawyer in Johannesburg, regarding the estate of my biological father. There had been a small amount of money owed, which my adoptive father settled – they weren't short of a bob or two. The only thing that they received from his estate was this."

William nearly dropped his gin. It was a stone. "Good God! Let me see that." He studied it closely. "What was your father's name?"

"I've no idea? But it was wrapped in a handkerchief embroidered with the intials…"

"S.M.?" interrupted William.

"S.J.M. to be precise. Do you think it's the Samuel Morgan mentioned in the Stonelore?" Eric went quiet. A disturbance behind them made him turn nervously.

"What is it?" asked William, noting a faint smell of perfume.

Eric looked around furtively. "Nothing. I've been carrying that thing around with me ever since, on and off. You don't think I'm going to get cancer and pop my clogs, do you?"

"No!" said William, unconvincingly. "Well, I never! I know it's not in the spirit of things, but I suggest you keep your discovery to yourself. In the meantime, I advise you to leave the stone here under lock and key until we return. It would be in everyone's best interest."

"Righto!" confirmed Eric.

"Oh! That's given me an idea," said William. "Would you do the same with the Stonelore trunks while we're away? It seems daft to be dragging them around with us. Help yourself to them in the meantime. I'll know if anything is missing!" William winked menacingly for effect as he ushered Eric through to supper.

William found himself seated between the Australian and Argentinian delegates. Mossi had drawn up the table plan. He introduced himself to a lady from Darwin. She was deeply tanned – perhaps early fifties.

"Professor of Australian Aboriginal Culture, if memory serves," stated William.

"That's right! Kirstin Blanch. And I know about your family's exploits, Mr Greenwood – rather a bizarre set of circumstances."

"You wouldn't be the first to describe it as such. How do you know Mossi?"

"We've been arguing for years by letter, and met face to face for the first time today. I once wrote a paper on Sumerian influences on Aboriginal Australians. Their belief systems have curious similarities. That's what piqued Mossi's interest in me – I studied Cuneiform script and Akkadian at Uni. He thinks the Egyptians were in Australia, and I've spent the last fifteen years trying to prove they weren't. Oh! And we don't have any pyramids as far as I'm aware. Ayre's Rock or *Uluru* – but no pyramids."

William enjoyed her company. She was amusing, and knew a surprising amount about wine.

173

The Argentinian delegate, Mateo Gomez, was more guarded. He spoke quietly, making it difficult for William to tune into his conversation amid the hubbub.

"I also studied the Piri Reis map," said Gomez. "I agree, the navigational details are extraordinary, as is the use of Mercator projection, but I'm not convinced it depicts Antarctica free of ice. I'm no expert, but there are many who think the original mariner became disoriented in the currents around Tierra del Fuego and continued north up the coast of Chile – or Piri Reis may have copied it incorrectly."

"Interesting theory. Forgive me, Señor Gomez, but I didn't catch your area of expertise."

"I'm a doctor – a psychologist. I worked for twenty years in a clinic in Buenos Aires. My expertise is in treatment of traumatic events – deaths in the family, murder witnesses and torture victims. Recently, I made a breakthrough using plant-based psychotropic compounds. Unfortunately, the bureaucrats think my work is dangerous and unethical, so I'm currently out of work. And I needed a holiday."

Mossi wound the dinner up soon after 9.00pm and the delegates drifted to bed. Once in his room, William found an envelope on his desk. It contained a few maps and a note.

William,

Please have a look at these. Once we reach Blantyre, I need you to guide us into the Eastern Highlands of Rhodesia. We will have local help, but by then many of the delegation will need incentive and clear instructions. I request that you go with JJ to the National Museum in Dar-es-Salaam. They have extensive map records. Find out all you can about the area. We will wait for you in Dodoma.

Mossi.

XXVIII: Exasperation

Makgadikgadi Salt Pans
Jan 23rd 1930

Temba opened his eyes, squinting in the glare of the dawn sun. Lying prostrate, his limbs were bound with rope and secured with steel tent pegs, bludgeoned into the rock. His head was ringing.

Roddy stood over him, blocking the sun. In his hand was the stone. He thrust it in Temba's face.

"What is this?"

"It's a stone."

"No kidding. Where d'ya find it?"

"It was given to me."

"By whom?"

"A man. He's dead."

"Where'd he find it?"

"I don't know."

Roddy pocketed the stone. Crouching, he covered Temba's face with a tea towel and held it firmly in place while Andre, the Afrikaner, poured a bucket of water from the pool over it. Temba spluttered, bucked and choked.

Roddy removed the towel. "What does it do?"

Temba vomited and coughed to clear his throat. "I... I don't know what you're talking about." He tried to catch his breath. "It's a memento... a keepsake from my emancipator. It's a stone... no more... no less."

Roddy and Andre repeated the exercise. Temba couldn't breathe: his throat was tightening, his sinews taut, straining against the ropes that bound him.

"Liar," barked Roddy. "Tell me!"

Temba's throat burned. Roddy took a knife and began to unpick the scar tissue from Temba's wrists. Blood ran freely – Temba hissed through gritted teeth as the ropes tightenend, burning his wrists.

"It's man-made – an ancient artifact," said Roddy, holding Temba's mouth and nostrils shut. "I was gonna have the guys look at it in Jwaneng, but you ran. I had good ol' Haskins track you down."

Temba shook off Roddy's hand and croaked, "I've no idea what you're talking about." He dismissed Roddy's suggestion, even if it explained how Edward had made such a timely appearance in the Selebi Phikwe Chapel on Christmas Eve. "Edward wouldn't do that!"

Roddy laughed, and slid the knife under Temba's chin.

"I've had a lot of practice skinning, Preacherman. Where's your God now?" Roddy ran the point down Temba's chest, piercing the flesh that covered his ribs. Roddy suddenly pushed down, sliding the blade underneath Temba's breast flesh and peeling back a flap of skin, just above his heart.

"Stop!" shrieked Temba. "STOP!"

Roddy ordered Andre to refill the bucket. "If you don't die from blood loss, this water will kill you. Quick death – short death – you choose." He signalled for Andre to pour the rancid salt-water over Temba, who shrieked in agony until his voice was hoarse.

Time began to distort: all that happened seemed to unfold in slow motion. Just like the encounter with the Tokolosh, Temba was able to study the path of every drop of falling water, mingled with his blood. He felt no pain – no fear. Instead, a seed of a thought germinated in the dark recesses of his mind. He sensed its power, yearning to be released – hope and strength:

'God is our hope and strength, a very present help in trouble.'

Over and over he repeated the words in his mind like a mantra.

Roddy covered Temba's face again. Another bucket rained down in slow motion – but Temba was at peace. He searched for the seed: it began to take root and grow. Its power surged like an overwhelming urge.

He released it with all his might.

In perceived, almost temporal stasis, a twisted eight-inch steel peg spun balletically through the air, the rope clipping Temba's cheek as it passed. The peg burrowed itself inch by inch into Andre's right eye socket, sending a plume of jelly-like humor towards Roddy.

Andre screamed and dropped the bucket. He grappled around for his rifle, half-blinded, but Temba's right arm was free.

Within the time warp, Temba sat upright. He studied the graceful, ballistic path of the second tent peg as it entered Andre's gaping maw and tunnelled its way through the back of his skull; the rope cord still attached, oscillating in simple harmonic motion.

Temba was mesmerised. It was as if some primaeval instinct had overridden any sense of humanity. He lifted his tethered right foot and used his own blood to slide down the rock, allowing slack in the ropes that bound his feet. Placing his right boot on the Afrikaner's chest, Temba grabbed hold of the cord dangling from Andre's open mouth. Rather than one sharp tug, the force Temba exerted on the rope was mighty and long drawn out. He felt a sickening crack as the back of Andre's cranium imploded – the peg recoiling, dislodging Andre's jawbone from his skull.

The passage of time corrected itself. The steel peg flew out of Andre's mouth, showering Temba's face in blood and shattered bone. Temba kicked Andre free – and lifeless.

Roddy had run to the truck for a rifle.
Undeterred, Temba released his feet from the knotted rope, stood and faced his adversary.
"Stop, Temba!" shouted Roddy, his rifle raised. "Tell me about the stone. You're a dead man."
Temba grimaced, acutely aware of the pain emanating from his flayed chest and the blood draining from his wrists.

"Yea, though I walk through the valley..."

Roddy fired a bullet into Temba's left thigh.
Temba fell to his knees: his life ebbing away.

"...I shall fear no evil."

Roddy took the stone from his pocket and held it out for Temba to see. "Tell me, Preacherman! If it's worth dying for... what does it do?"
Temba struggled to his feet and spat out a mouthful of Andre's blood and hair. "Worth? You think it has value? More value than your sister who you left out here to die?"
"She was dead anyway – and a colossal pain in the ass."
Temba couldn't believe what he was hearing. He shouted angrily, struggling to keep upright. "The stone creates a portal – a door between two worlds – the conscious and the subconscious mind – where time is of no importance. Time is merely a human construct – a means to interpret a sequence of sensations."

"What? You're crazy! A whack job!"

"You've seen what it's capable of!"

"Yeah? Well, if you won't be straight with me, I'll find out for myself."

Roddy cocked Trusty Girl and aimed at Temba's head.

A shot rang clear and bright in the granite amphitheatre, and far out across the salt-caked sands. Temba fell.

****

Edward Haskins sat with his head in his hands, and then punched the frame of the wagon. Guilt was eating him alive, as were several mosquitoes. He was desperately thirsty, and knew that if he took the water, Rhona would certainly perish. He had betrayed a friend for profit. The least he could do was get Rhona to safety. He calculated the odds of surviving the journey back to Francistown without fresh water – it was now or never. If Temba had located the McTaggart party, he was dead for sure. If he hadn't, there was no guarantee that they would make it to the borehole in Gweta, and there were precious few clouds to suggest they were due anything from above.

He punched the frame of the wagon again, and heard a murmuring: Rhona had stirred from her slumber. Edward kept quiet, hoping she would doze off.

"Temba?" Her voice was weak. "Temba?"

Edward knew that she'd recognise him immediately. What if he didn't give her the opportunity? Temba had left his *shemagh* for her as a pillow. All he had to do was press it down over her face. How long for? He had never killed a man before, let alone an ailing, defenseless woman. The more he considered it, the more he felt the urge to abandon Temba to the mercy of Roddy McTaggart or the scalding Makgadikgadi. Temba was a dead man either way.

Tethering the horses, Edward used the last of the fat to grease the wheels. He reached up for his water canteen and jumped out of his skin. Rhona stood above him, her hair hanging down in tresses, clutching her brother's Trusty Girl.

"I know what you did, Ed. Where's Temba?"

"I don't know." He faltered, stepping backwards. "He's gone."

"What d'ya mean he's gone? Did Roddy take him?"

"I… I don't know."

Rhona struggled down from the footplate, using a wagonwheel for support. She re-aimed the rifle. "What happened to him?"

"He went to look for your brother."

"Where?"

"He headed north."

"How long ago?"

"Maybe an hour."

"Take me there."

"And leave the horses?

"Precisely."

Rhona cocked the rifle.

"OK! I'll do it."

Edward pointed towards Temba's tracks.

Within twenty minutes, Rhona and Edward had begun to skirt the apex of the granite outcrop, rising above the saltpan. It exuded dry heat like a sauna. Rhona lost her footing and Edward steadied her, inadvertently cluching her rifle.

"Don't even think about it!"

Rhona regained her balance.

They were suddenly aware of voices and a splash of water.

"Move! Quick!" snapped Rhona.

Edward clambered along a ledge that ran round the side of the outcrop. Agonised howls were followed by another splash of water – Temba's suffering gnawed at Edward's conscience.

Suddenly, Rhona slipped again, weakened from the exertion. Edward saw his opportunity – he snatched the Winchester from her grasp and scrambled up the few remaining rocks.

Another scream: this time it wasn't Temba's voice that pierced the air. Edward spotted a tree growing out of a crevice and used its branches to hoist himself into a position to see the origin of the blood-curdling shrieks. Edward heard Temba shouting and then a shot rang out. He peered over the top of the rocky amphitheatre. One of Roddy's Afrikaner guides was lying on his back, blood pooling around his head. Temba was on all fours, struggling to stand. His face was bruised; his chest mutilated.

Roddy stood fifty feet from Edward, his rifle cocked and trained at Temba's head. Edward didn't hesitate: he pointed and fired. Roddy flinched, stepping back in shock as the rifle slipped from his hands. Temba crumpled, exhausted, hitting the rock hard. The American recovered his rifle, groggily. Edward emptied the second chamber: Roddy staggered backwards, and toppled off the rock.

179

Fighting to remain conscious, Temba saw what he thought were two people. One of them had long brown hair. Rhona? Edward was standing next to her, holding a rifle. He passed out.

****

"Get a fire going, Ed! You'll find all you need in the truck."

Edward raced to the vehicle while Rhona took Roddy's medicine chest up to where Temba was moaning in delirium. Mopping Temba's blood as she worked, she cauterised the loose flap of skin on his chest. The bullet to Temba's thigh had passed through cleanly. She sterilised a needle in alcohol, and began to swab and sew.

Edward dragged Roddy and Andre's dead bodies from the rock plateau and bundled them into a shallow grave, covering them in sand to keep the flies off. He had a fire raging by the pool. Using the drenched tea towel, he hauled another bucket of boiling water to where Rhona attended to Temba. She had staunched the bleed from his wrists, plunging cotton swabs into the water and dabbing them onto his wounds. Sterilising a hypodermic needle, Rhona injected fluid from a vial into Temba's arm.

"What's that?" asked Edward.

"It's an experimental drug extracted from mould – it's really for the horses. Mixed with a few other ingredients, it kills bugs – something my Dad's company's been working on for a few years. It saved me, and I hope to God it'll save him."

She sat back exhausted.

"Temba said you have malaria," said Edward.

"He was wrong – or he was lying to you."

Edward shifted uncomfortably. "I'm sorry."

"Sorry for what?"

"Everything. I was stupid… I didn't think…"

"Think what?"

Edward stepped away and turned to look out over the saltpan. "I betrayed him."

"If he pulls through, you can ask his forgiveness. In the meantime, we need to get the truck running. I think flies carry the disease. We haven't got long before the horses succumb. I'll give them a dose of this bug killer, but I'm nearly out of western *muti*."

The truck's engine was flooded, the oil low and the radiator bone dry. Rhona tended to Temba while he slept. He was running a fever, but her main concern was his fluid levels. She set up a shade cloth and held a cool, clean tea towel to his forehead.

Edward joined her by the pool, wiping the grease from his hands. "How do you know so much about medicine?"

"The McTaggarts make their money in the drug industry. I was sent to school to become a doctor – my mother's a progressive thinker. My ol' man said if I graduated, he'd pay for me to travel wherever I wanted. So I put my finger on a map, and hey presto! Here we are."

"Your father must have been very proud of you."

"Huh." She laughed. "Roddy was his blue-eyed boy. He couldn't put a foot wrong. Not until he left me to die. Honours even, I think."

"If you say so," said Edward, gravely.

"Let's boil more water. I need a drink. How's the engine?"

"It's low on oil, but the radiator's full. I'm pretty sure she'll start."

"Good work. Why don't you bring the horses round? They'll be thirsty. I'll dose them."

Edward hesitated, considering his options – what if she took the truck, leaving him stranded without water? Words failed him.

"Cat got your tongue?" asked Rhona. "I'm not going anywhere."

"OK," replied Edward, relieved. He handed her Trusty Girl. "Not so trustworthy after all."

Rhona elected not to comment.

Edward filled both his canteens with cool boiled water, climbed out of the rock amphitheatre and headed south on foot.

Rhona burst into tears. Circumstance had transformed her into the daughter her mother had always wanted. She wasn't prepared for the outpouring of emotion, nor did she have any idea what to do next. If Edward absconded, she would be left stranded with a dying man in the relentless heat of the Makgadikgadi. In spite of her surgical skills, Temba's wounds needed constant attention, and he was burning up. The pool water looked grim, with crusts of soap and congealed blood. Their clean water supply would barely see them to Francistown.

Her fear of abandonment was allayed when, eventually, Edward returned with the wagon and horses.

Edward called out, "I'll saddle them, just in case I can't get the truck going."

Rhona didn't trust him. In her eyes he was a weasel, and she'd been brought up in North Carolina to shoot weasels.

Sure enough, the engine started, kicking out black, foul-smelling smoke. Edward helped Rhona carry the unconscious Temba into the back of the truck, and lashed him down so that he wouldn't rip his stitches. She closed the tailgate, jumped in the cab and pressed the throttle. The exhaust kicked out another black cloud. The truck jolted forward to a stall. She tried the ignition again and, mercifully, it started.

"Steady on those gears," shouted Edward. "High ratio on the salt, or you'll get bogged down. I'll tether the chassis to the horses so if you get stuck, we'll provide momentum."

He might be a weasel, thought Rhona, but he was her best chance of surviving the Makgadikgadi.

They transferred the kit from the wagon to the truck and moved out steadily, following the wagon tracks south on the spit that separated the two vast saltpans. Once on firm ground, Edward untethered the horses and rode alongside the truck.

Storm clouds were amassing to the west.

They reached the southernmost point of Sua Pan at dusk, and the horses recognised the route.

"Temba and I built a shelter up ahead," said Edward. "I think we should camp out the night."

"Looks like we might get some rain," said Rhona. "I'll stay with Temba in the back of the truck. Do as you wish."

Temba's flesh was swollen and hot to the touch. Rhona rubbed what was left of the alcohol over the stitches, and injected the last of the antibiotic into his arm. She whispered in his ear. "There's not much more I can do for you, my friend. You've risen from the dead once – time to do it again." She noted a flicker under his eyelids, and then a smile. Whatever Temba was dreaming about, it clearly amused him.

Edward appeared by the tailgate. "We should talk."

Rhona agreed and hopped down. She was by no means fully recovered, but her resolve was strong.

"Do you intend to turn me in, Rhona?"

"That depends."

"On what?" asked Edward.

"If I approach the British authorities, I've no doubt you'd wriggle your way out of jail – but word gets around. Your business is struggling and corporations are undercutting you for mining contracts. The gossip would crush your reputation."

Edward nodded in agreement.

"I have a solution, Edward."

"Anything."

"I'll mediate for you on a deal with Roddy's mining interests in Jwaneng. If you manage his affairs, it'll save me the hassle."

Edward puffed out his cheeks. "That's not what I was expecting considering..."

"Don't think I'm gonna make this easy for you, Ed," said Rhona, firmly. "In return, I want forty-nine percent of your business interests in Francistown, in perpetuity, and for you to exert your influence on any contacts in Southern Rhodesia. We need safe passage – – no questions asked. You understand?"

"Half my business?" Edward scoffed.

"Forty-nine percent. Take it or leave it. You can draw a salary from the Jwaneng operation, and I'll sign over some of my shares to you. You won't be out of pocket."

Edward had underestimated Rhona's business acumen by a country mile. He had to accept. He knew all too well that business in colonial Africa was built on reputation alone. She could sweep his entire livelihood from under his feet. His family would be hounded out of the Protectorate. Her deal was a lifeline – and he owed it to Temba in recompense for his betrayal.

"I accept."

"Good. Let's get some sleep."

"One last thing."

"What?"

"I took this from Roddy before I buried him."

XXIX: Murder on the Dodoma Express

Dar-es-Salaam, Tanganyika
June 12ᵗʰ 1940

William bustled his way from the docks to the Museum through hot and dusty streets. JJ proved his weight in gold, extricating William from throngs of hawkers. Their arrival had been anticipated, and they were met in the foyer of the Dar-es-Salaam Museum with damp hand towels and cups of refreshing lemon tea.

They set to work; hand-copying maps of Nyasaland and the eastern highlands of Rhodesia, but without any clue of their intended destination, William became agitated. "I've had enough, JJ. Time to go."

They packed up and thanked the curator.

It was sappingly hot when JJ went out to commandeer a rickshaw. As William boarded, he couldn't help but notice a black Mercedes parked a hundred yards away in the shade of a tamarind tree. Intrigued, he peered around the canvas curtain and watched the car pull away.

****

As luck would have it, the overnight charter train to Dodoma for the delegation was delayed: a magnificent oil-powered steam locomotive from the Vulcan foundry in Lancashire, England.

The passenger attendant carried William's bags to his sleeper cabin while he monitored the last of the expedition baggage being loaded into the adjacent storage wagon. Thirsty and peckish, he headed straight for the buffet car. Alexander Knapp and Boris Kuriagin were already planted in a berth.

"William! Did Mossi give you any clues as to where we're headed?" asked Boris.

"Frustratingly, no. I've spent most of the day familiarising myself with the eastern highlands of Rhodesia – an area I barely knew existed."

"We're none the wiser," said Alexander. "Only that Rosalind passed through here a few months ago, and Mossi's just had the decency to let me know."

"Actually, I knew as well. JJ processed her paperwork. Sorry, Alexander, I didn't think to mention it last night."

184

A waiter arrived to take the order, as a group of delegates entered the dining carriage for afternoon tea. An attractive lady in her mid-thirties offered William her hand.

Boris took the cue. "William, this is Miss Adams."

"Call me Evelyn."

William stood in respect. "Please to meet you. From the USA?"

"Right, Mr Greenwood. I've heard a lot about you."

"Ah! You mean my ancestors. Crazy by all accounts."

"Takes one to know one."

William smiled and nodded approval, in spite of her insinuation. He sensed a wildness about her – a rebelliousness, perhaps.

"Miss Adams' family own mining and hunting concessions in the south. And she trained as a nurse! Did I get that right?"

"You certainly did, Boris," she giggled. "I thought you were too far gone to remember." The comment was coquettish, yet sobering.

"So what brings you on our adventure, Evelyn?"

"I've spent the last ten years trading curios and all sorts – and trying to keep on the right side of the British."

"Very wise!" laughed Alexander.

"Mossi thinks my knowledge of African customs and culture might come in handy. I enjoyed reading about 'Stonelore' by the way."

The three men sat up, charmed, blushing like schoolboys.

"Strange little things, these stones," continued Evelyn. "Any idea what they're made of, or who made them? Their legacy is quite something – if it's to be believed."

The train suddenly jolted to pick up slack. The three men shrugged, distracted.

"Oh! I think that's my cue to leave. Gentlemen, I bid you a pleasant evening."

Evelyn left the dining carriage as the whistle sounded. The train lurched again, and inched out of the station under a cloud of steam.

Dinner arrived at seven o'clock sharp: mutton curry and rice – intensely spicy – with sweet naan breads and coconut water. It was tasty, even if it gave William heartburn and a raging thirst.

"Well, I suppose it's my round," said William, attracting the waiter's attention.

Two other delegates had finished their meal, and were preparing to join them.

"Any objections?" asked an oriental gentleman wearing a swish safari suit.

"Not on my account," said Alex, bidding him sit.

Henry 'Harry' Tan was not what William had in mind of a citizen of the communist Republic of China. He was dressed expensively, westernised and yet hugely proud of his country's history. He began arguing that Boris's father's analysis of the Chinese pyramids in Shaanxi Province was tantamount to desecration. Boris dug his heels in and an argument ensued. Alexander and William filtered out the noise, turning their attention to the Mexican delegate, Jesùs Rousseau. It was his research on Olmec and early Mayan culture that Mossi had incorporated into the dossiers. William got stuck in.

"I assumed it was the alignment of the foundation structure to the pole star that indicated their true age."

"Yes," replied Jesùs. "That's part of it. But my analysis of soil composition and the presence of stone cutting-tools confirm that the Olmec were a displaced culture. They came from Polynesia and Africa originally. Well... that is what I'm trying to prove. I found stone carvings in Guatemala, depicting a vast maritime culture concurrent with northern hemispheric freezing."

William took it in. He hadn't considered the possibility that northern latitudes might experience a cooling, while southern latitudes might not. He stifled a yawn, and registered how long he'd been in the dining carriage. It was just after 9.00pm. He hadn't even collected his cabin key from the attendant. Excusing himself, William bid his colleagues goodnight and located the attendant several carriages down, near the back of the train next to the storage wagon. He was busy changing a light bulb, and only too happy to show William to his cabin nearby. William was half-expecting another dossier or file. Mercifully, there were none. The attendant slid the door closed, and William slumped into a chair.

Seconds later, he heard a loud shriek and the breaking of glass in the adjacent cabin.

William dashed out and knocked. "Hello! Are you OK?"

There was no reply. The door was unlocked. William slid it aside to reveal a man slumped on the floor by his washbasin, covered in broken glass.

"Are you all right?" William put his hand on the man's shoulder, only for the body to topple backwards. Blood oozed from a hole in his chest onto a white cotton vest.

Jesùs Rousseau appeared in the doorway from the other adjacent cabin. "What happened?"

"He's been shot. Did you hear or see anything?"

"I heard glass shatter and a scream – and you call out."

Teodoro Alvarez, the Peruvian delegate, arrived next on the scene.

"Did either of you hear a gunshot?" asked William.

They shook their heads.

"Odd," mused William. There was no exit wound, no hole in his dressing gown or blood spatter in the room. "Do you know this man?"

"He's the Japanese delegate, Yoshi Morimoto," replied the Kenyan delegate, Kioko Kamau, from the corridor.

"Could you please find Dr Chamberlain? And, for God's sake, would someone pull the emergency stop cord!"

Morogoro outskirts
June 13th 1940
Midnight

"Miss Blanch is missing too!" announced Boris.

"Who would want them dead?" asked William.

"We've no idea," replied Alexander.

"According to the inventory," added William. "Whoever shot Yoshi, stole his briefcase and a leather medicine bag. All that was left were clothes and personal items."

"This is a disaster!" remarked Mossi, entering the dining carriage. "He was a brilliant chemist, the son of a Japanese industrialist, with links to the arcane and occult. Not only was he a financial backer, he was an expert on psychic manifestations. He saw ghosts, apparently – a spirit medium. I was hoping he might shed some light on your dreams, Boris."

"Who was this lady... Miss Blanch?" asked Alexander.

"We disagreed about most things," replied Mossi. "That's why I liked her so much. One of the smartest women I have ever known. A brilliant linguist, she could crack most languages given time. Ugh!" Mossi took a large swig of water. "One of her specialties was linguistic lineage in Polynesia. It lends weight to many of the delegates' theories about Ice Age trading societies. I can't think why anyone would want to harm her, nor do I see any academic reason why she would want to harm poor Yoshi."

187

Eric entered. "I've taken care of Mr Morimoto's body and I've posted armed guards in each of the passenger carriages. I've asked them to report to me if they see or hear anything suspicious."

The night passed without further incident as the train rolled on towards Dodoma. William performed a quick headcount at breakfast. The delegates were jittery. A search of Miss Blanch's room and belongings had shone no light on her whereabouts whatsoever. Her clothes had been set out, and her valuables and research papers were safely stowed.

Mossi attempted to calm the delegates. "We've interviewed all the locomotive company personnel and they are all as shocked as we are. Dr Chamberlain will oversee the transport of Mr Morimoto's body back to Dar-es-Salaam. In his absence, Miss Adams has kindly offered to take over as expedition nurse for the foreseeable future. As to the identity of the perpetrator – I'm at a loss for words. Please be vigilant. Let's hope that there is no more foul play."

"You mean we should watch our backs?"

"Foul play? Who was next on her hitlist?"

"Did she steal anything?"

The delegates barked out questions, until Mossi retook control.

"Please! Who's to say that Miss Blanch isn't a victim in all this as well? I assure you, guards have been posted in the passenger carriages for your safety. William, would you care to make a list of who has what in the way of firearms, and might I suggest that we collect and stow them safely."

"What?" crowed Harry Tan. "And leave us vulnerable?"

"I also request, Mr Tan and esteemed colleagues, that you all allow us access to your cabins for a search. William Greenwood will take your statements. That will be all." Mossi left the carriage to prevent any further discussion on the matter.

William stayed in the dining car as the delegates dispersed. He took a newspaper. France had signed an armistice with Germany and Winston Churchill had commented that Britain would 'never surrender' in response to German forces massing in northern France. An attempted invasion seemed inevitable.

"Things are escalating quickly," said William.

"Here or further north?" asked Alexander, noting the reading matter.

"Both. Do you think Miss Blanch shot Yoshi? Or have you any idea who else might have a motive?"

"No. But if I wanted to keep my nefarious agenda under wraps, a spiritualist mind reader would be my first target."

"You can't believe all that *Gewäsch*, William?"

"Who said I did? Besides, who sat with him at dinner in Dar?" asked William.

"Miss Adams and the French delegate, Quentin Baraise. He's the son of an Egyptologist. It was Baraise who sought permission for Mossi and I to study the scrolls from Edfu in Paris. I can't see why he might have reason to kill two people he'd barely met."

"Something's amiss – no audible gunshot and no clear motive. There was no blood spatter in the room, or on his dressing gown. Did Eric say anything to you, Alex?"

"No. But I helped him bag Morimoto's body."

William began interviewing the delegates, trying to find a motive, or at least a connection between Miss Blanch and Mr Morimoto. The French delegate, Baraise, was cooperative whereas the South African Physicist, Thys Myburgh, was thoroughly unhelpful. He was more interested in scanning the Bush for birdlife as the train rolled past. He eventually relinquished his binoculars when the bell rang for elevenses.

The Peruvian delegate, Teodoro Alvarez, seemed anxious. He explained that he had been taking herbal tea in his room along the carriage from William, when he heard the breaking of glass and a short blast of something. He couldn't confirm conclusively, but he felt he might have heard either a gunshot or a door slamming. But that would have been ten or so minutes before William had arrived in the carriage to collect his key from the attendant, who swore blind that he hadn't seen anyone passing along the carriage.

Jesùs Rousseau invited William to his cabin. It was the closest cabin to the storage wagon. In between was a passenger access door. The door to the storage wagon was locked, so they called out the attendant who opened it and flicked the light switch. The bulb had blown. The attendant returned moments later, apologetic, with two battery-powered torches and a new bulb.

The storage wagon was packed high with supplies: baggage, collapsible tables, food, medicine chests, rolls of canvas and wooden tent posts. Nothing looked out of place. As William and Jesùs stepped back into the passenger carriage, the attendant locked the door. William pulled down the passenger access door window. He withdrew his hand

---

189

quickly. There was a crust of blood on the outside handle, and a second smear on the inside. William wiped his hands with his handkerchief. Could the assailant have jumped off the train? Could the murderer be Miss Blanch after all? At 9.00pm it would have been pitch dark, the middle of nowhere, in the savage African bush.

William reported his findings at lunch.

"Still no motive?" asked Mossi.

"No. But Miss Blanch jumped off or was pushed off. I found blood. Either way, there should be more evidence."

"I'll inform the police in Dodoma. Keep at it, William. The truth will out itself, mark my words."

The Indian and Kenyan delegates were seated in the dining carriage. Both professors of Anthropology, Ravinda Singh and Kioko Kamau were fixated on their game of backgammon. Both had cabins in the front section of the train, and neither had been disturbed by the night's events. The same was true for the Norwegian, Italian and New Zealand delegates: Kasper Iversen, Georgio Rizzo and Stephen MacDougall. All were oblivious, and all had alibis.

William wasn't surprised to see Teodoro Alvarez shuffling towards him.

"Might I have a word, Mr Greenwood?"

"Please, Señor Alvarez."

William steered Teodoro out of the dining carriage to his cabin.

"I should have come forward sooner, William. I asked Miss Blanch to examine a cloth I brought out yesterday morning, but she was busy talking. She told me to 'catch her' after supper."

"What's special about the cloth?"

"It was given to me five years ago in Cusco, Peru. It's not a secret – Mossi is aware of its existence, as are several of the other delegates. I showed it to Dr Iversen and Professor Singh. Mr Morimoto was sitting across the way at the time, talking with the American lady – Miss Adams. They all helped translate the characters, which happen to be mostly runes and Sanskrit. It's a prayer reputedly written by a Greek monk in the sixteenth century. The monk lived high up in the Andes Mountains near the ruins of Tiwanaku by Lake Titicaca on the Bolivian side."

"I remember reading about Tiwanaku in the dossiers."

"Yes. I put the information together for Mossi."

"Ah! Of course. Please continue."

"The monk was an advocate for the people of the Titicaca region, until he withdrew and became a recluse. On the cloth he wrote a prayer in several languages and added the Greek words 'αυτοι που φευγουν' – 'afti pu fevgoun' – forgive my pronunciation – 'those who flee'. At first, I thought it was a reference to the Inca fleeing the Conquistadors, but Tiwanaku was already a ruin, and the indigenous people didn't flee. In the prayer he mentions the name *Apu Qun Tiqsi Wiraqutra*. You might know him as Viracocha or Kon Tiki – a creator-being appearing regularly in early Incan artwork and mythology. The prayer describes 'a mother of many, who discovered a secret in the deep darkness'. I wanted the straight-talking Miss Blanch to examine it before I presented the evidence to Mossi."

"Who's to say the monk didn't make it all up?" asked William.

"I was summoned by the Cusco elders to a house. Inside, I found a very elderly woman on her deathbed. She handed me the cloth and a perfectly spherical stone, and told me that the monk had made contact with star people who had visited the earth in spaceships thousands of years ago."

William smirked. "Sorry? Spaceships?"

"Hear me out, Mr Greenwood. I'm aware of how crazy this sounds, but the woman was no cracked pot. According to her, the alien visitors came from a dying world, bringing wisdom and understanding to the ancient people of the Andes in exchange for vital resources. Both our worlds were on the brink of catastrophe. The visitors gave her ancestors the tools to survive. But the people became greedy, and turned against them. The star people had no option but to flee – but they left behind their legacy in stone constructions as well as clues to the founding of their civilisation. The old woman said something about a land of ice and a door. I remember her drawing a triangle with her finger in the air before she passed away."

"Ice? Door?" blurted William. "Have you the cloth?"

"No." Alvarez looked uncomfortable. "That's the problem. I haven't been entirely honest with you, William. When I found Miss Blanch last night, she was having a cigarette out of the window by the storage wagon. There was enough light in the corridor for her to examine it there and then. Suddenly, we heard a strange noise – a cough or a sneeze – it seemed to come from the storage wagon. Miss Blanch tried the handle – it was unlocked. She turned the light on, but the bulb blew almost immediately. She pulled the door shut and shoved me along the corridor back to my cabin, saying that she'd examine the cloth presently."

"What time was this?"

"Half past eight – maybe later. I can't say exactly."

"And you didn't see her again?"

"No. But I heard someone running down the corridor. I thought it was Miss Blanch and worried, so I followed, but I couldn't see her among the other delegates. I knocked on her door but there was no reply."

"And you definitely didn't see Mr Morimoto."

"His door was shut, as were all the doors in the carriage."

"So the map is gone?

Teodoro nodded miserably.

"What happened to the stone?" asked William.

"I gave it to Mossi several years ago."

"I see. Anything else I should know?"

"I have a transcription of the cloth, which I'd be happy to share with you. There are a few hieroglyphs on the back, starting with the Djed emblem for Osiris, and a snake."

"Leave it with me, Teodoro. We've only an hour to go before we arrive in Dodoma. Get some rest."

William returned to Kirstin Blanch's cabin with the attendant and searched high and low for the cloth. There was no sign of it.

William knocked on Mossi's door and gave him an update.

"A land of ice," remarked Mossi.

"Yes. Although, I thought you might have queried 'spaceships' first."

"Well that's just preposterous," said Mossi dismissively. "I'm aware of the cloth's existence, but Alvarez didn't tell me what was written on it. He wanted to assess it himself. The stone – you know about. Don't mention this to Boris. He'll be bending my ear on the possibility of a hare-brained trip to the South Pole. I struggle enough in temperate climes. So what are we going to do about Miss Blanch?"

"There's a window of merely twenty minutes when she got off or was pushed off the train. That equates to a five-mile stretch of track between Dar and Morogoro. The police will be able to pinpoint it better."

The train rumbled into the outskirts of Dodoma just after 3.00pm. There was no news regarding Kirstin Blanch. No one had definitively heard the gunshot that had killed Morimoto, and the only piece of evidence that seemed to link it all together was gone. Why was the storage wagon unlocked? And what had Miss Blanch witnessed in there?

Thys Myburgh, the birder, took William aside. "This might not be relevant, but yesterday I saw the same black Mercedes three times. If I didn't know any better, I'd think it was following the train." Myburgh held up his binoculars. "The last time I saw it was dusk."

"*Dankie*, Professor Myburgh." William elected to not mention that he'd seen a similar vehicle at the Museum. After his experience in the Austrian Vorarlberg, he was now deadly suspicious of any black Mercedes.

XXX: On Safari

The Dodoma Hotel, Tanganyika
June 14th 1940

William liaised with Mossi after disembarkation. Eric Chamberlain had arrived back in Dar-es-Salaam with Morimoto's body and possessions. William informed the police about Kirstin Blanch's disappearance and felt it prudent to mention the black Mercedes.

Mossi called a meeting before supper. The delegates assembled in the beautiful gardens of the Dodoma Hotel, in the shade of several impressively tall palm trees. "Lady… and gentlemen, I assure you, we are doing everything we can to find Yoshi Morimoto's killer, and to locate Miss Blanch. In the meantime, I'd like to begin this evening's seminar with a talk from Professor Kioko Kamau."

All the delegates had worked out that Mossi was looking for evidence of pre-Ice Age civilisation, and all were keen to please. Professor Kamau was no exception. Unbeknown to William, there was rather a large body of evidence, ranging from Mali to the lakes of the Rift Valley, which suggested that Stone Age Man was far more technologically advanced than assumed by mainsteam Anthropology. Kioko wound up his talk referencing a tribe called the Dogon whose faith system incorporated scaly, tall, fish-like beings from the star system of Sirius. There seemed to be a linguistic connection between the tribe and Egyptian Arabic.

"That'll please Mossi,' whispered William to Alexander. "Shame that Miss Blanch is absent!'

According to Kioko, the French Anthropologists who studied the Dogon said that they were aware of astronomical details from as early as 300BC that could have only been distinguished using modern telescopes.

After supper, the party remained in the dining room to dodge the mosquitoes.

Harry Tan sidled up to William. "You seem to be in charge of the murder investigation, Monsieur Poirot."

William puffed out his cheeks. "I suppose so. Not that I'm qualified. Terrible bloody business."

"Did you know about the Dogon?"

"No. It was news to me," sighed William. "As Mossi says – 'keep an open mind'."

Tan mumbled something seemingly dissenting in Mandarin that William didn't catch, before continuing. "The Dogon myth is similar to that of the Sumerian gods, the *Apkallu*, as mentioned on the *Enûma Eliš* cuneiform tablets – fish-human hybrids called *Oannes* dispensing advice. It also has resonance with the *Dogu* – animal-human hybrids from Neolithic Japan. The only two people that Kioko discussed the Dogon with on our first night in Dar… one is dead and the other, missing."

"Hm. Now you mention it, I forgot to ask Professor Kamau what he was doing in the carriage shortly after I discovered Morimoto's body. Are you saying you think he was involved?"

"I'm not accusing anyone. I just thought the information would be useful, circumstantial or not. While Mossi tries to brainwash us all with his views on a once global civilisation destroyed by cataclysm and rebuilt by the Egyptians…"

"What makes you so sure he's brainwashing us?"

"I overheard Alexander and Boris talking last night. They're convinced that Mossi has this all worked out, and wherever or whatever he is leading us to is supposed to bring us all into line. You know what he's like, William – the devil's in the detail – scientific objectivity and empirical analysis. No – he's a storyteller – and a good one to his credit. The only two people capable of shooting down the Dogon story are dead. Mark me."

Harry left William chewing the end of his pencil; feeling bereft of any 'little grey cells'.

Next to grace the lectern was Boris and his proposal that the Groenewald stones stored ancient technology within their crystal cores. William kept glancing towards Harry Tan, who was clearly irritable and making no attempt to take notes. Boris couldn't resist linking his proposal to the Seven Scribes of Edfu and the story of the Dogon. He had clearly spoken to Teodoro about the cloth as well. Though he mercifully avoided any reference to alien visitors, Boris was fixated on Alvarez's story of the dying woman in Cusco and the land of ice. William caught Mossi rolling his eyes. Boris segued neatly into Piri Reis' evidence for a landbridge between Argentina and the frozen subcontinent, and the deluge stories of Meso-America and Sumer.

Ravinda Singh added several intriguing statements alluding to sea-inundated cities along the coast of India and Pakistan from the Bay of Bengal to the Gulf of Kutch, and evidence of a man-made landbridge connecting Ramanathapuran in India to the island of Ceylon. This was supported by claims made by the New Zealand delegate, Stephen MacDougall, regarding continental drift and volcanic and tectonic activity in Polynesia. William remembered it was MacDougall who had supplied Mossi with extracts from Churchward and Le Plongeon's legends of Lemuia and Mu. MacDougall speculated on the oceanic spread of ancient people who colonised and traded all over the Pacific at a time when equatorial sea levels were considerably lower. William was grateful that no one had mentioned Atlantis, but Quentin Baraise put paid to that.

Baraise presented evidence of trade routes from the Azores to the Canary Islands and the suggestion that there was a structure in the Mauritanian desert similar in dimension to Plato's fabled city called the Richât. He reasoned that if the Sahara was more fertile and Lake Chad existed, as well as other Paleolithic lakes in Africa (as gleaned from geological surveys and the odd, speculative, near-illegible map) it would have displaced a significant amount of water from the ocean. These inland seas could only have been maintained with greater rainfall and a cooler climate consistent with thousands of years of ice build-up at the poles. Quentin closed by describing a bulging planet; the weight of ice at the poles causing the earth's crust to protrude and equatorial sea levels to drop. William was animated – it was the most cogent argument he'd heard based on his understanding – with no hint of a spaceman.

Mossi called the meeting to a close, and JJ detailed the delegates on the following day's manoeuvres. They were to meet in the foyer after breakfast. JJ had hired three trucks to carry porters, provisions and tents. The delegates would be escorted to the stable quarters.

The thought of a week on horseback both excited and worried William. He hadn't ridden for years, and his fears were realised the next morning when he was introduced to Saba. The three-year-old mare was not keen on her new rider, and twice tried to throw William. Eventually, he asserted his 'dominance' with a handful of oats, and trotted out of the stable quarters to join the others.

The trucks had pushed on ahead to set up their first encampment fifty kilometers south-west of Dodoma in the Huzi region. The ride was pleasant to begin with; the road maintained by the district farmers. By mid-afternoon, in the heat of the sun, the horses veered off into the bush following the truck's tyre tracks in the soft volcanic soil.

William had never seen such an abundance of wildlife: herds of Thompson's gazelle, zebra and wildebeest. He rode alongside Giorgio Rizzo, the Italian delegate, who was experiencing some discomfort.

"I've not ridden for a while, either." William broke the ice.

"It's not that – my back is not good."

"We've not really spoken, Giorgio. You're a Physicist, right?"

"I'm a Meteorologist – I study weather patterns."

"What do you make of Quentin and Stephen's global cooling conjecture?"

"There is no doubt that the earth experiences periods of cooling and warming. But whether it's enough to cause excessive bulging is, as you say, conjecture. I've seen evidence of African inland seas, and I've read Mossi's dossiers on the subject. I'm not sure they correlate with great ancient civilisations, though. You'd have to excavate the Sahara to find out – and as for the presence of Atlantis…" Giorgio shrugged his shoulders. "My real passion is the earth's magnetosphere – a magnetic field or dipole created by the earth's core."

"Ah, yes. I read your article. It absorbs or deflects radiation from the sun?"

"Deflects, with any luck. Life as we know it wouldn't exist without it. Harmful electromagnetic particles that penetrate the magnetosphere form auroras at the poles. I've witnessed them. The auroras migrate north and south depending on the magnitude of incident electromagnetic radiation and the strength of the magnetosphere itself. This is my field of research – I create plasma in my laboratory to see how it is affected by magnetism and the electromagnetic spectrum. One of my theories is that the efficacy of the magnetosphere to deflect particles is relative to the strength of the magnetism derived from the earth's molten iron core. In periods of weakening, the earth seems to experience anomalous weather patterns. If the weakening were to coincide with a solar flare there might be hurricanes, tidal surges and deadly plasma events. I've seen evidence of this in rock petroglyphs all over the world."

"Plasma events?"

"Super-lightning storms – discharging electricity from the ionosphere, and vast amounts of heat. The temperature is high enough to melt rock and boil seawater." Giorgio chortled. "It's a theory anyway."

The riders arrived at their encampment as the sun was beginning to dip. The Maasai porters, dressed in ill-fitting white suits, served tea and anything to numb the riders' aching posteriors.

"How are you, William?" asked Mossi.

"Good, thank you. Stiff, obviously."

"I saw you talking to Giorgio – an extraordinary mind. I think he's on to something. I've seen evidence of superheating in the desert – glass fragments and plastic deformation to structures. I've always wondered why there are so many underground passages built under mastabas and pyramids. Maybe they were sites of refuge?"

"Sounds plausible."

"Is there anyone you haven't spoken to yet?"

"Kasper Iversen and Ravinda Singh. Apparently, Teodoro had them translate some of the writing on his stolen cloth."

"Ah! I've been meaning to talk to you about Kasper. You should show him your journal – let him see the runes that Boris drew. It can't hurt."

After dinner, William found Kasper Iversen in his tent. By coincidence, he was reading Alexander's notes on the Stonelore.

"While we're on topic, Kasper, would you mind casting your eye over some runes?"

"Sure. Let me see them."

Iversen studied them and looked at William, puzzled.

"I'm sorry, Kasper. My rendering of them is poor."

"It's not that, William. Where did you find them?"

"They're my best interpretations from the Stonelore journals of dreams that Boris Kuriagin has been experiencing for some time."

Iversen took a moment to study William's sketches. "I've seen this sort of writing only once before – on the cloth that Teodoro showed me. I gather it's missing."

"Sadly, yes. It appears Miss Blanch may have taken it. What's the significance of the script?"

"I get the sense of it – but whoever wrote the cloth map and dreamt up these characters was not a Norseman in the classical sense. The runes are clumsy, almost childlike and resemble a dialect more akin to Icelandic. They show no semblance or congruency with anything I've analysed before, apart from..." Iversen paused. "Could Boris have seen Alvarez's cloth before he 'dreamt them up'?"

"I hadn't considered it. I doubt it. He's not been to Peru or Bolivia as far as I'm aware. I could ask."

"Don't!" snapped Kasper abruptly. "Leave it with me. Something's not right here."

"But what does the message mean?"

Kasper searched through a pile of notes. "The cloth says something like 'Children of the almighty seek protection from heaven and sea. From the underworld we celebrate the divine change of the birth mother'. 'Mother' can also mean 'mother earth'. Boris's runes say 'from a land of ice and hunger, we bring knowledge'."

William scratched his head. "That statement could be applied to anyone at any time throughout history. It could refer to a volcanic eruption in Iceland, for instance."

"I agree," confirmed Iversen. "Did this message come to him through the stones?"

"So he says," replied William.

"Pardon me for being sceptical."

The next morning, Thys Myburgh woke William, banging on his tent flap. He had risen early. A herd of elephant had passed not far from his tent, and left large mounds of dung.

"Care to join me?"

"Give me five minutes," replied William.

"Watch your feet!"

The pair left camp and stood by a miombo grove to watch the beasts feed.

"Can you hear the matriarch?"

"Yes," replied William, tuning in to a low rumble.

"She's telling the younger cows not to let the calves get too close to us. But her ears are flapping back and forth, so she's calm."

"Sound waves are your specialty, Professor Myburgh?"

"Infrasound in particular – elephant and whales. But I also design earthquake sensors for Geologists, and more recently sonar arrays for the Royal Navy in Simonstown."

"Gosh!" exclaimed William. "That must keep you busy."

"For sure!" laughed Thys. "I gather you're a British citizen, *Meneer Groenewald*."

William smiled and nodded.

"I put two and two together – Greenwood, Groenewald."

"It's no secret." William smiled.

"I only found out why I'm here last night," said Myburgh, nebulously. "That's why I was a bit short with you on the train. Mossi wants me to examine the stones, and analyse their capability to absorb and emit low audio-frequencies."

If what Myburgh said was true, could Mossi be undermining Boris or wanting a second opinion, or trying to keep the stones away from the Russians? What if Boris had a hand in Morimoto's murder? Had Morimoto seen through Boris's elaborate dreams? Was the cloth a hoax?

It was lunchtime when William and his horse, Saba, finally caught up with Ravinda Singh. The handsome Indian gentleman was an equestrian and a polo player. His mount was a magnificent Arabian gelding.

"You seem to be in your element, Professor Singh!" said William, out of breath.

"And which element would that be?"

"Ah, I forgot! You were a Chemist originally."

"Indeed. You're here to talk about the cloth."

"Amongst other things."

"Kasper said you would. He's right, by the way. Even the Sanskrit is… eggy. If Boris wanted to fool us by getting Alvarez to fabricate a cloth, surely he'd make a better job of it? If Alvarez's monk or dying woman story is to be believed, the monk might have had access to rudimentary Sanskrit and runic dictionaries. But Mr Ockham is right – '*Entia non sunt multiplacanda praeter necissitatem*'. The most logical explanation for the writing on the cloth is that it's authentic. But it doesn't stop me being sceptical too."

"Well I'm glad we cleared that up."

"Hardly!" laughed Singh before suddenly turning serious. "Why kill Yoshi Morimoto? That's what I want to know. He was a user by the way."

"A user?"

"I noticed a bottle of laudanum in his smoking jacket pocket at supper in Dar-es-Salaam. And he spent the evening bragging about a new psychedelic compound he'd synthesised from peyote or mescaline."

"His smoking jacket, you say?" remarked William, making a note. William hadn't seen Morimoto's smoking jacket when he had searched through his belongings, or a bottle of laudanum.

Singh took Saba's reins and led both of their horses to the makeshift stable *boma*, leaving William to think. Suddenly, something occurred to him – then a few pieces fell into place. He had to get word to Eric, but it was two days' hard ride back to Dodoma. He wanted to be with the party for Mossi's big reveal, and Mossi needed him to get the party safely through the mountains west of Blantyre. He decided to keep his suspicions to himself. If he were right, any imminent threat to the delegates was gone. The truth would 'out itself'. It was only a question of when.

SANCTUARY

The Premek trekked north on their quest – led by Ckan and Lek – and guided by the stones. Colossal, towering stormclouds drenched them in cleansing rain, lightning storms forced them under cover and swollen rivers halted their progress for days at a time. The savannah grasslands were awash with fresh green shoots. Vast herds of antelope brought an inexhaustible supply of meat, clothing and vital materials. The Premek feasted and grew strong, driven on by frosty winter nights and the chill spring air.

Since leaving their troglodyte existence, the Premek's physiology had quickly adapted to the turbulent terrestrial world. Their scaly skin had softened and better resisted punishment from the sun. A few of the clan had lost their greenish hue in exchange for a light tan. Their eyes accommodated bright light, making progress by day bearable, while their night vision remained acute. Their diet also changed to incorporate more plant-based foods: citrus fruits, berries, wild plaintains and root vegetables.

The Premek elders had urged Ckan to find a more permanent sanctuary – somewhere less exposed – where three of the Premek women could give birth. Ckan didn't hesitate to give consent: his wife, Hekket, was heavy with their first conception.

On their travels, the Premek were seeing more evidence of human survivor society: villages, felled trees, firepits, domestic livestock, recently butchered carcasses left for the scavengers and rocks decorated to demarcate territory. Eventually, they came into contact with roving bands of dark-skinned men and women who feared the giant Premek; fleeing, and sometimes returning in numbers to pelt the Premek with rocks, spears and arrows. Although the incidents were innocuous, Ckan worried that soon they might sustain attack from a more formidable foe.

The Premek's tiring search for a new home was rewarded. Scouts had reported a cave system in a range of sandstone and granite mountains. The elevation provided lookout points, and there was a constant supply of fresh water. Trees were abundant – for lumber and firewood – as was game for food. It seemed ideal. Ckan sent Lek on ahead to confirm its suitability, staying behind to build a temporary camp to protect the clan in the foothills of the range.

Ckan rested alongside Hekket under the clear night sky, and closed his eyes. He rubbed her swollen tummy and imagined a world full of mystery and awe: his child growing and flourishing, hunting and fishing, building friendships and playing in the sunshine. What would the future hold for the Premek? What awaited them far to the north? What were the stone edifices that he had seen in his dreams? Who had built them? What was their purpose? And what was contained in the granite box that Tsuk and he had retrieved from the underworld? Who had left their imprint on the warm, wet rock of the bioluminescent chambers, hidden deep in the earth's belly? Was it a warning? Instructions? How long had it been there?

His visions merged with the sonorous voices of his kinsfolk, entertaining children by the fire.

The eagle slumbers.
Pinpricks of light dance above him.
Stars converge:
shades of earthly creatures,
Each engendering human qualities
— human frailties.
Betrayal — blindness.
Titan releases his thunderbolt:
shattering the Mountain, splintering bone.
A fissure opens up,
the gaping maw of the behemoth
consuming its next victim.
A six-point star, chiselled into the rock,
encircling an empty recess.
Darkness gives way to light:
cacophony to orderliness;
balance, harmony and resonance.

THETU'S LULLABY

The children sit attentively.

"He is the titan, the eagle – the all-seeing eye.
The scarab brings fertility, fear not his lullaby.
The lion is our guardian, the protector of Kings.
The jackal is existence, onto which all life clings.
The crocodile: longevity – yawn – as time passes by.
The cobra is a demon, one bite and then you die!
Hiss! Aagh! Aaargh!"

The children scamper off in fright,
returning moments later.

"Thetu! Thetu! The ibis! The ibis!"

"The ibis brings forgiveness
and rewards you when you're good…"

"Ah!" plead the children. "I'm good, I'm good, I'm GOOD!"

"The ibis watches over you.
He knows your rights and wrongs.
He writes them in his little book
And turns them into songs."

"Again! Again! Again!" cry the children.
"NO! NO!
It's time for bed."

XXXI: The African Queen

Lake Nyasa, Nyasaland
June 23rd 1940

As each day passed, William became more anxious, thoughtful and restless. Conversely, the delegates became more at ease and outspoken. The waters of Lake Nyasa were deep blue in the winter sun. Clouds tumbled in from the west and fizzled out. Likewise, gossip regarding Yoshi Morimoto and Kirstin Blanch had evaporated. The odd argument had broken out, as was inevitable with so many strong opinions in close confinement. As a distraction, Thys Myburgh had converted the entire delegation into avid birdwatchers. He organised competitions to see how many species each could spot along the shoreline. The cruise along the length of Lake Nyasa on the chartered steamboat *The African Queen* was a fitting end to the safari.

On the last night on the water, William had an opportunity to test one of his theories regarding the death of Yoshi Morimoto. Just before the final lecture given by Mossi on Akhenaten and monotheism, Kasper Iversen was suddenly taken ill. William assisted Evelyn Adams, expedition nurse, to convey Iversen to his cabin.
"I'm sorry. I feel terrible," winced Iversen, clutching his gut.
Having diagnosed Iversen with food poisoning, Evelyn asked William and one of the porters to liberate the substantial medicine chest from Mossi's cabin. Mossi nodded approval. She dosed Iversen with a seltzer and a sleeping draught. She then asked William to find a sachet labelled 'quinine extract'. Making up a solution with sterilised water, glucose and salt, she injected it into a vein in Iversen's right arm. "He has a fever. I doubt it's malaria, but just in case I'm wrong... It's better to be safe than sorry."
Iversen slumped back onto his pillow. William replaced the sachet carefully, and studied each bottle in the medicine chest.
"Asleep already?" asked William.
"Like a baby," replied Evelyn.
William closed the door to Iversen's cabin and spoke in hushed tones, showing Evelyn a bottle labelled with Japanese *kana* characters. "I think I know what happened to Yoshi Morimoto."
"Who was it?"

"I can't say yet. There's something I need to know first." William suddenly noticed Evelyn brandishing a scalpel. Stepping back in surprise, he put his hands up in submission. "Wait! No. I meant..." He studied Evelyn's pained expression. "Please, Miss Adams. I don't think you had anything to do with it."

Evelyn slowly sheathed the scalpel. "Pardon me, William. I thought you were insinuating something."

"No. Not at all! But maybe you could start by telling me why you're really here."

"I'm here at Mossi's behest to discuss both African and North American relics. I've always had an interest in Egpytian antiquities. Mossi and I have had a dialogue for almost ten years – ever since I began to trade in curios. And I want to know more..."

"Tommyrot!" interrupted William playfully. "Relics? Piffle..."

And then the penny dropped... "Good God, Evelyn. The Eye of Horus pendant: you knew that Alexander Knapp would spot it in the Swiss broker's inventory and... Bless my soul – You know why we're here!"

"Don't mistake femininity for fragility."

"Clearly not!" William scratched his head. "How much does Mossi know?"

"Nothing, I hope. He invited me along for the ride out of courtesy. Maybe he suspects me – maybe he doesn't."

"Care to elaborate?"

Evelyn stared back at William, pursing her lips.

William dwelt on her admission. "I've no idea what your endgame is, Miss Adams, but my gut tells me that we should let it play out?"

"It would be better for us all if you did, William."

"Righto. Mum's the word," he replied soberly. He couldn't think of a good reason to blow her cover. "Do you know anything about Yoshi Morimoto's death? Or Miss Blanch's disappearance?"

"No," she shook her head. "Do you think Morimoto hid his secret potion here deliberately?"

William considered the question, and handed her the bottle. "I can't say. I'm guessing it contains mescaline, or a similar psychedelic compound?"

Evelyn studied the Japanese writing and sniffed warily at its contents. "I have to say, William, I didn't expect you to make the connection to the Eye. You're smart – trustworthy – a gentleman... and you've given me an idea."

In front of William, Evelyn poured Morimoto's concoction into a fresh bottle. She rinsed Morimoto's bottle out with distilled water and filled it with a cocktail of tinctures. She labelled the fresh bottle with a 'skull and crossbones' and handed it back to William, who hid it among several nasty looking chemicals. He then replaced the bottle labelled with *kana* in the medicine chest where he had found it.

"Let's have some fun," she beamed. "We owe it to poor Mr Morimoto."

Mossi had been waiting for William and Evelyn to return, and was relieved to hear that Kasper Iversen was comfortable.

"My talk today involves, in my humble opinion, the greatest paradigm shift in Egypt's long history. How and why did Akhenaten change the belief system of a civilisation that had embraced polytheism for over two thousand years? Why was he known as 'the mysterious', and how much say did Queen Nerfertiti have in the matter?"

His last clause caused a ripple of amusement.

"We all can agree that after Akhenaten died there was a systematic dismantling of his legacy by his son, Tutankhamun. If we look at this relief we see Akhenaten, uncommonly tall with an elongated skull, depicted with a sun or moon disc. I theorise that the disc is a metaphorical depiction of one of our stones, pouring wisdom down from on high as the sun god, *Aten*. You will also see in the photograph that Nefertiti is also depicted wearing a peculiar headdress and her children have elongated crania."

He paused for the delegates to review the images, translating the hieroglyphs for them.

William zoned out, trying to piece together Evelyn's motives for attracting Mossi's attention with the Eye of Horus. Was Mossi aware of her involvement? Was Evelyn aware that the pendant had housed another stone?

Mossi continued. "Boris Kuriagin may have stolen my thunder, but I believe Akhenaten or one of his forebears came into contact with 'Groenewald' stones that may well have been brought to Egypt by the Seven Scribes of Edfu, thousands of years before. You will also see that Akhenaten's entire body is cruelly misshapen, unlike the depiction of any ruler of Egypt that preceded him. The beauty of the mask of Tutankhamun, discovered by Howard Carter in 1925, suggests two narratives – restoring the god-like form of the pharaoh, and a quality of craftsmanship that supersedes almost anything that went before. Boris has already raised the question – were the stones responsible for the leap in technology after a period of cataclysm? I think the answer is indubitably, 'Yes'. But did the pharaohs have a love-hate relationship with the stones thereafter? And what happened to them after Akhenaten's dynasty?"

"Is it true that Nefertiti reigned after Akhenaten?" asked Quentin Baraise. "And was Tutankhamun really Akhenaten's son? There seems to be no physical similarity, no elongated cranium – and the timelines are awkward. King Tut was reputedly born well after Akhenaten's death."

Before Mossi could answer fully, more questions rained down on him. Eventually, the conversation gravitated towards the pyramids at Giza and their significance.

"So was Khufu really buried in the King's chamber?" asked Harry Tan. "And what's the significance of the Queen's chamber?"

"What's underneath The Great Pyramid?"

"How long did it take to build?"

"Who was Hemiunu?"

Mossi attempted to answer them all, and eventually put his hands up. "It's time to finish, but before we do, I'd like for us to consider the Sphinx. We believe it was constructed in the image of Kafre – The Lion – son of Khufu in the 4th dynasty, and the builder of the second pyramid at Giza. I'd like to draw your attention to the weathering around the base of the Sphinx. It suggests a time of deluge or precipitation coherent with our estimations of successive periods of flooding and drought. It brings into consideration that the Giza plateau might have once been part of the Nile floodplain, or that Lower Egypt was once an extension of a fertile land. My calculations suggest that a mega-drought changed all that over four thousand years ago."

"If I may go back?" asked Quentin Baraise, checking his notes. "I was expecting you to say that work began on the pyramids after the Great Flood. And we agreed this happened around 5000BC."

"Thank you, Quentin," replied Mossi. "I believe that the Great Flood destroyed a thriving culture in Mesopotamia, as well as a global economy based on trade from land and sea. Evidence from Sumerian cuneiform tablets shows this to be the case, as do records discovered in the Indus Valley and China. The same cataclysmic event obliterated the original inhabitants of the Nile delta who had reached an advanced level of culture and sophistication. There followed a passage of time where much of the earth was uninhabitable. Pockets of humanity sought refuge underground or in mountainous regions, isolating themselves for over two thousand years until the planet's atmosphere, land and sea permitted mankind to rebuild. It is during these periods of isolation that, I believe, humans bred similar features within their populations, discernibly distinct from other communities and governed by their environment. We have Wallace and Darwin to thank for that explanation. I was going to bring in Kirstin Blanch here to discuss how the diversification of religion and linguistics might corroborate my theory, but alas…" Mossi's brow knotted, revealing his frustration.

"As for my theories regarding advanced Ice Age civilisations – as indicated by the presence of inexplicable ancient megalithic structures, including submerged pyramids or land pyramids buried under metres of soil, sediment and plant growth – I suggest this cycle of global destruction and redevelopment has been occurring for millions of years. The problem is – the periods of stability seem to be getting shorter."

The assembled were strangely quiet, until Stephen MacDougall yelled, "Hear! Hear!"

The delegates began to applaud. Irrespective of 'Stonelore' hocus-pocus or alien intervention, the delegates were united: the world was spinning perilously towards the next unavoidable cataclysm.

"One very last comment before we retire," said Mossi with a twinkle in his eye. "It doesn't really matter what I think. In a week or so from now, and I stake my reputation on it, we will have more answers."

William looked towards Evelyn, who was pretending to smile while avoiding Mossi's gaze.

"If that hasn't whetted their appetite," mumbled William to Alexander. "Nothing will."

XXXII: Ruffled Feathers

Blantyre, Nyasaland
June 26th 1940

A cavalcade of horses, porters and equipment moved slowly west through the leafy outskirts of Blantyre. The plan was simple — make camp in the foothills of the eastern highlands of Rhodesia, where there should be plentiful food and water, and send out reconnaissance groups with local guides until Mossi was satisfied they were on the right track. Frustratingly, Mossi had still not revealed his secret. The delegates were getting itchy feet and, thought William, it wasn't just the fungal infection that was doing the rounds!

The road was graded, cutting through a range of low-lying hills and tea plantations. Sadly, for William, Mossi had requested that JJ stay in Blantyre with his uncle's family. William missed his banter. He had, however, received news from Eric Chamberlain that shoes belonging to Kirstin Blanch had been recovered from the Bush west of Morogoro. The information provided William with a rough timeframe for their disposal, but with no sighting of Miss Blanch, William feared the worst.

By late afternoon the delegates were weary. Kasper Iversen's condition had improved sightly, but he was still experiencing discomfort. A full day's ride had not helped. The camp was erected quickly before the porters lost the light, just north of the Thombani forests. Evelyn Adams forced some broth into Iversen before knocking him out with a mild sedative. She caught William on his way to debrief Mossi on the region's topography.

She kept her voice down. "Boris is also experiencing gut cramps. The level has dropped a fraction again in Morimoto's bottle. Just thought you should know."

"Thanks." William winked and entered the main tent.

"Our guide says that the border guards ahead are expecting us," said William, stretching a map in front of Mossi. "After that, we're on our own."

"Not quite, William," corrected Mossi. "JJ has arranged for us to pick up porters tomorrow at the border. They've agreed to lead us into the Highlands that the locals call Nyanga. Then it's over to you."

"Do you actually know where we're going, Mossi?"

"That will be all, William," he replied frankly.

Biting his lip, William rolled his maps smartly and left, but not before noticing Boris, sitting in the corner of the tent, staring at blank canvas.

After supper, Mossi announced the news that Professor Myburgh was to take over as chief researcher into the infrasonic capabilities of the stones on his return to Cape Town. Myburgh seemed pleased, whereas Boris's demeanour did not change: he seemed lost in his own world.

William leaned over to Alexander. "Is he OK?"

Alexander replied, "He's not been himself for a while now – ever since the boat trip. And he's off his drink."

The meeting continued with an inventory of the stones. Mossi had provided the delegates with a document revealing where they had been discovered, and their purported movement.

"We have four stones with us on this expedition, and it's my belief that we are likely to locate at least one more in the next few days. What some of you will already know is that Boris Kuriagin exhibits sensitivity to a stone that has been in his possession for many years. He had no idea of its significance until Alexander Knapp broadcast his findings. It had been my intention to analyse Boris's dreams *in situ*, with the help of Yoshi Morimoto, may he rest in peace. Nevertheless, under the supervision of Dr Gomez, Boris has been taking small doses of a psychotropic drug to help with the dissemination of information from the stones. We have determined that not all the stones produce as powerful dreams or visions as each other, which suggests to us that either their effectiveness is wearing off with age, or that he is simply not as sensitive to some stones as to others."

"Well that explains a few things," said Alexander to William under his breath. William remained poker faced, unsure as to quite what Alexander was referring to. Irrespectively, William had known for a few days that Dr Gomez had been dipping into what he thought was Morimoto's miracle drug. Boris looked awful. What had Evelyn concocted?

"As you are aware," continued Mossi. "Boris is obsessed with the Seven Scribes of Edfu, and we must be mindful of this when we form an opinion regarding his interpretations. In spite of Mr Morimoto's absence and thanks to Dr Gomez, it seems that we have made a breakthrough regarding the number and purpose of the stones. Boris's dreams have revealed a constant – a recurring geometric six-point star pattern with a central locus. So why do I mention the Seven Scribes? Because Boris believes that 'seven' refers to the total number of stones in existence."

"Where does Huw Williams's stone in South Africa fit in?" asked Dr Kamao.

"Ah! The Mankwe stone," replied Mossi.

"Are we to recover it?" asked William.

"William," Mossi said, somewhat patronisingly. "I know you've been champing at the bit to test your theory regarding the eagle and the pyramid from Huw's journal. As it happens, you were right."

"How so?" replied Alexander.

"Because I have the very stone here." Mossi held it up for all to see. "Boris believes this to be the stone that Huw Williams tried to rid the world of."

"That's impossible!" gasped Alexander.

"Give me a moment to explain," said Mossi. "Boris's dreams give us a glimpse as to how each stone was found. But what's more curious – this is the very same stone that I removed from the Eye of Horus pedant that turned up in a broker's inventory in Geneva last year."

"But that means your whole Hemiunu theory is dashed," said Jesùs Rousseau.

"Not necessarily," interrupted Boris. Everyone stopped and stared. "Forgive me – I'm feeling a little fragile." Boris pulled himself to his feet awkwardly. His eyes were bloodshot and his skin pale. "Mossi's right. The stone in his hand was the inset Eye of the pendant. It is, indeed, the stone that Huw Williams took to his death. I saw it in my dreams – the man was chased by a firestorm, hounded by a mechanical demon, harried by the four horsemen of the apocalypse and sucked into a gaping void."

Laughter broke out instantaneously: the delegates didn't hesitate to express their utter contempt for Boris's explanation. Most of all, it was totally contradictory to Mossi's directive, to avoid supposition and superstition at all costs.

"Before anyone commits me to Bedlam," said Boris. "I am more than aware of how absurd this sounds. In truth, I fear Huw Williams drowned. That is consistent with William Greenwood's theory of the stone being cast into a lake. Somebody retrieved it."

Again, the delegates fell about, while Mossi tried to retake control. Boris ignored the fracas nonchanlantly. William clocked him looking about the main tent, as if searching for someone.

"But what of the Hemiunu theory?" pushed Rousseau again. "Explain yourself, Mossi!"

"Maybe I can answer that," said Alexander, indicating that the delgates be seated. "Mossi uncovered the Eye of Horus in Tanis, complete with original inset stone. It was stolen soon after. Whoever tried to sell it in Switzerland, must have swapped the inset stone for another. With Boris's information, we have to consider that the broker was delivering a message. It doesn't affect the Hemiunu theory – the hieroglyphs in Hemiunu's serdab speak for themselves."

"Am I right in thinking that the Eye turned up in the Geneva inventory before William discovered the location of Huw Williams's Mankwe stone?" queried Ravinda Singh.

"So it seems," said Alexander.

"That means only one person could have retrieved it."

"Five, technically, Professor Singh," stated William. "If Alexander is right and the dealer was aware of the significance of the stones…" William lost his way momentarily. "Er… but one of those possibilities is so unimaginably remote that we should immediately discount it."

He was baffled by Alexander's clarity of explanation and timely revelation. Were Alexander or Mossi, or both aware of Evelyn's identity as the pendant's trafficker?

Suddenly, Kasper Iversen dashed into the tent. There was a disturbance outside, raised voices and a crack of gunfire some distance away. William instinctively reached for his pistol, but it was under lock and key with the other firearms.

"It's Miss Adams! She's taken a horse and crossed the border. Two ostlers went after her."

"Did she take anything else with her?" asked Mossi, shooting a furtive glance at Mateo Gomez and then the medicine chest.

"She had a rifle," reported Iversen. "She came into my tent to dose me looking scared out of her wits, and then bolted."

"Please calm yourselves, gentlemen," shouted Mossi above the commotion. "She can't have gone far. We'll post a guard by each of your tents. In the meantime, please be seated."

"What the devil frightened her off?" asked Alexander.

"I've no idea," replied Iversen. "She was terrified, poor thing."

"Has someone got it in for the fairer sex?" added Harry Tan.

After minutes of pointless questions, William stood and asked the assembly to return to their seats.

"You and your bléssed stones, William!" barked Stephen MacDougall. "There are more important things in life. Take living, for example!"

"Please be seated!" shouted Mossi. "Whoever scared her off – it can't have been any of the delegation. Apart from Kasper, we were all present."

Eyes turned swifty towards Kasper Iversen.

"Don't be daft. I was barely awake when she came in to dose me!"

****

Evelyn rode for half an hour; the dirt road lit by the full moon. Ahead, were lights – fires burning – and the smell of cooking. Slowing her horse to a trot, she picked her way through silhouetted thatched huts. Folk were gathered in the centre of the village by a larger brick building. A Christian cross on the roof signified that she had reached sanctuary. Dismounting, she led the horse through the crowd. The people parted to reveal an elderly priest serving stew to his flock.

"Peace be with you, my child."

He pointed towards the chapel. Evelyn tied up her mare by a flight of stone steps and entered. The altar was illuminated with candles, but the nave was dark. Alone, at the end of a pew, was a figure sitting motionless, shrouded in a woolen blanket. Evelyn walked slowly to her and sat softly.

"How are you, mother?"

"At peace."

"Are you in pain?"

"Not any longer, my child. How are you?"

Evelyn was overcome with emotion. She sniffed back tears, summoning conviction and poise. "They know about the pendant. Boris Kuriagin saw me in his dreams."

****

"That's preposterous!" shouted Quentin Baraise.

"No it isn't!" argued William, trying to maintain order. "There were four people at the Driefontein Mission. All had access to Huw's journal, and we know what a pulling power these stones have. The most likely scenario is that Temba Schmidt went to find Huw's remains. Perhaps the temptation was too great."

"But you said 'five' possibilities," added Giorgio Rizzo. "What's the fifth?"

"That someone else stumbled upon it."

The tent erupted in laughter.

"Nonsense!"

"Twaddle!"

Alexander stepped in to defend William. "How the stone was discovered is irrelevant. The whole thing is conjecture anyway. We know what the stones are capable of…"

"We know nothing!" said Stephen MacDougall. "Boris could be making the whole thing up. Maniacal demons? Horsemen of the apocalypse? Mossi, I'm sick of hearing about these stones. They could be circumstantial artefacts. I need proof. We all do!"

Boris didn't react, staring into space.

Mossi indicated to Mateo Gomez to bring forward a briefcase. Mossi unlocked it. Inside were three more stones, individually housed in lead-shielded boxes.

"The mind boggles!" Stephen MacDougall gazed at them a moment, and exploded. "I want nothing to do with this hocus-pocus!"

Mossi's patience had worn thin. "Hocus-pocus, you say! I wondered why a Japanese industrialist was so keen to have his son join this expedition. It became clear when we found Yoshi Morimoto had tried to steal one of them!"

"You killed him?" queried MacDougall in amazement. "For a stone?"

"No," replied Mossi, immediately recoiling. "I did nothing of the sort. Mateo Gomez found it amongst Yoshi's personal items."

"What?" asked William astounded. "And you didn't think to mention it?"

"Sorry, William," confessed Mossi undoing his collar button. "It didn't seem relevant."

"Good God, man!" snapped William. "I've had Eric, the police and goodness knows who else searching for that bloody briefcase! Please don't tell me that you know something about Miss Blanch's whereabouts as well."

Mossi shook his head remorsefully.

"This is a circus!" belly-laughed Harry Tan.

The delegation was unraveling quickly.

"And where is this proof?" asked Stephen MacDougall.

Suddenly, Mossi slammed the box shut. "If I had proof, this whole bloody expedition would never have happened. Do you honestly think I gathered you all for a jolly holiday in the African sun? I risked my career – No! – my life to bring you all here. I deceived my King!"

All were stunned into silence.

Mossi composed himself. "Stephen, I'd like you to return to Blantyre. Wait! Let me make this plain. If any of you have doubts – after breakfast tomorrow – you may take your leave. JJ will arrange your transportation from Blantyre. Now get out of here before I do something I regret."

The delegates scuffled out of the tent. William and Alexander stayed put.

"All of you!"

****

After breakfast the next morning, the extent of the ill feeling became apparent. Kasper Iversen was the first to apologise to Mossi: he wasn't fit enough to continue. Giorgio Rizzo and Quentin Baraise were next in line, followed by Stephen MacDougall and Ravinda Singh. Harry Tan was last to go. They all cited personal reasons or problems associated with hostilities in Europe and further abroad. Several of the porters were detailed to return with them. Mossi promised that they would receive a partial reimbursement to diffuse the situation. With the South American and African contingent opting to stay, it brought the expedition party's numbers down to nine.

Mossi summoned Alexander, Boris and William to his tent – his threadbare veil of verisimilitude had been rent from top to bottom. Nursing a glass of water, he stared at the heavy locked briefcase. "If you have anything to say, do it now. Get it out of your system."

William plucked up courage. "I think you should have said something about Yoshi and the theft. We lost their trust."

"Well it's too late for that," said Mossi remorsefully.

William continued. "We have to accept that we don't really know what the stones are, what they do or where they're from – and that's hard to swallow…"

Boris stifled a laugh. "Really, William? I can't believe my ears."

"Next, Boris will be saying that he's wrong about the Seven Scribes," added Alexander jovially. "Incidentally, Boris, are you finished with the stones? You look as rough as hell."

"It's like a terrible hangover. But I've seen some damn strange things, and not all of them in my sleep, if you catch my... er." His concentration wandered off.

"Drift?" finished William.

"Er... no... meaning. Whatever you lot think, I know there are seven stones in existence. The fifth and sixth are in the mountains." Boris stopped, stood abruptly and headed out. "I'm off for a nap. Let me know when it's time to go."

William sat quietly, contemplating Boris's prophecy. Did he know of Eric's heirloom as well, the seventh stone, locked away in the Customs House in Stone Town? Something didn't feel right. William had kept the existence of Samuel Morgan's discovery from Alexander, but Alexander had worked it out by himself. Had Eric told Alexander or Boris or Mossi of Samuel Morgan's discovery? Was Alexander, too, not prepared to lay his cards on the table quite yet. And more to the point – what would happen if the seven stones were reunited?

Mossi coughed, breaking William's train of thought. "What are we going to do about Evelyn Adams, poor girl? What the hell frightened her off, and where is she headed?"

William's confidence in Mossi was waning, and his suspicions were growing fast. The man could not be trusted.

XXXIII: The Child

Nyanga Districts, Eastern Highlands
Southern Rhodesia
June 29th 1940

Evelyn led her mother's horse into the mountains. Clouds clung to the sides of steep cliffs. Squalls of rain dampened the ground. Her mother was contemplative and said little apart from the odd curse. The bandaging covering her face prevented her scratching at the persistent itch from the sockets where her eyes should have been.

"We should rest," said Evelyn.

Her mother took a deep breath and pulled at the reins. "This was a mistake. I'm useless to you now."

"But we're so close, mother!" pleaded Evelyn. "Just another few hours to the village, and I'll get you comfortable."

****

William Greenwood passed up the opportunity for lunch to peruse his sodden maps. One of the porters had picked up the tracks of two horses leading up a valley on a muddy path.

"Alex, look here! She can't be far ahead of us."

"We have to stop. Boris is flagging and I'm soaked through."

Whatever Evelyn had concocted in Yoshi Morimoto's bottle had turned Boris's guts inside out. It was also further evidence that someone had been trying to administer Morimoto's psychotropic compounds, and the only person in the expedition party that had sufficient expertise to do so was the Argentinian Physician, Mateo Gomez. It didn't, however, explain why the Japanese chemist had to die.

Boris waved the party on. Thys Myburgh and two armed porters stayed with Alexander and William. They pressed on up the steep winding path, following the horses' tracks, until they spied a village through the mist. The settlement comprised fifty or so dwellings that spread up the hillside, and a modest stone Mission chapel. The path became so slippery that the horsemen were forced to dismount and continue on foot.

"We've been spotted," announced Thys Myburgh. "I don't think they'll be sending a welcoming committee."

"Just keep an eye out," remarked William. "The Manyika live up here for good reasons."

The path widened as it entered the village. It looked deserted. Two horses were tethered outside the Mission chapel.

Alexander stayed with Thys and the porters, while William approached tentatively, tied up his horse and entered the chapel. It was dark, lit only by a few meagre candles. He smelled cooked food. The floorboards were damp, slippery and rotted through in patches. Four parallel rows of pews guided William up the aisle to the altar. He made the sign of the cross and looked for the source of the smell: a vestry, with a light flickering inside. He drew his pistol and nudged the door open. Sitting on a wooden chair tending a fire was an elderly woman, hunched over; a woolen shawl pulled tightly round her. Her hair was matted, her face obscured.

"Who's there?" she croaked.

"I mean no harm."

The woman didn't react. Instead, she picked up a bowl and spooned soup into her mouth.

"May I come in?"

Again the woman ignored William. She placed the bowl on the floor and pushed her hair back. A soiled brown bandage covered her face.

"Rosalind? Heavens! What happened?"

Rosalind turned away, moaning and clutching her knees to her breast. William knelt and tried to hold her, but she pushed him away.

Alexander and Thys burst into the room.

"It's Rosalind! Thys – my medical supplies, please."

Thys returned a minute later. Alexander had stayed rooted to the spot. Rosalind's distress was clear to see. She rocked back and forth, mumbling to herself, batting off any attempt by William to touch her. Gone was the elegant, snappy-talking Irish lady, and in her place was a dried up husk of a soul, fighting to keep her sanity.

"He took my eyes, Alex. My eyes!"

Rosalind allowed William near her. He removed the bandage carefully: sparkling green gems had been replaced with deep dark pits.

"Who took them?" asked Alexander.

"My boy. My precious boy!" Rosalind howled. "He's a monster. A monster!"

"Temba? Why? What happened?"

219

Rosalind rocked in her chair, weeping.

"We must get her back to Camp, Alex," said William. "We have to find Evelyn. She'll know what to do."

"She's gone after him," interjected Rosalind. "Leave me here… but she…" Her words tailed off in anguish. "He took her boy. There's no reasoning with him. He's lost."

"Who? What boy? She has a son? Temba took her son. Your grandson?" asked Alexander, kneeling beside her, weeping and stroking her hair. "Is that what this is all about?"

"Alex!" shouted William. "We need to stop Evelyn before she suffers a similar fate – and we have to go now before we lose the light. Rosalind, do you know where she's heading?"

Rosalind mustered strength. "Take the path up the valley. She's only been gone a hour. There's a waterfall up there. She knows you're coming. And her name is Rhona… not Evelyn." The exertion caused her to collapse back into the chair.

"Rhona?" queried William. "Thys – stay with Alex. I'll head up there with the porters." William turned to Rosalind. "Is he alone? Temba? I mean – is it just him and the boy?"

Rosalind shook her head uncontrollably. "No. He has followers. They're mad devotees… disciples… they'll protect him at all costs. The local Manyika villagers fear them. They stay away from the mountain. It's an evil place. Evil!"

"Let's go," said William. "Alex – what do you want to do?"

"Thys and I will take Rosalind back to main Camp."

"Thank you, William," said Rosalind feebly. "Be on your guard. They are armed."

William detailed the porters. They weren't keen at first, but crossing of palms seemed to do the trick. Together, they headed up the path as the weather broke, sending shards of needle-sharp sleet into their faces. The path was treacherous, punctuated by slippery rock and deep puddles. By the time they caught sight of the waterfall, they were soaked to the skin and shivering. The path channelled them into a narrow gorge and against a raging torrent. The porters began to chatter.

"What do you see?"

One of the porters pointed to the right of the waterfall. It was Rhona wearing a leather jacket, her hair tied back, brandishing a rifle. William put his hands up in submission. She waved them up the final stretch, pointing to various hand and footholds in the cliffs beneath the falls. The water level was rising fast.

Rhona called down to them. "Take care. This is the worst part."

William focused on the climb, but his hands were numb with cold. His boots slipped on algae and moss, clumped around fissures. Rhona seemed to disappear, only to materialise beside another cataract.

"Hold your breath!" With that she walked straight through the white cascading water.

William and the porters followed her, bracing under the chill and force of the cataract. A cave system had been gouged out underneath the main river course. Rhona had lit a fire.

"Dry yourselves." She hunkered down with the porters while William wrung out his shirt and jacket.

"Alexander and Thys are taking Rosalind to the main Camp, and I think you owe me an explanation."

Rhona rubbed her hands together for warmth. "Ten years ago, Temba Schmidt and I settled near Bulawayo and discovered a market for curios – some I'd ship back to the USA. One day, an old German soldier came into the store and revealed an Eye of Horus pendant to me. God knows how he'd got hold of it, but he was dying of cancer and his mind was frail. I gave him a woeful price for the relic – turns out it was priceless."

"And the inset stone?"

"Huh." Rhona smiled sarcastically. "Temba saved my life – I was left for dead by my brother, Roddy, in the Kalahari. In rescuing me, Temba was gravely wounded. I knew he'd recover – it was the second time I'd brought him back from the dead. First time he healed good and clean, but second time round… let's just say, there were complications. But they didn't manifest till after I'd fallen for him, married him and bore us a child. We were happy for a while. Then I stupidly left the Eye of Horus lying around in the office. He spotted it and became transfixed on the inset stone. Just my luck – another damned stone! I took it from him, but he got pissy. It seemed to rekindle his obsession, and he began to sense the presence of his own stone that I'd buried under our house. I told him it was lost to the sands of the Kalahari, along with my brother. He didn't believe me – he was so messed up that he started digging around the property. I couldn't lie to him any longer. I handed it to him one day thinking it'd calm him down, and stop the digging. Big mistake, girl! Next thing – he vanishes – gone for weeks – and then turns up all smiles. He'd found another stone – the one that Huw Williams had tried to discard at the bottom of a lake. I mean – he wouldn't tell me how he found it, but I knew it was unnatural. I tried to reason with him, 'But Huw died trying to hide that damn thing!' It didn't matter to Temba. He was all about power and possibility. Well, he found power all right..."

"So, it's true! The stones aren't just filled with messages from the past."

"No sirree! They mess with your body and your brain."

"So what did you do?"

"I located Rosalind in Austria and wrote her everything. She came up with a plan. I swapped out the inset stone of the Eye of Horus, replaced it with the one Temba had recovered from the lake thinking that he mightn't notice. When he did, I put the plan into operation. I had my curio trading partner visit and got 'em to add the Eye to a trafficking inventory in Switzerland. Rosalind knew it would pique Alexander's interest."

"So you and Rosalind orchestrated this whole expedition?"

"Uh. Well, she did in truth. I think, by now, Alexander and Mossi must have worked out that this recovery mission isn't just about the stones."

"Well it explains rather a lot," said William. "But why did you swap the stone in the Eye pendant?"

"I needed to know the truth! You live with a man like Temba, and you learn a few things about these stones – Boris isn't far off the scent with his Seven Scribes theory. Each stone has its own particular animal familiar. How they were imbued with this characteristic is a mystery to me, but the stones were once the property of a group of travellers, survivors from a cataclysmic event. Temba's stone took the form of an eagle, and the stone he recovered from Mankwe Lake was a jackal. The Eye of Horus stone was a crocodile. I swapped the croc for the jackal to see if he'd notice."

"And you say he did?"

"He sure did. It drove him insane. And when he found out what I'd gone and done, and shipped the Eye of Horus off for his 'own good', things went from bad to shitty. Up until that point, he'd never shown any aggression or violence to either me, or little Katlego. But the fury... Woah!" Rhona shook her head.

"Did he strike you?" asked William.

"No." Rhona chuckled nervously. "We had an oil-powered generator fitted at the property. It was primitive, but we had light and heat in winter. One day he flew into such a rage that all the lightbulbs blew, tripping the generator, but not before burning out the valves and transformer. He knew he'd messed up. Such was his remorse, he vowed that he'd keep his temper in check."

"Gosh! Did he?"

"Three weeks later he disappeared and took Katlego with him. No note. Gone. *Vamoosed.*" Rhona untangled a moth from her hair and tossed it angrily on the fire. It fizzled and popped. "My boy had just turned seven."

"How long ago was this?"

"A year or thereabouts. It took me months to trace him. And when I did…" Rhona's voice trembled.

"He was unrecognisable?"

Rhona nodded and began to well up.

"And your boy… Katlego?"

"Didn't even recognise me. I tried to infiltrate Temba's cult of worshippers… blend in… make amends. But he knew what I was up to. He didn't let me near my boy. I spent five months up in these mountains listening to his bullshit. They call themselves The Children of the Premek – something to do with these ancient travellers, The Primaeval Ones or the Seven Scribes. Eventually, I had my fill and left. It crushed me to leave my boy up there. When I got home, I got word from Rosalind that she was headed here, and that her plan had worked. I was overjoyed. We met up on the border at a Portuguese Mission, and I prepared her for what she was about to witness. Of course, being Rosalind, she just thought she'd storm in, give Temba a clip round the ear and all would be well."

"Clearly not."

"What he did to her was barbaric! I got her out. Well… he didn't want us around would be a more accurate assessment. He's dangerous, William, and I don't think a bunch of antsy scientists are gonna scare him off. He has powers. He can manipulate thought and…" Rhona hesitated.

"What else?"

"He causes things to spark. Just like when he blew out our generator. I don't know how he does it, but my guess is he draws power from the stones. If we're going to rescue Katlego, we need to steal the stones away, or distract him somehow."

"Sounds like rushing in would be a fool's game. We need to plan this carefully. Where is Temba?"

"From here it's several hours climb into the mountains. His disciples don't come this side of the range. It's treacherous – almost inaccessible in the rain – but the river has carved a pothole system in the soft limestone. This cave leads deep into the mountain and opens up about half a mile above us. If we can get to Katlego, we could smuggle him out through here. I doubt Temba's loonies would follow – I doubt they even know of the tunnel's existence."

"You know that even if we were to get Mossi to sanction a recovery mission, he'll want something in exchange."

"Two stones and the proof that they are something out of this world? That would appease his critics."

William scratched his head. "We might have a problem there, Eve... I mean Rhona. Half of the delegates turned back before the border. There's only a handful of us left – and twelve or so porters. I'm not sure they're battle hardened."

Rhona looked crestfallen. "You mean?"

"I mean we're woefully low on numbers. And I don't know how Mossi will take the news that his entire expedition was a ruse to rescue your boy. Negotiating will require a delicate touch, not to mention the conscription of mercenaries. How many Premek disciples does Temba have up there?"

"Sixty – maybe more."

"Crikey! Are they armed?"

"They have weapons, but mostly old rifles and I don't think they've ever had cause to use them. The Premek are brainwashed loyalists, who adhere to Temba's rhetoric. They did nothing to stop him maiming his mother, and they wouldn't hesitate to lay down their lives…"

A porter caught their attention. They were losing light but the rain had stopped.

"Time to regroup, Rhona. Let's get back to main Camp. It's a few hours ride from the Manyika village. We should manage the last stretch in the dark."

"Wait, William! I can't stress enough – Boris is no phoney – he's the real deal. We must be cautious."

She braced herself, and slipped through the watery curtain.

XXXIV: The Hero of Nyangani

Mount Nyangani, Eastern Highlands
Southern Rhodesia
July 4th 1940

"It hasn't escaped my attention that today is Independence Day." William grinned at a pensive Rhona and checked his wristwatch: It was ten o'clock. "At least the weather's holding."

Rhona was hunkered down in a patch of heather, high on the mountaintop. Through her binoculars she picked out a procession of Premek carrying food and provisions up the valley. "There's no sign of Katlego. Any idea what time the mercenaries will be ready?"

"Mossi says they should be ready to deploy by half past one. If it wasn't for JJ, they'd be stuck at the border."

"And he's prepared to wait for payment? I'll have the diamonds by the end of next week."

"He took you at your word. JJ says that rumours spread quickly in Blantyre. He was literally fighting off requests to join your militia. Let's hope you were right about the Premek's paucity of weapons training."

"How did he take the news?"

"About Katlego or the pendant?"

"Both."

"Ha! I think he's secretly in love with you. Alexander said he paced around all night chuckling to himself. I think he suspected that Rosalind was in some way involved. You? I'm not so sure. I'm sorry that she…"

"And Boris?" interrupted Rhona. "How are his guts?"

"Settled."

"Any nearer to discovering what happened to Yoshi Morimoto and Kirstin Blanch?"

"Now you mention it – thanks to a squirrel – yes."

"A squirrel? Hang on!" Rhona cut him off.

William turned his binoculars towards a column of khaki-clad soldiers mustering at the bottom of the valley. "There goes the element of surprise!"

"Let's head to the rendezvous point."

William and Rhona skirted the slopes of Mount Nyangani. It was steep and slippery in places, but not as treacherous as the eroded fissures masked by vegetation. Ahead they noticed movement. Ducking down in the heather, Rhona saw two men.

"It's Boris Kuriagin and Thys Myburgh!" Rhona waved to draw them out.

"Stop, Rhona!" hissed William. "They're telling us to keep hidden. Something's spooked them."

Rhona dipped down and unsheathed Trusty Girl from her shoulder holster.

"Nice piece!" whispered William, noting the Winchester.

"It's a long story."

Whatever had spooked the men had passed. Boris and Thys continued to crawl along a ridge above a recess in the cliff face. They shimmied towards William and Rhona.

"Mrs Schmidt, I presume."

"Right, Boris. No flies on you!"

"Ha! I miss this," said Boris, rattling his rifle in childish ecstasy. "We've found the secret entrance. We'll stake it out – if anyone tries to escape. BOOM! Ha-HA!"

Both Thys and Boris were heavily armed with grenades and backpacks containing dynamite and timer-controlled detonators.

"Please don't go anywhere near my boy with those!"

"It's a distraction," said Thys. "We're going after the stones. Tell me again – they're embedded in the statue, correct?"

"Yes. There's a massive star-shape carved into the back wall of the cavern. The statue is cut into a central recess. It's twenty-four feet tall. I measured it. Predictably, the stones are in the eye sockets – but they're out of reach. You'll need to blast out the legs to topple it. When I have Katlego safe in my arms, William will give the signal."

"Have you secured the ropes for your descent, William?" asked Thys.

"Yes. We've hidden harnesses, ropes and torches for our extraction through the pothole system to the east."

"That's trusting your boy cooperates," added Boris.

"You leave that to me," replied Rhona curtly.

Thys started back up the ridge.

"And thank you, Boris!" called Rhona.

"What for?" asked Boris.

"You know."

Boris winked. "See you later."

226

Suddenly, a thunderclap ricocheted off the surrounding rock. The temperature dropped and a mist closed in around them.

"That's not good!" exclaimed Boris, holding his ground.

"On the other hand, it means you won't be spotted making your way back," said William.

"I hope you're right," said Boris.

"Let's hope that the Premek see sense and surrender," said Rhona. "If they don't, wait until they engage the mercenaries and head in. Keep well away from Temba. Don't underestimate him, Boris. He's inhumanly strong and a skillful marksman – if you get a chance to take him down, it might be your last."

Boris followed Thys back onto the ridge to take up position, high up on the far side of the cavern entrance.

"Come on," said William. "Let's go meet your army."

Rhona and William hurried down the mountain, giving the valley leading up to Temba's stronghold a wide berth. As they descended, the clouds cleared. The troops amassing below could not have escaped the attention of Temba's disciples. Rhona's anxiety grew, worried that Temba would have her boy moved or hidden.

By the time they reached basecamp, the sun was shining and it was dry under foot. They entered the main tent to find Mossi detailing two uniformed officers using a map that William had drawn.

"Ah! Mrs Schmidt. Please meet Colonel Fernandes and Sergeant Sántos. They will be helping to coordinate your son's rescue operation. I trust you've completed your preparations?"

"Thank you, Mr Nkosi," said Rhona, taking water before shaking hands with the officers. "Boris and Thys are in position."

"Colonel Fernandes has been briefed that we intend to resolve this peacefully," said Mossi. "However, we think it's best that I negotiate on your behalf."

"What?" exclaimed Rhona. "That's not what we agreed."

"I'm sorry, Rhona. I've made up my mind. You concentrate on rescuing your boy, and I'll conduct the operation – and deal with any hostility, should it come to that."

"But what if I can appeal to him?"

"The matter has been discussed, and the decision has been taken. I will speak with your husband."

William placed his hand on her arm, but she pulled away.

"You have no idea what he's capable of. He's a monster. You can't trust anything he says!"

"How do you Americans put it?" said Mossi superciliously. "This is not my first rodeo, Mrs Schmidt. Now please take your position on the mountain top, and this will all be over by teatime."

William barged Rhona out of the tent before she could unleash.

"Thanks for nothing, William!"

"Calm down, Rhona! Think about it. We can sneak in with Boris and Thys, and find Katlego. It's better this way. Temba doesn't know Mossi, and the sight of a hundred armed militiamen is bound to affect him somehow. And if the Premek engage, his attention will be elsewhere."

"The stones are all Mossi cares about."

"That's as maybe. But you tricked him, remember?"

Rhona didn't answer. She turned and retraced her steps up the mountain.

****

Mossi stood at the front of the column with Fernandes and Sántos as the militia made its way up the valley. It was quiet – ominously so. After an hour, Mossi called a halt so that scouts could recce the upper reaches. There was a chill in the air, but no rain. The higher they ascended, the more precipitous the sides of the valley became, until it was a gorge so narrow it blocked even the midday sun.

"I see the entrance." Mossi gave the order to Colonel Fernandes to distribute the men evenly up the sides of the valley. They took cover in the rough vegetation and trained their rifles. Then they began to crawl slowly towards what looked like a tall slit in the rock at the top of the gorge. It had been reinforced with concrete, just as Rhona had described.

Mossi continued up the well-worn path in full view of the fissure.

"Stop!" A voice rang out.

He did as he was told. All went quiet. The voice was unfamiliar – high-pitched – childlike.

****

From the top of the gorge, Rhona and William peered down with their binoculars. They heard the voice ring out a second time.

"It's Katlego!" Rhona fought her instinct to call out.

The boy stood on a rock, in front of the cavern entrance, dressed in a leather suit embellished with a thick mat of feathers.

"Hello, young man," called Mossi. He stood fifty yards from the boy, flanked by Colonel Fernandes and Sergeant Sántos. "What is your name?"

"I am Tetu-Mor Premek, son of Kan-Mor Premek – divine leader of The Children of the Premek. Why are you here?"

"We'd like to talk to your father." Mossi was clearly flabbergasted. "It's rather urgent."

"Talk?" replied Katlego. "You bring these fighting men to talk? The Premek are men and women of peace – we seek only wisdom and understanding. The divine matriarch, Tsuk-Premek, would not approve of such aggression. My father is right, 'Mankind has not learned the lessons of the past'. He will not speak with you. We wish to be left alone."

The boy turned to go.

"Wait!" shouted Mossi. "Let me speak with your father." Mossi signalled for Seargant Sántos to train his rifle on the boy, causing Rhona to grind her teeth. "Or we will have to force him to listen to our demands."

Katlego turned and hesitated, as if he was receiving further instructions through an invisible earpiece.

"We do not want bloodshed," insisted Mossi. "This can be resolved peaceably."

"Bloodshed?" replied Katlego. "We are but cosmic dust."

"We don't have time for this, boy," shouted Mossi.

Seargant Sántos pulled back the firing pin.

"Time is inconsequential. Life is paramount." Katlego recited the mantra several times, walking out of Mossi's view.

"Fire, Sántos!" commanded Mossi.

From Rhona's vantage point it looked as though Sántos had shot at the boy. She screamed, her voice reverberating along the rocky steep-sided valley. She watched as her son entered through the fissure unscathed. It settled her nerve.

Mossi looked up towards her position and tutted.

Again, it was quiet. No one moved for several seconds. Mossi felt a strange tingling sensation in his fingers. He dismissed it as hypertension. Colonel Fernandes waved for the right flank to move closer to the fissure. Two sappers, with packs containing explosive, crept forward slowly. The left flank mirrored the right until the entrance was surrounded.

From the fissure came a booming voice. "You must leave. This is your final warning."

It was Temba.

Mossi waved impetuously for the sappers to edge forward along an outcrop. Suddenly there was a crack of gunfire. Seargant Sántos fell backwards with a bloody hole in the centre of his forehead.

"Damn it!" Mossi's jaw dropped. He ran for cover and looked back towards the fissure. There was no sign of Temba: it was too dark to see inside. Fernandes had also taken cover and was crawling towards Mossi in shock.

"Call off your men!" called Temba in a booming bass voice. "Or there will be more reprisals."

"That's enough talking! You've gone too far."

Mossi gave the signal and Colonel Fernandes whistled loudly. A fusillade opened up from both side of the valley, targeting the fissure. The sappers took the explosives forward and began to unravel the connecting wires. The cover fire seemed to do the trick. When the sappers had withdrawn a safe distance, Fernandes ceased the cover fire.

"Temba! This is your last chance. Let the boy go, or we will obliterate you."

Again, Mossi felt the tingle in his fingers. He counted to twenty, taking a few deep breaths.

"Fernandes! Blow the rock to smithereens."

Fernandes relayed the signal to the sappers.

Nothing happened.

"What's wrong? Detonate the explosives!" barked Mossi.

Fernandes called out in Portuguese to the sappers. They replied with a shrug. One of them edged forward to check the connection, but was thrown back against the rock as a bullet ripped off the side of his face. He fell limply from the ledge. Again, Fernandes ordered cover fire. The second sapper edged nervously to check the connection. He managed to scramble to his position and signal that all was fine. Once more, Mossi noticed the tingling sensation, and once more the explosives failed to detonate.

****

"He's using his powers," said Rhona to William. "He's disrupting the electric field. I told you, these stones... pah!"

230

"The men will have to go in with grenades, but it'll expose them."

Sure enough, several men charged forwards and launched grenades at the fissure. Most of the barrage landed short of the mark, and two men were felled in the process.

"Temba's picking them off one by one!" said Rhona. "Maybe Boris and Thys can help. Call them on the radio set."

William tried several times but there was too much static interference. "We'll have to do it ourselves."

Rhona nodded. William climbed to the top of the ridge above the fissure to where Boris and Thys were waiting by their rappel lines. They had already figured out what William was about to suggest and met him halfway.

"We'll drop a pack of TNT from above," shouted Thys.

"Good," replied William. "Set the detonator, and do it now before Temba picks off any more of the troops."

Mossi noticed movement from high above the fissure, and ordered the men to stop firing. Through his binoculars he could see Thys Myburgh teetering over the edge of the cliff, attached to a rope above the fissure. Thys let go of the explosive and scrambled for cover. The detonation rocked the entire valley.

Mossi's ears rang with a high-pitched whine.

When the dust cleared, he could see that the blast had ripped out the prefabricated concrete and rock from the fissure entrance, making it wide enough to access – the strewn rock providing cover for his men.

"Go! Go! GO!" yelled Mossi to Fernandes.

****

Rhona watched as the troops rushed forward to the cavern entrance. She saw another soldier fall, but with sustained grenade attack the men breached the widened fissure. Rhona and William edged to the side of the gorge for a better view. They could hear the battle raging inside the mountain and noticed a soldier dragging out an injured comrade.

Mossi gave the signal for Rhona and William to mobilise. Above the fissure near where Thys had dropped the explosive, a crevice had opened up exposing a rock gallery in the soft sandstone.

Rhona called over to William. "We can enter through here. Let's hope Thys and Boris got in safely."

The passageway was cramped, but it led Rhona and William into a crawlspace above the main chamber.

"The shooting's stopped. Do you think it's over?" asked William.

"I doubt it. The fissure leads into a small chamber, but the main chamber and living spaces are easily defensible. With any luck, Mossi will hang back and wait for our signal.

****

Mossi and Colonel Fernandes saw what Rhona had described. They were pegged back outside the main cavern. An army medic was attending to the fallen.

"Sixteen down and five injured – including Sántos – he was a good soldier," reported Fernandes, gravely. "We need to hold our position. I've posted scouts to keep an eye out for any rearguard reprisals."

Mossi peered over the edge of a rock and into the main chamber, lit by vast firepits and convex mirrors. On the back wall was a huge six-point geometric star, and carved into the middle was a twenty-foot statue of a strange long-limbed humanoid with an elongated skull. "My gods!" exclaimed Mossi. "What the hell is that?"

Bolted into the rock, and linking the points of the star, were what appeared to be chains. He caught sight of Temba – tall and muscular. He was too far away for a clear shot, and obscured behind a curtain of long, steel chains suspended from the rock ceiling. Suddenly a bullet ricocheted inches above Mossi's head. He bobbed down and up again, glimpsing young Katlego, rifle aimed. The second shot would have taken his head off had he not ducked – the bullet impacted in the exact same spot above his head. Mossi crawled back to where Fernandes was loading his pistol.

"We can't just storm in there," reasoned Mossi. "They'll pick us off one by one. How many grenades do we have?"

"We used most of them to breach the fissure," replied Fernandes.

Mossi looked over to a pile of dead Premek. Their clothes were rudimentary, but crafted meticulously. He felt the same tingling sensation. This time he was aware that it had been sensed by all of the men. The air around them was filled with static electricity.

****

"Stop crawling," whispered Rhona. "We're right above Temba."

William peered down. "Woah!" It was a hundred foot drop to the floor. He recoiled before steadying himself. "What's with all those chains?"

Temba walked back and forth in front of the statue muttering; masked by swinging chains.

"I can't get a clean shot," said Rhona. "The chains are a recent addition."

At once, both Rhona and William felt the crackle of static electricity. The chains began to vibrate and spark, whipping back and forth. The Premek disciples knelt and began to hum at different pitches. The cavern was filled with strange mesmeric music. The rock amplified the resonant frequencies, causing William and Rhona some discomfort. Above the commotion, William heard Temba's bass voice cry out, louder and louder. William watched as the possessed man grasped hold of the steel chains, which crackled and fulminated, showering the Premek in plumes of dazzling light.

"My head!" hissed William covering his ears. "It feels like it's going to burst!"

"Ugh!" moaned Rhona, clutching her head. "I can't move!"

The humming grew in intensity, as did Temba's bellowing as he gripped the steel chains tighter and tighter, contorting his body. His roar was deafening. William wailed in agony. Rhona screamed as she felt her eyes burning in their sockets. The rock around them began to shake. William saw Temba's disciples topple one by one, deep in trance, writhing and wailing.

All of a sudden, a blast ripped through the cavern. The ground shook violently. The humming stopped, and immediately Rhona felt the burning sensation in her eyes abate. She looked down. Several of the chains had broken, trapping Premek underneath.

"Now, William!" shouted Rhona.

William barely had time to recover. Rhona holstered her rifle and leapt. Catching hold of a chain, she slid to the chamber floor, burning the palms of her hands. Katlego was close by, crouching behind a raised platform, his rifle trained on the narrow entrance to the cavern and Mossi's men. Without a second thought, Rhona ran at Katlego, bundling him to the floor. Straddling him, she held her son's face in her hands.

"Katlego! My boy! It's me!"

The boy's eyes were glazed, and showed no glimmer of recognition. Instead he wriggled out from underneath her, picked up his rifle and pointed it at Rhona.

"'Lego! Stop! It's me – Momma – PLEASE! DON'T…"

****

Boris and Thys had set the charges on timers, and had to sneak out to reset them repeatedly. The Premek were taking flack and retreating into the main cavern, pushed back by Fernandes's men. A group of women ran towards Boris and Thys's position, clutching their children. Hiding in the wood-lined living quarters, it was only a matter of minutes before Boris and Thys would be discovered.

"We need to detonate now!" snapped Thys.

Sonorous humming and droning filled the cavern.

"*Eina!* Boris! We need to detonate now or we're all dead!"

Boris shrieked; his cheeks turning beetroot, convulsing from head to toe, contorting his face wildly. Suddenly, his eyes blinked open, and his body went limp.

"Boris!" Thys shook him but there was no response. He grabbed his rucksack and rummaged around for his headphones; plugging them into his radio set and cupping them over his ears. The wireless static seemed to counteract the noise and ease the pain. Leaving Boris unconscious, Thys scrambled to the bottom of the cavern down some loose boulders and reset the charges for the last time. Igniting a stick of dynamite should they fail, he ran for cover.

The blast ripped out the walls of the living quarters, sending a cloud of wood, splinters and sand across the cavern floor. The rock ceiling collapsed behind him, hemming Boris in with the women and children.

Fernandes's men swarmed in and overwhelmed the first line of Premek defence. A dozen fell, some of them already injured by falling debris.

Thys picked his way through the splintered wood towards the suspended chains, and leaned with his back against the rock wall for cover. Through the steel curtain, he spotted Temba taking cover on the far side of the cavern. He was picking off incoming soldiers at will. Not far from Temba, Thys caught a glimpse of Katlego, his rifle trained on Rhona. They were talking – No! She was pleading for her life.

Thys watched William descend from the roof of the cavern, and open fire. The bullet struck the boy's rifle, knocking it out of his tiny hands and sending him sprawling backwards. Katlego's head hit the rock wall hard. Rhona scooped him up, aided by William.

Thys then saw that Temba had clocked William; his rifle poised. Miraculously, the shot clipped a steel chain and whistled inches past William's face, impacting with the rock and sending up a shower of sand. William and Rhona carried the boy to the cavern entrance, and out of Thys's view. With Temba's attention diverted, he seized the moment. The statue was no more than thirty feet from him. He could see the stones inside the eye sockets. Using the last of the charges, he set the explosive to detonate in five seconds, and threw the pack towards the statue. The blast amputated a leg, but the statue stood firm. When the dust cleared, Thys saw Temba staring back at him. He ran for cover but his escape route was filled with fleeing Premek.

Suddenly, Boris appeared.

"Boris! I thought you were…"

Thys didn't see the blade that was thrust into his guts.

****

"We'll have to carry him out," yelled William.

Rhona was whimpering; her eyes blinded by tears. William picked up the unconscious Katlego, and eased him up and over his shoulder. Using a group of Colonel Fernandes's men as cover, William ran to the cavern entrance. Mossi was there, pistol primed, taking pot shots at the Premek.

"Go, William, get the lad to safety. We're losing men fast."

Able-bodied Premek had regrouped with Temba on the far side of the cavern near Thys's body. Their retaliatory fire was forcing Fernandes's men back to the entrance.

"What about the stones?" asked William.

"If we don't fall back now, we'll be massacred," replied Mossi. "Go, Rhona! Get your boy to the Manyika village. Porters are waiting there with horses."

Katlego began to stir.

"'Lego!" called Rhona compassionately. "Katlego! Can you hear me?"

William put the boy on his feet, but his legs buckled.

"He's concussed," said Mossi, noting the blood on the back of the boy's head. "You need to go now!"

Rhona and William supported Katlego's lean light frame and carried him out of the small cavern through the fissure. Rain poured down on them as they slid over the rocks to the path leading up the steep sided valley. As they tightened their grip, the boy began to moan. Below them, Fernandes's men were flooding out of the fissure into the storm, carrying their injured. Rhona spotted Mossi running for his life.

When they were hidden from view, William called a stop. They laid Katlego gently under a bush to catch their breath.

Peering over the edge of the gorge, Rhona watched as the last of the troops exited the fissure, running for cover in disarray. Fernandes made it as far as the path before he was gunned down. Temba marched over to him and kicked his body over before firing a second round into him, point blank. Behind him stood Boris.

"Christ! He's turned Boris," said Rhona clutching the crucifix round her neck.

"What do you mean turned?"

"Brainwashed him – bewitched him. That's what the humming was all about. I told you! Boris is sensitive. He must have succumbed."

"And Boris knows where we're heading! Come on!"

Rhona and William dragged Katlego over coarse vegetation to the pothole system. The water table was high, swollen by recent heavy rain. Rhona connected their harnesses to the belay ropes, and carefully lowered William in with the unconscious boy strapped to his front. There was barely enough room for them both to squeeze in. The rushing water aided their descent into the darkness. Katlego began to squirm, weakening William's grip on the slippery rock.

"Hurry!" whinnied William.

When Rhona was inside the main conduit and her footing secure, she pulled out two torches from William's backpack. "No one said this would be easy."

William lay back with the boy on top of him, and felt for footholds. Rhona belayed them down a steep gulley. At the bottom, to William's relief, the pothole system levelled and opened up into a wider channel. Soon they were able to wade waist-deep through head-high conduits. The water was cold, but neither of them noticed, pumped full of adrenaline.

Again, Katlego began to stir. "Momma?"

Rhona hugged the boy, almost breaking William's nose in the process.

"Katlego! It's Momma! I'm taking you home. Stay with me."

"Momma? I'm scared. Where's Daddy?"

The boy squinted into the darkness.

"I can't see, Momma. Where are we? I'm cold."

"Don't worry, my love. You'll be warm soon. Can you walk?"

Katlego suddenly realised that he was strapped to a strange man and began to buck in panic.

"Shh! Calm down, my love. It's OK. It's OK! Shh! This man is helping us. He's our friend."

William heard voices above them. "He's found us. Boris is with him. We have to hurry."

"Daddy?"

"No. It's not Daddy," Rhona lied. "We have to go. You're a big brave boy, and this is a big adventure."

The frigid water forced William down several hundred metres. Every now and then he lost his footing, only to be righted by Rhona. Temba and Boris were closing in, their voices amplified by the tunnels.

Suddenly, Rhona caught a whiff of smoke. "Almost there, 'Lego."

William caught a glimpse of light above them. The water followed a sluice to the left. To the right, a scree of collapsed rock led up to the light.

"You go first, Rhona. Drag us up with the rope."

William could barely feel his legs wobbling under their combined weight. Rhona called up, and two porters appeared. They grabbed the rope and hauled William and Katlego up the scree.

The porters untied Katlego, who was shivering uncontrollably. He had regained his balance even if his vision was still blurry.

"Katlego!" came a voice from somewhere below.

"Daddy?"

The roar of the waterfall masked the boy's reply.

The porters had pitched a ladder, and the descent from the cataract was swift. Once out of the river gorge and onto the path, William felt his strength return. The rain had stopped too. They hurried down, dogged by the fear that Temba and Boris weren't far behind. Katlego stumbled and fell. The porters needed no instruction. They took it in turns to piggyback the boy down to the Manyika village.

William caught sight of Temba; his leather jerkin ripped and an ammunition belt slung around shoulder and torso. His first shot clipped a bush, metres from where Rhona had stopped to look back. It spurred them on.

As they entered the village, William ran to untie the horses while the porters carried Katlego as fast as they could to the safety of the chapel. Rhona mounted her mare, and William hoisted Katlego into her saddle. Another shot fizzed past. Rhona sped off. The porters mounted and rode off after her, leaving William to untether his horse – but the gunfire had startled the beast, tightening its reins to the post. William fumbled the straps, yelling in fury and desperation at his useless frozen fingers.

Temba's next shot found its target. William's right shoulder exploded, showering the horse in blood. The beast bucked and snapped the wooden post. It galloped off, dragging splintered wood with it. William scampered around the chapel to dodge another bullet. Close by, two thatched Manyika huts might provide him with cover. He sprinted over clutching his useless arm, and hid.

It went quiet. William could only hear his own intermittent breathing and the patter of rain on thatch.

"William?" called Boris, mockingly.

William couldn't catch his breath. "He's brain... brainwashed you... you fool. Boris! Snap out of it!"

William began to sob in pain and exhaustion. He tried to reach his pistol but there was no sensation in his right arm. He had never shot with his left hand. Now was not a good time to query whether he could or couldn't.

He stepped out from behind the hut in the pouring rain, aimed the pistol and fired.

Boris stood still in surprise... patted down his torso... and began to laugh. "You missed!"

William dropped the pistol, and raised his left arm in surrender. A firm hand grabbed him by the collar and threw him into the churned up mud. William fell face first, unable to support his weight. He squealed, writhing to free his busted shoulder.

"It's over," said Temba, placing his right boot on William's back. "You stole my boy. Feel my wrath."

XXXV: The Squirrel

Manyika Village, Nyanga Districts
Eastern Highlands, Southern Rhodesia
July 6th 1940

William's eyes were caked in mud. He wasn't sure if he was hallucinating. A mounted division of uniformed soldiers cantered hurriedly through the mud towards the chapel, draped in oilskins and wide-brimmed hats; rifles drawn.

****

He awoke lying next to a small fireplace. He wanted to scratch his nose but his right arm resisted painfully. His left hand sufficed. He regressed into memories: Anthony, his son, standing on the harbour wall in Southampton; his poor wife, distant, abandoned.

****

William was roused by the sound of rain, beating down on the iron roof above him. The fire was hot – someone had added logs. He was thirsty. He tried to sit up, remembering the trauma to his right shoulder. Easing himself into a seated position on his canvas pallet, he studied the room. He was in the chapel vestry where he'd found Rosalind, blind and distressed. His shoulder had been dressed with bandages, and sensation had returned to his hands. Someone had left a tin mug and water canteen on a table. William tottered over and drank. He looked down at his bare feet. A pair of clean trousers hung off his hips, loosely. Pulling a blanket over his naked torso, he tucked it under the bandaging and sat in a chair, raising his legs onto the pallet in front of the fire. Within minutes he had nodded off again, only to be awakened by a familiar voice.
     "Alex?" William took a moment to orient himself. "How long have I been here?"
     "A day. We must go. I've brought clothes." Alexander Knapp pulled back the threadbare curtains. It was dark outside.
     "What time is it, Alex?"
     "God knows! It's morning."

William struggled to get dressed. His boots were dry and polished. "Did you do that, Alex?" asked William fondly.

"You need to look your best," said Alexander, packing up the canvas bed. "Want me to tie your laces?"

"Yes. That would be capital."

Sunrise had brought a fresh, dry, cleansing breeze. William's horse had been retrieved, groomed and replenished with tack.

Alexander helped William into the saddle. Several Manyika villagers milled about, sweeping out their huts and watching intently.

"They seem friendlier," said William.

"They're much happier now the Premek are gone. The Manyika were under duress to supply them... and not just with food. We returned two young men and a woman who was heavily preganant. They were grateful."

"Tell me, Alex? What happened?"

"What are you referring to?"

"Here. What happened? I can't remember. I thought I was imagining things. I saw horsemen. I thought the stones were playing tricks on me."

"You didn't imagine that. That was the Rhodesian Regiment. They were training for deployment in the mountains."

"Well they deployed in the nick of time."

"*Ja!*"

Alexander yawned and trotted off, sheepishly. Ahead, William spotted a group of riders waiting on the path. He caught up, and rode alongside Alexander when the path widened.

"You're not telling me something. How's Rosalind?"

"She's being treated at main Camp. In the meantime, you need to know that Boris was captured and is under guard. Mossi went back yesterday with the Regiment to flush out any remaining Premek."

"And to recover the stones?"

Alexander nodded. "Mossi has them. He used the remaining explosives to bring down the cavern roof, steel chains and all. There's nothing left up there."

"What about Temba?"

"He didn't go down without a flight. It took several of the Rhodesians to restrain him. He suffered a heart attack in the process and died. His body was taken by the Regiment to Umtali."

"Gosh!" It took a moment for William to process the information. "What about Rhona and the boy? Are they OK?"

240

"She wanted to get him as far away from here, and as soon as possible," replied Alexander. "And there's the small matter of the diamonds she promised Mossi."

The Rhodesian riders saluted William, who had completely forgotten his rank and station. It took him several seconds to return the salute – and not before twinging his right shoulder in the process.

"How many men did we lose?"

"Too many – Fernandes and Sántos, and thirty other mercenaries."

"Yes. I saw what Temba did to Fernandes. What about Thys Myburgh?"

"He's alive, but barely. When I left, he was stable. He lost a lot of blood, hauling himself out of the cavern before the whole system collapsed around him. He says that Boris stabbed him in the guts."

"Good God!" exclaimed William.

"Boris says he doesn't remember any of it."

"Boris was brainwashed."

"Hmm."

"You don't sound convinced, Alex."

"Tell me, William…" Alexander ignored the insinuation. "You said you had a hunch about Morimoto's killer."

The path widened into open *velt*. The Rhodesian riders rode them hard for several miles.

"I still need to tie up some loose ends," said William, picking up the thread.

"Tell me anyway."

"When I left the museum in Dar-es-Salaam, I noticed a black Mercedes observing me. Thys Myburgh told me he'd also seen it from the train. When I found Morimoto, slumped in his cabin, I was immediately perplexed by the lack of blood spatter and an audible gunshot. Then Kirstin Blanch disappeared, and the only things linking her to the incident were Teodoro Alvarez's map and a smear of blood on the handle of the train door. Teodoro told me that he and Miss Blanch had both heard a disturbance coming from the storage wagon, and that Miss Blanch had opened the door – a door that should have been locked. She saw something that startled her."

"What? Or Who?"

"My first impression was Morimoto, shooting up laudanum. Ravinda Singh spotted a vial of the drug in his smoking jacket pocket the night before. But he could have done that in the privacy of his cabin. It didn't make sense. Then there was the jumble of sounds that various delegates had heard. No one could conclusively say they heard a gunshot. Plenty of bangs and crashes but no gunshot."

"So what did Miss Blanch see?"

"There's more. When Kasper Iverson was taken ill on *The African Queen*, Rhona – or Evelyn, as she led us to believe – opened the expedition medicine chest. I took the opportunity to search through the medicines, and found a bottle labelled in Japanese *kana*. It leant some weight to my idea that Morimoto had placed it there deliberately – for safekeeping, or to hide it. I had no proof either way, but the pieces began to fit into place. Rhona poured out the bottle's contents into an empty bottle and replaced it with a cocktail of all sorts. I watched her label Morimoto's mystery substance with a skull and crossbones for safety."

"What did you do with the bottles?"

"We left them hidden amongst the other medicines. But when we reached Blantyre – remember Boris's health quickly deteriorated? I had a suspicion that someone had found Morimoto's bottle and had been administering it to Boris thinking it was Moromoto's secret potion – I guessed it was the Argentinian physician Mateo Gomez. Ravinda Singh told me that Morimoto had been bragging about a new compound he had synthesised, similar in function to mescaline. Of course, Rhona's concoction turned Boris inside out. Judging by the twinkle in her eye, she replaced the psychedelic with an emetic or some sort of bowel irritant. Now, I realise – she was trying to slow Boris down, to stop him exposing her."

"Ha! So what was Morimoto's medicament?"

"That's what I needed to find out."

The Rhodesian riders began to kit up against a strengthening squall. They signalled that the main encampment wasn't far. William struggled a poncho over his head.

"Did you? Find out, that is," asked Alexander.

"After a fashion. I needed a subject to test my theory, so I trapped a squirrel in the grounds of the hotel in Blantyre, and injected it with a small dose of 'skull and crossbones'. The poor thing died in seconds."

"*Gott im Himmel!* It was poison?"

"Deadly. I felt sorry for the poor critter. I nipped off to try and find a way of disposing of it, but my mind was preoccupied. I cornered Mateo Gomez, accused him of dipping into Morimoto's medicines, and he confessed right away. In fact, he led me to his room and produced Morimoto's missing medicine bag. Mossi had told him to keep it hidden. I went storming off to find Mossi and suddenly realised the implications of leaving a dead squirrel in my room in the heat of the day."

"And?"

"Well, bless my soul. There he was, nibbling on his nuts!"

"So he wasn't dead"

"No. Just resting, it seemed. So… being curious I gave him another dose."

"You did what?"

"I gave him a slightly larger dose this time, and again he keeled over. I felt for a pulse, and was quite sure that I'd murdered him good and proper."

"And had you?"

"This time I waited… and waited… and by suppertime I was convinced I'd succeeded, so I locked him in a cupboard and went to dinner. I'd had time to think by then, and decided it best that I didn't mention Mateo Gomez's admission to Mossi. Besides, I was sure that Gomez wasn't the murderer. Then I had a light bulb moment during one of the speeches."

"A light bulb moment?" asked Alexander.

"Yes. PING! Inspiration!"

"Oh! I see."

"Actually… literally – I remembered that when I went to collect my cabin key from the train attendant, he had been fixing an electric light fitting. And when we opened the locked storage wagon, the light wasn't working."

"Someone had blown the lights?"

"I'll wager that whoever Kirstin Blanch saw in the carriage, removed, smashed or shot out the lightbulb with a silenced pistol."

"Someone who shouldn't have been there."

"Correct. Someone she knew and feared."

The horses sped up as the terrain underfoot flattened out for the last mile into Camp. Alexander struggled to keep up with William's horse.

William continued. "Whoever Miss Blanch saw wanted to mask their identity. In breaking the bulb in the storage wagon, they probably tripped the electricity supply in the next carriage."

"Was it the killer?"

"This is where it gets hazy, Alex. Remember the squirrel?"

"How could I forget? Don't tell me... resurrection?"

"Yup! He was up and at it when I returned from dinner."

"No!"

"I think the sight of Morimoto and our mystery guest scared Miss Blanch, and unwittingly she hid in Morimoto's cabin, breaking a glass and cutting herself in the process."

"I suppose that makes sense of the blood."

"I returned from supper to see the attendant fixing a light fitting, but he wouldn't have known necessarily about the bulb in the storage wagon – made evident by his embarrassment when I opened it up to find that the light wasn't working."

"What happened next?"

William dismounted gingerly and tied up his horse in the stable *boma*. Alexander was flapping at his heels. They wandered over to the main tent.

"At first, I thought that Kioko Kamau was involved, as I heard himidentify Morimoto's body. He shouldn't have been there as his cabin was in the front carriage. It turns out that he'd had a drop too much, and found himself at the wrong end of the train!"

"Ha! *Unglaublich!*"

"Teodoro Alvarez did, however, have a cabin along the corridor. He said he heard footsteps hurry past, a glass break and a door slam. I think that amongst the commotion, Miss Blanch leapt from the train, taking Morimoto's smoking jacket with her for warmth."

"But Morimoto? When was he shot? And why?"

William stopped just short of the tent, and turned to Alexander. "It was staged. It was Morimoto chasing after Miss Blanch down the corridor. As soon as he realised she had given him the slip and alighted, Morimoto hatched a plan. He made a hole in his nightshirt, withdrew his own blood – after all, Morimoto would have had no aversion to needles. Waiting for me to return to my cabin next door, he had time to hide his magic potion in the medicine chest, fabricate a wound and apply the blood. Hearing my arrival, he injected the drug, covered himself with broken glass and cried out to get my attention."

"*Mein Gott!* So he's alive!"

"I believe so. A bit elaborate, one might say, but not if Morimoto needed a disturbance to allow his accomplice to slip from the storage wagon unnoticed – or, more likely, off the train. I called for the emergency stop to be triggered. That's where the black Mercedes comes into picture. It was the getaway vehicle."

"But why didn't Eric Chamberlain say anything when he examined Morimoto? I watched him bag the body. And why was a stone found amongst Morimoto's belongings? Had he really stolen it?" asked Alexander, looking doubtful.

William shrugged his shoulders, opened the tent flap and ushered Alexander in.

"William!" exclaimed Mossi. "The Hero of Nyangani! You must be exhausted."

William was surprised to see JJ and shook his hand warmly.

"Congratulations!"

William monitored Alexander's expression as he put the pieces together.

"I've been detailing the delegation," said Mossi. "We'll have some explaining to do when we get back to Blantyre. In fact, Eric Chamberlain has come up with rather a good idea to avoid all the red tape. We've decided to push on south into Southern Rhodesia and then on into South Africa. We've no reason to go back – we have what we came for. JJ can man the inquest in Blantyre and distribute monies to the 'quick and the dead'. Eric can detail the captain of the Isis to meet us in Durban. There is something I'd like to see before we leave for Cairo. It seems that Eric found a clue in the Stonelore journals that throws light on a Samuel Morgan discovery." Mossi opened the locked briefcase to reveal five lead-lined boxes. "Two to go!"

Alexander suddenly cleared his throat in readiness, but was cut off.

"That sounds like a splendid idea, Mossi," said William. "We can take the train. I think we all deserve a rest."

He turned to leave and invited Alexander to join him.

"Mossi, I know it's a bit early, but I think we deserve a drink. Gentlemen, adieu!"

Walking a safe distance from the tent, William stopped abruptly and muttered. "So, Alex? Have you worked it out then?"

"It was Chamberlain in the storage wagon?"

"Perhaps… probably not… but he's involved somehow. As for the stone found in Morimoto's possession," William shook his head. "I think Mossi made that up to save face."

"But this opens up a whole new can of fish. If not Chamberlain, then who?"

"Worms," corrected William. "I don't know… but I have a horrible suspicion that our progress has not gone unnoticed. Coffee?"

"I have to see Rosalind. The Rhodesian Regiment is escorting her to Umtali tomorrow to bury Temba. After that, she wants to stay with Rhona, here in Rhodesia – to help raise Katlego."

"I see. How is she?"

Alexander shook his head, overcome.

XXXVI: The Assignment

Oslo, Norway
October 15th 2016

"Are you there yet, Mark?"

"Just landed."

"I've sent you an email. It's encrypted. You need to read it before contact."

"What does it say?"

"Just read it! Now piss off and do your job."

Timothy Gordon hung up. Mark Watts swore.

Mark checked into his hotel and took a hot shower. He found a pub on *Karl Johans gate* called 'The Scots Man', screening a recent Glasgow Celtic versus Rangers match. He settled into a booth with a large single malt whisky, opened his laptop and Gordon's email attachment.

"Bloody hell!" remarked Mark under his breath. There were pages and pages of scanned transcripts. "This is going to be a long night."

Mark's phone rang at 7.00am.

"Did you read it?"

"Mostly," yawned Mark. "How much am I supposed to believe or just accept?"

"You must have an opinion?"

"An opinion suggests I might have some learning, background knowledge or understanding of the subject. I don't. I have a perspective."

"Typical," remarked Gordon. "Just get to the Embassy."

"So you were at Prep school with this guy?"

"I trust him, if that's what you're insinuating."

"What about the other dude?"

"I was… sort of with him at school too. You assess him and make the call. Just don't be late. I've got to go. Speak later."

Mark bought a sandwich in the *Aker Brygge Marina* and continued along the fjord.

"Who knows I'm here?" asked Mark, fumbling his phone.

"Yes, I see. Young white male," said Gordon. "We're patched into the CCTV. Any chance you could give him the shake?"

Mark checked the route on his phone, crossing a bridge over the dual carriageway. "Yup. Out."

The path doubled back to a railway underpass. Out of sight, Mark paused and used his iPhone camera to peer around the corner. His tail had broken into a jog. Mark's elbow connected with the bridge of his pursuer's nose, and a swift crack to the windpipe left the man clutching his throat. Mark supported the dazed man's weight and shoved him up against the wall. Removing his wallet, Mark released the man and took out his ID. The man collapsed, breathless and bloody. Mark tossed the wallet in the gutter.

"It's our German friends. Any sign of Anna on the facial recognition?"

"No. Just get to the Embassy ASAP."

The path from the railway skirted the back garden of the South African Embassy. Mark walked nonchalantly up the road, pretending not to notice the shiny black Range Rover with German plates parked nearby. He picked up the pace and ducked under a tree, jogging the final hundred yards to the front door of the Embassy. He rang the bell and the door opened instantaneously.

"Come in, Dr Watts."

Mark held his breath and smiled.

"Timothy Gordon called ahead. He said you might be a little tardy. You're early, as it happens."

Mark extended his hand.

"My name is Mukwa."

"Mukwa? As in Mukwa Greenwood?"

"Indeed. Come through." Mukwa ushered Mark into a large drawing room. "Your Excellency, this is Mark Watts."

An elegantly dressed South African woman in her late fifties stood up from her desk. "Dr Watts. Can I offer you coffee or tea?"

"I'm good. Thank you, your Excellency."

"Take a seat. You're up to speed with the operation?"

"I'm getting there," replied Mark, shooting Mukwa a curious sideways glance that revealed that he hadn't a clue what was going on.

"Good. Well, things have escalated since you extracted the bodies from the Neumayer Station. The stunt you pulled created a great deal of red tape. And it's taken an equal amount of negotiation to get any form of cooperation from Dr Jan Schneider, head of the EU

Antarctica Project at the Neumayer base, not to mention the Norwegian Navy and various irascible NATO personnel."

"When I last looked, South Africa wasn't in the North Atlantic," said Mark petulantly.

A knock at the door broke the tension.

"Dr Watts! Samuel Walker. Thanks for coming." Sam shook Mark's hand and turned his attention to the Ambassador. "The German Embassy is on the phone. Mark, it seems you've already introduced yourself to one of our collaborative security detail."

"Ah! Sorry," said Mark unapologetically. "I hate being followed. Is he OK?"

"Yes. Fine. A broken nose and bruised windpipe – he's learned his lesson," replied Sam.

The Ambassador's face was stony. "Dr Watts, I've been ordered by a NATO syndicate to put together a multinational task force." She cleared her throat. "You've been chosen to coordinate and lead the team that will go after the artifact, although it occurs to me that you are the least informed and equipped for the job. Someone must believe in you."

Mark took a moment to digest the information.

"You look confused, Dr Watts."

"Forgive me, Ambassador. Would you mind if I just call my Head of Section at MI6 to remind him that he's a colossal arsehole."

Sam laughed out loud.

"Why?" asked the Ambassador.

"It's complicated."

She stood and smirked, indicating that he should follow. Mark got up reluctantly, politely ushered forward by Mukwa and Sam. He followed the Ambassador down a staircase. At the bottom was a reinforced steel door. She punched in a code on a wall-mounted keypad. An internal mechanism made a clunking sound.

The Ambassador eyed Mark disparagingly. "You have a map and a key. What's complicated about that?"

XXXVII: An Unusual Alliance

Waterval-Boven, Eastern Transvaal
South Africa
July 20th 1940

The skies over the South African *highveld* were crystal clear. It was cool and dry, and the skin covering William's knuckles had cracked. The motorised convoy of three army trucks struggled up a rocky track, throwing the passengers about like rag dolls.

"Not far now, according to Eric's map," shouted Mossi from the front passenger seat.

Alexander leaned in to William, who was concentrating hard on holding down his breakfast. "Curious that Eric didn't want to see this for himself."

William nodded before unbelting and thrusting his head out from under the canvas roof of the truck. Wiping his mouth, he struggled back to his seat. "I think I told him too much back in Stone Town. Besides, how did you discover Samuel Morgan's secret? You only had half his memoirs."

"I found a scrap of diary entry that pre-dated his meeting with Huw Williams. It mentioned a trip he'd made to inspect a goldmine in Blaauboschkraalspruit. My contacts down here confirmed that they were no such gold reefs under investigation at the time. But they said there's an old earthwork up on the plateau. The local *Bokoni* people were supposed to have built it five hundred years ago, but the presence of erected monoliths suggests it's a henge from the Neolithic period."

"Why didn't you mention this, Alex?"

"Why didn't you mention it to ME, William?"

The truck stopped abruptly by a grove of eucalyptus trees.

"Mossi. Why have we stopped?" asked Alexander.

"We have company," replied Mossi, stepping out.

"Here goes," said William. "Keep your wits about you, Alex."

William checked his pistol, as did Alexander, and they clambered out the back of the truck. The other delegates began disembarking from the supply trucks. Blocking the track ahead were three light khaki Landrovers. A man wearing a brown padded airman's jacket approached slowly and removed his hat.

"Eric?"

"Mossi. We need to talk."

Mossi followed Eric to one of the Landrovers. There was a heated yet curt conversation before Eric opened the front passenger door for Mossi to get in.

Alexander relayed the information to the Messrs Gomez, Rousseau and Kamau in the second truck while William helped Teodoro Alvarez ease Thys Myburgh out of the front of the third.

William took out a cigarette and offered one to Alexander. "Who do you think's in there?"

"I've had a bad feeling about this for a while," replied Alexander.

Mossi got out of the car and beckoned them. "Our plans have changed." His face was flushed, despite the cool temperature.

Eric opened the back door of the Landrover. The occupant stepped out uncomfortably with the aid of crutches. His black coat enveloped him, and his clothes hung off him like a scarecrow.

"Gerhard Stoltz!" snapped Alexander. "*Warum bist du hier? Du Drecksau!*" (Why are you here? Swine!)

"*Ruhig, Alexander,*" said Stoltz calmly, concentrating on his footing. "*Wir müssen reden.*" (Quiet, Alexander. We need to talk.)

William was preoccupied by Stoltz's considerable weight loss.

"Mossi! Don't listen to him," shouted Alexander. "He's not to be trusted. Bloody Nazi scum!"

"Unfortunately, that isn't possible," replied Mossi.

The rear door to the second landrover opened. Boris alighted, closely followed by Yoshi Morimoto.

The delegates edged closer. Thys Myburgh appeared alongside William. He was still in a bad way, but mustered the strength to floor Boris with a well-directed punch to the jaw. William restrained him, while Boris gathered himself.

"I'm sorry Thys. I wasn't myself."

William took over. "It was you in the storage wagon, Stoltz, wasn't it? Hurt yourself getting off the train, did you?" He scoffed, pointing at Stoltz's plastered ankle.

"Yes, William. You're right – it's broken. At least you kindly stopped the train for me. It could have been much worse."

"And you, Morimoto?" barked William. "A bit elaborate, don't you think? I'd love to know more about your reincarnation drug. What were you after? Stones, map or information?"

"We can discuss this later, Herr Greenwood," said Stoltz.

"No! You will discuss it now!" snapped Teodoro Alvarez. "Where's Miss Blanch and my map?"

251

Stoltz shook his head. "I confess, I don't know. Time with the Aborigine has, I'm sure, provided Miss Blanch skills sufficient to cope with African Bush."

"Kirstin Blanch recognised you and fled with Alvarez's map. Didn't she," barked William.

"I must remind you, Herr Greenwood, that we are at War!"

"She was a spy?" gasped William.

"*Genau.* But your side got to Fraulein Blanch first."

"A double agent?" exclaimed Alexander.

"So where is my map, Eric?" snapped Alvarez. "Or are you working for these pigs too?"

Mossi slammed his fist on the hood of the truck. "Gentlemen. We need cool heads. It seems that if we are to achieve our goal, some concessions will have to be made. Teodoro, you have that transcription of the cloth, right?" Mossi lowered his tone. "He has our balls in a vice. We have no choice."

Teodoro nodded reluctantly.

Alexander spat on the ground in front of Stoltz. "My nephew was right. I should have killed you while I had the chance." He stormed off to the back of the truck.

The convoy continued to the top of the plateau, whereupon the porters began to build an encampment. William was itching to talk to Eric, and found him examining an eroded stone wall.

"Explain yourself."

"I have a family, William," replied Eric dolefully. "Stoltz arrived in Stone Town a few days before the Isis docked. You need to hear what he has to say. Don't worry. The Stonelore is safely locked away, but I had to relinquish my stone. Stoltz gave it to Mossi as a peace offering."

William began to chuckle. "Ironic, don't you think, that your father found the stone here all those years ago. But why did you bring us here? There has to be some significance."

Eric sighed. "I found a connection in the Stonelore, as I'm sure you did. I also found a series of seemingly unrelated symbols that actually have a distinct correlation to Alvarez's cloth."

"Go on."

"Samuel Morgan found an inscription somewhere here. If I'm right, it unlocks an ancient cipher.

"And we have a link between two pieces of evidence from two different continents – and Boris's testimony," concurred William.

"Exactly!"

"But why did you release Boris? He should be tried for attempted murder."

"That was one of Stoltz's demands," replied Eric. "If Boris has the ability to communicate with the stones, maybe he can find the inscription. He might be our only lead."

"Might?" scoffed William. "If you're wrong, I'll make sure that Thys Myburgh reserves the right to the first shot."

"William! Be reasonable!"

"Reasonable? Where were you, Eric, when we were being gunned down at Nyangani? Quaffing tea with Nazis?"

In the mess tent, the Camp porters had prepared *potjekos* for the assembled: a thick spicy lamb stew with ample mielie-maize pap. The food seemed to settle tension, though William doubted it would last.

Yoshi Morimoto sat next to him – he seemed younger than William remembered.

"Mr Greenwood, I must apologise. And I'm impressed that you figured out my deception."

"In my experience, compliments are often the most insincere form of flattery. Tell me about the drug."

"Tetrodotoxin. It's a deadly poison extracted from *fugu*, or Japanese pufferfish. In micro-doses it lowers vital signs and can make the subject appear dead. I combined it with a powerful psychotropic and a stimulant that takes a while to be assimilated into the bloodstream. Not for the faint hearted – but a wonderful way to explore a dream."

"Impressive, if not crazy. How long have you been working for Stoltz?"

"My father sent me to school in Berlin. Prodigious young chemists don't go unnoticed."

"But spying for the Nazis? Don't you see what they are doing is reprehensible?"

"Yes. But what choice do I have? If I run, they'll kill me. Better to be here than cooking up poisonous gases and explosives in a laboratory in Berlin. My conscience is clear. Stoltz is in trouble with his superiors. The only way he could avoid a sticky end was to tell them about the stones and their arcane properties. It seems that Alexander Knapp's original correspondence asking for help to determine the function of the stones, made it to the top."

"The top? Not Heinrich Himmler, surely?" gasped William.

Yoshi nodded. "Stoltz was granted a reprieve from *Reichskriegsgericht* or court martial, and ordered to find the stones and any associated information. I'm afraid the Nazis know all about the Stonelore journals and the stones."

William put his head in his hands. "Oh, Eric!" he groaned through gritted teeth. "Now I see what Mossi means by 'our balls are in a vice'."

"I'm afraid so. Stoltz is using the Stonelore trove as leverage."

William pondered, prodding his supper with his fork before using a napkin to clean his spectacles. "Well, for what it's worth, it seems that the only one harmed by your stunt was Stoltz." William chuckled, imagining the scene. "What did he want?"

"I was ordered to steal Alvarez's map, but Miss Blanch saw us in the storage wagon. Stoltz sneezed on his snuff..."

"She hid in your cabin."

"I guess so. The last place I'd look," said Yoshi. "It was dark. I ran down the corridor..."

"She cut herself, grabbed your jacket for warmth..."

"And I assumed she'd jumped. The next part, was as you say, elaborate. But it worked. The problem was..."

"She took your laudanum."

Yoshi nodded in shame. "My vice. I wouldn't have lasted long."

The explanation seemed plausible to William. "You know that Mateo Gomez tried to dose Boris with your resurrection potion?"

"No. My God! He could have died! How did he..."

"Survive? He has Rhona McTaggart to thank for that. She switched out the contents for emetics or some... you know..."

The sight of William Greenwood and Yoshi Morimoto giggling like schoolchildren elicited a look of intrigue from the other diners.

Though Alexander was still fuming and couldn't bring himself to acknowledge Gerhard Stoltz and his treachery, he was bemused as to the cause of the hilarity. "Tell everyone about the squirrel!"

SONGS OF THE PREMEK

The-tu-Hade-d'abju-Moona-Jil (the storyteller who sings like the Ibis) was the next of the Premek cataclysm survivors to receive a stone from Ckan. His talent for documenting the history of the Premek in Song was prodigious. The children adored him, as did their parents. As well as a musician and a wordsmith, Thetu was a brilliant craftsman, solely responsible for sculpting a huge effigy to the Matriarch Tsuk-Premek in the rock wall of the Premek's cavern home, high up in the mountains.

Protected by a plateau of limestone and granite, and shrouded in cloud, Ckan encouraged the Premek families to construct habitations within the caverns with whatever resources they could gather, providing them with privacy, comfort and relaxation from forays for building materials and food.

In the cool of the evening, Ckan would call his brethren to muster in the midst of a square of four blazing firepits, and in front of Thetu's statue of Tsuk. Carefully measuring out a large geometric star shape formed from bidirectional equilateral triangles, Ckan placed Tsuk's stones equidistantly from one another. In the centre of the circle he placed his own precious stone. Humming softly on a low pitch, Ckan encouraged his kin to intone in ever-increasing harmonic chord complexities, firing synapses in their brains and connecting ganglia that had lain dormant for generations until some, but not all, fell into a trancelike state. The harmonics reverberated throughout the caverns and resonated far through the water-eroded passages of their mountain domain. Their music shook the very foundations of their habitation and covered the Premek in fine sand that rained down from the ceiling of the cavern. Sometimes, small pebbles would rise and fall, and light anomalies would dance off the rock walls, sparking and discharging in multicloured flashes like shooting starts burning up in the earth's atmosphere.

In time, all the Premek learned to commune with the stones, retrieved from deep within the polar continent. Tsuk-Premek had understood the danger they posed to her descendants. But she also believed that they had been crafted by some higher bygone intellect: crammed with knowledge by some forgotten race – and why they needed to be disinterred from the deep phosphorescence-illuminated galleries of the polar underworld. She believed the stones contained images and information from a distant past, and would provide the

Premek with glimpses of their destiny – visions that they interpreted as future events: cities rising and falling, ships swept away by typhoons and tsunamis; distant worlds populated by divers races and cultures; machinery of terrifying proportions and capability; armies crumbling to dust; cataclysmic upheavals; and the vast panoply of bright stars exploding into a seemingly infinite expanse of dark space.

The children would wake screaming – disturbed by nightmares – to be soothed by Thetu's lullabies. Only once the children had settled and were fast asleep would the adults discuss openly the meaning of their visions. The Premek elders would officiate on interpretation, using logic and understanding gleaned from lifetimes of experience and spoken accounts passed down by their ancestors. They were in no doubt as to the wonder of the stones, but it was another matter trusting Tsuk's legacy implicitly.

As leader of his kin, Ckan erred on the side of caution. As a new father, he was in no rush to leave their safe haven and abandon their home. The stones were urging them north to great fertile plains, where visions of men and women fished vast inland seas, strange horned and wattled beasts pulled iron ploughshares, great pyramids rose from still waters fashioned from enormous blocks of gleaming white stone. The present was a time for rest, recuperation and preparation. Neither Ckan nor any of the Premek had any comprehension of what Tsuk had also disinterred from the subterranean polar paradise. Locked away, undisturbed in its granite sarcophagus lined with acacia, was the dismantled artifact of smooth flat circular stones; metallic discs; plates of polished crystal and gold wires. The collection was conspicuously absent from the Premek's visions – and until any of the Premek could fathom its function, their journey northwards would have to wait.

To be continued…

Glossary

Abydos ancient city of Upper Egypt; famed for its temples and burial sites; built circa 3200BC.

acacia tree: *aka* wattle, thorntree.

Afrikaner people: socially dominant among white South Africans; Dutch origin; Cape of Good Hope settlers in late 17th century.

Afrikaans language: west Germanic root; evolved in southern Africa from Dutch vernacular in the 18th century.

Armistice a temporary suspension of hostility; Treaty signed by the Allies and various German signatories on November 11ᵗʰ 1918.

Axis Powers military alliance forged between Germany, Italy and Japan in the 1930s.

Baalbek geography: *aka* Heliopolis; city in Lebanon famous for its monoliths including the unused quarried stone called 'the pregnant woman'; reputedly weighing 1000 tonnes.

baobab tree: *aka* upside-down tree; barrel-shaped tapering trunks and branches.

Batswana people: plural noun of Tswana: southern African people living predominantly in Botswana and South Africa.

Bechuanaland Protectorate: area of southern Africa established on 31st March 1885 by the United Kingdom of Great Britain and Ireland; now Republic of Botswana (since 1966).

Bellville Hoerskool High School: founded in 1937; situated in the suburb of Bellville, Western Province, South Africa.

biltong food: cured and dried meat cut into strips; *aka* jerky.

boet/bru *Afrikaans* slang for brother.

boma *Kiswahili* enclosure: made of wood to house livestock.

chloroquine medicine: drug used to prevent and treat malaria.

cholera disease: potentially fatal bacterial disease of the small intestine; causes vomiting and diarrhoea.

dagga boy biology: a bull buffalo that has left the breeding herd; highly aggressive; dagga (*Afrikaans*) refers to mud they are often seen wallowing in.

Diocesan College school: *aka* Bishops; private boarding school for boys established in 1849 in Cape Town.

Djoser Step Pyramid archaeology: found in the Saqqara necropolis north-west of Memphis, Egypt; reputedly built around 2600BC, it is deemed to be the first cut-stone man-made construction.

drongo bird: black with a forked tail; bird call mimic.

Edfu geography: city on the Nile near Aswan famous for The Temple of Horus; reputedly built on the site of an earlier temple; (context: built by the 'seven scribes' to store early accounts of the founding of Egypt).

Eina! *Afrikaans* expression: Ouch! (Nama Bushman derivation).

emetic medicine: drug that induces vomiting.

familiar mythology: an animalian daemon; (context: an animal into which a human might transform).

Flinders Petrie, Sir William Matthew (1853-1942) English Egyptologist; reknown for his systematic methodology, preservation and curation of ancient Egyptian archaeological artifacts.

gemsbok biology: (pronounce with a guttural 'g') large straight-horned antelope of the oryx family; suited to dry habitats.

Great Zimbabwe city: capital of Zimbabwe during the Iron Age (11th century) abandoned in the 15th century; ruin; suggested links to prior trade with Arab merchants; unconfirmed reports of artifacts from Phonecian dynasty (c2500BC).

Gruppenführer rank: German paramilitary rank of the Nazi Party; (context: SS officer).

Hemiunu *aka* Hemon: born c.2570BC; reputed architect of the The Great Pyramid at Giza.

Himmler, Heinrich (1900-1945) German politician and leader of the SS (Schützsstaffel); leading member of the Nazi Party; lifelong occultist; eugenicist and perpetrator of the Holocaust atrocities.

Homo floresiensis biology: archaic hominin that inhabited the island of Flores, Indonesia (c50,000BC)

Homo neanderthalensis biology: archaic hominin that inhabited Eurasia until about 40,000 years ago.

hominin biology: taxonomically related to humans and chimpanzees but not gorillas.

Highveld geographical area of South Africa with an altitude over 1500m; covers most of the south and west Transvaal (now Gauteng Province).

hyrax biology: *aka* rock dassie or coney; short eared rabbit-sized rodent.

Imhotep history: chancellor to Pharoah Djoser and reputed architect of the Djoser Step Pyramid in the late 27th century BC.

impala antelope with glossy red-brown coat; widespread.

Islay geography: pronounced 'eye-lah'; an island off the west coast of Scotland famous for its whisky distilleries.

Kalahari desert in Botswana spanning into Namibia and South Africa; home to the San Bushmen.

kana *Japanese* syllabaries or sound units in written Japanese.

Khoi language that connects the Khoi and the San people.

Khoikhoi people: nomadic pastoralists from south-western Africa who first made contact with the Dutch settlers in the mid-17th century.

KhoiSan people: overall term for all indigenous people of South Africa (the KhoiKhoi and the San people).

Khufu *aka* Cheops: King of Egypt c.2580BC; commissioned the building of The Great Pyramid at Giza.

laager *Afrikaans* defensive circle of wagons; encampment.

Mafikeng/Mafeking town in north-west South Africa; misspelled by British (Mafeking); became Mafikeng in 1980 when it was incorporated into Bophuthatswana; changed to Mahikeng in 2010.

magnetosphere a region of space surrounding the earth, protecting it from the solar wind, charged particles and cosmic radiation that would otherwise damage living organisms at a cellular level.

Makhadzi geography: picnic site on the Kumba River, Kruger National Park; (context Bush Camp).

Matabeleland geography: region formed in 1840 from the Bakalanga, Lozi and Nguni people in west Zimbabwe.

Mankwe *Setswana* mother leopard; (context: a lake in the Pilanesberg region).

mescaline naturally occurring hallucinogenic found in certain cacti (peyote) and beans.

mielie *Afrikaans* maize plant; 'sweet corn'.

miombo biology: sparse deciduous woodland of east Africa.

MI5 UK national counter-intelligence and security agency.

MI6 UK international counter-intelligence and security agency.

mooer *Afrikaans*: murder

Mohenjo-Daro geography: built around 2500BC it is one of the largest cities of the Indus Valley Civilisation in Pakistan.

monna *Setswana* man.

mopani (alt. mopane) tree: pea family; distinctive butterfly-shaped leaves; widespread in the north of South Africa.

mopani worm emperor moth larva; large edible caterpillar.

muti *Setswana* bush medicine

Nazi member of the Nazi Party (1920-1945) or anyone associated with their propaganda and beliefs whether voluntarily or not.

Nikola Tesla Serbian inventor and engineer; credited with the design of the modern alternating current (AC) supply system.

oke *Afrikaans* slang for man.

Oubaas *Afrikaans* outdated term of endearment for an elderly 'employer'.

phosphorescent chemistry: light emitted by a substance without combustion.

Pilanesberg geography: mountainous area in the north-west of South Africa; site of an ancient eroded volcano.

plasma event astronomy: *aka* coronal mass ejection; solar flare; massive burst of electromagnetic radiation from the sun; (context: earthbound electrical storm triggered by a solar flare and weakened magnetosphere.)

Polaris astronomy: *aka* North Star or Pole Star; the brightest star in Ursa Minor.

precession astronomy: gradual change of the earth's axial orientation within its elliptical orbit around the sun. One complete cycle takes just under 26,000 years.

psychotropic medical: classification of drugs that affect a person's mental state.

Puma Punku geography: built c.540AD; part of the Tiwanaku site in western Bolivia; famous for its precision-cut stonemasonry.

Queen Maud Land geography: region of Antarctica claimed as a dependent territory by Norway in January 1939.

Rhodesia (Southern) British Crown colony named after Cecil Rhodes between the Zambezi and Limpopo rivers (1923-1965); gained independence in 1965 and renamed Zimbabwe in April 1980.

rooibos *Afrikaans* herbal tea made from the leaves of the red bush plant.

Sacsayhuamán geography: city on the outskirts of Cusco, Peru; reputedly built by the Killke culture around 1000AD; famous for its mortarless, interlocking, polygonal wall stones.

sagittal suture biology: dense fibrous connective tissue between the two parietal bones of the skull.

San Bushmen people: first nations people of southern Africa; hunter gatherers from the Kalahari region.

Sangoma *aka* Shaman: traditional healer.

Setswana language of the Batswana.

shemagh (schmog) *aka* kufiya: traditional Arabian cotton headdress.

shufti *Arabic* slang for 'glance over' or 'recce' in military jargon.

snowcat caterpillar-tracked enclosed vehicle.

Solon Athenian lawmaker born c.630BC; researcher of antiquity.

Soutpiel/Soutie *Afrikaans* (derogatory term) literally meaning 'salt' and 'penis' suggesting that one foot is in Africa, the other in the UK, with the penis dipping in the Atlantic Ocean.

Spetsnaz Russian special forces.

suffa *Arabic* sofa.

Sumerians people of Sumer: ancient civilisation from the Mesopotamia region between the Tigris and Euphrates rivers (4500BC to 2000BC).

Tanis geography: city in the north-eastern Nile Delta, built in the reign of Ramasses II circa 1075BC.

Tiwanaku geography: ruins in western Bolivia near Lake Titicaca; built around 110AD (by modern concensus).

Tshukudu *Setswana* rhinoceros.

Tsonga people: southern African people predominantly from Mozambique.

Tswana people: singular of Batswana: a member of the southern African people living predominantly in Botswana and South Africa.

veld *Afrikaans* uncultivated grassland

veldskoens *Afrikaans* field shoes; strong leather or suede boots.

wildebeest (blue) *Afrikaans aka* gnu; large antelope with blue-grey coat and short up-twisted horns; migratory; widespread.

Winchester (rifle) series of lever-action repeating rifles; (context: the Winchester .405 was a classic sports' rifle in the late 19th century.)

ACKNOWLEDGEMENTS

My work as an opera singer has taken me far and wide. Accordingly, much of this book was written in Opera House canteens and digs, particularly Austria (Festspielhaus Bregenz), Switzerland (Geneva and St Gallen), Glasgow (Scottish Opera), London (Royal Opera House and English National Opera), Oslo (Den Norske Opera & Ballett) and Cardiff (Welsh National Opera).

Unsurprisingly, the locale features heavily in the book, or has been hugely inspirational.

I'd like to thank Dr Jake Willson, Robert Worrall, Susan Abraham, Gina Brees-Marcovecchio, Kelly Patterson Galpin, Murray Hipkin, Wilf and Barbara Stout, Andre Swanepoel, Miklós Sebestyén and anyone who helped, taught, advised and inspired me.

ABOUT THE AUTHOR

David Andrew Stout was born in Oundle, England in 1974. He joined the choir of Westminster Abbey in 1983 and became Senior Chorister in 1987. He was awarded a Music Scholarship to Uppingham School and later attended The International School of Bophuthatswana (now The International School of South Africa in Mahikeng, North West Province) before reading Zoology at Durham University and Biology/Science Education at Homerton College, Cambridge while singing in the choir of St John's College. He taught Biology and Physical Education at Epsom College from 1998 to 2003. In 2006, he graduated with a Masters degree in Musical Performance from the Guildhall School of Music and Drama and has since enjoyed a fruitful career as an operatic baritone. He lives with his family in Glasgow, Scotland.

Printed in Great Britain
by Amazon